NIGHT WINDOWS

NIGHT WINDOWS

Jonathan Smith

An *Abacus* Original

First published in Great Britain by Abacus in 2004

Copyright © 2004 by Jonathan Smith

A CIP catalogue record for this book
is available from the British Library.

ISBN 0 349 11531 1

Typeset in Bembo by M Rules
Printed and bound in Great Britain by
Clays Ltd, St Ives plc

Abacus
An imprint of
Time Warner Book Group UK
Brettenham House
Lancaster Place
London WC2E 7EN

www.twbg.co.uk

ACKNOWLEDGEMENTS

I would like to thank Richard Beswick, my editor, for all his advice; John Hann for his generous help on police matters; Philippa Harrison for her enduring support; and my daughter, Becky Quintavalle, who has encouraged me on this from the very first day to the last.

for John Inverarity

In between 1987 and 1994 the author was the victim of identity theft and fraud. This narrative grew out of that experience.

1

It all began just after lunch on 5 November – Guy Fawkes Day, in fact – and Patrick Balfour was sitting at his desk, pencil in hand, drafting a letter. He always drafted in pencil, using a soft 3B, before transferring the words to the screen. It was a difficult letter, this one, to difficult parents about a difficult pupil.

Patrick liked to think he wrote a good letter, a natural letter, a friendly letter, but this sort could take him ages. There were easier things in the world than telling parents that their child had behaved very badly, that the apple of their eye could not only be naughty sometimes but was also capable of being a nasty little sod. But, by inserting a few phrases and by moving around a word or two, he was trying to catch his more conciliatory tone: to suggest that this was the kind of boy who deserved a last chance, and that he was the kind of man, the kind of head, who always liked to leave the disciplinary door open.

Well, he was trying too hard. Because when he read through the new version he found that, far from improving it, he had succeeded only in making himself sound pompous, and pomposity was one of a headmaster's occupational hazards that Patrick was most keen to avoid.

So he stood up, as he often did when he was irritated with the world or (as here) with himself, and walked round his study, up and down, round and round. It was on the first floor, his study, a spacious book-lined room with a high ceiling, and a room with some of the best views in London.

To the south the Thames flowed by not fifty feet away, with the Globe Theatre and Tate Modern on the far bank. The Thames, full of tugs and city cruisers, lapped the bank with its grey water, the surface bobbling with polystyrene cups and empty plastic bottles. The embankment ran both ways, full of joggers and pigeons.

From his west window he had a snapshot of his school – a timed snapshot, too, because the clock tower was directly opposite him – and these snapshots gave him a feel of the place. Indeed, by looking down on the comings and goings in the quad below he could pick up more than anyone realised; almost at a glance he could see from the body language in the quad whether the school was purposeful and bustling or looking a bit ragged at the edges.

Some days Patrick felt he could be even more specific: in a split second he could spot that a new power group was forming down there, or, on a more individual level, he could sense from her shoulders and walk that the under-achieving girl who had just crossed the quad – the one they had been talking about in last Tuesday's staff meeting – was not so much moodily adolescent as downright depressed.

Patrick liked to think he knew every one of them by name – he prided himself on it – and sometimes as he stood at the window he would test himself. And as he looked down on the quad below, in amongst the moving mass would be the hard core, the lads, the boys with their

2

shirts out, the ones with their top buttons undone, with their shoe laces missing, with their ties half down, with their different colour socks and their non-school shoes (and, in one case, with a letter soon on its way to his parents).

Milling around with the lads, of course, would be the in-girls, the outnumbered girls (the school was not yet fully co-ed), and in amongst the outnumbered girls in all probability would be Alice, his daughter Alice. He always noticed her. She was now one of the gang, one of the sixth-form girls with their low-cut strappy tops and half-hidden tattoos and partly exposed midriffs. She was now one of the in-group, one of those boys and girls who eagerly grasped every available opportunity to get up the school's nose, or rather the management's nose, or in Alice Balfour's case her father's nose, by exploiting the dress code, by being late for lessons and by letting the place down as badly as possible in public.

And Patrick was glad they did that. Well, not let the place down *too* badly but took them on. Even when they were a bit of a pain and pushed you to the limit, he thanked God for the unmalleable young. The difficult ones were usually the ones who did something with their adult lives, did something extraordinary, and as an extraordinary man himself Patrick liked to see extraordinariness reflected in his school.

As for the grumbling teachers, the long-term malcontents, the ones who were always threatening to leave but never quite got round to handing in their resignation, he could tell them a mile off. It was the way they met in the middle of the quad for a five-minute moan, then glanced up and tossed their heads in the direction of his study, the place where they felt the real problem could be located, little knowing that the real problem was up there looking

3

down on them. As Patrick often said to other heads, 'Difficult pupils come and difficult pupils go, but difficult teachers go on for ever.'

But on this occasion, on Day One, on that drab, dreary afternoon of 5 November, none of that was catching Patrick's eye. For a start everyone was in lessons. No, on this occasion he could see a blue Volvo circling the quad, looking for a parking space, and it was the slow, unhurried way it was proceeding, its rather dawdling feel, which struck him as unusual. There wasn't a parking place – on their cramped central London campus there rarely was – and the car paused with its engine running while a man in a grey suit got out from the driver's seat and walked over the cobbles to the porter's lodge. There was something about the man, the suit, the way he took his time, the way he carried himself, which suggested that he was not a parent. He did not quite seem to fit.

Come on, Patrick said to himself, you can't stand here like this all day: get back to your desk, you've got a pile of work. Back to that letter you're supposed to be writing.

In an altogether brisker mood, he had just finished the letter and signed it when the internal phone rang. It was his secretary. Patrick had no doubts at all that he had the best secretary in the world.

'Yes, Daphne.'

'Two things, Patrick.'

'Yes.'

'The BBC have just rung again.'

'Yes.'

'Amanda Martin from *Newsnight*. About next Thursday. She really wants you to go on.'

'Will it be Paxman?'

'I didn't ask.'

'Anyway, I can't, we've already told her I can't.'

'Yes, we have told her that but she –'

'And it's the Lower Sixth Parents' Evening.'

'I know that, Patrick.'

'And there's no way I can get out of that. Michael would go mental.'

'Well, you know what Amanda Martin's like, Patrick, she never gives up.'

'Look, I can't do any more this week, Daphne, I really can't.'

'I'm just telling you she rang, Patrick. I really do not need to be told the state of your diary.'

Daphne's voice was, unusually for her, just short of sharp, betraying a tone of controlled annoyance. This usually meant that Michael Falconer, Patrick's deputy, was having one of his days. If Daphne was tetchy it probably stemmed from Michael coming in and out of her office every quarter of an hour, pressing her for an immediate meeting with the headmaster 'if by any lucky chance he is in'.

'And,' Daphne added, 'there's an officer from the CID here.'

'We weren't expecting anyone, were we?'

'No, but he'd like to see you, Patrick.'

'About?'

'I'm afraid I don't know.'

'It's not that business on the Waterloo platform? The mobile phone thing.'

'No, as far as I know Michael has sorted that one out.'

'Fine, send him straight over, would you?'

'And you've got Mrs Colley at three-fifteen. The yellow file's on your desk.'

'Yes. Got it, thanks.'

The police.

Within seconds of putting down the phone he heard the footsteps coming across the wooden, echoey upper hall.

The police.

What was it this time?

What was Patrick Balfour thinking on that grey afternoon of 5 November, if what was happening in his head at that moment could even be called 'thinking'? In the ten seconds or so that it took before the knock on his study door Patrick was caught on his whistle-stop tour of horrors:

a fatal accident on a school trip, with one of his staff held responsible

someone with a gun on the premises

anything to do with sex

a suicide in the Thames, the note blaming persistent bullying

a senior member of his staff arrested for shoplifting

his bursar embezzling

more or less anything to do with the chaplain.

And would whatever it was get into the press? His school might not have been the most prestigious in the country, it wasn't Eton or Westminster, and it wasn't right at the top of the league tables, but it was now the school in England most featured by the media and the one most talked about on the circuit. Because Patrick Balfour, by hook or by crook, had made it so. It was now a school to emulate. Even his rival heads, seething with envy at his high profile and over what he had achieved, would concede that much. Which meant that it was also a school to throw mud at. Which meant that any misdemeanours got the school, or rather Patrick Balfour's face, on to page three. Or, in the worst of all cases, on to page one. If you live by the sword, Patrick's enemies said, you die by the sword.

The ten seconds were up. There was a knock on the study door.

'Come in.'

Patrick walked round his wide desk to greet the man in the grey suit he had seen getting out of the blue Volvo.

'Mr Balfour? Mr Patrick Balfour?'

'Yes, what can I do for you?'

The detective took out his badge, a small black leather flap-over wallet with the Metropolitan Police crest. Patrick nodded at the identification and almost smiled at the routine. Alone, with only a bottle by way of company, he tended to watch too many cop shows on late-night television.

'I'm John Bevan, Detective Chief Inspector Bevan.'

They shook hands. Bevan sounded as if he might be Welsh.

'Do sit down.'

'Thank you. Before I do so could I just confirm, Mr Balfour, that you have two addresses in London?'

Bevan was Welsh all right.

'We do. We have a flat here, on the next floor up, over the shop you might say. It belongs to the school, of course. Our own house is just off the Gloucester Road.'

'And your address there is . . .?'

'64 Finley Place.'

In fact, Bevan was as Welsh as they came, from South Wales, with that singsong valleys accent Patrick had never much liked, though it was unusual to hear one quite as strong as his in London. Bevan went on in a relaxed, almost friendly way,

'And you use both your homes, Mr Balfour, do you?'

'Yes. I'm there some weekends and sometimes in the week. If I can get away.'

'I see.'

7

'Not always easy, of course, in a school like this.'

'No, I can imagine. You're a busy man.'

'My wife and daughter are at Finley Place much more than I am, more or less permanently.'

'So you are quite often here, in the flat, at the weekends?'

'Yes.'

'Alone?'

'Quite often, yes. Not always.'

'Thank you.'

The detective chief inspector turned and settled on Patrick's wide leather sofa, the one on which parents always sat for their first interview with the headmaster. Bevan was in his late forties, pale-faced and plump, greying at the temples, with the look of a sportsman who had gone to seed. He pulled up his socks (they were black and red) and nodded Patrick towards his own upright leather chair.

'May I suggest you also sit down yourself, Mr Balfour?'

Though irritated by the way the chief inspector so readily assumed higher status, Patrick did as he was asked. The detective then took a moment – for Patrick's taste a moment too long – to look at the dark oak bookcases which reached high and wide to the ceiling, to nod appreciatively at the thousands of leather-bound books, and to glance up at the evenly spaced portraits of three nineteenth-century headmasters, all solemn clerics – two wearing beards, one a moustache – which hung on the wall behind the headmaster's desk.

The detective also took in, nodding again to himself as he did so, the cluster of family photographs, the silver-framed ones of Patrick, Caroline, Jamie and Alice. These were on the mantelpiece, in amongst the fixture cards and the formal invitations. If he were being honest, Patrick had always felt uneasy about the way he had this group of photographs placed just so, photographs too at ease with themselves and their beholder. It was all too calculated. It was all part of the kit that he liked to think he despised, the kind of aren't-we-a-happy-family cluster that second-rate headmasters tended to have on their mantelpieces because it was the sort of photographs they believed that their prospective parents liked to see.

There was one of Caroline looking young and glamorous. As she once had been. And there was the obligatory wedding-day pose. Then there was one of Alice before the teens kicked in, about twelve-ish, a bit toothy and gauche but sun-tanned and healthy on her horse. Next along there was Jamie, uncomfortable in his suit but impressive in gown and mortarboard on his graduation day. Then one of Caroline and Patrick with the children in Norfolk, a photograph Patrick had asked a passing Japanese holidaymaker to take.

Of all the photographs the one that meant the most to Patrick was not, however, in this silver-framed cluster or visible to Detective Chief Inspector Bevan. It stayed, a touchstone, in his desk; and every morning Patrick Balfour opened the top right-hand drawer just a little to look at it. It was a black and white one of his father, a headmaster himself, surrounded by his staff in the playground of his primary school. His father's unwavering eyes were on Patrick, saying, *Do what you can to help, Patrick.*

The detective chief inspector was now nearly ready. After briefly studying the ends of his fingers, he sat up a little on the sofa, his stomach bulging hard against his belt as he leant forward.

'Mr Balfour, I have to tell you there has been an allegation made against you.'

'An allegation?'

9

'And that allegation, together with some other information and material which has come into our possession, has given me cause for concern.'

Part of Patrick wanted to laugh. Perhaps it was the way the chief inspector delivered the phrases *come into our possession* and *cause for concern*, like a policeman in a rather pedestrian school play, or perhaps it was the ludicrous nature of the moment, but he managed to keep his face straight and his voice steady as he said, 'What material? What are you talking about? What information?'

'I don't think this is the time or the place to go into that in detail.'

2

When Patrick told Daphne to cancel all his appointments for the rest of the afternoon she looked him full in the eye before picking up her shorthand pad. He told her that he was going off with Detective Chief Inspector Bevan to the police station to clear up some misunderstandings. He insisted that no one, but no one, be told anything. One word in a school community, as they both knew only too well, and it was all over the place. If pressed about where the headmaster was, by Michael Falconer or indeed by anyone at all, she was to play the straightest of bats and say it was an urgent family matter.

Daphne knew all about straight bats. She did not blink. Indeed, there was only the slightest of wobbles in her voice when she asked, 'Do you want me to ring Caroline?'

'No, thank you. I will later.'

'Or the Chairman?'

'No, I'll do that.'

'If you're not back by four-thirty, what about the Heads of Department Committee?'

'Michael will have to take it.'

'I'll tell him.'

'Too bad if they don't like it.'

As Patrick recrossed the wide wooden hall to his study, Detective Chief Inspector Bevan was waiting for him just inside the door. Patrick tapped his pockets to check he had his wallet and his mobile phone with him, and on his way out he remembered to pick up his reading glasses from where he had left them, face down on that disciplinary letter.

'Right,' he said, 'let's go.'

But the detective chief inspector did not want to go just yet. He wanted, if the headmaster wouldn't mind, to see the headmaster's private flat, and he went ahead of Patrick up the curving staircase with that nimbleness peculiar to slightly overweight men. On their way up, passing the early Munnings watercolours and the prints of Patrick and Caroline's Cambridge colleges, he questioned Patrick on the issue of keys to the flat.

'Does anyone else have one?'

'My wife, of course.'

'And your daughter?'

'Yes.'

'But they're not here now?'

'No, my daughter is in class. Or at least I hope she is.'

'So she's at school here then?'

'Yes.'

'Does that cause you any problems?'

'Not that I am aware of.'

'Can't be easy, though.'

'We get on very well.'

'And how old is she?'

'Seventeen.'

'Very nice. Same as mine. But she . . . lives with her mother?'

'Mostly, yes, as I've told you. She sleeps over there most nights.'

Patrick opened the door to the flat, but Bevan paused on the threshold, looking at the lock.

'Anyone else have a key to this flat? Outside the family?'

'Joan. She pops in to clean each morning. She's been with us for years.'

'Reliable, is she, this Joan?'

'Totally.'

'And that's all? All who have a key?'

'The Clerk of Works will have a set. He has a key to every property in the school.'

'Why?'

'He has to get in if there's a burst pipe or whatever.'

'And what about all those who work for the Clerk of Works?'

'They'd be under the Clerk of Works' control, the keys.'

'And you don't mind all these people having access to them?'

'Why should I? What is all this?'

'Just that a lot of people in your position, Mr Balfour, have to guard their privacy.'

'Schools like this don't work like that.'

'Is that so?'

'It's more like a goldfish bowl.'

Patrick stood aside to let Detective Chief Inspector Bevan go in first, and followed him from room to room. He felt like a confused vendor unexpectedly dealing with a prospective buyer. This is the kitchen, and that's the bathroom; you can just see the dome of St Paul's, and then we have the three bedrooms, my daughter's, it's a bit tidier than usual, but then she's rarely here, as I just said, and this is my son's, but he's in America just starting his Ph.D, and this is where my wife and I sleep, well no, it's where I sleep, and here's the sitting room, which has most of my paperbacks and a small study area over there in the corner. Nice view of the Thames, isn't it?

13

But Patrick said none of this.

Instead, as he watched the detective move around, all he could hear replaying was Bevan's singsong voice in his study downstairs, and the words *We won't go into the detail of it now, Mr Balfour, but they are serious matters* and the words *There are things I need to discuss with you* and the words *I wouldn't be here otherwise, would I?* and the words *No, it's not 'an arrest' as such. To be technical, you'll be our guest.*

Patrick was also thinking about Caroline, and about his children, and about what he might have to tell them. In his mind he was phoning them all or, which was worse, speaking to them face to face. He was thinking about *Newsnight*, and he was hearing the question in the television studio, *So tell me, Mr Balfour, why were you arrested?* and he was thinking what the hell is going on here, and he was thinking what on earth do you mean by *We've got something to show you.* Bevan interrupted these thoughts.

'And you work up here sometimes, Mr Balfour, do you? You're comfortable up here.'

'What do you mean by "comfortable"?'

'You can relax up here on your own?'

'Yes, I sometimes bring school stuff up here, but I might come up to have a quiet read, or do some writing. I write as well.'

'But more often you're downstairs?'

'Well, that's where all the files are and where my secretary is. That's my public study.'

'And if you see any of your students you see them in your downstairs study? For disciplinary matters?'

'Well, I see my pupils on many matters.'

'But always downstairs?'

'Of course.'

'Never up here? You never see a pupil up here?'

'Good God no, this is strictly private.'

14

'I see.'

'I have to be myself somewhere.'

Bevan smiled.

'Of course, yes. So at weekends, when your wife and daughter are in Finley Place, and your secretary's not in, you might well be up here?'

'I might be, yes. I might be doing any number of things.' The detective opened no drawers or cupboards. Nor did he seem interested in the family snaps or what was on the bookshelves, beyond taking Patrick's novels out and looking at the author's photograph and at the biographical details inside the back flap. Patrick knew only too well the narrow panel of words Bevan was now reading. After all, he had to agree the details each time with his publisher.

Patrick Balfour read History at Cambridge where he was awarded a double first. As well as being a headmaster he has written historical novels about Robert Louis Stevenson and Auguste Rodin.

A Fellow of the Royal Society of Literature, he is married with two children and lives in London.

Bevan put the books back on the shelves and peered out of all the windows, one by one, and, turning around each time, made rather a point of looking back at the room from every angle. Intensely irritating though Patrick found the whole thing, especially the ponderous pace at which it was conducted, he was damned if he was going to demean himself by asking, 'So what exactly are you looking for?' He stood in the middle of the room as impassively as he could be until the detective chief inspector spoke again.

'That's fine. Thank you, Mr Balfour.'

By now Patrick was less concerned about this visit to his flat than about whether, on his way across the quad to the thankfully unmarked police car, he would have to walk side by side with the policeman, even though detectives did not wear uniform. He had only five minutes until the bell to end lesson six and he did not want to walk through the quad when it became a millrace of pupils.

In a school, in the goldfish bowl, headmaster-watching went with the territory. There were thousands of windows, scores of buildings, and Patrick knew there were eyes, curious eyes, hostile eyes, eyes focused on him every hour of the day. The last thing he wanted (short of bumping into Michael Falconer and having to say 'Oh hello, Michael, this is Detective Chief Inspector Bevan') was to run the gauntlet of hundreds of pupils and a handful of staff, a point he made to Bevan while closing the front door of the flat behind him. The detective chief inspector was instantly accommodating.

'By all means, let's meet by the porter's lodge in a couple of minutes, shall we? My car's a blue Volvo.'

'I know, same model as mine. I saw you arrive.'

Bevan's eyebrows picked that up and he half-smiled the acknowledgement. However, as they turned the corner at the bottom of the staircase, there, dammit, was Michael Falconer hurrying up the opposite staircase to his office, to the deputy head's office, where most of the day-to-day school discipline was administered.

Michael Falconer saw them both, and Patrick could see that Michael saw enough to register 'Who on earth is that with Balfour?' but neither made a move towards the other, and Michael hurried on. Patrick had little doubt that his deputy would hurry on. It was part of Michael's management style to hurry on, to run from room to room, from meeting to meeting, and to suggest that by dashing in this way from place to place he was saving the school from falling apart. It was also outside Michael's door that those boys and girls sent to him for bad behaviour had to stand and stew. Indeed, there was a guilty looking bunch standing there at this very moment.

Well, Patrick reflected, it was at his own door that some big stuff had now arrived, some very big stuff indeed, but as he stepped out into the quad he was more determined than ever to appear effortlessly in control. Part of being a good head, as Patrick knew better than most, was in looking the part. He made sure that he was always well dressed, and he took particular care each day with his shirt and tie.

The quad was more or less empty of pupils, just a few piles of books left lying where they shouldn't be, and the usual sprinkling of sixth-formers lounging against the wall, with their shirts right out. As Patrick walked towards the unmarked blue Volvo he realised that one of them, the boy they were all huddled around and listening to, was Hugo Solomon.

In catching Hugo's eye, Patrick caught a look he knew only too well from many previous encounters, a look more subtle and soiled than a simple schoolboy sneer. It was the look of someone who was never surprised by any development, the look of a mind with a low view of humanity, the look of a contrarian who enjoyed conflict for its own sake.

Suddenly, when Patrick was about ten yards from the group, they all glanced his way, burst out laughing, and then turned quickly back towards each other. Sometimes Patrick heard that sound, at exactly that artificially increased volume, as he left a classroom or turned the corner of a corridor. He could usually tell if it was personal, if it was verbal ink thrown at the back of his jacket. This laugh sounded like one of those.

17

3

Primary schools. Patrick could never forget them, because his father had been the head of one, and because all primary schools had their own distinctive smell. As did police stations. This he found out during the long afternoon of 5 November. With police stations, he noticed, it was an altogether different smell. It was a mixture of beer and sweat, of unwashed clothes, of skin deeply ingrained with nicotine, and, above all, the smell of an indefinable fear.

Detective Chief Inspector Bevan, light on his feet, walked ahead of him along the narrow, brightly lit corridor. As Patrick followed he could hear, through a wall or two, a distant drunk banging on a cell door, banging and shouting.

'Give me my fuckin' trainers back, they'll be nicked.'

'Shut it!'

'While you got me in 'ere some fuckin' thief'll nick my trainers.'

After a pause a voice, the voice of a policeman bored with the man in the cell and all those lowlifes like him, called back, '*Shut it*, scumbag.'

They passed some uniformed officers. As so often when

Patrick Balfour walked in a London street or along a railway station platform, a few eyes flicked his way, half-recognising him. It was a glance Patrick knew only too well. They had seen that face before, they knew who he was, who was it, come on, on telly, who was he on with the other night?

Then Bevan turned left and ushered Patrick into a small interview room.

It was a plain room with a table, two chairs and no natural light: about the size of a study in a boys' boarding house. There was a double tape recorder bolted to the wall with a small square microphone above it. There was nothing on the walls, nothing at all, just black paint. But in the air hung the same lowlife smell.

Detective Chief Inspector Bevan asked Patrick if he wanted his solicitor present. Patrick did not. He said he had done nothing wrong and he did not intend wasting his solicitor's time. The solicitor was one more person to know. He did not want this nonsense to go any further. Instead, in passing, he asked Bevan why someone who was locked up would not be allowed to have his trainers.

'Don't want him hanging himself with his laces, do we?'

'Is this being recorded?'

'No, Patrick. This is a preliminary discussion.'

Ah, Patrick now, is it?

So, now he was on their side of the street, it was 'Patrick'. Bevan sat opposite Patrick, and the first thing he brought up, in his most casual way, and in his most singsong voice, was why it was that Patrick had driven off from the forecourt of a petrol station in the Mile End Road without paying for his fuel.

'What's a man like you, Patrick, doing getting involved in bilking?'

If Bevan wanted a reaction from the headmaster facing him across the table he wasn't disappointed. Patrick exploded in an anger so sudden that it took both of them completely by surprise. He brought both hands down flat and hard on the table.

'You can't have brought me down here for this rubbish! I've been through this! You know that perfectly well.'

A few weeks earlier, in October, Patrick had been phoned by the police to ask if he had forgotten to pay for £35 worth of petrol in the Shell garage on the Mile End Road. The garage had reported the non-payment incident to the police, quoted his car registration number, and the police had rung the school. Patrick told them not only that he had not been driving in the Mile End Road at that time but he had not been down the Mile End Road for at least five years. Which was true, apart from the five years bit, which was none of their business. The garage had made a mistake, as he had explained at the time, the garage had got the wrong car and that was their problem and that was it, full stop.

'Is it?'

'It is, full stop.'

Bevan spread his hands and shrugged his shoulders as if to say 'Maybe, Patrick.' The detective was composed, at ease, genial, his voice warmer and more South Wales by the minute, and by the second more maddening.

'And that's all you have to say on that, is it, Mr Balfour?'

Back to 'Mr Balfour', are we?

'Yes, so why have you brought me down here to ask me again?'

'Because it's not full stop. You see, I have now seen the video.'

'So you've seen it.'

'Yes, and it *is* your car, with your number plate. The garage did not make a mistake. I checked in your school yard this afternoon, and there's no doubt at all.'

20

'In which case it was stolen from me.'

'The car was? In the middle of the day?'

'I imagine so.'

'Without you knowing? Big red Volvo stolen in broad daylight from your usual parking place? Reserved For The Headmaster it says in big white letters. Right between the one Reserved For The Deputy Headmaster and the one Reserved For The Bursar?'

'Yes.'

'And then returned to the same place? Big red Volvo? Still in broad daylight?'

'There's no other explanation. It must have been.'

'Take a bit of doing, wouldn't it? Pretty crowded car park, it looked to me. Lots of people around. Porters, security people, CCTV and so forth. Bit of a goldfish bowl, you said, a bit of a Fort Knox too, and a car that everyone must recognise as the headmaster's. It's the only red Volvo I saw down there. Shouldn't think many teachers could afford one.'

'Look, I'm sorry, but this is absolutely ridiculous. Is this all you want to talk about?'

Bevan looked a touch amused.

'And, another thing, it *is* you getting out of the car to fill up the tank. Some of these garage CCTVs are a bit grainy, a bit vague, I admit that, but in this instance it isn't. It is you.'

'What do you mean, it's me?'

'I've studied the film.'

'And I've just told you it isn't me. It wasn't me. It can't have been. I was driving back from a conference in Brighton, I came up on the M23 to the M25. I didn't even come in to London on the eastern side.'

'It's you, same clothes, same suit, same height. Even the same walk.'

21

'In which case it's someone who looks like me.'

'Come on, Patrick.'

Patrick eye-balled the detective. 'No, there's no "come on, Patrick" about it. Don't tell me to "come on".'

Bevan sat back in his chair.

'Well, let's leave that for a moment, shall we?'

'No, let me see it. Where's the tape? I'll stop this in its tracks now.'

'We can arrange that. But first things first.'

First things first! Patrick's patience was going. It was going fast.

'Do you think I would ruin everything, jeopardise my career for the sake of £35? Do you know who I am?'

'I know very well who you are, Patrick.'

'I'm "Mr Balfour" to you.'

'That's fine, Mr Balfour.'

'I can't believe you're bringing all this up again.'

'People do very strange things, Mr Balfour.'

'Well, I don't.'

'The most unlikely people. You wouldn't believe it, Mr Balfour. Even writers, even politicians, even people who appear on radio and TV. Some of them are in prison even as we speak.'

'Yes, well, thank you for that insight into your working life but I don't.'

'You're sure, Mr Balfour?'

'Not unless I've had a nervous breakdown, and if I had I'm sure my secretary would have pointed it out by now. Or unless I've got Rory Bremner on my staff.'

Bevan raised his eyebrows as if he were assessing that last remark.

'I've also been looking at the press cuttings. You're not exactly a stranger to controversy, Mr Balfour, are you?'

'And you're not to cliché.'

'Always in the papers, it seems. There's a huge lot about you.'

'I'm a public figure, yes, and public figures attract gossip, but what has that –'

'Yes, I heard you when I was in the car the other day. You spoke very well; *Start The Week*, wasn't it?'

'And some reporters sniff around my private life; it goes with being known.'

'Quite a risk, even so. For a man in your position. Quite a risk with your career. For a headmaster. Five days in a row it was in the press, lots of photos, you and that woman. Two Sunday spreads made a real meal of it.'

'They did, yes.'

'So it didn't exactly fade away, Mr Balfour, did it, as a story?'

'No.'

'But your governors supported you.'

'As they should have done.'

'And your wife did.'

'Yes, she did.'

'Very loyal of her.'

'Yes.'

'And your staff.'

'Most of them did.'

'Not all?'

'No, some of them thought I should have resigned, or been sacked. That little detail was leaked to the press too. I'm sure you've read it all up.'

'But, despite all that, your governors still backed you.'

'Yes, they did.'

'But your governors could have argued it was damaging the school's reputation.'

'They could have.'

'Because the thing is, correct me if I'm wrong, but the

well-off middle classes don't like spending all that money and sending their kids to a school where the head's having it off all over the place, do they?'

'I wasn't *having it off all over the place*.'

'Still, doesn't go down too well on the old competitive dinner party circuit, does it?'

'Good schools aren't damaged that easily. And it was a private matter.'

'Which got into the public domain.'

'And what has any of that got to do with any of this?'

'Just that people do surprising things. Under pressure. That was my point. That's all. Whiter than white is what you blokes have to be, isn't it? Can't be easy, mind, watching yourself all the time, all that self-control. Too much self-control can do things to you.'

'I know that.'

'Even to media-hardened headmasters like Mr Patrick Balfour.'

'That is an insulting term. Can we move on to something more important?'

'Certainly we can, Mr Balfour. I am arresting you. And I am now going to caution you.'

'You're *arresting* me?'

'And I am now going to caution you.'

The detective looked above Patrick's head and intoned the words he knew by heart: 'You do not have to say anything. But it may harm your defence if you do not mention, when questioned, anything you may later rely on in court. Anything you do say may be given in evidence.'

'Why are you arresting me?'

'Because I'm not satisfied with your answers.'

Patrick pushed his chair back hard. Bevan went on.

'Would you like your solicitor now?'

'No.'

'You're sure about that?'

'I'm sure.'

'Think you can look after yourself?'

'Yes, I do.'

'All right then, let's go along to the duty sergeant, who'll read you your rights and book you in.'

Bevan stood up. Patrick rose to face him.

'So this is the point, is it, at which I cease to be your "guest"?'

'Yes, it is. And there are a few things I need to check out before we talk again.'

4

When Patrick became headmaster of his first school one of the first things he did was to get rid of the dais from every classroom. He disliked their symbolism. He had remained of that view, telling the Clerk of Works to remove every single one from his second school. He did not give a damn what tradition dictated. The raised platform had for centuries insisted that pupils look up at their teachers and had allowed, if not encouraged, teachers to look down on their pupils. The raised platform smacked of the past, of the cane, of the mortarboard, of deference, and above all of the I'm-in-charge power game. There would be none of that in any school that Patrick Balfour ran. As far as he was concerned they were better off as fire wood or round the back yard in the skip. So when it comes to decisions on the fate of the dais, the Clerk of Works joked to Patrick, the only person still left standing on the raised platform is you.

Whatever might have changed in his schools, Patrick found that the old ways were still going strong in the Metropolitan Police. Although Patrick was just over six feet tall the floor on which he stood was at least two feet lower than the level on which the duty sergeant, armed with his paperwork, sat. The duty sergeant, his white bald head shining in the harsh striplight, took his time, leaning on the counter and looking down on Patrick. He gave Patrick his rights and offered him free legal representation, and, with painful slowness, filled in Patrick's answers. C stream, Patrick thought, C stream at best. But he swallowed hard and took it. Then he was searched.

'We're required to do this, sir. First your hair.'

'My *what*?'

'Your hair, sir.'

'What about it?'

'We have to examine it.'

'Examine it!'

'There might be a sharp pin in it; you wouldn't believe what weapons some people come in here with.'

'I'm not in the habit of sticking pins in people.'

'I'm sure you're not, sir. Thank you, now if you would just loosen your collar and take your tie off . . . just routine, sir, now under your arms . . . And if you'd just empty your pockets . . . and now . . . your legs. Legs apart, sir.'

Patrick spread his legs.

'Thank you.'

The duty sergeant placed Patrick's wallet and mobile phone into a plastic bag, then put that in Box Number 4 in the locker behind the counter.

'Can I keep my glasses and my shoes?'

'Yes, you can.'

'Not a suicide risk then?'

'Let's hope not, sir.'

Patrick was put straight in to a cell. The door banged behind him. Inside there was nothing but a rubber mattress, a lavatory bowl without a seat and a bench.

It was in here, in the disciplinary technique much favoured by Michael Falconer as well as the Metropolitan Police, that Patrick was left to stew. And while he was stewing, a new seeping stench – that of stale urine, of unflushed loos – joined and overpowered all others. But even though the air quality was very poor, Patrick did some deep breathing. He also tried to decipher some of the names scratched on the door by previous occupants.

Dave D
Rog Selwood
up your arse
Normal Norman
a good few swastikas
suck my cock
Sammy

Switch off, Patrick said to himself. Switch off now.

Over the years Patrick had developed the ability to switch off, or, if not quite to switch off at least to desensitise himself, to bring his body and his emotional temperature down to freezing point, to turn the volume around him right down so that whatever was going on in front of him – particularly if it was distasteful or tedious – was no more than a kind of half-heard murmur, rather like a radio left on in a distant room. He found this a particularly helpful technique in staff meetings when they still hadn't got past item three and Barbara Bingham was boring for England.

Switch off.

Switch off. Choose your attitude.

And, strangely enough, when he was in the cell in Charing Cross Police Station there was something else, something quite specific which helped him, a particular sentence which was at work in his mind. While Patrick had been shaving that very morning, the morning of the day on which he was arrested, he had heard 'Thought for the Day' on Radio 4. It was about Victor Frankel. Until that moment Patrick had never even heard of Frankel – a philosopher and logotherapist and a survivor of Auschwitz – but, with half his face covered in soap, Patrick put his razor down and stood staring in to the bathroom mirror. He was held by Frankel's life and by the way the man had come through his appalling experiences. And of all the excellent things Frankel said the line that hit Patrick hardest was 'Our last freedom is to choose our attitude.'

If Victor Frankel could come through Auschwitz and be positive, the very least Patrick Balfour could do was put up with being kept waiting in a piss-soaked police cell.

So he sat there and repeated to himself Frankel's words: *Choose your attitude, Patrick.*

An hour and a half later, with the smell of urine now in his shirt and in his hands and in every breath he took, and with the man in the next cell still complaining at the top of his voice about his trainers, Patrick was taken back to the interview room. This time, Detective Chief Inspector Bevan explained, the interview would all be recorded. When Bevan then asked him, 'Do you understand that?' Patrick cut back, 'You mean, do I understand the words "This will be recorded"?'

That was how long his *choose your attitude* attitude had lasted, about fifteen seconds. Unperturbed, Bevan pressed play and record.

'I am DCI Bevan. I am interviewing Mr Patrick Balfour. The date is 5 November. The time is 1600 hours. Before the commencement of this interview I must remind you that you are entitled to free legal advice. I understand you do not wish to have a solicitor present. This interview is being conducted in the interview room at Charing Cross Police Station. At the conclusion of this interview I will give you a notice explaining what will happen to the tapes. I will now once again caution you.

You do not have to say anything. But it may harm your defence if you do not mention, when questioned, anything you may later rely on in court. Anything you do say may be given in evidence.'

Then, having broken the numbered seal of a plastic bag, DCI Bevan spoke as much to the mouth of the plastic bag in his hand as to Patrick.

'I am opening a plastic bag and taking out Mr Balfour's wallet.' He handed it to Patrick. 'Your wallet, Mr Balfour.'

'Thank you.'

'Very nice. It seems very new.'

'It is.'

'How long have you had this one?'

'This one?'

'That's what I asked.'

'Three weeks. Or thereabouts.'

'What happened to your previous one?'

'I lost it.'

'Did you report it?'

'I didn't think it worth bothering. There wasn't much money in it, I don't carry much, as you've doubtless found out; somehow I've got into that habit. I suppose I've become rather spoilt by my secretary's arrangements.'

'No credit cards either?'

'Yes, I rang up my three credit card companies straightaway.'

'Which cards?'

'Gold Card, Visa and American Express. I rang to cancel them. Luckily nothing had been spent on them, no shopping bonanzas, so I got new cards and a new wallet. The one you've just seen. End of story.'

'Maybe.'

'What do you mean?'

Bevan looked steadily into his eyes. 'Well, you keep

saying "full stop" and "end of story" as if you're running the show. The thing is you're not. I'm not one of your students. All right?'

Patrick seethed but chose his attitude and said nothing. He breathed deeply. The detective smiled no harm done and went on.

'Were you upset about losing the wallet?'

'I was irritated. Not upset, no.'

'I would be.'

'I'm too busy to worry about that sort of thing for too long. I'd suffered no financial damage.'

'You weren't concerned about any other damage it might do you?'

'I don't follow.'

Bevan stood up and hitched his trousers up over his stomach. 'When did you last see that wallet?'

'The afternoon I went to Hatchard's.'

'Hatchard's?'

'The bookshop in Piccadilly.'

'You were buying something there?'

'No, signing copies of my latest book.'

'Oh, yes, of course. Was this one fact or fiction?'

'Fiction.'

'Do you enjoy fiction?'

'Yes.'

Did Patrick spot the slightest of smirks flit over the detective's face, a kind of Hugo Solomon smirk? He couldn't be sure, but the very thought of it unsettled him and he was annoyed to hear a defensive blustering note in his voice as he said, 'Well, a mixture I suppose. A bit of fact, a bit of fiction, sometimes I'm on the line between. I write . . . historical novels.'

'Interesting, that. I'll read them. So, how long were you in Hatchard's?'

'I'm not sure, an hour or more. An hour and a half. When I got home and realised my wallet was missing I rang them, of course, but it hadn't been handed in.'

'No, but it was handed in to the police at West End Central.'

Patrick sat up a bit in his chair.

'Well, it's good to know there are still some honest people out there.'

'There are plenty of honest people out there, I'd say.'

'I know that.'

'Do you?'

'It was a silly comment. I was joking.'

'Were you?'

'You're making too much of it.'

Bevan stared at him in silence. Then he opened a drawer in the table and took out another plastic bag. Inside it Patrick could see another wallet, the black leather one he had lost. It still had the yellow Post-it on it, the one to remind him to buy a birthday card for Caroline. He had forgotten to buy the card, but Daphne, who always kept some spare cards in her desk, had (and not for the first time) saved the day.

'What was in it when you last saw this particular wallet?'

'In it? I can't remember.'

'Yes you can.'

'Not much. Pretty boring stuff. My driving licence, some photos of my family, nothing of interest.'

'And that's all?'

'That's about it.'

'Well, this wallet has some interesting things in it, Mr Balfour.'

'Really?'

Bevan opened the wallet and carefully slipped something out. 'These cards.'

'Cards?'

'As well as some telephone numbers. Quite a few cards, and quite a few numbers.'

'What sort of cards?'

'These.'

The room lurched, the floor tilted, my legs went weak, my mouth went dry, I couldn't believe it was happening to me. Patrick had heard them all said, all those phrases, and he had read them all, and each time he had heard them or read them he had felt superior because his professional life had taught him to reject such clichés, to put a red line through each and every one, to put such books back on the revolving stand.

Well, the room lurched, the floor tilted, his legs went weak, his mouth went dry, and he could not believe it was happening to him. Dry-mouthed, Patrick said, 'Anyone could have put these in my wallet.'

'But that is your handwriting, Mr Balfour?'

'Where?'

'On the back of the pink card?'

Patrick turned over the card. He looked and looked again, holding the card closer. It was not his writing on the back but it was as close to his writing as dammit was to swearing. But, dammit, lots of people could do that. Copying signatures was a schoolboy's game. As a schoolboy himself he had been an expert at it: he used to practise writing all his friends' names exactly in the way they did, and as a forger he was always in heavy demand and frequently offered free packets of cigarettes to sign order forms.

Bevan passed over another card.

Patrick took it. The numbers on the back of this card were also formed in just the way that he formed his numbers, most especially his characteristic 3 and 7. The handwriting was very small, as was his. The ink was the same colour and strength as he used, a strong black ink. But in particular his eye was held by the way that the letter 'r' was formed. That 'r'. His heart kicked into another gear. How the hell could anyone know about that? It was an 'r' he had briefly appropriated from a much cleverer contemporary who had dazzled him at Cambridge. But he had not used that 'r' for many years, in fact not since his undergraduate days.

He smelt his fingers. It was no longer the smell of his own body. It was the smell of other people's urine. His shirt was now sticking to his neck, to his back and clinging under his arms.

Bevan went on talking, in his whispering Welsh boyo way, as he wandered round the room. He then stood right behind Patrick's chair, a technique Michael Falconer had told Patrick that he favoured when leaning on a suspect.

'We rang the numbers, Patrick.'

'Did you?'

'Yes we did.'

'Well, I never have.'

'Come on, Patrick. We've got a record of the calls you made . . . from your number in your flat . . . one-thirty in the morning, two in the morning. The calls are listed.'

'It must have been someone else.'

'Not very nice. Schoolgirls. Offering a bit of female discipline for the teacher. A bit of caning. Bottoms up for teacher. In her twelve-year-old's school skirt. Tied up to the desk with her school tie. That's what she said she was best at. Bit of a speciality. And the twelve-year-old's dress and white socks. And when one of the girls takes her clothes off it's a boy. Not what I'd like to think any son or daughter of mine was up to. Not, I imagine, Mr Balfour, what you'd like to think your son or daughter was up to.'

Patrick's voice croaked, 'Keep my children out of it!'

Bevan opened his hands in a gently untroubled gesture. 'I was making a general parenting point. You've written a book on parenting, you see, and I've read it. Bought it off the internet. Got very good write-ups. And you mention your children in it. You brought your children into it quite a lot. Jamie and Alice. You're very interested in the young, aren't you?'

Patrick stared at the cards. His blood was beating in his ears. 'Who handed it in? My wallet?'

'A man came in to the station and left it.'

'When?'

'On the same afternoon as you were in Piccadilly. The afternoon you were in the bookshop.'

'What was his name?'

'We don't know.'

'You don't know or you won't tell me?'

'We don't know.'

'But you must take the name and address of whoever hands things in?'

'Usually. But he just came in, said he'd found it and left.'

'Bit odd, isn't it?'

'It is a bit unusual, but it does happen. Police stations are very busy places.'

'Why don't you find your unknown benefactor and ask him? He'll be on your CCTV, then you can give him his cards back.'

'At the moment I am asking you some questions.'

'Are there any more? Any more things in your drawer?'

Detective Chief Inspector Bevan seemed to enjoy that. 'Why do you ask that, Patrick?'

'Things tend to come in threes. And you've got that look about you.'

'But I haven't finished with the wallet yet.'

'Well, I've left a busy school behind and a busy day.'

'I'm sure they can do without you for a while. And they'll have to: you're now under arrest.'

'I'm aware of that. And it's a disgrace.'

'Well, it's not very nice, I agree, but then nor is what you've been up to.'

'Up to?'

'Yes. With the young.'

Patrick could now feel the blood pulsing in his temples. He flexed his fingers and tried to control his breathing.

'I've been up to nothing. Someone else has.'

'Well, they all say that.'

'Do they?'

'Oh they do. All of them. Are you interested in photography?'

'Photography? Why?'

'Are you?'

'I'm interested, yes. I've got a camera, if that's what you mean.'

'What sort?'

'It's a digital.'

'Good at it, are you?'

'No, not myself, not as an art form, but I like going to exhibitions. At the National Portrait Gallery, that sort of thing.'

'Very nice.'

The detective seemed amused. Patrick tried to ignore it. He kept going.

'And there are a couple of promising photographers at my school. One girl at the moment is particularly good.'

'And that's it?'

'Well, as I said, I sometimes go to exhibitions at the National Portrait Gallery, if I'm walking past.'

'You walk around London a lot?'

'Yes.'

'On your own?'

'I like walking, I like fresh air, I like to get out of my study.'

'But you don't take photographs yourself?'

'No, my wife does. Well, I'm sure over the years I've taken a few bad snapshots, like all parents, but no, I don't take photos. As such.'

'Really?'

'What is this?'

'Well, that's the point, that's what I am hoping you can tell me, because of more concern to me, Mr Balfour, than the contents of your wallet are what I have here.'

Detective Chief Inspector Bevan half-gestured, this time with an almost apologetic here–we–go–again–nod, towards the drawer beneath his stomach. He then took out another plastic bag, undid another numbered seal, this time containing an envelope of photographs. As he opened the envelope and described for the benefit of the running tape what he was doing and handed the photographs to Patrick, one by one, as one might pass across some recent holiday snaps to a friend over the dinner table or around the fire, he spoke very quietly and very courteously in his stroking voice, his face not far from Patrick's ear:

'Snappy Snaps in High Street Ken phoned us last week. They said they were developing some photos that worried them. We went to see the photographs. They sometimes ring us if they feel some concern. We have an arrangement. The prints were the ones you are looking at again now, Mr Balfour. The person who took them in, the name and address given by the person taking them in, 64 Finley Place, and the person captured on the shop's security camera collecting them, is you. In you come and say can I have some prints made from my digital camera, and you've

37

brought the memory card along, the digital flash card, and they say yes, just put it in the machine there and follow the instructions, and they give you a receipt and you can pick them up tomorrow. And you do. Once again, I have checked the CCTV film. Many times. And it's a very clear film this one, better even than the garage one. No doubt about it at all.'

Patrick could not speak. All he could feel was a falling and an incoming wave of pain, and then another, and then another.

After a few standard landscapes, pretty places that could have been almost anywhere in southern England, flower beds and woodland scenes and some conventional shots of churches – East Anglian wool churches by the look of them – came photos of a young boy. A boy turning to look at the camera. Of the last batch, before returning to a final landscape of a Kentish oast house and a rural lych gate, six were of a boy, all taken from different angles.

With a terrible new jolt Patrick recognised the background. In the last few the boy was lounging provocatively on his sofa, the sofa in the sitting room of his upstairs flat. The boy was smiling straight at the photographer, with one hand seeming to stretch out in welcome while the other hand dangled D. H. Lawrence's *The Boy In The Bush*.

It was Patrick's sofa all right. There was no argument about that. They were his paperback bookcases. No doubt at all. If you looked closely you could see some of the titles on the shelves, the rows of his early orange Penguins, from which the Lawrence volume had clearly been taken. And the boy was as at home on the sofa as he could possibly be. He was, as it were, patting the place next to him. Come and join me, his smile seemed to say, come on, come and feel me.

38

Patrick's voice, when it came, rasped a little: 'Who would do this to me?'

'Would you like a glass of water?'

'I have never seen these photographs. I did not take them.'

'But you do take your flash card to Snappy Snaps in High Street Ken.'

'No, I don't.'

'Snappy Snaps is where you get your prints made.'

'No, I go to Jessops.'

'We'll leave that. But it is your flat?'

'It certainly looks like my flat, yes.'

'It is your flat, Patrick. I've been there this afternoon with you.'

'Yes, it is.'

'At least we're agreeing on the flat then.'

'But how they came to be taken there I simply haven't any idea.'

'Did you take them?'

'No. I did not.'

'Oh, come on, Patrick.'

Patrick just shook his head. Sweat was running down his arms. 'I did not and I would not.'

'Pat-rick.'

'And I have no interest, in that sense, in young boys.'

'It's quite common in your profession. It's what draws some in to it. Isn't that the case?'

Patrick swallowed. 'Yes, that is true.'

'But not you? I know it can be difficult to talk about this sort of thing. You start with the mags, with *Vulcan*, yes? with *Euro Boy* . . . and you just had to look, and then you just had to click on, and then you just had to go to the swimming pool, yes?'

'No!'

'Teachers can do a lot of that, easy for them, it's tailor-made for it, come on, the changing rooms, checking out the pants and the boxers, stealing a pair, the pair of a favoured boy, fingering the name tape, checking the showers, standing under the diving board, and all, of course, in the cause of making sure there's no bullying and showing an interest in their education and following the swimming.'

'This is terrible.'

'It's not nice, I agree. But it's the risk, isn't it, the risk of being found out, that's what gives it the . . . spice. And it's the caring smokescreen that gets you in. How does it go: make the friendship, seal the friendship, abuse the friendship. That's what I'm told. Isn't that it?'

'You tell me.'

'And it's not just teachers who abuse. It's not just you, Patrick, it's out there among all the carers. Who knows, there may be policemen at it even as I speak.'

'Perhaps you're one of them,' Patrick bit back. 'You seem to know a lot about it.'

'If you don't want me to help, Patrick, I won't go on.'

They sat facing each other in silence. Patrick broke eye contact and covered his face with his hands. Neither said a word for a few minutes. When he next spoke Bevan was looking at the tape recorder.

'So, Mr Balfour, someone in your car looking exactly like you drove off from a petrol station in the Mile End Road without paying, and two weeks later your wallet is handed in, a wallet you admit is yours, and it contains names and addresses of pornographic services, and ones with an educational bent, and phone calls are made from your school flat to these pornographic services, and worrying photographs are taken in your flat of a young boy, and you agree it is your flat, and the man on the camera driving away from the petrol station and the man on the camera handing in the film to be developed looks exactly like you but you deny all knowledge of any of it. It's all nothing at all to do with you?'

Patrick opened his eyes and stared at the table top. Where could he turn? He had to talk to someone. He knew who. He needed to talk to her, he needed to talk to her more than anything else in the world. Not a solicitor. Her. But that was not possible. He would never see her again. He had promised, promised both of them.

'I'll ask you again, Patrick. You deny that all three things, the bilking, the contents of your wallet and the photographs, have anything to do with you?'

'That's right. Nothing at all.'

'You deny it all?'

'I do. Of course I do. It's disgusting.'

'Right, I am now returning the wallet which was handed in and the photographs to their bags. I am not going to charge you or hold you any longer now, Mr Balfour, but, pending further enquiries, I am bailing you, without conditions, to return to this station in four weeks' time. That will be on 2 December. Do you understand?'

'Yes, I understand. December the second.'

'Fine. Here is my card in case you wish to meet me or to ring me or to talk in the interim. After you have thought things over you may find you wish to do so. Right, the time is now 1715 hours. You will now go to see the custody sergeant. He will provide you with a notice telling you how you can obtain a copy of the tapes, and he will explain the arrangements for your bail. And that concludes this interview at Charing Cross Police Station between DCI Bevan and Mr Patrick Balfour.'

41

5

He knew the number. He would never forget the number.

'Hi, it's me.'

Long pause. His heart was hammering. Was her heart too? Was it him? Yes, it's me. Look, I know we said we wouldn't, but sometimes something happens, something very big happens to you, something so big that it overrides all the previous agreements, it overrides caution, you know what I mean, don't you, and you don't care any more because you're stuffed and when you're stuffed you turn to those you . . . you turn to those you cannot stop thinking about, to those you still love though you still try to deny it.

'Patrick?'

'I'm calling from a police station. Well, just outside.'

'Sorry? Come again, I didn't catch that.'

As he stepped out of the police station into the streets of London, out to the bangers and the cannons, out to a sky exploding with all the colours of the rainbow, that call remained Patrick's first instinct, a tug, a draw which, even though he twice started to dial her mobile number, he just managed to control.

No, he said to his fingers.

He would not make that call.

He put the mobile back in his pocket.

It was not right to burden her with all this. It was not right, especially in his present state, to reopen things. If he did, as he knew only too well, if he once touched her again, even her hand, even her hand would be enough, or had a long vulnerable conversation, which was more or less the same thing, and brushed her loose lips, tasted her loose lips, he would be back in as deeply as he ever had been. And his life as a headmaster would be over. His marriage would be all over. Caroline and Jamie and Alice might have forgiven him once, but not twice.

Patrick walked along the Embankment. *Any spare change, please?* He stepped around the cadging man sitting on his sleeping bag, then, ten paces on, turned back and gave him some pound coins. A rocket hissed away into the night and showered yellows. He passed someone eating chips, the air sharply edged with vinegar.

Patrick did not want a taxi. He could not face a bus. All he could see were the photographs on his sofa and Bevan's accusing eyes. All he wanted was the gathering November night and the anonymity, the cold cleansing night, with no one looking at him, the November night air, even if it was edged with vinegar, that's what he wanted. Air that did not smell of piss, air that did not taste of fear.

Breathe in, deeply, Patrick, breathe out. Breathe in, deeper this time. Every hundred yards he could feel some of the smell going out of his lungs and some of the fur coating easing off his tongue. Each hundred yards his shirt was unpeeling from his back, his suit was losing its heavy moist feel. A few minutes further along the Embankment and his tongue felt a little cleaner.

On both sides of the river, more early evening fireworks, now green, now yellow and red and blue, were chalking lines on the sky and reflecting off the Thames.

Coloured dots arced and traced their way upwards before bursting and flowering over London, while below, in thousands of gardens and parks beneath those pretty lights, the cannons were banging and the effigies were burning.

So, Patrick asked the sky, who was intent on roasting him?

All right, so he had enemies, he knew that. Who hasn't? You can't publish a book or get to the top of any profession, let alone be a regular on television, without putting some people's backs up, without sticking in someone's gut enough for him to want to stick a knife in you. Anyone worth his salt had someone, some inadequate soul, some disappointed challenger, targeting him. Famous people were pestered. Fact. Famous people had to take out court orders. Fact. Famous people were gunned down by stalkers they did not know. The world was full of failures and tossers, full of envy and bitterness. But no enemies that Patrick Balfour had ever made, in all his years of teaching, in all his years as a head, would go this far, would ever go down this sordid route.

Except, Patrick, that someone somewhere most certainly had gone down that route. Well, who for example? Well, for example, Liz's husband. Roger? Why? Why not? Why wouldn't he want to ruin you? Come on, Roger Nicholson hates you. Roger threatened to do you in. Justin Pett hates you as well. No, well yes, Justin may hate me, and Justin would do a lot, but he wouldn't do this, he wouldn't go this far.

Patrick walked on, the water reflecting the sky, the sky a sudden sunflower-yellow.

What about an inside job?

What about the staff?

Who would? What on earth had he done recently to justify this, to trigger all this? When his head cleared he would think about it properly. As Patrick watched the fire-works he heard the voices all over London, the muttering Common Room critics and the dinner-party know-alls. If any whisper of this got out, any hint of any kind, it would be a field day for all of them. *If this ever gets out . . .*

'Well, he must have done *some*thing, mustn't he . . .'

'There's no smoke without . . .'

'I've always said there was something about Balfour, can't quite put it in words but . . .'

'If he was so innocent the police would never have gone to such lengths, would they?'

'With a man of Patrick Balfour's public profile they wouldn't want egg on their faces, would they?'

After Blackfriars Bridge Patrick leant over the low Embankment wall and made the most straightforward call of them all, the one call to a woman he could be absolutely sure was right: he rang the loyal, the blessedly non-judgemental Daphne. She would be going through hell wondering what was going on and sooner or later he'd have to fill in the gaps. That would not be too difficult because Daphne would say nothing. No rack, no electric shock, no sleep deprivation or toenail torture would ever get Daphne to break a confidence.

As for telling Caroline.

That would be less easy.

And what about the Chairman of Governors, Alex Colthorne? The professional thing, the recommended thing, the sensible thing would be to ring him straight away. But Patrick knew he would not. Nor, on getting back to his study, would he tell Michael Falconer. Michael Falconer and the Chairman of Governors went back a long way. They had played rugby and cricket together at school. And for the old guard playing rugby and cricket together was where most things began: on the playing fields, in the showers, in the bar, in school teams. Tell Alex or Michael, tell one and you'd told both. Get one against you and you got both because his Chairman and his deputy longed for the day that Patrick Balfour finally left the school, the school that he had changed beyond recognition.

'Daphne?'

'Patrick? I'm so glad to hear you.'

'Look, I won't keep you long, Daphne, just a moment or two, if I may.'

'Where are you?'

'First of all, sorry to leave you so suddenly, with all that rearranging to do, such a bore.'

'Don't be silly, Patrick, it's not a bore at all. Where are you now?'

'Not ten minutes away.'

'What was that! That bang?'

'It's Bonfire Night.'

'Is it? So it is.'

'Don't tell me you hadn't noticed?'

'Are you coming back to the office now?'

'The office?'

'I'm rather hoping you'll say you're not.'

'No, I won't, if that's all right. I need a bit of a regroup, I'll fill you in on it in the morning. And, look, Daphne, why don't you go home?'

'I'll be about another hour. Oh, and Caroline rang.'

'You told her?'

'No, of course I didn't, you told me not to. But she said whatever it was she wanted to say wasn't urgent.'

'Was it difficult holding everyone else off?'

'No, not at all. Euan Stuart wants to see you sometime about things in the theatre.'

'Fine, book him in. What about the Heads of Department Committee?'

'No problems at all.'

'Really?'

'Really. Michael said they were like lambs.'

'No other crises? Hugo Solomon hasn't blown the place up?'

'Not that I've heard.'

'Because this is exactly the day he'd choose. And one more thing, before I forget, ring *Newsnight* and say I'll do Thursday week. Do that now, would you, before you go home?'

There was a pause. He knew only too well the full power of his secretary's lengthening pauses.

'Really? Even after . . .?'

'Especially after this. I'm not letting whoever's done this stop me.'

'Done what, Patrick?'

'If you don't mind, I won't go into the details now, but let's just say they've taken the handcuffs off.'

'The handcuffs!'

'For the moment.'

'Oh, don't joke, Patrick, please.'

'Anyway, there we are, another day in the life of a modern head, another chapter in the unwritten autobiography.'

'And there's nothing I can do to help?'

'No, really.'

'It's just that I'm so much nicer a person when I *am* helping.'

'You're always a nice person, Daphne.'

'So I'll leave some sandwiches ready for you when you come in? How about smoked salmon?'

'Perfect. And some cheese and chutney, that real ale chutney. And an apple.'

'I'll tell Susie.'

'Thanks, Daffers. You're a star.'

Patrick ended the call, looked at his phone again, considered the number again, and once again did not dial. For goodness' *sake*, Patrick berated himself, you must play it straight, now more than ever.

Two children, weaving their sparklers in dizzying circles and expansive loops, ran excitedly past him, followed by a mother hurrying to keep up. It suddenly hit him what they were doing. They were writing their names in the night air.

'Stand well back from the fireworks, Patrick.'

'Yes, Mum.'

'Patrick!'

'What?'

'Don't be silly. You're being silly!'

'I'm not.'

'Dad's about to light them. It's dangerous.'

'It's not.'

'You could get hurt.'

'I won't, I won't.'

'Pat-rick!'

6

Patrick rang Caroline over his second cup of coffee at 7.30 the following morning. He could have gone straight to Finley Place from the police station and got the whole damn thing off his chest. That would have meant facing a further round of questioning when he was exhausted but he would at least have seen his daughter and spent the night with his wife. Or he could have rung Caroline at any time from 1.51 a.m. onwards as he was awake all that time. Instead he waited until 7.30 in the morning and rang her and said in the most casual way that he could muster, look, why don't we meet for dinner tonight at La Poule au Pot. It was one of Caroline's favourite restaurants; they usually went there on her birthday.

'Any special reason?' she asked, her voice brushed by irony.

'No,' he said, as if a little hurt by her implication, 'does there have to be?'

'No, there doesn't have to be, but there usually is.'

'I just thought it would be nice to talk.'

'Oh, fine,' she said, 'see you there then, eight-ish.'

'You're not too busy? Because if so, let's leave it.'

'No, it'll be lovely not to have to cook.'

Patrick did not sleep well, even at the best of times, and that had been the worst of nights. 1.51 . . . 2.20 . . . 2.47. At half past three he switched on the light, got out of bed and opened the window. Through the drizzle he could smell the smoke of dying bonfires; or, as his Head of Chemistry might have put it, what you're inhaling, headmaster, is not as romantic as you arty types may suppose: it is sulphur dioxide, carbon monoxide and nitrous oxide. After a few gulps of all that unromantic air he closed the window.

Patrick noticed his sock drawer was half-closed. Mechanically he took out all his socks — they were all black or blue or blue-black — and started to put them into pairs on top of the bed. When he had seven pairs and nine with holes in the heel and three odd ones, he gathered them all into a pile and stuffed them back where they had come from.

He took the school list from his jacket pocket and sat on the sofa. Then, realising it was the very sofa on which that boy had been photographed, he stood up immediately and moved quickly to one of the hardbacked upright chairs in the kitchen.

The termly calendar had every bit of information anyone in the school community could ever need. Every telephone number, every address, the personnel of every academic department, all full-time staff, all part-time staff, other staff, the secretary of every society – you name it and it was there, the works department, the secretariat, the bursary, the pupils by forms, the pupils by houses, every boy and every girl and their subject choices, the daily and weekly events, the plays, the concerts, the sporting fixtures, the porters, caterers, laundry staff, even helpful London bus numbers and the nearest underground stations etc.

On the very first page, after the school crest and motto, *Let the truth prevail*, came the staff list. The very first name was that of the headmaster, P. S. Balfour, MA, FRSL, followed by the deputy headmaster, M. D. Falconer, MA. Next year, when there would be almost as many girls as boys in the school, there would be two deputies, one male and one female, another development that Michael would not find easy. Patrick ran his eye, as he had done so many times before, down all the names in the Common Room, all eighty-three of them: from Christopher Adams to Sarah Wainwright.

This was something of a ritual even on a normal day, something he found himself doing, sometimes alone in his study, sometimes across his desk with Michael. A problem with a member of staff popped up and out came the list. Taking the list out of his pocket had become a reflex action with Patrick whenever there was a promotion to consider – was there a dark horse in the field, a name he had missed? – or, more often, when a nasty administrative job, like running the examinations, came vacant. Who the hell could do it? Who on earth would want to do it?

Or, in this more serious instance, at this unearthly hour of the morning, he asked himself who on this list, which man or woman among the eighty-three, was sick enough to try to destroy him in this very detailed and public manner? Feeling something of a detective himself, he ran a finger swiftly down the names.

No, it couldn't possibly be him.

He couldn't, wouldn't, no.

Impossible, shit no.

Good God no, ridiculous, no.

Mmm? Possibly? Just might? Got a nasty streak.

No, well, put him down as a possible.

No, she wouldn't, no.

No.

No, she's a fan.

No.

No, he'd die rather than do it.

Umm, er, mmm? . . . may . . . be . . .

The first run-through the list didn't take long.

Then, getting his pencil out, Patrick did it again. More slowly this time, with less despatch, with more criticism, with more self-criticism, and it hurt him more the second time, much more, as he faced up to every colleague on the staff, to every name and to every possibility. He felt he was looking into their eyes. He also felt he was running the gauntlet: he, the headmaster, was now the potential whipping boy of every teacher.

The exercise was as bleak and dispiriting as the hour. Patrick started to feel dirty himself, guilty even to be considering x or y. The trouble was that, in a close-knit community, whenever you started to get suspicious – for example, whenever there was persistent stealing in the school, and you let your eye run over the faces in chapel or at lunch or in the quad – you started to suspect everyone. Everyone was now a potential thief. Everyone was light-fingered, every pocket contained someone else's credit card or cash. Everyone you sat next to might be the villain, even the girls and boys you most liked and trusted. After all, when push comes to shove, who could you trust? In no time at all you stopped being an optimistic headmaster and became a detective. It was horrible.

Even so, as he moved down the list, there were three names he question-marked, three names against which he put a very small pencil mark, and they were the same names that had come up to him through the smell as he sat, his head whirling, his head in his hands, in the police cell.

They were *Euan Stuart, Casey Cochrane* and *Max Russell-Jones*. They were the three people who caused the most discord in the Common Room, the three people who most often looked up in disdain at his study window. And when the Patrick and Liz Nicholson story hit the papers all three of them had signed the letter to the governors calling for the headmaster's resignation.

Patrick did not tick the name Barbara Bingham, who probably despised him even more than the three men did, because a woman, unless she was a cross-dresser, would have needed a male accomplice to do this. Perhaps it was a failure of his imagination or a sad version of sexism but Patrick could not see any woman, not even Barbara Bingham, becoming mixed up in anything quite like this.

Each of the men, though, had reason enough to want Patrick Balfour destroyed. *Euan Stuart*, a brilliant teacher and mimic, was corrosively bitter because the headmaster had passed him over as Head of English not once but twice, on the second occasion for a young woman, Myfanwy James. Euan now spent less and less time on his English lessons and more and more in the new theatre. (Indeed, Alice Balfour was currently rehearsing day and night in his latest production.) To Michael Falconer's amazement and great annoyance, Patrick had recently made Euan Stuart the new Head of Drama.

As for *Casey Cochrane*, the Head of Computing, he had openly criticised Patrick in Common Room meetings. Patrick did not like being openly criticised, especially for not spending amounts of money which would with a double click have wiped out the whole school budget. Michael Falconer had, however, found out that Casey had also been making a fortune on the side by writing programs for violent computer games, not to mention moonlighting for a special-effects firm in Soho. Patrick had immediately hauled Casey in. He told him to stop both these out-of-school activities and put him on an official warning. The headmaster and the Head of Computing were now barely on speaking terms.

Max Russell-Jones, Patrick's third pencil tick, had come to teaching late. After university, he had trained as a librarian before switching to the BBC World Service at Bush House (where he briefly teamed up with his old Balliol friend, Roger Nicholson, who just happened to be married to Liz Nicholson). More to the point, Max was married to an Italian who also taught at Patrick's school, and when Patrick closed down Italian because there were too few takers he had at a single stroke halved the Russell-Jones family income and doubled their hatred. At his own request, Max had recently left the classroom to become the senior librarian, a job at which he was proving to be superb.

At four o'clock in the morning of 6 November, these were the three names on Patrick's mind. At four o'clock on that morning he had never felt more low, more bitter and more embattled.

To combat this he had a shower, the palliative he tended to turn to when suffering from a hangover. He had a long shower, washing his hair, soaping himself all over, letting the water wash away the sweat of anxiety, wash away the last vestiges of the police station, hoping the water would also wash away the images of the boy on the sofa. In the shower Patrick's mind was a vapour trail of theories, his mind fast-forwarding, back-tracking, fast-forwarding, reviewing, editing, pausing, trawling his life while letting the water run all over his face and back.

He then sat on the cane chair, wrapped in a large white towel, and let himself drip dry and watched his toes tap involuntarily on the bathroom floor.

He stood, put the towel on the rail and looked at his body in the mirror and, another reflex action of his when alone, turned sideways to see if his stomach was still flat.

Or flattish. How would he look to a woman eyeing him across the bedroom? And when had that last happened? Then he looked in the close-up shaving side of the mirror. His face was pasty, his eyes rimmed red. Seen in that mirror each hair on his face, each blemish, each variation in skin colour was a surreal enlargement. And that, he feared, was how the future might be. If this story broke, his whole life, every detail of his past and his private life, would be exposed to that zoom lens of pitiless scrutiny. In comparison, the business with Liz would be as nothing.

He walked naked, feeling a little cooler and looser from the shower, his head clearing, and went into the kitchen where he grabbed a handful of biscuits, then carried them back to the bed he now rarely shared. He tried three pillows behind his damp shoulders but his legs started to jump again and his toes began another spasm of involuntary twitches.

So he padded around from room to room, the last trickles of water running slowly out of his hair and down his neck and down his spine, and made his way into Alice's room, and sat on the edge of her bed, the bed where she used to sit up, so upright, her eyes so wide, as he read to her about Jemima Puddleduck and Timmy Tiptoes. The bed where he used to answer her questions and talk to her. That is, when he used to talk to her properly.

Patrick squatted in front of her bookcase: *The Wonders of The Universe, Go Well, Stay Well, The Puzzle of God, Families and How to Survive Them, Clever Polly and The Stupid Wolf, Pride and Prejudice, Taking Drugs Seriously, Fantastic Mr Fox* and *Anger, Sex, Doubt and Death.*

Oh well, Alice, that little selection just about sums it up. Life.

Her walls were plastered with posters, pin-ups and postcards. The posters of Siena and Seville were from recent school trips. There were male models with bodies better than Patrick's: muscly boys with bleached or streaky hair; some androgynous boys without muscles; some soulfully self-obsessed couples kissing in Paris streets; and the obligatory James Dean.

For no particular reason – he just watched himself doing it – Patrick pulled open Alice's bedside table drawer. It jammed half-open. The letters inside were so thick, so heavy and so numerous that he found he could not move the drawer backwards or forwards. To ease it he slid out the top three letters, but the thought of reading them only made him put them straight back as if he had been caught *in flagrante* (and he knew only too well what that felt like).

Then, as the drawer would not now budge either way, he had to take out even more letters to free it up. Lower down he saw an empty cigarette packet, some Mates and a few loose matches.

You should not be doing this, Patrick.

Hey, Alice, You're great, and it's not just me who thinks so, but it's me that matters, but you didn't ring me and you said you would . . .

and the next one

Hi, sexy, I saw you today in rehearsals. Has anyone ever told you just how . . .

No, Patrick, these letters are none of your business. Absolutely none of your business. This is not how a father should behave. Put the letters back in the envelopes now, now I said, and close the drawer carefully to cover up your snooping.

Anyway, he knew his daughter was sexy. He knew this only too well, and from personal experience, because the last time he had been on a beach, in Italy only two summers ago, he had fallen asleep face down on his towel and raised his head bleary-eyed to see this beautiful woman

56

with a great figure walking between him and the sea, about thirty yards away, and he thought my God that woman has really got it, and then, as his eyes cleared, he realised with a jolt it was none other than his fifteen-year-old daughter.

It was now 4.55 a.m. Patrick walked through to the sitting room and thought about ringing Caroline. Never mind the hour, that is what he should do. Never mind the hour, that is what Caroline would want him to do. Instead he drifted along the passage into Jamie's room, into the smell of old trainers and musty tracksuits. A boy and a girl, a son and a daughter of the same parents, and as different as a boy could be from a girl. Here there were photographs of mountains in Nepal and India, where Jamie had spent two summers. A book on rock music (*Small Talk, Big Names*), books on economics and politics, travel books. Boy books.

In the spirit of even-handedness Patrick felt he owed it to Alice to pull open one of Jamie's private drawers. It opened easily . . . to reveal only keys, loose change, a photograph of Granny in better days, a stopwatch, health club membership cards, mints, sunglasses, a student railcard and some spare passport photos which bore no resemblance at all that he could see to Jamie Balfour.

Patrick shook his head.

A bit disappointing really: no contraceptives, no love letters, nothing much given away, no sign of an interior life at all . . . until he found a bulging large brown envelope. Inside was every birthday card Jamie had ever received from his parents. To Jamie with lots of love on your 5th birthday, with lots of love on your 6th birthday, on your 9th, 10th, 11th, 13th birthday . . . with lots of love from Mummy and Daddy. They were always signed by Caroline and he knew that it was Caroline who would have bought every single one of them. As Jamie grew up the cards

57

changed from pop-up tractors to footballers to mountain bikes to Himalayan scenes, and Mummy and Daddy changed to Mum and Dad.

Patrick sat on Jamie's bed, turning the years over, and heard himself whisper aloud to the empty flat: 'Well, Jamie, well, Alice, your Daddy . . . your Dad . . . your father's in trouble. I think there's little doubt about that.'

At six the gas-fired hot water clicked on. The pipes started softly clanking, then expanding, then gurgling. Still sleepless at six-thirty, he smacked his face in the shaving mirror and told himself that during the coming day he was going to have to put on the performance of his life. He put on some Eau Sauvage aftershave.

You've got to perform, Patrick.

Choose your attitude.

Compared with what Churchill faced this is peanuts.

What was the Nike ad?

Just do it!

Don't buckle. You've just got to go out there, Patrick, and do it.

7

At nine o'clock, Patrick, with Michael Falconer at his side, stepped on to the stage of Old Big School. There was silence. After double-checking that the microphone was turned on, he looked down on the whole sixth form, both the upper and the lower sixth. There were more than three hundred of them packed into the hall for their weekly assembly with the headmaster. In amongst them, probably keeping her head down near the back, would be Alice – but he made no attempt to spot her. When talking to large numbers Patrick never focused on one face, not even his daughter's, choosing to set his eye line just above the audience.

Many heads used captive audience occasions such as these to read out the results of the school matches or to run through an MOT check list of trivia. That was not Patrick Balfour's way.

'Good morning. Sit down, please.' He waited for them to settle. 'I imagine that all of you – even those of you who do not study history or politics – will know that in 1940 Winston Churchill, the greatest Englishman of the twentieth century, became Prime Minister. I would guess that rather fewer of you will know that he was already sixty-five years old. At the age when most of us have long since picked up our senior railcard, when most of us are only too ready to step down from an active life, Churchill stepped up. At sixty-five he took on the most demanding job in our country and he took it on in our darkest hour. Throughout the war his motto was Never Give In, and that motto, embodied by his character, inspired not only this nation but the whole free world.

'I would also guess that even fewer of you will know that in 1951, at the age of seventy-seven, Churchill was returned to Downing Street for his second premiership. At seventy-seven years old. His wife Clementine, as Martin Gilbert put it, "accepted the ballot box with a sinking heart". She thought her husband had already achieved quite a bit. But while she was not too pleased with this turn of events, many millions of people in the country were.

'Today I want to tell you about something that happened two years after that. When Churchill, still the Prime Minister, was seventy-nine.

'The year is 1953.

'1953: the year in which we – or rather a New Zealander and a sherpa from Nepal – climbed Everest, the year in which our Queen was crowned, and the year in which we – and the cricket fans amongst you will all know this – the year in which we regained the Ashes.

'A year, then, of great celebration.

'In the very middle of 1953, only two days after the longest day of the year, on 23 June to be precise, Churchill, while making a speech at a dinner party for the Italian Prime Minister, suffered a serious stroke. He collapsed at 10 Downing Street. He slumped in his chair. The Italian Prime Minister and the other guests were hurried away. His doctor, Lord Moran, was sent for. Was this the end? Had we heard the last bark of the bulldog?

'Well, you might say, so what, quite frankly, he was

60

seventy-nine, he'd had a good innings, well past his sell-by date, we all have to go some time, and he'd probably overstayed his welcome. Time, surely, to hand over to his long-time deputy, to his loyal deputy, Anthony Eden, who for many years had been waiting, an increasingly frustrated man, in the wings.

'The only problem was that on that very same day, 23 June 1953, Mr Eden himself was in Boston, undergoing a third operation on his poisoned bile duct. It was by no means clear that the Deputy Prime Minister would survive this long and dangerous operation. Mr Eden was very frail.

'So in mid-summer 1953 this country was without an active Prime Minister, and the Deputy Prime Minister was on an operating table in America. Mr Churchill was whisked away by car to Chartwell. The cabinet was not told. The country was not told.

'While the stricken Churchill fought for his life, the three greatest press barons, Beaverbrook, Bracken and Camrose, were called down to Chartwell and while pacing the lawn – what good television this would make – all of them agreed to gag the story. Imagine that today! The press do not tell the story. The press have the scoop of their lives – both Prime Minister and his deputy at death's door, who's in charge of the clattering train, government in crisis, no one at the helm – but they do not tell it.

'Not only were there no headlines there were no twenty-four-hour news bulletins; there were no bulletins at all. Furthermore, no one at Number 10 or at Chartwell sold the story. Imagine that! No leaked memos. No need for the shredder. No leaked e-mails. The story that would have destroyed the reputation of the government and rocked the West was kept private.

'Gradually, with huge courage, Churchill recovered his speech and his ability to walk. No one saw him in his wheelchair. No one saw him struggling to enunciate those memorable phrases he so loved to roll. But he was up there, in his spartan bedroom in Chartwell, and he was not giving in. He still had a role to play. He felt he was still needed.

'Was he kept going partly by the belief that he himself was up to the level of events, but that his deputy, Mr Eden, was not? With Stalin dead – he died earlier in 1953 – did Churchill believe that he alone could bring lasting peace to the West?

'I don't know. But in the long hot days of July 1953 Churchill did start to recover. His legs came back. His words came back. He found he could still fertilise a phrase. Indeed, in October of the same year, only four months after his stroke, he stood upon the platform at Margate, a platform very like this one, and gave a thirty-six-minute speech to the Conservative Party Conference. He did not step down. He did not give in. Mr Eden, no doubt boiling inside, was to be kept waiting even longer.

'There is much more to be said about this episode, about this little-known footnote in history. There are many personal, moral and political questions which arise out of it. Should a man aged seventy-nine be the leader of his country? Should a matter of such magnitude as the Prime Minister's incapacity be kept out of the public domain? What precise form does "the right to know" take? Was Churchill gaga? Does power corrupt? Do some of us cling on too long because we cannot face life without our hands on the reins? If the next generation is frustrated for too long do we stoke up further problems in the future?

'I'll leave you to ponder all those. But one thing is clear. Churchill confronted not only Hitler and the Nazis but also his own health problems with the greatest fortitude. In today's jargon, he toughed it out.

'We are not Churchills. But in your own lives I would

62

urge you to fight, to fight back from any disappointments and setbacks and injustices you may face here. In so far as you can, try to confront your public tests and your own inner demons. You won't be facing the Luftwaffe, and with any luck you will not be facing an incapacitating stroke, but you will and – indeed are – being faced every day with your own challenges. Try not to give in today. Try not to give in tomorrow.'

On his way down the four wooden steps from the Old Big School stage, with the sixth form now all standing and with Michael Falconer at his side, Patrick's face suddenly darkened. He heard something. To his left, a few rows from the front, he had heard the sound of an imitation Spitfire and a snigger. Eyes burning, he swung towards the source of the sound. He made no accusation. He told three pupils, including Hugo Solomon and Hafiz Iqbal, that they looked a complete and utter mess and to do up their ties and tuck in their shirts. They looked as if they were about to laugh.

The sharpness of Patrick's actions, particularly following so hard on the tail of his moving words, stunned the hall. In an even deeper level of silence the headmaster and his deputy strode out.

At nine-thirty Patrick interviewed and hooked some prospective parents. At ten he caught up with his mail, as ever laid neatly out by Daphne on his desk. He then worked on his strategy for the next Arts Development Committee in which he intended to drive through his plans for the new integrated arts centre. After that Patrick's energy levels dipped somewhat. He sat, spent and white-faced, at his desk.

He did not go to the Common Room for break, nor did he look down on the quad from his study window. Instead, bunkered over tea and biscuits, he gave Daphne an outline of what had happened at the police station without being specific on the nature of the photographs. Daphne held her hands firmly together on the top of her shorthand pad and did not blink.

For lunch he went to the staff dining room. As a rule, and to ensure that he kept in touch with all his constituents, Patrick tried to sit at a different table each day. Rather than search out his most trusted colleagues he liked to make it his business, his daily professional practice, to sit more or less at random. To take his chances. It might be that he would take a seat next to the scientists, which could of course be something of a trial, but he would bite the bullet with a don't mind if I join you, do you? Or he might drop in on the ever-multiplying musicians. Or even break into the hermetically sealed circle of computer geeks led by Casey Cochrane.

On this day he joined a table of whom Max Russell-Jones was one, and Max, he could not help noticing, was unusually solicitous, ministering to his every need, tactfully hovering, murmuring headmaster this and headmaster that, passing the pepper and salt, filling up his water and capping it all by getting him his favourite blackcurrant yoghurt. (All this served only to remind Patrick of his wife's theory: that the pupils Caroline suspected of making obscene phone calls to her in the days when she was a classroom teacher were always the ones who were extremely nice to her the next day.)

After lunch Patrick, back to his most masterful, chaired a Curriculum Review Group, in which he cut short Michael's attempts to question the time allocated to the creative arts; then, protected by Daphne, he grabbed an hour's rest on the bed, and it was while he was up there, awake but with his tired eyes closed, that the wheels loosened and even threatened to come off, and before Churchill came to the rescue he even considered ringing the Chairman of Governors to offer his resignation.

Keeping this crisis all to himself was a risky strategy. He

needed no one to tell him that. He knew that he could very easily pay with his job and his reputation, but it was a risk he was going to take. More than that, it was a risk he embraced.

So, one way or another, in some shape or fashion, and with a fair bit of Never Give In and to hell with them all, Patrick fought his way through the day. At seven-thirty (fortified by a decent whisky) he took a taxi to La Poule au Pot. But as he walked in and kissed Caroline on the cheek, Patrick could not help noticing that the background music – of all the music they could be playing – was Oscar Peterson's *Night Train*. The track, he also could not help noticing, was 'I Got It Bad (And That Ain't Good)'. They settled into their favourite corner table.

'You look good,' Patrick said.

Caroline opened her napkin.

'Thank you. Everything all right?'

'Oh, you know, muddling along.'

'What sort of day have you had?'

'Pretty average, nothing unusual.'

'Bad night?'

'Well, you know how it is.'

Her brown eyes were as sharply focused on him as the shaving mirror. 'You look tired, Patrick.'

'You always say that. I'm fine. I really am.'

'Do I always say that?'

'Yes.'

'Really?'

'Yes, you're as bad as my mother.'

'In what sense?'

'On telling me how I look, I mean. Look, I need a drink, that's all.'

He waved to the wine waiter. At the next table sat an elderly, elegant American couple. Patrick tried to hear what they were talking about. Caroline leant forward.

'You take stress better than anyone I know, but it's obvious you're overdoing it.'

'Nice place this, isn't it? Nice atmosphere.'

'You're not drinking too much, are you? The tireder you get the more you tend to drink.'

He spelt out his reply, as if to an irritating child: 'No. Caroline, I am not. Drinking. Too much.'

Caroline, quite unbullied, went on. 'Have you heard from Jamie?'

'Is that what you rang about yesterday?'

'Yes. It's just that I've been thinking about him a lot.'

'Well, he's fine. Just had one of his typical e-mails. He's fine. Sorry I didn't get back to you.'

'So you're fine and Jamie's fine and it was a one-sentence e-mail so everything's fine?'

'More or less. You know Jamie.'

'I do, and I miss him.'

'I know you do. So do I.'

Caroline suddenly turned away, biting her bottom lip, her eyes filling with tears. She scrabbled around for a tissue in her handbag, muttering 'Sorry about this.'

'Not at all, it's probably my fault.'

'God, I do miss him. He's a lovely boy, isn't he?'

'Yes, we've got the best son anyone could ever wish. *And* the best daughter.'

'It doesn't always feel like that.'

'She'll be fine, she really will.'

'You think so?'

'I do.'

'Where's it . . . all gone, Patrick?'

'It hasn't all gone.'

Her eyes were clearing. 'You don't think so? Us? You really don't think so?'

'Hey, come on.'

Patrick pressed her arm. How long was it since he had last touched her? With a kindly touch? With any kind of touch, let alone a touch of any other kind?

'So. So, how's Alice?'

Caroline looked across at him, on the edge of an unconvincingly brave smile.

'I was going to ask you the same question.'

Caroline sniffed and they both laughed just a little and they both, very briefly, felt better.

'She's living with you, Caroline.'

'But she's at your school all day, isn't she?'

'Yes, but you know what it's like for me. I hardly ever see her. Is she doing any work, that's the main thing? You know, in the evenings, I mean?'

'When she's in, yes.'

'What does that mean?'

They could both feel it unravelling.

'She's seventeen, Patrick.'

'So she's not in much?'

'It varies.'

'And when she is?'

'When she is, I don't know. She's writing an essay, I imagine, or learning her lines.'

'For her play with Euan Stuart?'

'I suppose so.'

'What's it about? The play?'

'God knows. And if she's not learning her lines she's on the telephone to someone. Running up my bills.'

'Being a normal girl, I suppose.'

'Whatever.'

'Any special friends?'

'Sorry?'

'Has she any special friends?'

'Oh, just the usual gang, I think.'

67

'Who's that?'

'Pat-rick, you're sounding like Paxman.'

'Am I?'

'Yes. We're out at a restaurant. We're out to have a nice chat, or so I thought, and all you're doing is being a bully.'

'Am I?'

'Yes, so stop it.'

The American woman was looking hard at Patrick.

'So . . . So who is Alice's usual gang?'

Caroline audibly breathed out. 'The usual gang? Well, Sally. Katie. Ruth. I don't know.'

'Just wondering.'

Caroline took her reading glasses out of her handbag. 'Hadn't we better order?'

'Sure. What do you fancy?'

'Give me a moment; it all looks so delicious. I could always eat every single thing here.'

They looked at their menus.

'No boys, then?'

'Do you mean me or Alice?'

'I was meaning Alice.'

'Nobody special, as far as I can tell.'

'Well, you'd know.'

Caroline put her menu firmly down and took off her glasses. Her eyes were unsparing. 'No, I'm not sure I would. Not necessarily. Why do you suddenly ask?'

'Was it sudden?'

'It's not like you to ask straight out like that. You've never been the intrusive type.'

'It's just that I found some contraceptives in her bedroom drawer.'

'In the flat?'

'Yes.'

'Well, she's probably got some at home too. Girls carry them.'

'So you don't mind?'

'What were you doing looking for them?'

'I wasn't looking for them.'

'So what were you doing?'

'I don't know really. I was sort of wandering around.'

'Sort of wandering around?'

'Yes.'

'It's not like you, sort of wandering into Alice's room.'

No, Patrick thought, it's not like me to snoop, and it's not like me to be a bully, and it's not like me to interview my wife and to ask myself questions as if I am the detective in the flat in which they think I photographed a tart of a boy.

'No, sorry, I shouldn't have mentioned it.'

'You shouldn't have looked in her bedside drawers, isn't that the point? Surely you didn't suggest this dinner for us to talk about contraceptives?'

'No. Let's order.'

Something about her always moves away from me.

They each stared again at their individual menus and they each stared at their individual lives, and Patrick knew all over again why they did not see much of each other any more. You can't pin it down, he thought, or put a date on it; you can't say it started on this evening or at that event, it just steals up on you and you know you have grown apart just as surely as you know that evenings at an expensive restaurant like this aren't going to bring you together again.

They had first met over coffee in the University Library tea room at Cambridge: Patrick was in his last year reading History, Caroline in her last year reading Modern

69

Languages. In the tea room she was head-down reading Zola or Flaubert because, even over a cup of coffee or on the top of a bus or in a dentist's waiting room, Caroline was the kind of undergraduate who had to be reading, had to be improving her mind. Not for her a cheap novel and a bit of student gossip. She'd looked up and seen Patrick. Patrick was drinking his coffee and thinking he was a bit too big for Cambridge and looking at Caroline's legs and coming out of his Dinah Washington phase and going into his Billie Holiday phase.

Patrick was also wondering how much longer things could go on with Viola. He and Viola had been together for over a year, in and out of each other's rooms, in and out of each other's beds, doing things together every day of the term and every day of the vacations. Hitch-hiking in France and Italy, climbing in Greece. No, it wasn't going to be easy ending it with Viola. She would take it badly.

Caroline was left wing and rich – unlike Patrick – but, like Patrick, she wanted to teach. She was full of hope for the world. Patrick was not so sure the world could be saved but he was full of energy and drive, and he was keen to teach and he was keen to publish.

Caroline was a good mother from day one, a very good mother, and she still was. But after bringing up the children she did not, as she confidently claimed she would when first pregnant, return to teaching. It was not so much that she did not need the money as that she had never really enjoyed the classroom experience. Whatever her hopes at Cambridge, and whatever her successes with some individual pupils, Caroline was the first to admit that most of the kids in her classes did not learn much French and certainly did not love France. When she remonstrated with them in French they told her to fuck off in English.

Patrick's pupils thought he was inspiring. As for his col-leagues, he dazzled or alienated them in equal measure. Every staff room he split fifty-fifty into pro or anti Balfour camps, but he moved on and in no time at all he had been appointed to his first headship. He was thirty-five. He was far too young to be a headmaster but far too young to know it. He liked to think he was more than ready. Soon they (well, Caroline) bought a house south of Kensington Gardens, just off the Gloucester Road, not five hundred yards, in fact, from 28 Hyde Park Gate where, on the morn-ing of Sunday, 24 January 1965, Churchill breathed his last.

And on Sunday mornings, in the happy years of their marriage, after walking with Jamie and pushing baby Alice over to Kensington Palace, and then helping Jamie to sail his toy boat on the Round Pond, Patrick liked to bring the children back for lunch via a detour to Churchill's final home. Standing outside Number 28 Hyde Park Gate, and sensing the great man was himself still standing at his window, Patrick told his children the Churchill stories that they – and his pupils – would hear often.

Caroline had grown up on a large country estate in Staffordshire, in a sizeable house with the most superb formal gardens, and in their handsome high-ceilinged London home she soon put her mind and her hands to the patio/terrace at the back and to the balcony at the front. What she created in those confined spaces stunned every visitor. The effects also caught the eye of passers-by who happened to glance up from the pavement below.

In no time word got around, and her friends and acquaintances were soon ringing for Caroline's advice on the best way to mask a retaining wall or to discuss with her the best position for their sweet-pea divider. In their exclu-sive part of London, in every gate, in every mews, in every place, there was always someone whose back yard tap

71

could spout as a cascade, whose small pond could be surrounded by ferns and a catalpa, whose fire escape could lead to exotic foliage on the roof garden or whose warm wall could take plums and peaches. Even the tiniest of spaces, Caroline told them, could be enlarged by mirrors or a *trompe-l'œil*.

Her new post-teaching life took off. In six months it was a close-run thing over who was making the more money, Patrick, as an increasingly high-profile head, or Caroline. Her face and her town gardens started to appear in magazines. Patrick made only one contribution to her business and that was in coming up with the name. For a month or two Caroline had favoured Tantalising Trellises but he advised her against any twee alliteration, suggesting it was OTT.

'OTT?' Caroline said. 'Do you think so? I quite like it.'

'No, Caroline, that's the name you should go for, Over the Top trellises, roof gardens, terraces and patios. Get it? OTT.'

'Are you taking the piss, Patrick?'

Well, he was and he wasn't, but the phrase grew on her as quickly as it grew on the lips of her customers, and she was soon ordering headed notepaper.

'You always were good at titles,' she admitted.

And as OTT boomed her involvement with his life and the life of his school steadily dwindled; indeed, it had dwindled to the point where Michael Falconer and other senior staff would now tell anyone who cared to listen that the Ice Maiden, Mrs B, the Headmaster's Wife, had all but disappeared from the scene. Caroline had never much cared for playing the role of Mrs Patrick Balfour At Home, but in recent years she had put in no more than a few token appearances at Speech Day, the Carol Service and, most recently, the opening of the new studio theatre.

72

As Patrick looked across the table, his eyes not taking in the menu, he tried to catch again what he had seen at Cambridge, to feel once more what he had once felt walking with her by the River Stour in Dorset. Even to recognise it. Even more, to understand what had kept them together, if you could call this dinner for two 'together'. All the questions, he'd asked them himself a thousand times, all the usual questions, and, as for answers, all the usual answers, he had given them himself thousands of times.

What keeps you two together?

Stop it.

Family, of course.

Jamie and Alice, of course.

Shared memories, of course.

Lack of alternatives.

Well, you did have an alternative.

Would we still be together if it weren't for her money?

Could I operate quite as I do without her money?

But it's more than that.

Patrick had faced up to what had ended it with Liz, with whom (he guiltily admitted to himself) he would far rather be having dinner.

Drop it.

Do not even think about this.

Patrick did not want this next series of self-questionings, any more than he wanted the others in the middle of the night, but he was as unable to close down the insistent voice in the restaurant as he was to close down the Welsh accent of Detective Chief Inspector Bevan.

What ended it with Liz, Patrick?

What ended it with Viola?

Things had run their course.

The last he had heard of her she had gone abroad.

No, forget Viola, what ended it with *Liz*, Patrick?

Getting caught ended it.

My position in society. What a ghastly phrase.

Her husband's violence. Roger Nicholson's violence.

And desire, the desire which made it impossible not to want her.

Well, he couldn't have her. He couldn't have everything.

When you are grown up, Patrick, you have to accept that.

As in cake (not having and eating).

Oh, for God's sake, stop it.

Look at the menu, the food here's good.

Say something kind to Caroline, that was more to the point, *say something now, it doesn't have to be intelligent*, something less crass than the contraceptive stuff, something civilised, something funny or droll, come on, some cut-and-paste highlights from school, hell, even (if all else fails) fabricate a Michael Falconer story or a Casey Cochrane malapropism, say something about the theatre, what's wrong with a rewrite-and-edit of some Common Room row? Come on, Patrick, do the decent thing.

How about *It's nice being here with you*?

Or, *You've been a great wife.*

But he couldn't. He was played out.

In the early years of their marriage, though, he couldn't keep anything from her, even the way he had overspent her money. There was a time when, if he heard the door slam, he'd be out of his seat before her car keys were hung on the peg and he would call out loud, hello, hi, is that you? her walk crisp as they hurried to see each other, how was it, good day or not, given her a kiss, given her a hug, felt her breasts against his chest, guess what happened, come on, what? I'll make you a coffee, you'll never guess,

74

go on, what? it's incredible it really is, seriously, don't muck about, what is it, no you'll never believe it: I've got that headship, you haven't! Or, they're doing a feature on me in *Homes & Gardens*. That's great!

Well, how about *I've just been taken to the police station.*

Now, on the rare occasions that they were in the same house, when he heard the door shut, not slam, and the keys slide across the polished walnut table, there was a muted half-heard hello, no hug, no kiss, just a sort of low-level so how was it, oh you know so-so, anything special, nothing much, you name it, just the usual, and you? same here, nothing? not really no, nothing, shrug, I'll have a shower, do you want a drink, as he watched her back go upstairs, not yet I've got a bit of a headache, you sure? yes, you go ahead, see you later, you look tired, turning at the head of the stairs to say it doesn't help being told I look tired, sorry, if you need me I'm down in my study, bit of school stuff to finish, if you need me, weary-why-would-I-need-you smile, shall we eat at the usual time? fine, why not?

So, she to her shower or her migraine pills; he to the drinks cupboard. She to the cleansing and the revitalising, to the emollient creams and the talcum powder and the extra-comfort moisturising lotions and a close examination of her face in the misty mirror; he to the drinks cupboard and his fist round a large whisky. Time was he'd have wandered into the bathroom to watch her shower, to watch her breasts, to watch her dry herself, to watch her talc herself, better still to dry and talc her body for her – well, dry and talc her body for himself and allowing his hand to stay there while she closed her eyes and slowly sat on his knee. Now, alone in his flat and far from such excitements, Patrick allowed his hand to pour the spirit for a second longer into a larger glass.

75

Now, talking of this and that in La Poule au Pot, he waited for his moment, guilty only in his self-control, worried only by the ease of his unruffled, masked delay, half-troubled that in his marriage everything was now filtered and percolated and released at the most strategic time, yet half-pleased, more than half-pleased that even on a day like this he could still function fully, well, if not fully function at least get through.

Whoever was doing this had not broken him.

He gulped some wine. And some more.

He felt a rush.

And whoever had done this was not going to break him.

Then Patrick put down his glass. If he could not share this with this wife, this thing of all things, this thing which had happened only yesterday, what did the future hold, what kind or quality of sharing was left?

'Actually, Caroline, I have got something to tell you.'

'What?'

Her eyes were on him, those unsparing eyes that knew him only too well.

'Well, when I said nothing unusual had happened . . .'

'Go on.'

And he went on, speaking slowly and clearly, as if he were giving a skilful summing up in the final of the school debating competition, as if he were defending himself in court and holding his corner well under pressure from the prosecuting counsel. Furthermore, he tried to make it sound as if the whole topic – the police car, the cards in the wallet, the pornographic photographs – could really have been any topic, any bit of adolescent misbehaviour, any old bit of troublesome school business that might suddenly arise to ambush a modern head.

It didn't work.

Caroline was very still. Her eyes became larger but her face seemed to shrink. From Patrick's side the table suddenly felt twice as wide, the table cloth was now as broad as a king-size bed. Shrinking from her eyes he breezily swung the other way, quickly trying to be more upbeat, attempting to be more combative. His voice became more assertive. So did Caroline's. He was punching his point home with a raised finger.

'It's complete bollocks, of course.'

'You don't have to say that, Patrick. I know it is.'

'Absolute and complete bollocks.'

The elderly Americans at the next table stirred and glanced over.

'It's horrible,' she said, 'the whole story. Absolutely disgusting.'

'Shh . . . not so loud, Caroline. I know it's disgusting, OK?'

'From start to finish. Horrible. How on earth have you become the victim of such a thing?'

'God alone knows.'

'And I'm very upset that this happened thirty hours ago, *thirty hours ago*, and you wait until now to tell me.'

'I didn't know how to react. I was completely thrown. I couldn't think what to say.'

'I doubt that. I doubt it very much.'

'That's not very nice, Caroline.'

'Nor is keeping it from me.'

'Anyway, I'm bailed for a month while they look further into it.'

Caroline's face was white and rigid. 'What does that mean?'

'What it says, I suppose. Any idea who might have done it? That's what intrigues me?'

'No.'

'No one come to mind?'

She shrugged a little, then said, 'Justin Pett? Max Russell-Jones?'

'Justin? Justin Pett! But we're friends.'

'Were.'

'Yes, all right, were.'

Patrick sat back. Caroline leant forward.

'And he's capable of it.'

'You think so? You really think so?'

'Yes, he could. He'll never forgive you.'

'The school thing, you mean?'

'More the Rodin.'

'My novel?'

'Yes.'

'But you agree he had to go? You said that at the time.'

'Yes, he had to go.'

Patrick drank some more, still right back in his seat, nodding OK to himself. 'OK. Justin Pett might have. But what about anyone on the staff now?'

'I wouldn't know, would I?'

'Yes, you would. I trust your instincts.'

He took the school list out of his pocket and offered it across the table. Caroline looked away.

'I wouldn't know where to start, Patrick.'

'But you've met most of them, and know some of them, all right, maybe not as well as you used —'

'Knowing you, you've already run your eye down the list. How about Max Russell-Jones?'

'You think so?'

'Well, he did organise that letter to the governors about you.'

Patrick felt his energy going, going fast. His heart was sinking. He slowly put the list back in his jacket pocket.

'The trouble is, Caroline, when a detective walks in and

78

takes you to a police station and puts you in a cell and then accuses you of that kind of thing to your face, and shows you photographs like that, you can't help feeling defensive.'

'Why, when it's nonsense and you can prove it's nonsense?'

'Are you serious?'

'I can see why you'd be angry and upset, but not defensive.'

'You really can't see it?'

'No, I really can't. Why *defensive*?'

He leant forward, speaking with quiet intensity: 'Putting me into the porn category, that's the worst thing you can hit a head with. Basically he thought it was me, that detective thought it was me, in *our* flat! He really did. Detective Chief Inspector Bevan thought he'd got his man.'

'Well, so would you in his shoes. Just because someone is respectable doesn't rule him out. The police have to keep an open mind.'

She pointedly put her hand over her glass as Patrick again lifted the bottle of Chablis.

'Are you sure? Oh, go on.'

'No. These glasses are too big for me.'

So Patrick, making rather too much of his point, filled his to the brim. 'I mean, what the hell was I meant to say?'

'You never have any trouble with words, Patrick, you just have to tell the truth, don't you?'

'But you've no idea how suspicious he was, Caroline.'

'But I'm not a policeman.'

'I know that, for God's sake.'

'And I'm not suspicious.'

'I know that.'

'Even when I should be. As you also know.'

Patrick should, he immediately realised, have seen it coming. In his deluded, masterful, headmasterful way, he had allowed himself to think it was all rolling along on the tracks in the way he had planned; he liked to think that he was controlling it all, the day, the pressure, the crisis, the evening, the wine, the conversation, the confession, handling it all as well as could be expected, even shaping its direction.

And then, bang, she brought up Liz Nicholson. That was all it needed. Not by name, of course: that would have been beneath Caroline. But that's what she meant, that was exactly who she meant. Just because you've lied to me before, Patrick, and led another life and had a second diary and a second mobile and a second bed and dragged me on to page three doesn't mean I think you're always a liar or that you've been touching up young boys on our sofa.

Patrick felt his stomach collapse. He needed to blur the edges. He needed to ease the pain. For an hour or two he needed to block out the past and to inhabit a gentler present. He looked round for the wine waiter.

8

You just have to tell the truth, Patrick. When he said to
Caroline that no names beyond the school gates sprang to
mind Patrick was not, strictly speaking, telling the truth. In
fact, he wasn't telling the truth at all. One name immediately sprang at him and smacked him in the face and
kicked him in the balls: the name of the man who had
promised to do exactly that to Patrick if ever their paths
crossed again, and it wasn't the name Justin Pett.

It was Roger Nicholson.

Patrick had met Roger, a friendly sandy-haired
Yorkshireman who loved radio drama and Sheffield
United, at the very same party in Goodge Street as he had
met Justin. A fateful night. Justin and Patrick were already
discussing the tragic love affair between the two sculptors,
Auguste Rodin and Camille Claudel, and Roger's ears
pricked up and his nose sniffed a story and he turned
round ('Did I hear the name Auguste Rodin?') because
Roger had always been a fan of the randy old frog, as he
called him, especially those fast studio drawings he did of
naked Sapphic women, and what's more he had always
fancied directing a play about him.

'You don't know Liz?' Roger had asked Patrick.

'Liz? No, I don't think I do.'

'She's in publishing is Liz, she might be interested in it too.'

'Really?'

'As a novel.'

'Is she here?'

'No, she's in Frankfurt.'

'Frankfurt?'

'The Book Fair.'

'What a pity.'

'Camille Claudel's her kind of stuff, wronged women and all that. I'll get her to give you a ring.'

But, as so often happens, nothing did happen: Frankfurt came and Frankfurt went and there was no phone call. Life, school, the trivial round, the common task took over again, so that Patrick felt his chance meeting with Liz, and the dramatic way it hit him, must somehow have been 'meant', though as a fully paid-up agnostic he tended to scoff at any such beliefs in the pre-ordained, let alone in someone up there.

It was raining for the fourth successive day that June and . . .

Look, do you really want to rerun this, Patrick, I know it's your favourite video, your secret fix, but are you really sure you want to see it again, to sit through it all again, all the joy, all the pain, all the loss?

Yes?

Yes, because it always overrides all the other videos.

All right, Patrick, on your own head be it, press play –

It was a Wednesday, and Patrick had hurried over to see his mother, as he always did on a Wednesday, and he had taken her for a brief spin in her wheelchair and then had hurried away from her on the excuse that he had a meeting back at school with the spooky Casey Cochrane

82

about buying even more computers (this time for the library). But he didn't have any such meeting arranged and he was now hurrying up and down the Charing Cross Road and St Martin's Lane, looking for a first edition of Robert Louis Stevenson's fables, when a beer lorry going past him in the road not four feet away ploughed right through a huge puddle and the spray that hit him full-on might just as well have come from one of those Paris water cannons they used to repel the rioting students in 1968. And that was it; that was enough for Patrick, his hair wet, his socks soaked, his trousers clinging to his shins, that's *it*, he said, bugger this country, I'm emigrating, I'd rather live in Australia, running through the swing doors into the National Portrait Gallery and half-knocking her over, half-catching her arm, apologising as she spun, shaking his head like a black labrador climbing out of a river. His hand catching her arm, the words spilled out:

'It's good you're light on your feet.'

'I need to be.'

'I'm really sorry, I wasn't looking. Do forgive me.'

'Do you think it's easing off?' she asked.

'Easing off?'

'Out there.'

'Easing off! Of course it's not easing off, it's just going on and on, isn't it, on and on until we all crack.'

She looked as if she was going to laugh, and that was when he first noticed her mouth and her teeth, and while she looked as if she were going to laugh Patrick wiped the rain off his neck with his handkerchief and pursued his theme.

'And if I were you I wouldn't be looking for any sign of a clearing, any sign of a break in the clouds or any general lightenings in the east or in the west because there aren't any breaks or lightenings in any direction, and do you want to know why, because *the rain is here to stay.*'

Taken by his syntax, attracted by the roll of his sentences, she laughed. Her teeth, her mouth, her energy, her mouth at his level, she was just below his height. She looked over her shoulder.

'You've come to see the photographs?'

'What photographs?'

'They're great. Street kids in Bolivia, they're really disturbing, but great.'

'No, I only came in to get out of the rain.'

Patrick turned to watch the rain coming straight at the doors at throat level and solar plexus level and sock level, the sort of rain that gets you everywhere, and he asked her if she wanted a coffee, it's the least he could do, may I buy you a coffee, but she'd just had one, but she wouldn't mind another, but a coffee meant going out again into *that*, and suddenly without discussing it any further they were both straight out there again, he couldn't get any wetter and she thought it was funny splashing across the road with this distinguished looking bloke she'd never met, and as they stood in the café they introduced each other.

'Liz Nicholson.'

'The publisher? Didn't I meet your husband a couple of weeks ago?'

'Roger? You might have done.'

'I'm Patrick Balfour.'

'The novelist headmaster!'

'Well . . . yes!'

And with a mock ritual they concluded all that by shaking hands. Hers was warm, his still not quite dry.

'And I've read *Silver*,' she said. His novel about R. L. Stevenson and W. E. Henley.

'You've read it?'

84

'It's very good.'

'Thanks.'

'Very good indeed.'

He did his wow gesture. She laughed. Her mouth. Her teeth. Her eyes.

Help me, God.

'You know, I'd never have guessed you're a headmaster.'

'Fan-tastic. That has made my day.'

'Why, do you try hard not to look like one?'

'Oh, all the time.'

'I don't believe you.'

And that's how it started and that's how it went on over the coffees and the Danish pastry and the ashtray which he moved to the next table. He could talk to her.

Liz took off her coat and put it over the back of her chair. A black dress, a red scarf. Nice earrings. He liked the way her hair was cut short. He took off his wet coat, wiping some more drops off the back of his neck, and felt conscious of his formal suit. But they talked on and on. She told him that she had not known until reading *Silver* that Long John was based on Henley. That got Patrick going on the one-legged Gloucester poet, and he told her about Henley's courage and how Lister saved his remaining leg in Edinburgh Infirmary and how Henley was the first to champion the art of Rodin in England.

She mentioned Patrick's 'very Stevenson surname' Balfour, though it wasn't Patrick Balfour in *Kidnapped*, it was *David* Balfour, wasn't it, and he told her that she was the first person he had ever met who had actually read *The Body-Snatcher* and *The Beach of Falesá*, let alone heard of Stevenson's fables. They talked about how much research you had to do to get a historical novel right, about how difficult it was to judge the point where you didn't need to know any more background. That's right, she said, because if you're not careful you start shoe-horning in your research.

They just talked.

What a simple sentence that is.

They just talked.

What a dangerous sentence that is.

We just talked. It can speak volumes.

By the time the weather had cleared and they'd both looked at their watches and both exclaimed at the hour and both had said it was nice to bump into each other, well, we literally did, didn't we, sorry again about all that, there's really no need for you to say sorry again, and both had gone their separate ways, Patrick was out into the most familiar streets of central London and well and truly lost.

Patrick had always heard voices. As a child it had bothered him that the voices were louder and more compelling than the voices of his parents and the voices of his teachers. Louder even than the voices of his playmates in the school yard. The voices made him wet the bed long after other boys his age had stopped. He could not mention the voices to anyone else so it worried him that he might be alone in hearing these competing claims on his attention. For a while, when he was a clever teenager, he rationalised all this (he rationalised everything when he was a clever teenager) as the promptings of an overactive conscience, as a debate between the good angel and the evil angel (viz. *Doctor Faustus*, which he was reading in his lower sixth English class). And, for a while, that made the voices go away, or at least made someone turn down the volume. But they never left him alone for long, and after meeting Liz Nicholson they returned with a vengeance.

Oh, Patrick, what have you done now?

86

I didn't mean to, honestly.

That's what young children say, Patrick.

I wasn't looking for her.

Fortune brings in some boats that are not steered.

But you could have walked away.

You could have apologised and left it at that.

I know.

And she's younger than me.

I know.

But it doesn't matter.

Thirty-four. She is thirty-four.

That fact, her age, Patrick found out later, but the more important point he found out at that very first meeting: that he could not think about anything or anyone else. When he was talking to Michael Falconer in his study about problems in the theatre or about tightening up on the dress code, when they were deciding to have a blitz on the boys who were walking around with their shirts out and on the girls showing more and more of their stomachs, or when he was chairing a committee on new directions in the curriculum, or when he was talking with such winning fluency in a Common Room meeting, whatever he was doing you couldn't really tell anything was wrong with Patrick, if wrong's the word, because all the right words were coming out of his mouth.

Patrick was doing a perfectly professional job. He was keeping up with his correspondence. He was meeting parents and winning them over. Not only was the school full to bursting, there was a waiting list. He was communicating with colleagues in a perfectly sensible way, and talking to Daphne over a coffee about how they were going to sort out his terribly overcrowded diary, and taking a tough line with Euan Stuart's disloyalty, but he was always going through the swing doors or leaning over the table top, or catching Liz as she fell, or looking at her mouth, wondering what she would be like on top of him in bed, picturing her walking past the house in Heriot Row in Edinburgh where Robert Louis Stevenson lived, or seeing her naked on the South Sea island beach at Falesá.

He had, he realised, never been in love before. He'd had women, of course; at Cambridge there was Viola Hutcheson, and then there was Caroline, there was Caroline, of course. Of course there was Caroline. But after he met Liz Nicholson most pop songs, even those with the most banal lyrics, suddenly started to sound profound. Car radios – especially car radios – got him going, the way she walks, the way she talks, I love you because you understand me, baby you've got it, I'm crying over you, she's a mystery girl, she's a mystery girl, what the hell was going on in his head?

Patrick felt very numb and very far away and very alive. The panic, the choice of clothes, the panic in your heart and mouth, the absence of everything else, the unheard conversations, the muzzy head, the unfocused eyes. And when he watched sentimental films on his own late at night, videos with Meryl Streep and Clint Eastwood, *The Bridges of Madison County*, and what was the other one, yes, you know, the rework of David Lean's *Brief Encounter*, oh what on earth was it called, *Falling in Love*, that's it, *Falling in Love* with Meryl Streep . . . they were two Manhattan commuters, yes, it was Meryl Streep again and . . . and Robert De Niro. Yes, Robert De Niro. Well, after meeting Liz, those films did not seem sentimental any more. They seemed true. They seemed real. He popped into Tower Records in Piccadilly and bought a double CD of Country and Western songs. *Country Gold* it was called.

Are you OK, Patrick?

Patrick, are you OK? his friends asked him.

Yes, fine, why?

Oh nothing, just something about you, I was a bit worried, that's all. No, I'm fine. I'm absolutely fine. Sure? Sure. As sure as I'm a bloody liar. Patrick now knew that once you fall in love with another man's wife, once that happens, you become more careful, more cautious, more devious, more economical with the truth, more aware, more quiet, more enigmatic, more on your guard for unforced errors or dangerous slips. If you don't want to give the game away – and you don't – you start behaving not only a bit like a criminal but a bit like a detective. The price of lying is eternal vigilance. So is the price of being in love with another man's wife.

What the hell is going on, Patrick?

Well, you have a film running in your head and it runs on a loop and you can, if you like, try to laugh it off and try to keep it in proportion and you can use pejorative words and phrases like 'affair' or 'romantic love' and say it won't last, you'll grow out of it. Balls. Don't make me laugh. You just carry on, you just go deeper into it, that's the only route. Whether you go on or turn back, either way it hurts and neither way do you grow out of it.

It took a week for Patrick to think he might move to Liz Nicholson's publishing house. He did not tell Caroline what he was thinking. He met Liz for lunch in Covent Garden. He did not tell Caroline where he was lunching. He and Liz were witty and lively and sharp together. And he felt guilty that they were witty and lively and sharp together. He felt guilty that he felt so alive. Liz liked to dress in bright colours – and the colours brightened his day – or in black. Her black brightened his day. She had reread his novels. She was outspoken about his work. She was volatile and funny. He tried to think how many funny women he had met and he couldn't think of many.

She would love to edit him, she said, but if he wanted the next novel to be a bigger seller than the Stevenson then he needed to write with a greater reach, to flesh out the scenes, and at the same time to cut harder and sharper to the moral crises; to be more like Brian Moore, more direct in his storytelling. In a nutshell, Patrick, you need to write big.

'Especially this novel you're going to write for me on Rodin.'

'Am I?'

'Yes, Patrick, you are. The Rodin is a great idea.'

'Right. Better get on with it then.'

'Yes, you'd better.'

'Are you like this with all your authors?'

'No.'

'Why not?'

'Because all my authors aren't as good as you. And this idea is a winner.'

'You really believe that, Liz?'

'I do. It's more important than your job. And it will be your breakthrough book. I'll see to that.'

9

Some headmasters Patrick knew, headmasterly colleagues of his 'on the circuit', tended to describe their Common Room or their Staff Room as a form of enemy territory, as almost a no-go area. These heads claimed to find the Common Room an unwelcoming place where backs were turned and voices lowered whenever The Boss Intruder was spotted coming on to their patch. The Common Room, these heads were made to feel, was for the assistant teachers, for the workers, for the hewers of wood and the drawers of water. That kind of thing.

Patrick did not go along with this off-limits stuff. Nor, to be honest, had he felt it to be so in his case. And even if he had done, he would have resisted any attempt to freeze him out. If he walked in and a back was turned or a voice was lowered, too bad, so be it. Let them get on with it. It was part of the game. He could take that. If his skin was that paper-thin he shouldn't even be in the job. No boss should be a coward.

Besides it was also a good thing not to know everything. If you knew what everyone else was saying about you behind your back, what knives they were throwing at your shoulder blades as soon as you left the room, what they were saying about you as they watched you join the salad queue at lunch, what they were saying about your absentee wife, you'd never get out of bed in the morning. You'd turn over and face the wall. If Patrick had conspired with the bursar to have the Common Room clandestinely bugged, and if he had then secretly tuned in to the behind-the-scenes chat about himself, he'd be finished; he knew that. Much better not to know.

In much the same way, if you knew what the future held in store for you, you wouldn't bother to go to work. If you knew you were going to have a head-on car crash, to keel over with a heart attack, to catch this disease, to be hit full in the face by that stroke of fate, you'd give up. What's the point in being hopeful, of staying fit, of saving money, of investing in a top-up pension, of keeping an eye on your booze intake and your waistline, of not getting involved with too many other women, if you know you're going to be zapped on this or that preordained minute?

So Patrick popped up to the Common Room whenever he could, often for no particular purpose other than that it kept him in touch and gave him a feel for things, often climbing the staircase against the flow of traffic, pausing on the bend to allow through a line of teachers hurrying down to take their classes.

Being seen up there in the Common Room, browsing in a natural way, also gave members of staff a chance to settle various matters with him on the hoof.

Patrick was usually addressed in one of four ways. To some teachers of all ages he was simply an approachable 'Patrick'; others preferred the respectful or at least neutral but rather arms-length 'Headmaster'; a number eschewed titles altogether, while a tiny few avoided any kind of greeting or eye contact. The last ones cut him as if he had the pox.

So the typical greetings were:

Michael Falconer: 'Morning, Patrick. Do you have a minute?'

Max Russell-Jones: 'Ah, Headmaster, something rather disturbing has just turned up in the library.'

Euan Stuart: 'Will you be in for lunch? I'd like to catch you for a word.'

Or the Casey Cochrane Cut.

If no one wanted to buttonhole him or complain to him or suck up to him, Patrick tended to flick through the daily papers and then glance at all the society activities and sports results and forthcoming lectures. It was amazing how busy the school was, how busy *his* school was, and how much photocopied paper circulated around the place.

Anyway, why would he need a purpose to go to the Common Room? If Euan Stuart and others of his critics periodically enjoyed telling him (and they periodically did) that the morale in the Common Room had never been lower, Patrick enjoyed looking unruffled and saying oh really, strange you should say that, I was only thinking this morning how bracing and lively the place was feeling.

Ever since he had become a head, even when he was a very young one, Patrick liked to think that he mingled well with the staff, particularly the outnumbered women – he enjoyed talking to women – and especially the younger teachers, male or female, who had not yet settled into any of the defensively closed-circuit groups. After all, he liked teachers. He *was* one, dammit, and he enjoyed the professional exchanges, he loved the way that they cared for each pupil, he enjoyed the banter, and if there was any laughter going he was glad to be part of it. It made him feel normal.

And he had never felt more like feeling normal than on the morning of 9 November, four mornings after the police station and three after his difficult dinner with Caroline. Each time he visited the Common Room the first thing he did – in a reflex action much like checking his school list or his stomach in the bathroom mirror – was to clear his pigeonhole of any internal mail. (His external mail was taken, as soon as it arrived each morning at the porter's lodge, straight to Daphne's office.)

When he got to his pigeonhole on that morning, a bit heavy headed from too much late-night whisky but trying, above all, to look as if everything in the life of Patrick Balfour was business as usual, he found about the usual amount of bumph, plus the minutes of the last Games Committee meeting (chaired as usual by the games-loving Michael Falconer), a few lists, lists of those who had done good work, lists of those who had done bad work and just one letter.

There was no stamp on it. That was not unusual because most of his internal letters, most of the sycophantic or stroppy notes he got from the staff, were placed in there. BY HAND was typed on the outside. That was unusual, but not as unusual as what Patrick found inside the envelope.

It was a sheet of A4 paper. That was all, with no address, no date, no signature, and carrying only this one typed sentence:

Only a fool would ever forget the opening of *The Trial* (1925).

He looked round to see if the shock he felt in his hands and on his face had registered with any of the staff still left in the Common Room. No, it hadn't; they were all doing their own thing. Only Euan Stuart might, he felt, have been looking across at him. No one else. No, he was being paranoid, Euan wasn't looking at him at all.

Patrick slowly folded the piece of paper, as if it were neither here nor there, put it in his inside pocket, browsed around the notice boards a little longer, with the body language of a boss who was relaxed enough and organised enough to have a little time left on his hands, and then walked down the Common Room steps.

Walk, Patrick.

Don't run.

He crossed the quad, telling himself not to change any of his habits, telling himself to walk at his normal pace. Above all, don't run. It must not show.

Indeed, if you were a visitor to the school, a prospective parent, say, or a policeman, or a press photographer, and had passed Patrick Balfour at that precise moment he would probably have struck you as every inch the head-master: perhaps a little preoccupied, perhaps a little pale, perhaps a little distant, perhaps a touch arrogant, but then that was no more than hard-pressed heads allowed them-selves the right to appear.

Patrick knew where the sentence was. He could see the page. He could almost see where the cover had over the years browned a little at the edges. But he controlled his stride all the way across the quad, and while doing so he almost bumped into the head porter who was carrying some reams of paper to the photocopying room.

He then hurried up past his study, aware that a protec-tive Daphne had spotted him through her half-open door, wanting to remind him of his meeting with Michael, until – turning the bend in the stairs – he let loose the reins, bounding, two steps at a time, up to his flat, in to his sitting room, moving behind the sofa on which the boy had been photographed, to the shelves of paperbacks, to the rows of his early orange Penguins, hundreds of orange Penguins which he set out in more or less alphabetical order. Even if his life was in turmoil, Patrick still liked some sort of order in his books.

As he was running up the stairs he even remembered where he had bought the novel. He could almost see himself handing over the cash; no, it wasn't cash, he had put it on his account, on his book account that became so big that he had to spend most of the vacation not with Viola but working on a building site to pay it off. He had an account in Bowes and Bowes, on the corner of King's Parade and Trinity Street, now the bookshop of the Cambridge University Press. He could predict how his handwriting would look (small and in black ink even then) when he opened the front cover. And he could predict how his signature would look, with that appropriated 'r' in Patrick and the appropriated 'r' in Balfour.

He could see again the seat in the University Library (North Wing Four) where he had started the novel in a state of altered reality; and he could see his room in Second Court, his cold room in his second undergraduate year, the cold room in which he had, at three the next morning, in a state of some shock, finished it.

And by way of background music he could hear again what was on his record player: Billie Holiday. And when it wasn't Billie Holiday it was Dinah Washington singing 'September In The Rain'.

He knew exactly where on the bookshelves to look, where to direct his gaze. It was halfway along, third shelf down, in the Ks.

Kafka
Kant
Kesey
Kipling
Koestler.
It was Kafka, of course.

He knew the sentence, it was on the tip of his tongue, it was tantalising, one of the most famous opening sentences in all modern literature. Even in those first few stunned seconds up in the Common Room he had half-formulated it, although he was not sure he would get it exactly right. Precise quotation had never been Patrick's strong point. But even if he could not get it exactly right there was no way he could ever forget its force, never forget the way it first hit him as he sat reading it, an excited undergraduate, with a cigarette and a coffee.

With his older hands now trembling slightly on the cover, there it was once more, page one, sentence one of *Der Prozess*, of Kafka's *The Trial*:

Someone must have slandered Joseph K, because one morning, without his having done anything wrong, he was arrested.

10

Patrick had fifteen minutes before his meeting with Michael Falconer. The headmaster and his deputy saw each other most mornings for daily business at 9.30 in his study and, if he was to be in any sort of shape for that meeting, Patrick knew he would need every one of the fifteen minutes. He suddenly felt terribly tired, drained of the spurious performing energy he had pumped into himself. The Churchill tap had been turned off.

That letter in his pigeonhole.

Right. The main thing was, he wasn't taking any more of this. He'd had enough, more than enough, and he was going to ring up Detective Chief Inspector Bevan. That was the first thing to do. He needed Bevan back on the case, and he needed him on his side. The letter in the pigeonhole would prove that it wasn't him. Bevan had to know that the whole thing, far from being over, now looked as if it was only just beginning. Patrick had to tell him that, as well as being impersonated as a petrol-stealing petty criminal and a pornographic pervert, he was being watched, being psychologically stalked, inside his place of work and very close to home.

He took John Bevan's card out of his wallet and moved

towards the phone. But almost as soon as he started across the carpet he stopped in the middle of the room, the decision involuntarily made by his body. Patrick heard himself say 'No'.

Sometimes he heard his 'no' voice speak out loud, unbidden – and it always surprised him. Usually it happened when he was on a walk, out in the middle of nowhere and alone and screaming inside, far away from buildings and other people, and he would hear himself calling out aloud at the cows and the sheep and the trees. But he had never before heard his voice inside his flat say, as it said now, 'No, don't. Not yet.'

His body, still taking the decisions, set off towards the kitchen and put the kettle on. He watched his hands take the top off the kettle and run the cold water into the kettle, and then put the top back on the kettle, as if someone else was doing these mundane things, and he watched his right hand put the plug in the back of the kettle and he watched his left hand press down the switch on the kettle. Good, that's done then, glad to confirm that the kettle still held water and that the kettle still boiled water, and that, generally speaking, kettles still did what kettles were told to do.

His lips were sticking to his gums. He loosened them with his tongue. He spooned some coffee into the cup.

What if this wasn't an outsider? How had he (whoever he was) got into the Common Room? You couldn't just walk in off the Embankment and tap in the entrance code and pass Laura in reception and go upstairs to the Common Room, someone would notice. Well, you could, you might get away with it, if you did it confidently enough. Do anything confidently enough in a school and you had a good chance of not being challenged. Walk in confidently enough, dammit, and you could eat in the staff dining room twice a week and someone might think you were one of the peripatetic piano teachers or taking a judo class. The only person brass-necked enough to challenge anyone trying that on would be the bursar, because he enjoyed ruffling feathers. But on average you could get away with an awful lot of deception if you strutted around and behaved as if you belonged.

Hang on, Patrick thought, whoever-he-was didn't have to walk in himself, did he? He could have asked or paid someone else to do it, he could have asked or paid someone/anyone on the teaching or non-teaching staff to put the letter in the headmaster's pigeonhole. For example, someone in the bursary. Or asked a porter or a cleaner. Or the tea lady. The wider school community ran to hundreds of people. (Patrick had passed two women the other day he'd never seen before, one with nice legs, and later found out they had both already been working for three months in accounts.)

No, it was far more likely to be an insider. And the point was this: whoever sent this typed sentence also knew about the visit of the police. He knew. And he was mocking Patrick about it, winding him up, taking the mickey. Whoever typed this letter had either seen him going off in the police car or had known it would happen or had happened.

So was he in league with the police?

Hugo Solomon had seen him with Bevan.

Don't be daft.

Sit down, Patrick.

He looked at his watch.

Michael in eight minutes.

He sat down at the kitchen table and stirred his coffee and ran his fingers around the rim of the cup. He noticed the small brown dots on the surface of the coffee which had not yet dissolved. He noticed some age spots on the back of his hands. It was a similar brown. As were the small brown spots he noticed on the yellowing pages of the Penguin paperback of Kafka's *The Trial*. Bodies and paper: they both aged. His mother's skin was now almost paper thin.

1925.

That the stalker put the date was surely significant. He was making a statement: I am educated. He was flagging the fact, I am educated and up yours. I know about such things. I like to put in the scholarly detail. That's what he's saying.

So he knows the year of publication, Patrick thought, and he wants me to know that he knows it. So he is one of the academic staff. Isn't he? Or was one. Must be. Perhaps one of those who just passed me on the stairs? One of those who cut me. Or one of those who smiles at him, the smiler with the knife under the cloak. Face it, Patrick, there is someone here, in your school, who hates you *that* much.

He pressed his fingers down hard on the top of the table and closed his eyes. He sat like that, eyes closed, breathing deeply, until his heart steadied and the trembling in his hands began to stop.

Deep breath. Who was behind this?

Deep breath. Why?

Keep your eyes closed, Patrick, and think.

Casey. Max. Euan.

No, no teacher, no colleague of his would do this, not even those men, no one who worked with him or for him or knew how much time and love he put into the school would stoop this low. No one in his school was that low, that sick. The school was a civilised place, a famous school, a school to emulate, and full of fine young people.

You may say that, Patrick, but it is happening, isn't it? Open your eyes. Some teachers are paedophiles. Some vicars are paedophiles. Some accountants are. Some scout-masters, some swimming instructors are. Some prep school headmasters are. Some policemen are paedophiles, Detective Chief Inspector Bevan said as much. There's plenty of it, or enough of it, in the caring professions. Because that's where the young are. And you are a teacher, Patrick, all right a famous headmaster, but you are still a teacher, and a few days ago you were treated like a pervert in the police station, for three hours, and you're on bail. In a cell for an hour and a half. Fact. And you have just picked this very nasty envelope out of your pigeonhole. Fact.

But did teachers who not only read Kafka but knew the dates of his novels also steal cars? Did teachers who read Kafka steal your wallet and put porn cards in it? Well, someone had stolen his car and his wallet and been in his flat and pretended to be him, had gone to great lengths, to dangerous and criminal lengths, to get him arrested. If you could do all that, it wasn't much of a challenge, was it, to type out a sentence of Kafka's?

Patrick's fifteen minutes of respite were up, and here Michael came. Picking up the sound of those familiar steps, those polished brogues, clipping across the bare wooden floor to his study, Patrick put on his headmaster's I'm-on-top-of-my-job voice.

'Come in. Ah, Michael! Good to see you. Take a seat, do.'

Michael took a seat and, as usual, took out his list of the points he wished to make, and to make firmly. And, as usual, Patrick could not help noticing, Michael Falconer had his Hawks Club tie on. Was there a day in the year, Patrick wondered, when Michael did not wear that striped gold and burgundy tie? It never failed to amaze Patrick – no, it never failed to irritate Patrick — that playing some games at Cambridge when you were between the ages of eighteen and twenty-one, and then being elected to a games club by a group of very like-minded games players of between the ages of eighteen and twenty-one at Cambridge, should be seen as the Ultimate Lifetime Achievement Award for a man in his mid-fifties. But, be it winter or summer, with whatever shirt (check or plain) and with whatever suit (grey or blue), Michael always wore his frayed Hawks Club tie. For a funeral he would forgo it for black but on all other occasions, holiday or term time, weekday or weekend, the Hawks Club tie was his chosen statement.

'I must say, Patrick, you were on terrific form.'

'I'm sorry?'

'With the sixth form the other morning. The Churchill.'

'Oh, that, was I . . . it seems an age ago.'

'You really were.'

'Thank you.'

'You had them all in the palm of your hand. It's a great gift, being able to do that, I wish I had it.'

'But you have, Michael.'

'No, I haven't, and it was, if I may say so, an object lesson in how to talk to a school. Short, personal and to the point.'

On balance, Patrick thought, taking everything into consideration, he's not such a bad bloke after all. And he does look very tired. Was he perhaps taking Michael too much for granted?

'It's kind of you to say so, Michael.'

'Hear a pin drop. Inspiring stuff. Really was. You must have been a great classroom teacher. Made me very proud of you.'

'Thanks.'

'Not to mention the way you sorted out that ghastly Solomon boy.'

Why on earth shouldn't he wear whatever old boy network tie he wants? Mustn't be petty.

But Michael immediately made rather a point of pulling himself together, of looking at his points-to-put-to-Patrick list as if to say, well it's all very nice for us to be sitting here having a bit of a chat but you and I, Patrick, have got a school to run. Only too aware of this, Patrick jumped in.

'So, Michael, hit me with your little list.'

'My little list?'

'Yes, sorry, don't know why I said it, can't stand Gilbert and Sullivan, never could. Sorry, what's on your mind?'

Put out by Patrick's pre-emptive strike, Michael stirred in his seat and bent down to pull up his socks.

'Well, three things really. The first concerns clashes between music, drama and sport.'

'What, *again*?'

'Yes, again. We're getting into a terrible tangle.'

Patrick stood up, his hands beginning to tick. At the moment he could do without this. At the moment he could do without the music/drama/sport saga.

'But I thought we'd sorted out the policy on this one. Each activity has a different priority time. I've spelt it out to the Common Room, Michael. At some length.'

'I know.'

'And it's all very clear.'

'We have a policy, yes, and it's very clear to you and me, Patrick, but it's being ignored.'

'In what way?'

'Well, when they should be playing games they still haven't been let out of their music or drama rehearsals. Then they have to change into their games kit and by the time they get to practice it's practically over.'

104

'Well, please remind the relevant heads of department of the policy.'

Michael breathed out through his nose, crossed his legs, pulled up his socks again and stared at his polished brogue toecaps, a characteristic gesture to suggest that inside those shoes there were the toes that he was about to dig in.

'If I hadn't already done that, Patrick, I wouldn't be wasting your time now.'

'And what effect did it have?'

'It had absolutely no effect. You can't practise scrums or line-outs if the hookers and line-out jumpers are still warbling or cavorting on the stage.'

'Singing and acting, you mean?'

'Which never ends on time.'

'Right, I'll speak to Euan and Harriet.'

'Water off a duck's back, I'm afraid.'

'You mean that whatever I say will have no effect on my staff?'

'It'll certainly have no effect on Euan Stuart. As you will know. But even so I'd be grateful if you would say it. Thank you.'

Patrick returned to his seat behind his desk, thinking, how trivial is this, how bloody trivial is this, and picked up his fountain pen, unscrewed the top and wrote down some notes. Before he had finished Michael spoke again.

'And I'm afraid the second thing, Patrick, is related to the first.'

Patrick's head jerked up.

'Go on.'

'To the new studio theatre in fact.'

'The snagging list, you mean? What's gone wrong now?'

'No, Patrick, the atmosphere in there.'

'The heating and ventilation, you mean, yes, I've spoken to the bursar and we're going to sort that out. The architect and the heating people are coming in on Friday. It's in my diary.'

'No, I mean how the theatre's being run.'

'How it's being run?'

'Yes. And used.'

'Used? It's being used for drama, as it is supposed to be.'

'It feels subversive.'

'Subversive? Sub-ver-sive?'

'Yes. It worries me. It's just my gut feeling.'

That Michael Falconer hated the new studio theatre was well known in the Common Room and almost as well known by the pupils. It wasn't just that plays took place in a theatre – and plays in themselves were bad enough – it wasn't just that plays involved dressing up and pretending to be someone you weren't, it was that the plays were now taking place in a converted building that had once been the gym. And the gym had been the heart of the school. Yes, all right, an out-of-date gym with water running down the walls, but still a gym. But now there was no gym, indeed no physical education at all, while there was a new place for drama, albeit a hot and cramped one with blue bench seats. The wonderful new theatre had materialised; the much-discussed sports hall had slipped further down the waiting list. The Balfour view of the school had won; the Falconer view was side-lined.

And, to add insult to injury, every day of his life Michael had to walk past the gym/theatre knowing that inside it the pupils were not doing something healthy like playing basketball or climbing the wall bars or lifting weights or fencing or practising jumping in the line-out but screaming at each other in role play, speaking incomprehensible Pinter, miming, dressing up, making faces at each other and monologuing. It was sacrilege.

'So what should I do about it, Patrick?'

'About what, Michael?'

'About the problem in the theatre.'

The problem suddenly on Patrick's mind was Detective Chief Inspector Bevan. The phone rang. Patrick snatched it up.

'Yes?'

'It's not a good moment?'

It was Caroline.

'No, it's fine. Problems?'

'No, just that I'm sorry I was unhelpful the other night.'

'No, it was my fault. Completely.'

'I don't think it was. Sometimes I'm carrying a lot of resentment.'

'About Alice?'

'About Alice at the moment, yes, and about you, and it's not good.'

'I understand.'

'Is there someone with you?'

'Yes, Michael is.'

Michael was putting his list back in his pocket, his other hand lightly tapping his knee.

'All right,' Caroline said, ' I won't go on but I just wanted to say that I should have been more sympathetic. I felt bad after you'd gone. Sometimes I just can't snap out of it.'

'I'm the one who should be apologising.'

'Has anything else happened? On the other front?'

'Could I ring you back?'

'Is that code for something has happened?'

'Yes.'

'Please do ring if you can find a moment. I know you're under pressure. Bye, Patrick.'

'Bye.'

Patrick put the phone down.

'Sorry about that, Michael.'

'Are you all right, Headmaster?'

'Yes, I'm fine, why do you ask?'

'It's just that the last couple of days you've not been looking well.'

'I'm just thinking about what you were saying about the theatre —'

'Because I know you think I'm against music and drama but I'm not.'

Patrick stood up, his stomach ticking fast. 'Oh, Michael, I thought you were.'

'No, I'm not.'

'You just resist every move I make.'

'I certainly do not.'

Patrick paced the study as he spoke. 'You made no secret of the fact that you disapproved of me making the school co-educational.'

'I did disapprove of us taking in girls, yes, and I still think it was a mistake and I think we will suffer for it, but I have always supported you throughout all the difficult —'

'And you resist every move I make to improve the cultural facilities, don't you?'

'No, I love music, it is my passion, but I do not like seeing the music or the drama department taking liberties.'

'Taking liberties?'

'Yes, I resist it, I resist it every time I see the liberal consensus so convinced that anything they do is OK, while anything sportsmen do is not. It used to be very sporty here and that was wrong but it's now swung too far the other way and we're losing every match. Now it's Orwell, four legs good, two legs bad, music and drama good, sport and games bad.'

'That is ridiculous. My son is an athlete.'

'And a very good one. I loved watching Jamie run.'

108

'So what is your point?'

'It's not just that I don't like much of what goes on in the theatre, it's that I resist their self-indulgence and posturing, and I resist them taking precedence over every other facet of school life as if they are of a higher order. Euan Stuart is the worst offender and you go and make him Head of Drama. He'll say whatever he has to say in committee or in the Common Room and then go and do exactly what he wants. At whatever cost to everyone else in the community.'

'So, put it to me again, Michael, would you?'

'I am saying the new studio theatre is not being properly run.'

'And you're an expert on theatres?'

'There's something wrong. I can smell it.'

'What can you smell?'

'People working against us, not for us.'

'Us? And you can smell that?'

'Yes.'

'Is there an "us" in this school? I sincerely hope not.'

'There used to be.'

'And what should I do?'

'Sort it out. That is what you are paid for.'

Patrick felt as if a wire band were tightening around his head. 'I'm afraid I don't intend to do anything at all.'

'I see.'

'Good.'

Michael's neck was bulging against his collar. The veins were standing out on his forehead. 'This is not an Academy for the Performing Arts, this is not a drama workshop, this is not London's second orchestra, this is a school for all-round talents. I'm sorry, Patrick, but it is. Or, rather, it was.'

'No, *I'm* sorry, Michael. In my view the drama department is doing new and exciting work, and that is precisely

109

what I want it to do. To fight complacency, to stir things up.'

'Whose complacency? We are the most self-critical –'

Patrick's interruption was as quiet and intense as Michael had ever heard, and finished as loud: 'And I want to hear no more this morning, or on any other morning on which I am still headmaster, about the studio theatre or your desire to return the school to the past! Do I make myself clear?'

Michael stood up, almost stumbling back over his chair as he did so.

'Yes, you do make yourself clear. Very clear.'

'Good.'

'But just because you are cleverer than I am, Patrick, and just because you are the headmaster, does not mean you are always right. You might recall Justin Pett.'

Patrick and his deputy glared at each other.

'So, Michael, what is the third thing you have on your list?'

'That can wait, Headmaster.'

'Why don't we sort it out now?'

'No, it's a personal matter. And it can wait.'

'Are you sure?'

'Yes, I am sure. Thank you for seeing me.'

11

The private line was ringing again on his desk. He moved towards the phone. Dammit. Damn, damn Michael Falconer for stirring that up. Damn Michael for making him lose his temper on this of all mornings. After answering this he must call Caroline straight back. He was the one who had to apologise. He grabbed the phone, his voice abrupt.

'Yes.'

'Dad, is that you?'

'Jamie!'

'How's things, Dad?'

'Great to hear you.'

'Great to hear you, Dad.'

'What a surprise! I can't believe this.'

'Believe what?'

'Well, believe it or not, I've just been talking about you. Well, mentioning you.'

'Really? Who to?'

'To Michael Falconer, he's just gone.'

Jamie laughed. 'Really? How is he?'

'Oh, in fighting form.'

'Give him my best wishes, won't you, when you next see him.'

'I will, I will.'

'Did I ever tell you there was a postcard from him waiting for me?'

'In Baltimore?'

'Yes, when I first got here.'

'No, you didn't say that.'

'Nice of him, wasn't it?'

Patrick sat down. 'Yes. Very. He's good like that. So. So, how's things?'

'Yeah, OK. Just felt like ringing you. Just felt like a bit of a chat.'

'How's Baltimore?'

'It's great, Baltimore's fine. Everything's fine.'

'And you feel you've settled in?'

'Yeah, really, no worries.'

Patrick felt a twinge of unease. 'Lovely to hear you. But, hang on, isn't it the middle of the night with you?'

'Yes, four-ish, but I was awake and I thought I'd catch you.'

'It's better than an e-mail, I'll tell you that! Not that I mind your e-mails, I love them.'

There was a pause.

'In fact, strangely enough, Dad, I was ringing about e-mails.'

'How do you mean? Is yours on the blink?'

'This is a bit of a difficult one, Dad. It's just that I've had one about you. That's why I'm ringing. I've had this . . . e-mail.'

'About me?'

'A really sicko one, saying, well, saying you'd been arrested, and so I just wanted to hear your voice, that's all, it's silly. I feel better now.'

Patrick looked at the mantelpiece. There he was, on his graduation day: a tall boy with a rather forced, shy smile.

'I'm . . . glad you rang. Really glad you told me.'

'It's not true though?'

'No, but something strange is going on here, something really odd. I'm being . . . set up. And I'm trying to get to the bottom of it.'

'Set up?'

'Yes. But I'll sort it.'

'You mean you *have* been arrested?'

For a few minutes Patrick filled him in, the barest bones, with Jamie silent in Baltimore.

'Jamie?'

'Yes.'

'Sorry, I thought I'd lost you. Have you had any other e-mails from England?'

'A couple, nothing special, one from Alice, a couple from you, that's all. Nothing on the same lines.'

'Where was Alice's from?'

'From school.'

'Did the other one spell out the reasons for my so-called arrest?'

Pause.

'Did it, Jamie?'

'Yes.'

'And did this come before or after Alice's e-mail?'

'After, I think. Hang on . . . yes, definitely. I'm looking at the screen right now. Yeah. The next day.'

'You haven't told her, have you?'

'I'm not stupid, Dad!'

'I know you're not.'

'Does Mum know?'

'Yes, she does.'

'She's pretty upset, I bet? God, she'd absolutely hate anything like that.'

'Yes, but don't worry about it at all.'

'I worry about Mum, Dad.'

'Mum can handle it, she's pretty tough, and I'll sort it.'

'Give her my love, won't you?'

'I certainly will. Why don't you ring her?'

'Dad! Dad!'

'What?'

'Dad, whenever you tell me to ring Mum what you really mean is that you don't ring her.'

'OK. Got the point.'

'And Al. What's she up to?'

'Acting. That's about it, as far as I can tell.'

Jamie laughed. 'Always the drama queen, eh? Hey, I miss you all.'

'We miss you too.'

'So, so who would do it to you?'

'That's exactly what's on my mind twenty-four hours a day. But, look, you get on with your life, will you? That's the best thing, and nothing will cheer me up more than thinking you're getting stuck in over there. Please, Jamie.'

A bit of delay on the line meant that Patrick heard his last few words echoing 'over there. Please, Jamie.' Then Jamie said,

'It was signed by you. Patrick Balfour.'

'What a joke!'

'Dad, it's crap, isn't it?'

'Yes, it's crap. Trust me. And if anything else happens, ring me. Well, keep ringing anyway because it's really lovely to hear your voice.'

'OK.'

'And forward me that e-mail, would you?'

'I don't want to do that, Dad.'

'I know you don't, and that's sweet of you, but I may need it for the police.'

'I don't want to.'

'It would help if you did.'

Pause.

'And there was an extra bit attached I didn't mention. A quote from Edward Thomas. He's the poet, isn't he?'

'Yes.'

'Thought so. Euan Stuart was always going on about him. You know, the one about a railway station.'

'*Adlestrop.*'

'That's the one.'

'Anyway, read whatever it is to me, would you?'

'It's not poetry though, this bit. Well, it's not set out like poetry.'

'Whatever.'

'It goes . . . "I expect your father will have heard of Edward Thomas. So he may know" (and this bit's in italics) "*My head is almost always wrong now — a sort of conspiracy going on in it which leaves me only a joint tenancy and a perpetual scare of the other tenant and wonder what he will do.*"'

'Right, I got the drift of that. On much the same lines. Send me that too.'

'Weird stuff, isn't it?'

'Yes, it is.'

'So what's all that about, Dad? All that tenant bit?'

'Look, I'm really not sure, just trying to unsettle me I think. Let's leave it for now, shall we? And . . . you're all right financially?'

'Yes, no worries.'

'How's the training? Running well?'

'Yeah, not bad.'

'Which means?'

'Yeah, OK.'

'Meaning?'

'Did 3.42 the other night.'

'3.42? 3.42, that's brilliant.'

'Not so much round here. The standard is fantastic, really incredible. Anyway, cheers, Dad. Glad I phoned you. You're a champ.'

'Did you say I'm a chump?'

'No, you know I didn't.'

'Bye, Jamie. Love you lots.'

'Love you too, Dad.'

Chastened and warmed, Patrick immediately rang Caroline back to say, guess what, her favourite son had just rung. Oh, how lovely. She was so happy he had and she'd love to talk but she was already late and about to dash out of the front door, in fact that very minute. Ring me again later, yes I'll do that, but before you dash, it won't take a second, he quickly told her about the Kafka and the e-mail and the Edward Thomas. She suggested he rang Detective Chief Inspector Bevan straight away.

12

Liz Nicholson had liked Patrick's writing and had, above all, loved his style long before she bumped into him in the rain. After she had tempted him to join her list she backed him at acquisition meetings and pushed up his advance and talked him up on the literary circuit. She also rang him regularly at school. That is until the best secretary in the world (or 'Daphne the Dragon', as Liz soon dubbed her) got particularly frosty with the headmaster's new editor, and from then on it was nearly all mobile phone calls or e-mails. Each morning, even before his first cup of coffee, it was the first thing Patrick did: check the screen to see if there was a late-night one-liner from liznich@hotmail.com.

Sometimes, his heart beating a bit harder, he got out of bed in the early hours to see if there was one waiting for him in his Inbox. He sat in front of the computer, urging it to warm up more quickly. He clicked on e-mail. If there was a new one he was excited. He would read it again and again. It was a turn-on. If there wasn't one, he overcame his disappointment by scrolling through all the earlier messages (and there were a lot of warm and witty ones) from liznich@hotmail.com.

Patrick wrote the Rodin novel like a man possessed. Sometimes he sat at his desk, 3B pencil in hand, from ten o'clock at night until gone two in the morning. Sharpening his pencil in a controlled hallucination, and writing. He was Rodin; she was Camille Claudel. He was older; she was younger. He was an artist; she was an artist. They gave each other everything, body and soul. She was naked in his studio; he was naked in her studio. He moulded the clay and moulded her body. She was moulded in clay and formed in marble. His sentences kissed her. In the school holiday he went to the Hôtel Biron, the Musée Rodin in Paris, and looked at *The Kiss*. He walked along the Embankment to Tate Britain and looked at *The Kiss*. Paris or London, the Thames or the Seine, they were *The Kiss*, he and Liz. And as he read her e-mails he could see her standing there across the *atelier*, Liz dressed in Camille's clothes, Camille taking off her clothes to reveal Liz, with the River Seine flowing by.

He was ludicrously in love.

Writing a novel about Rodin and Camille Claudel led Patrick and his editor not only into discussing the difficult matter of appropriation, but also towards even wider questions: the art of writing, the personality of the artist, the fine line between history and fiction and the competing claims of the Romantic and the Classical approach.

The following exchange (arising from whether he had got the tone right in his opening chapters) took place on the telephone after Liz had said:

'Because, if anything, it's all just a touch too . . . Classical for my taste. That's all.'

'Well, if that's so, Liz, I'm pleased.'

'You don't take the Romantic view, do you?'

'No, I don't.'

'Not even with a story like this.'

118

'It's the sense of shape I like, Liz, the form, that's what I'm after, plus a bit of what you might call eighteenth-century wit and elegance. I'd like to fuse that with their late nineteenth-century expressiveness.'

'Well, if you think you can pull it off.'

'Look, we've all toddled along far too long under the Romantic shadow.'

'You think so?'

'Yes, we're still all bloody Romantics, it's all me, it's all self-indulgence and confessions, all me me me, too much wallowing and letting it all hang out, give me the real world with a bit of edge. Give me a bit of Fanny Burney and Dr Johnson.'

'I've certainly got nothing against Fanny Burney and I've got nothing against the real world, Patrick. After all I –'

'Oh, I do hope you're not going to say that you publishers live in the real world and we teachers don't!'

'I certainly wasn't.'

'Good.'

Both their voices were high and excited by the tussle. Liz went on:

'But don't you also like the individual vision, that special –'

'Yes, yes I do, but –'

'Let me finish . . . that special . . . yes, Romantic, if you like, that Romantic inwardness, that's what so often gives art or poetry or music or the novel a burning impact. And I'll gladly trade a bit of form and shape for that. And, as your editor, that's really all I'm saying.'

And whenever they met over the next few months, Liz in her vivid reds or black, Patrick always conservatively dressed, he found he wanted to listen to her, to hear her criticisms of his later chapters, to lock intellectual horns, to hear her voice and (to be honest) to see her reaction to his own. She was tough-minded and wanted to make his novel better, and she was making it better. She also asked him if, when the novel was finished, he would ever consider writing his autobiography. He said no he wouldn't, he had quite enough voices competing in his head already and how could you judge which one to listen to, and when you start an autobiography you're inviting not only a reporter but a tape recorder into the room and that's another voice, an editorial voice, and which track, which reel does he/you listen to? And who even decides, in the first place, who the reporter should be? Sounds promising to me already, Liz said with a laugh, adding that it would also sell. Sometimes Patrick made funny faces when she was talking and quiet asides that tickled her and sudden confessions that touched her. One came up after she had pressed him on his energy and ambition. OK, forget the autobiography bit, she said, but how on earth did he manage to achieve so much in a day? Wasn't he worried he might burn out? Patrick said it all began when he first became a head and he decided that he wasn't going to give up his writing, people said you couldn't be a headmaster *and* be a writer, that it was a matter of either/or. Well, with him it was going to be both, and nothing, not the pressures at school or his marriage or his children, would force him to stop. Well, no, Patrick said, breaking eye contact and glancing out of the window, to be really honest it began even earlier. If I'm honest it began at Cambridge when I started to focus on my academic work. Really focus, I mean. I didn't just want to do well, I wanted to win, to get first-class honours, I wanted to be thought to be clever, I wanted to write history books, I wanted to write novels, I wanted it so much that even as a nineteen-year-old, even when I was in bed, even when I was in bed with my girl and some music was on, I was lying there and I know I should have been thinking about her – no, not Caroline, this was before her – but my mind was full of the opening paragraphs of my history essays, and the opening sentences of novels I was going to write, of alternative opening paragraphs, of crisp opening sentences, and with my eyes closed I would silently recite whole sections of the essay I was writing, or going to write, or reshape the sweep of my argument, and, another thing, d'you know what –

'What?'

He suddenly pulled up short. 'You think that's terrible, don't you?'

'No, I don't.'

'Yes you do, I wish I hadn't said it, you think it's off-putting, unattractive. Unpleasantly ambitious, typical man stuff.'

'No, I don't. Don't tell me what I'm thinking.'

'You're laughing at me then?'

'No,' she said, 'I'm not.'

Her mouth, her teeth.

'Yes, you are. You're trying not to but you are. We teachers can always spot it, we're famous for it.'

'It was just that . . . there I was thinking that all this sounds a bit more . . . well, a bit more Romantic than Classical.'

'Does it?'

'Yes. You're more Romantic than you like to believe you are. You're a Romantic all right, but under severe self-control.'

'Bloody hell, am I?'

'Yes.'

'What can I do about it? D'you know a good doctor?'

Then, over a lunch in Joe Allen's – it was a hot day outside but cool in the basement air – he told her his sailor in

121

Portsmouth story. It was no more planned a move than their first meeting in the rain; it just came out.

The story had first been told him, years back, by an English don at Cambridge. Although he read History Patrick spent most of his evenings with the English set. The English don and Patrick were discussing Henry Cockeram's 1623 dictionary, *The English Dictionary, or a new interpreter of hard English words*, in which Cockeram listed words of high register and then gave their low-register equivalent, and vice versa. Cockeram's pocket edition, a most original idea, allowed you to look up the most decorous or, if you preferred, the roughest way of saying something. Cockeram's dictionary offered you the high-falutin' or the vulgar, the court or the street. And it is Cockeram's dictionary, the English don went on, printed in 1623, the year of the First Folio edition of Shakespeare, which proves how sophisticated the issues of linguistic decorum were in the early seventeenth century.

Anyway, all this led, as such things do, to the English don telling Patrick about the sailor who a few years earlier had been arrested not far from the docks in Portsmouth. The sailor had been apprehended for behaving indecently in a public place, he had committed a lewd act, and was now up in front of the judge. And it was this story that Patrick, a good mimic, told Liz, herself as good a listener as he was, over her third glass of Chilean red.

'Anyway,' Patrick said, stalling. 'Any-way, in court, the sailor was asked by the judge to put in his own words exactly what had happened. But I'm not sure I should go on with this one, Liz.'

'Why on earth not? I'm hooked.'

'It's a bit crude.'

'Don't be silly, I'm a big girl and I watch naughty films.'

'Do you?'

'Yes.'

'All right then.'

Patrick checked Liz's eyes. She smiled him on.

'What!' the sailor protested to the judge, 'you're joking.'

The judge looked down on him. 'In your own words, my good man.'

'Well . . . no . . . I'm not sure as I can . . . Not sure as I want to, your honour.'

'Do take your time.'

'Well, phew, well, I'm a sailor, see, and we'd been at fucking sea for fucking months and I can fucking tell you, your honour, you get fucking sick of the fucking sight of it, not to mention your fucking mates. Anyway, we was coming up for some fucking leave and not before fucking time even if it was a fucking hole like Portsmouth and the captain who was a real fucker by any fucking standards said all right you lot you can fuck off, you're fucking useless, so we went into the first fucking boozer we saw and sank a few a bit fucking quick I can tell you. And there we was going from one fucking pub to another and if you've been at fucking sea for that long you don't need me to tell you what it's fucking like when a fucking girl walks in and anyway one fucking thing led to another and she had a few fucking gin and oranges, and I'm thinking fuck the money, who gives a fuck, spend it all, and like I said one thing led to another and soon we was out in the fucking car park and she was on her back on the bonnet of this fucking great Merc and . . . and −'

'Yes?' the judge said. 'And what, my man? And what?'

'Well . . .'

'Well *what*?'

'Well . . .'

'Come on, man. What happened?'

'Well, your honour, intimacy took place.'

123

13

Each Wednesday, personal crises and political pressures at school permitting, even after a blazing row with his deputy, Patrick went to see his mother – as he had been doing ever since she had come, three years earlier, to live in a flat near the school. In fact, just around the corner, barely ten minutes' walk. He had paid for her removals and he paid her rent.

'It's my final move,' she said.

And that was clearly to be the case. After months spent somewhere between hope and despair, between the hospice and her home, she had now resigned herself to her fate. Her system, in the words of her brisk doctor, was closing down. And she wanted to see the birds.

At the back of her ground-floor flat there was a tiny patch of south-facing garden, or grass at least, with boxes for the tits to nest in, and bags of nuts for all the birds she loved to see, the sleek nuthatch going down the tree trunk head-first being her favourite. When he called, letting himself in with his own key, calling out 'Mum, it's Patrick', she was often asleep. If she was, Patrick stood for a while looking down at her, feeling sad, feeling helpless, above all feeling grateful, remembering the powerful presence she had once been. Then he would shake her shoulder and lift her upright and get her out of bed.

'Come on, up you get.'

'I don't want to. I'm too tired.'

'No, you're not.'

'You've got no idea.'

He would open up her folding wheelchair and help her into it and push her over to the french windows.

'You know what the doctor said. You've got to move.'

'The nights are long, Patrick.'

'I know they are.'

'I don't like the nights on my own.'

All this cajoling and bullying, all this lifting and manoeuvring, swing your legs, all right, I know it's not easy but please try, try to sit up, that's it, up you come, one leg, then the other (how heavy her legs were), put your arms round my neck, hold on to me, hold on tight, Mum, careful, sorry, I'm a dead weight, no, it's not your fault, you're very kind, it's just that I bruise so easily, look at these marks on my arms, I've got them all over, that nurse who comes in can be a bit rough, like black clouds aren't they, the bruises, black blue and red, a bit like a Nolde sky, do you like his paintings, a bit gloomy for my taste, a bit of a German thunderstorm.

All this took Patrick most of the time he had allowed for his visit.

'There we are, Mum. You can see the birds now.'

'Come and sit with me. Come and talk.'

'Nice to see the sun, isn't it?'

'I've never liked the sun much.'

'It'll do you good. We don't see enough of it in this country.'

'Your father loved it, of course.'

'I know. He always went a lovely brown, didn't he?'

'Nutmeg. Had very nice hands, your father.'

'Yes, you've often said that.'

'So have you, Patrick, you've got nice hands.'

'Have I?'

'Yes. A man's hands are important to a woman.'

That's what Liz always said.

She peered at him, beckoning him to come closer. The rings, riding over her veins, looked too large for her fingers. Oh the opal. And the sapphire.

'How are you, dear?'

'I'm fine. Really I am.'

'You don't look too well.'

'Don't worry about me.'

'I do worry about you.'

'Give me your glasses, Mum.'

'What?'

'They need a good clean.'

He was not sure she had heard him, but instead of saying it more loudly he gently eased the glasses off her nose.

'Hell, Mum, how on earth do you see out of these? No wonder you're not reading so much.'

'I can't see the paper.'

'What about the large-print books?'

'What about them?'

'What's the last book you read?'

'One of yours. Whatsitsname. You know the one.'

'No, I don't.'

'That's the one.'

'Did you like it?'

'Yes. It's you. You on every page.'

Even the Rodin and Camille sex scenes?

He busied himself with his clean handkerchief on her smeared lens.

'There. That's better.'

126

'No point cleaning them, my eyes have gone.'

'No, they haven't. You said I didn't look too well.'

'I don't need to see to tell that.'

'So there's life in the old girl yet.'

'What do you mean?'

Patrick, laughing, gave her a kiss. She playfully nudged him away with her elbow.

'Are you listening to the radio, Mum?'

'I can't be bothered. Except when you're on.'

'Well, you must bother.'

'Why?'

'It'll give you something to think about.'

'I've got plenty to think about, thank you.'

'I'm on *Newsnight* again soon.'

'What?'

'I said I'll be on *Newsnight*, on TV.'

'I'm asleep by nine.'

'Are you?'

'You know I am. Angela comes at eight o'clock. Then I'm awake half the night.'

'Perhaps you'd sleep more at night if you slept less in the day.'

'Well, you don't sleep well.'

'Why don't you listen to the radio more?'

'I do, but there was this Kafka serial on. Horrible stuff. So, I turned it off.'

'Kafka? When was that?'

'Last week some time, I forget. Ah, there it is.'

'What?'

'The squirrel.'

Patrick went into a mock fascist rant, a game which always made his mother smile.

'They're everywhere, aren't they? They've taken over our country. Taken over our gardens. They breed like rabbits, squirrels. Taking our food, overcrowding the place, they're the problem, mate. Can't tell one from another. I'd send 'em back.'

They watched it running along the top of her fence, leap the gap and do a corkscrew skim up a tree. Basically showing off.

'How is school?'

'Oh, you know. So-so.'

'You always say that. What does it mean?'

'The thing is, Mum, to be honest, unless you're in it there's little point talking about it. It wouldn't make sense.'

'You can always pretend to want to tell me and I can always pretend to understand.'

'That's not you.'

'No, it's not you.'

Patrick and his unmollified mother watched the squirrel, nut in mouth, sprinting back along the fence, this time being chased all the way by an Identikit squirrel, which was being pursued stride for stride by another. They then all froze, as if for an athletics photograph, before zooming off again. How would the squirrel police ever be able to decide which squirrel had buried its cache?

'How's Jamie?'

'Safe and sound and enjoying it. He rang the other day.'

'He sent me a letter. From America.'

'Oh, did he? I'm so pleased about that.'

'He didn't say much.'

'That'll be Jamie. But you could read it?'

'Of course I could read it.'

'So your eyes haven't gone.'

She looked askance at him. He mustn't be sharp with her. Why did children, of any age, feel they had to be sharp with their parents? Why all this point-scoring now, now of all times? Why be sharp when it's all over? Because it sharpened her up, that's why. So you're sharpening her up for death, are you, Patrick? No, making her sharper for the few minutes he was there. For the last minutes she was there. That's the best he could offer. And the touching. He held her arm, making sure he did not press too hard. She wasn't exaggerating about her Nolde bruises. They looked bad.

He opened the french windows and looked at the patch of garden. The summer flowers had long gone. The sycamore next door, hanging over the fence, had black fungal spots on the leaves. In a week or so all the leaves, the yellow and the mouldy, would have gone too. The wet soil was smelling of damp mulch.

'Patrick.'

'Do you want me to close the french windows?'

'No, why did Jamie want to go all the way to America?'

'He likes it there, Mum.'

'Why?'

'He just does. It's a new challenge.'

'Why can't he do whatever it is over here?'

'It's a better course over there. It suits him better. And it's better for his running.'

She shook her head slowly, and gave up. After a while she said, 'And Alice?'

'Don't see much of her, Mum, to be honest.'

'Well, you should.'

'I know.'

'Girls need their fathers.'

'I know that.'

'Girls miss their fathers.'

'I know that, Mum. I miss mine.'

'Do you? Do you still?'

'Every day.'

'You're not just saying that to please me?'

'No, I do miss him.'

129

'Not as much as I miss him,' she said.

Every day you keep my letters in your drawer and every day I keep him in my drawer, his photograph, every day I look into his eyes, and try to measure up to Dad. And I know I don't.

'Sometimes he's right here beside me,' she said. 'It's uncanny. I still talk to him.'

Dad sitting next to her on the garden bench, sucking on his unlit pipe. Don't get into all that, it'll only upset her. Just hold her hand. That's what she needs, comfort and touch. And, sure enough, she soon closed her eyes. The strength had gone from her wrists these last few visits, so much so that she could no longer hold up a cup and saucer to her mouth. Another step on the final straight. Still, he liked to hold the cup for her. Doing something like that, doing something practical, was a help to them both, diminishing their shared sense of hopelessness.

When he was young and told her his worries she told him to be brave, and in later life she could be quite annoying and dismissive of his passing complaints. Don't go on about that broken toenail, Patrick, don't polar explorers lose two or three toes (or is it three or four fingers?) with frostbite, not to mention those uncomplaining people who don't have any legs at all. Don't rabbit on about your headache, Patrick, some people lie in darkened rooms for three days with kaleidoscopic migraines, so be grateful you haven't got a tumour in your head the size of a grapefruit.

She spoke with her eyes closed.

'Did you hear me, Patrick? Did you hear what I said?'

'Yes, I heard you, Mum.'

'She's stopped ringing me. Alice has.'

'Really?'

'She's always rung, Sunday mornings, eleven o'clock, I could set my watch by it.'

'She's probably still asleep at eleven o'clock.'

'Well, she shouldn't be. I've got a very soft spot for that girl, and she's stopped coming to see me. She can let herself in, she's got her own key, she can come any time she likes after school. Just for five minutes. I'm only just round the corner.'

'OK, Mum, but you know what teenagers are.'

'Not really.'

'All right then, but I do. It's my job, I suppose.'

'But you don't know what's up with your daughter.'

'Nothing's up.'

He held his mother and kissed her, knowing that however long she went on with the questions she would not ask about Caroline, knowing that he did not want her to ask. Outside her window a splash of sun touched some stones at the side of the lawn. Two money spiders, picked out by the sun, were moving across a web between the stones.

'Would you like a coffee, Mum?'

'No, thank you.'

'A ham sandwich?'

'I'd like a drink. A large brandy.'

'You shouldn't drink when you're on those pills.'

'I said I'd like a drink.'

'How many pills are you taking each day?'

'Four red ones, six white ones, my water tablets, and those purple ones. The tiny ones. Three of those. I can't get my fingers round them. The doctor says they're the strongest.'

'You can still count, then?'

'And I'm still your mother.'

'I know that.'

'So don't be rude. And Alice is still your daughter, Patrick.'

'I know.'

But I don't want her to know what I'm going through. I really don't.

'And you've only got one mother.'

'I know that too.'

'So I'll have a brandy.'

'The doctor said you shouldn't.'

'What does it matter either way?'

'You've got to listen to the doctor, Mum.'

'Why? I've had it.'

He went out to make himself a cup of coffee. He stood by the draining board, wiping up a plate and a cereal bowl as he waited for the kettle to boil. The cold tap was dripping. He tightened it but it went on dripping. He could tighten it all he liked; the point was it needed a new washer. He opened her small fridge and smelt the carton of milk. It was OK. Just about. Next time he came round he'd give the fridge a good clean and sort out the tap. He wiped down her draining board, stirred his Nescafé and poured her a Martell.

She was asleep, her head slumped to one side, her white hair thin on the top of her head, her shoulders bent, her mouth open. He moved her magnifying glass and placed the brandy quietly on her side table, the side table in which she kept every letter he had ever written to her. His letters were always in the top drawer, within her reach, big batches of them held together by blue elastic bands. And underneath those were the early drafts of his books: she liked to keep his first handwritten copies. She said she often found that raw drafts were often more interesting than polished final versions. He knew what she meant.

He sat with his hand lightly on her arm. The skin hung in folds off her bones. Any kind of pressure would make another bruise. Soon there would be no more thunderstorms, no more Nolde skies.

132

The sun came full on his face. Unwillingly replaying the Edward Thomas line, *a perpetual scare of the other tenant and what he will do*, Patrick too closed his eyes, allowing his arms and his legs to go loose. He would not sleep – he dared not sleep in case he crashed out and was late back to school – but he cat-napped. Churchill cat-napped. In a way he felt, for a moment, that he had touched his base. For a moment, sitting here with his mother, sitting here with the woman who had given birth to him, he was safe from the other tenant. Everyone needs a mother.

When Patrick was ill in the night as a child, and he often was, his mother always sat up with him, helping his breathing, filling the air with steam, breathe in, that's better it's easing now, you're sounding better, kettle after kettle of water boiling away in the kitchen until the croup in his chest cleared. Until, with a damp forehead, he slept. And whenever he wet the bed, she changed the bottom sheet and peeled off his clinging pyjamas and ensured he was snug and warm and dry again without ever making him feel bad about it.

Well, this was pay-back time. Crude though it might seem to put it this way, that is how he put it to himself as he sat next to her, holding her arm while she slept. He felt that this was the very least he could do. He would sit here, his hand on her arm, with the sun on his face, and if he was a bit late for his next appointment, he was a bit late, and if there was a crisis at school, Michael Falconer could deal with it, and if the police called, the police called, and if the other tenant wrote or e-mailed or put a letter in his pigeonhole, well he wrote or e-mailed . . .

Most hours of most days, even as he sat with his mother, there were now two reels running in Patrick's head: the one was what he was saying, the other what he was thinking.

133

Usually he could tune in to both, to both A and B, and yet keep the signals separate. But now they were competing in volume, owner and tenant, both going full-tilt, competing in pitch, and he was beginning to fear that the second reel was going to take over in public. What would happen to him if the internal policeman, the editor of his mouth, slipped off duty?

'Oh, I don't know,' Patrick heard himself say out loud to himself earlier that morning, looking out across the river from his study to the Globe Theatre. 'Oh, I don't know.'

How could it be, but it was, that a man who was so often turned to by young and old for advice, a leader who was often admired for his wisdom and philosophy and balance, a people-person who knew so much about the world and its ways, could stand there and sigh aloud to no one (though by chance Daphne heard him say the words and, unseen by Patrick, tiptoed back out).

'Oh, I don't know.'

Daphne noticed that he stressed none of the words in particular. It wasn't a weary '*Oh*, I don't know' or a petulant 'Oh, *I* don't know' or a table thumping 'Oh, I *don't* know' or an end of argument 'Oh, I don't *know*.'

It was said evenly and in a matter-of-fact way and without undue emphasis.

He did not know what to do, any more than he did when he was ten and nearly drowned. You can't get much closer to death than Patrick had been that afternoon. It was only a matter of seconds left for him when he was dragged out of the water, unconscious in Clevedon. And whenever he drove south from Bristol on the M5, going down to Devon and Cornwall to address some educational conference or to speak at some literary festival, he could feel the pull in his hands to turn off to Clevedon, to revisit the place of his near-departure. But he never did. He could

134

feel it pouring out of his mouth, the water, the burning salt and the retching and the dribbling, as he lay face down on the slippy, seaweedy side.

He had just learnt to swim.

And in Clevedon that day, instead of doing as his mother told him (*Walk out as far as you can, Patrick, and then swim back*) he had walked out as far as he could and then started to swim further out. When he got tired and put his feet down to rest, down he went. And down. And panicked and fought and gulped and swallowed and gulped and shouted and went down and filled up and he was finished.

End of Patrick Balfour's brief life, long long before Detective Chief Inspector Bevan paid his surprise call on Guy Fawkes Day.

Patrick had 'gone', he was a goner, a corpse, another not-waving-but-drowning little boy. But he was saved by a man. The man, whoever-he-was, told Patrick's mother that he feared he had been too late. From that day on, if Patrick was perched up on the top branch of the apple tree in the back garden and out of her sight for too long, his troubled mother would call out to see what he was up to:

'Patrick?'

'Yes.'

'Patrick?'

'Yes!'

'PAT-RICK!'

'YES!'

'What are you doing?'

'Reading.'

Or, as an overanxious variant:

'Patrick?'

'Yes.'

'Patrick?'

135

'Yes.'
'PAT-TRICK!'
'What!'
'What are you doing?'
'Thinking.'
Or, as a cruel variant:
'Patrick?'
'What!'
'Where are you?'
'I'm in the bath.'
'What are you doing?'
'Drowning.'

As Patrick, drowning all over again, tiptoed to the door, leaving his mother slumped asleep, with her brandy waiting on her side table, she called out:

'Aren't you going to tell me what's wrong?'

14

Caroline Balfour had always been a straight shooter, an uncomfortably straight shooter, and even before he was startled by the first envelope in his pigeonhole on 9 November and then got the call from his son, Patrick was taking the Justin Pett idea seriously. If Justin Pett was the first name that had come to Caroline's uncluttered mind, Patrick needed to give it his full consideration. Certainly Justin was tricky enough and clever enough, and – even more to the point – he was a man with time enough on his hands to carry it out.

Caroline was also right on a possible motive: the Rodin story, not to mention their final and abrupt parting of the ways. Justin Pett had always been a proud man, a man to bridle and to take offence. Given half a chance, Justin always festered in his own good time.

Justin Pett was an art critic, the author of books on Goya, Poussin and William Morris, an illustrator and an occasional lecturer at various London art colleges. Patrick first saw Justin, glass in hand, leaning back on a bookcase and complaining loud and long about the ludicrously small advance he had just been offered for his Goya. They hit it off straightaway, the sober-suited headmaster and the louche critic, yet again confirming Caroline in her view that Patrick had a pronounced weakness for 'colourful types'. If it was a 'weakness' it was one to which Patrick would very gladly admit. Somewhat constrained by his own social position, he found solace and excitement in the company of those who threw two fingers at the world.

Justin, loud and opinionated in his crimson jacket, was always a wonderful guide to any exhibition in London. He also was always wonderfully short of cash, and in a particularly difficult time – in the late spring of the year in question he lost not only his mother but also a lot of money in a Kensington casino – he turned to Patrick for help. Yes, of course he disapproved of independent schools, of course he did, he thought basically they were full of absolutely awful people, but needs must.

After overcoming some of his own doubts and reservations, and the even stronger doubts and reservations of Michael Falconer (the Falconer verdict was 'your Pett chap simply isn't a schoolmaster and never could be'), and after a bit of persuasion with the governors and some juggling with the timetable, Patrick was able to gave Justin a job for one term. Only one term, eight lessons a week, teaching History of Art. Not a lot of money but it was work, and the pupils were bright – and in one or two instances the boys were beautiful. There was also an excellent free lunch, as most of the itinerant musicians in London could testify.

It all started promisingly enough. In his first week in the classroom Justin Pett was an instant hit, as Patrick thought he might be. He was stimulating and demanding, original and tangential, generous and flirty with the favoured few, lending his expensive art books to anyone who was interested, as well as giving hour-long General Studies lectures to the sixth form on Velasquez and Ingres. And all this without notes. He was, without doubt, an intellectual roadshow, and Patrick felt that his intellectually buzzy school was buzzing even more than usual.

Also the way Justin crisscrossed the quad with his silver-handled cane ensured he was interviewed at considerable length for the school magazine. And according to the headmaster's daughter, Alice Balfour no less, who was in one of his classes, he conducted a lesson on Poussin while lying on his back with his head cradled on a large purple cushion.

'Well, as long as he's interesting,' Caroline said, remembering her own dog days in the classroom.

'Interesting, Mum? He's brilliant! He's the best.'

The next lesson Justin led them in a discussion of photography and David Hockney. The intellectual excitement in the air of his classroom was palpable. Alice told her parents that he asked them about images and truth and lies. With all the latest technology and 'computer manipulation', as Justin put it to them, were not photographs, since the 1980s, in danger of losing their veracity? Could you trust a photograph any more?

But Justin was drinking too much. In week three of the term he went too far with another group, upsetting some of the girls by saying how he would 'once and for all sort out those yobbos who spray-gunned our beautiful buildings'. And how would you do that, sir? 'Simple, my dears, I would sort them out by chopping their fingers off, one by one, and that would not be a problem because I myself would happily volunteer to do the chopping. And I have a splendid surgeon friend who will lend me the necessary. But only the fingers, you understand. At first.' In week four he turned up half an hour late two days running, and then, over the fish pie one Friday lunchtime, he called Michael Falconer a cunt.

Here was one crisis which did not immediately bring

139

Michael's brogues clipping their way across the quad to Patrick's study, but it was only a matter of hours before a note from the deputy headmaster arrived on the headmaster's desk. It read:

'Memo to PB from MF.

At 1.20 today, in front of six senior colleagues at lunch, Justin Pett spoke to me in a manner more offensive than anyone ever has in thirty-four years of teaching. I should also add, without spelling it out, that Barbara Bingham was among those present.'

Justin could hardly have chosen a worse target for the 'c' word. Because Michael Falconer, famously, did not swear. Michael Falconer hated foul mouths in all their manifestations. Whereas most people, when faced with rudeness, would say that they were bloody furious Michael preferred to say that he was more than affronted. As for the 'c' word, it was quite beyond the pale.

Patrick sent for Justin, who came across the quad tapping his silver-handled cane, with his big blue spotted handkerchief hanging from his sleeve, deep in dispute with Hugo Solomon about the rights and wrongs of Anthony Blunt's treachery. Unseen, and rehearsing how he would play the coming interview, Patrick peeped down on the animated couple, part-time master and absorbed pupil, standing below his window. It was the first time that Patrick had ever seen Hugo openly impressed.

But once he was up in Patrick's study, far from saying he was sorry or offering to apologise to Michael, Justin was the picture of aplomb.

'Yes, it's all too true, my dear, I did.'

'Look, Justin, you just can't say that.'

'But he is.'

'But why did you *say* it?'

'Well, I'm sorry, but he dismissed William Morris as a

dreary socialist. And the one thing you must agree, Patrick, is that Morris was not dreary.'

'Michael's the deputy head, he's a senior figure in the school.'

Justin did one of his theatrical shivers. 'And do tell me *why*. He's so bovine. Uugghh.'

'I inherited him.'

'Well, disinherit him. You historians know all about that. Defenestrate him from this very spot.'

'And you know as well as I do, Justin, that . . . that sort of language isn't acceptable in a school, it's not adult society. In a school you have to behave in a different way.'

Justin smiled a small, sad, half-pleased, half-alarmed smile. 'Oh, dear, Patrick. Oh dear oh dear.'

'What?'

'I never thought to hear this from you.'

'Well, I'm sorry, but there it is.'

'From you, of all people. From London's Most Liberal Head.'

'That's not the issue.'

'But you would agree he is one, wouldn't you?'

'It's not as simple as −'

'And you do know he's working against you every second of the day, don't you?'

'I think that's an exaggeration. We've had our difficulties but I −'

'Every time your name is mentioned to him he makes a face.'

'That's teachers. That's part of the way common rooms work. They make faces better than they make policy. Let him make faces.'

'Well, he shouldn't. He's meant to be your loyal deputy.'

'We're all human.'

'I think, my dear, that should be my line not yours.'

141

'And he's doing a good job. The school is his life and schools owe a great deal to such teachers. He works night and day.'

'He works night and day destroying you. Want to hear some of his lines?'

'Not particularly.'

And Patrick really did not want to hear what Michael Falconer was saying behind his back but Justin was now holding centre stage.

'Well, here are two samples of the wit of Michael Falconer . . . He passes Max Russell-Jones in the corridor. Max asks, "Haven't seen Balfour, have you, Michael?" Michael Falconer replies, "Haven't seen Lord Lucan, have you, Max?" Want another example?'

'Not really, no.'

'Well, you're going to get one. Falconer passes Hairy Harriet in the corridor. She asks, "Spotted the head today, Michael?" To which Michael Falconer, your loyal deputy replies, "Spotted a hoopoe, Harriet?"'

'As I said, that's all part of the game, that's schools, it doesn't bother me one bit, Justin.'

'Well, it should. You should sack him.'

'I can't get rid of good professional colleagues just because they disagree with me. Especially the deputy head.'

'He's frustrating your reforms at every stage. I've seen him doing it.'

'I know that.'

'So get rid of the cunt.'

'Whatever I may think you can't go around saying that kind of thing in this sort of place. You simply can't.'

Justin stood up. 'Well, I'm sorry, my dear, but I said it and we'll just have to learn to live with it.'

Patrick stood up and faced him. 'And *I'm* sorry, Justin, but I think it's best if you go.'

'Go?'

'I'll pay you to the end of the term, in full, so you won't lose financially.'

Justin walked to the open window, as if he were John Gielgud on a film set, and glanced down on the busy quad. He looked across the river at the Globe Theatre. It was a very hot day. The river was sparkling and slow. He then turned and looked above Patrick's head, as if he were at a gallery appraising the portraits of the three clerics high on the study wall. After a pause long held, he said, 'So you're flicking me off?'

'I'm saying you must go.'

'Just like that?'

'Yes.'

'You stand there, behind your desk, the smug master of all you survey, and flick me off.' And here Justin made an elegant flicking gesture with his finger and thumb.

'I don't see it like that.'

'So how do you see it?'

'I see it as something I have to do.'

'You know, you remind me of Ralph Lowe at Brasenose. Have you heard of him?'

'Name rings a bell.'

'His greatest achievement as an undergraduate – I remember it well – was pissing into an empty milk bottle from six feet. Ralph had absolute pinpoint accuracy in a field where the firing accuracy of the male member is, I think we can all agree, rare. And do you know who and where he is now?'

'No, Justin, I don't.'

'He is a High Court Judge, handing down some of the severest sentences in the land. Something, no doubt, he feels he has to do.'

'Look, Justin –'

143

'And what about that little piece of yours in the *Guardian*? Last week, wasn't it?'

'What's that got to do with –'

But Justin was now on a roll: 'If I remember rightly, it was all about the importance of firmness and sensitivity, yes, I'm sure it was, about getting the right balance between vulnerability and confidence. If you want to give a lead to the young, I think this was the gist of it, you need the strength and the humility to admit you have made mistakes. If you're prepared to appear vulnerable, you went on, you can be cornered but you also give people a chance to identify with you. *So* moving. And if we, as teachers and parents, could only *build* that awareness into our philosophy and practice we might give the young the best possible chance. Do you remember writing that? So puky, so accessible and exactly the sort of psycho babble the middle classes are now lapping up.'

'Look, Justin –'

'And I could see it as a minor cult book and being read on trains and selling stacks on the Waterstone's self-help table. It's that gift you have for *inclusivity*. My God, the more I think about it, the way this country is going you could be Prime Minister one day, Patrick. And what about the Rodin?'

'That is nothing to do with this.'

'I'm sorry?'

'I said Rodin has nothing to do with this.'

'You don't feel any guilt?'

'No.'

'About nicking it? The story of poor, wronged Camille Claudel. The story which made your name as a novelist.'

'I didn't nick it. You gave it to me. You offered it.'

'Because you are a friend. *Were* a friend.'

'All right.'

'And you didn't even mention it in your book. Not a whisper. Not even on the acknowledgements page. I mean, I wasn't expecting to be the *dedicatee* but I thought I might at least get a little mention. A little *mention* costs nothing. But no. You're like Rodin and his women. You're like Picasso. Picasso and his women. Balfour and his women. Even Balfour and his men, it seems. What does anything matter to you as long as you win, as long as everyone is talking about you and your wonderful energy and how you do three jobs while poor sods like me can't even do one part-time one without being sacked?'

'You're being hysterical.'

'*Don't* tell me I'm being hysterical. Don't take the high moral ground with me!' Justin was now screaming, with flecks of spit on his chin and lips. Patrick closed the window.

'Look, Justin —'

'Friendship counts for nothing with you. Only winning.'

'It's not as simple as that.'

'No loyalty, only treachery. No love, only using.'

'I have a job to do. I'm really sorry it has to end like this.'

'But it hasn't ended, my dear. Believe me.'

And that afternoon, while taking down his poster of Goya's cellist, Justin Pett told his sixth form — including Alice Balfour (who was staring hard at her desk) — that they had been the sweetest group to teach, they really had, but that due to some unforeseen circumstances he had to leave forthwith. It was all most unfortunate, so he would be grateful if they would kindly return all the private books he had lent them, but he did not wish to abandon them altogether so if they sent him their History of Art essays through the post he would happily mark them, and, assuming the Royal Mail or Consignia or whatever disguise the Post Office now went under could be persuaded to get off its collective arse, he would send them back by return.

It was at this point that Hugo Solomon timed his run.

'But why *are* you going, sir?'

'Why am I going?'

'Yes, sir. Why?'

'I'm afraid, Hugo, I could not possibly tell you why I am going.'

'But why not, sir?'

'No, my dear, my lips are sealed. Scouts honour.'

Hugo stood up and walked towards the door. 'I'll go and ask the head then. He'll tell me.'

'Oh, don't do that, it would only cause a flurry.'

'I'm going to see him now, sir. Balfour's always saying he'll be straight with us if we're straight with him.'

'No, Hugo my dear, you mustn't.'

Alice was in agony. Hugo opened the door.

'I'm going.'

'Please don't, I beg you to think of your own future.'

'All right, but only if you tell us.'

So, Hugo resumed his seat while Justin Pett explained, chapter and verse, why he was going, giving not only the cause of his dismissal but also the exact nature of the decisive dialogue with Michael Falconer in front of other senior colleagues over the fish pie. It was not a moment that the seven boys and three girls in the lower sixth History of Art class would be likely to forget.

15

Just as Patrick was beginning to recover from the Kafka and from Jamie's phone call – indeed only a few mornings after seeing his mother – it happened again. It was, in fact, the morning of the eleventh, but as far as Patrick's pursuer was concerned there was to be no cessation of hostilities. This 11 November was to be no Armistice Day.

As if to keep his victim on his toes, this tap on his shoulder, this envelope, was properly addressed to Patrick Balfour Esq., at school and delivered through the post. The postmark was London. It was typed, as before, without any home address or date. And, as before, it carried no signature.

It was headed PRIVATE & CONFIDENTIAL and he came across it, unopened, as he worked through the pile of mail left on his desk by Daphne.

Was this the kind of man they would send after him? Was he, wasn't he, was he? He didn't look like a policeman or a detective at all. He looked like a businessman, somebody's father, well-dressed, well-fed, greying at the temples, an air of uncertainty about him. Was that the kind they sent on a job like this, maybe to start chatting with you in a bar, and then bang! — the hand on the shoulder, the other hand displaying a policeman's badge?

Bang!

Patrick opened the widow of his study a little, even though that let in the smell of petrol and the roar of tyres, and breathed in, steadying himself, pressing his hands hard down against the windowsill. He stayed that way, gulping, for a few minutes. But it did not work. There was no way this churning would settle. And his eyes, when he opened them, were so unfocused he could not name any of the boys or girls crossing the quad below. He had ringing in his ears.

Who the hell was this, quoting Patricia Highsmith at him? He reread the passage. Was it from *The Talented Mr Ripley* or *Ripley Under Ground*, from *Ripley's Game* or *The Boy Who Followed Ripley*? Tom Ripley was the man who became someone else, but Patrick could not remember which novel . . . it was the first in the series, he thought. Or the second. It might even be another first page. But how on earth did anyone know that he had read the Ripley novels?

No, of course, *of course*. The Ripley novels were on his shelves upstairs. Like the Kafka. Like the Lawrence. Patrick had read the Highsmith quartet of stories two summers ago in France. He had read them sitting by the pool or under the tree in the village of Callian. Somewhat unexpectedly, Caroline had bought them as holiday reading and enjoyed them more than she had imagined she would and then passed them on to Patrick who, once they were back in London, passed them on to Jamie.

So, the man up there with the boy had photographed the shelves, then found an appropriate book, and then homed in on the appropriate passage with which to taunt

148

him. Tom Ripley did not allow anyone to prevent him getting what he wanted, including killing a man, including becoming someone else. That was the message. So this man was a bookish man, no doubt about that, this was a bookish crook. But Patrick sensed he was more than that. It all smelt of more than books. How would such a man get into such a world? Wouldn't a modern Ripley, a bookish crook, an identity thief, an obsessive e-mailer who would send that to Jamie, first trawl the internet?

New energy kicked into Patrick's veins. He turned in his seat and watched his fingers tap in *identity*. He watched his fingers tap in *crime*.

Identity, crime.

Separate words or a phrase? His head reeling, Patrick spoke silently to the screen.

Identity crime.

Click-click, search signs, he targeted and trawled far and wide. No, I don't want that, no, not that, yes, could be, hell-o, let's try this shall we, yes, type in that, this might be something, now we're getting somewhere, now we're cooking, there are lots of vendors, want a new number?

Patrick sat back, held by the screen. Just look at this, Netdetective, create a new address, be a credit card fraudster, know your employer's credit rating, know everything you want to know about your employees and your boss.

And if it was this easy and this quick to reach so far and so wide, and to drag in whatever support/help/dirt/info you wanted from every nook and cranny, what chance did Patrick have of knowing, on a headmaster's minor crime level, where his pupils' coursework came from? He followed the signs to DigDirt. Oh, what a lovely phrase that is. DigDirt would have made a quick meal of Churchill and the press barons cover-up in 1953.

Come on, DigDirt.

Patrick scrolled down. What have we here? Quite a list. Quite a few, quite a few of them. Becoming someone else is almost a genre.

The Modern Identity Changer.

How To Disappear Completely and Never Be Found.

The Fastest Growing Crime of the 21st Century.

Identity Theft, The Cyber Crime of the Millennium . . .

Patrick noticed that they were all American books. Published in? . . . in Colorado, in New Jersey and in Washington. So you could sit at home and work at becoming the other Patrick Balfour, could you? Do a nice little correspondence course in it. Probably even get a Ph.D in Identity Studies. Instead of getting into stamp collecting or doing jigsaws you could make yourself up or you could make up your new self, or make up your face to look like someone else and steal some other's name. It was that easy.

The screen was now giving him new advice, albeit a bit too late.

Avoid having your identity stolen.

Make the shredder your best friend.

Stop someone becoming you.

Patrick read the blurbs and synopses of the books and then ordered them, one by one, tapping in his credit card number. Even as he was tapping in his numbers he knew the risks he was taking. For DCI Bevan this would be evidence. Why give them your credit card number? Why give them the name Patrick Balfour? But he did not care. He trawled on, and as he trawled on, he was feeling . . . what are you feeling, Patrick?

He's feeling, *if he hurts Jamie I don't care what happens to me. If he hurts Alice I don't care what happens to me.*

Patrick's fingers are now well ahead of his mind and they are flying loose on the keyboard and he's feeling it's all too fast for me, it's all getting too much for me, and he's going through another emotional chicane again, chicane-chicanery, get someone else to pay your bills, the screen tells Patrick, and he won't even notice.

Patrick was not feeling well. He had to get out of his study but his fingers would not let him. The screen had its own pulling power. The screen pinned him to his seat.

The screen changed. Patrick leant forward.

What's this, you're not serious, I'm afraid so, look for yourself, there it is, it's a bad world out there, Patrick, it's all DogDirt, I can feel the bile coming up, no, there's no bile left, hold on to your seat, make your own ID, yes, you too can be a disappearee, Patrick, oh what a chummy phrase that is, *be a disappearee*, resurrect the dead, we will give you all the detailed documents as well as the layout advice, we will help you paintbrush your new passport photograph. You want a new passport photograph? Oh, yes, please, then I won't look like a criminal. You'll need a macro lens. You want to change the colour of your eyes, facial hair on or off? Hair-dye job plus trimming tips, Be The New Dorian Gray, Windows Paintbrush, create the impression you're dead, up-to-date instruction on the art and science of a new identity, be a spy-demon, heavy-duty disappearing techniques, leaving the country is made easy, what! you're joking, no, look, Patrick, it's there, in black and white, it's going on all over the world, hell's teeth, just tap into DigDirt, DogDirt, the complete pro-gram, names, pictures, take someone's identity in three weeks, click-click.

You could be someone else, Patrick.

Well, *I know that*, don't I! I'm a writer.

And writers like being other people.

Patrick had no more settled a purpose in going on the net than he did in opening the timetable file. More and more he was acting on hunches. In the file he checked to see which forms should now be up there during this lesson. He then crossed the quad, glad to be in the fresh air, passed the theatre, skirted round the squash courts and went up the steps to dig some dirt in the computer labs.

Every seat was taken, every screen glowing, the place packed with fourth-form boys and girls. Most were far too engrossed to notice the headmaster's entry. A few glanced up, hurrying to clear the games from their screens. There was no sign of Casey Cochrane who was timetabled to be teaching them all. No surprises there. Patrick was sure that Casey, his arms too long for his shirt, would be facing his own even bigger computer screen in his office, doing his own work, moonlighting, with his Do Not Disturb notice on his door.

Patrick stepped over the satchels and pencil cases and jackets and bags and knocked on the door. It opened immediately.

'Can I help?'

It wasn't Casey. It was a white-faced white-coated technician with a cup of coffee in his hand. Patrick may have seen him before but he did not know his name. This place was a rabbit warren.

'Yes, I would like a word with Casey.'

'I'm afraid he's not here.'

'But he is down to be teaching a class now.' Patrick nodded back at the computer lab. 'That fourth form in fact.'

'I'm covering for him.'

'And you . . . are?'

'Terry Perkins. Can I help?'

'You don't happen to know where Casey is, do you? I'm the headmaster and I want to trace something. And it is urgent.'

152

Not sure where to look, Terry settled for the middle distance. 'He popped out.'

'Do we know when he popped out?'

'Not exactly.'

'Do we know to where he popped?'

'He didn't say. Just asked me to keep an eye on things.'

Patrick was at his iciest. 'Fine. Two things, Terry, if you would. Please tell Casey to contact me as soon as he returns. I'll be in my study waiting for him to ring. And please go and supervise that class in the lab. Now. That is what covering a class means.'

'Yes, Daphne.'

'It's Casey Cochrane on the phone, Patrick.'

'Put him through.'

'Hello.'

'Is that you, Casey?'

'Yes.'

'I came over to see you half an hour ago.'

'I know, headmaster.'

'And you weren't teaching when you should have been.'

'No, I was in the theatre.'

'Why?'

'They were having some trouble and Euan asked me to help.'

'Shouldn't you be doing that in your free time?'

Casey half-snorted. 'My free time?'

'Yes.'

'What's that then, headmaster? I was asked to help so I did. I always try to help all my colleagues, especially on the creative side. Things were all covered here.'

'They weren't. That's the whole point.'

'The class knew what it was doing. Terry Perkins was here.'

153

'Terry Perkins was drinking a cup of coffee.'

'We don't stand over them, headmaster, and hold their little hands. There's too much spoon-feeding in this school. All they had to do was knock on his door.'

'You can't leave a class unattended.'

'I understand that, and didn't feel I had.'

'So what was the problem in the theatre? I thought we'd just sorted all those out.'

'It's a bit too technical to explain. Anyway, headmaster, Terry said you came over because you wanted my help as well. What can I do for you?'

'It doesn't matter now. You'd better get on.'

16

Patrick rang Caroline, as he had promised he would, and told her in more detail about Jamie's phone call and the Edward Thomas *tenant*. She said I can't bear it, not if Jamie's involved, I'm worried, please come round tonight and I'll do some pasta.

He went round to Finley Place and showed her the Highsmith *bang, hand on the shoulder* letter. They had a bottle of wine and a cosy supper in the kitchen. He told her what he had found on the internet and she didn't mention the speed at which he was drinking. He told her about his clash with Casey Cochrane and she said he had handled it well. He told her he felt he was beginning to lose control of his life. She said he would be fine and held his hand. She said why don't you crash out here. He said he would like to but where's Alice. Alice was staying with a friend.

Patrick did stay the night and he dreamt. He dreamt he was walking in the Greek mountains. It was a hot day and it was hard going so he sat down for a drink and unlaced his boots. Then he noticed that both his feet had been amputated and that his mother's heavy swollen feet were now grafted on in their place. He could not fit his climbing boots back on over them.

In the morning, glad to feel his own feet on the end of his legs, he and Caroline had breakfast together and chatted about this and that. It was as good as it had been for a long time.

Well, three days later he wished he had said nothing. He regretted saying a single word about the whole damn business to his wife because, after they had totally and utterly agreed on the absolute importance of not lumbering Alice with any part of what he was going through, Caroline told her.

Patrick had never been much taken by the way that women (with Daphne as a glorious exception) traded confidences. How did these things happen? They happened, he imagined, over a coffee or while the women were sitting with their feet up on a sofa, girlfriend to girlfriend, woman to woman, mother to daughter, and I really shouldn't say this blah blah, well you really mustn't then blah blah, but if you'd like to blah blah you can trust me blah blah and I'll tell you something I shouldn't blah blah but because we've both been terrible blah blah we won't feel so bad, well we will feel bad but we'll also feel nice and warm and special, while the blokes, the poor silly buttoned-up buggers we're talking about, try to bluff it out on their own and end up retching face down in the lavatory bowl.

What happened was this. The night after Patrick had slept there, Alice got back very late to Finley Place, *very* late even by Alice's standards, and she and her mother clashed the moment she walked in. Caroline was in her nightdress and Alice was in her as only a seventeen-year-old coming in very late can look, and they had the mother and daughter of a row about where Alice had been (Alice would only say that she had been 'with this very interesting man').

'Which man? Who is this man?'

'I'm not telling you, it's private. I'm old enough to have my own life.'

'You said "man" not "boy".'

'Yes, I did, and I'm still not telling you.'

But Caroline said, but why didn't you phone and what's the point of having a mobile in your handbag if all you're going to do is run up huge bills when it's not at all necessary to use it and then worry me frantic by not using the wretched thing when it is.

Caroline, of course, would not tell Patrick where exactly Alice had been, or precisely with whom, even if she knew, because that really would have been breaking a confidence, wouldn't it, and Caroline had absolutely promised Alice that whatever else happened she would 'not tell Dad' because if she did, as they both agreed and as we all know, 'Dad would go both ballistic and berserk.'

So, after tears and stamping and door slamming, they ended up red-eyed and pale-faced and soulful, or so Patrick imagined, over a women's-half-way-through-the-night-milky-drink, during which Alice confided that, although everyone said she was coping so well at school she was in fact very very stressed, and then there was this play she was co-writing, not to mention the ridiculous amounts of work being set in all her subjects, and every teacher saying that this or that subject was the most important subject, and then there's the you-don't-know-how-lucky-you-are-to-be-at-this-school, well, neither of you, neither you nor Dad has any idea how difficult it is *being me*, being a pupil at Dad's school, you really haven't, oh you think you have, but can you imagine what it's like being called Alice Balfour at Patrick Balfour's school, plus the fact that on the last three times she had passed Dad (in the corridor/the quad/the library) he hadn't even bothered to acknowledge her.

'As far as he's concerned, Mum, I might as well not exist.'

'Don't be silly, Alice, he loves you to bits.'

'No, he doesn't.'

'Look, don't drag Dad into all this,' Caroline said, 'it's not fair.'

But by all accounts, or rather by Caroline's account, Alice was now riding the wave, a seventeen-year-old river in full spate, staking out some of the suddenly appearing on the horizon martyr territory, and saying it wasn't that she wanted Dad to be all lovey in public, because he couldn't be, she knew that, headmasters couldn't be, she knew that as well as anyone else or better, but the very least he could do, and it wasn't asking a lot, was smile at her in a secret way or raise an eyebrow or nod or *something*. But Dad's got so stressy lately, he's no fun any more, Mum, and you can see why some of the boys are suddenly getting so nasty about him, he walks around looking so grim, I mean usually it's Falconer The Deputy Nob they all get after but now the guns are being turned on Dad, it's horrible hearing what the boys say, and it's not just Hugo and his lot, it's even worse than the Justin thing, it's some of the girls too.

'Well,' Caroline said, 'he's under a lot of pressure at the moment.'

'He's always under a lot of pressure,' Alice said, 'but he's never been like this with me before.'

'Yes, well —'

'Anyway, Dad loves pressure, you're always saying that.'

'Yes, but this is different.'

'In what way?'

'It just is.'

'Why?'

'Oh, in lots of ways.'

'Why?'

'I can't tell you, Alice, I'm sorry, I just can't.'

'You've got to tell me.'

'I've just told you I can't.'

'Is he ill, Mum? He's ill, isn't he?'

'No, he's not ill, but he could well be if he doesn't watch it. And he hates seeing his mother in the state she's in. Granny's not got long.'

'He is ill, isn't he, and you won't tell me. You're hiding it from me and Jamie.'

'No, I'm not.'

'Does Jamie know?'

'There's nothing like that to know.'

'Dad's been for tests, I know that. I saw it on his desk.'

'Dad has to go for regular health checks. That's in his contract.'

'Is that what you can't tell me? Because you think I'm not old enough to be told? He's got something terrible, that's why he's suddenly looking so grey and lined.'

'Don't be silly.'

'He's been to the doctor. I heard you saying that if I can go to the doctor's about my problems, why can't you go to the doctor's about yours. "*You men!*" I heard you say that, I heard you say that to him.'

'It's not that, it really isn't.'

'So what is it?'

So she told her.

17

The third note, nestling under an unexpected and hand-written apology from Casey Cochrane, was in Patrick's pigeonhole on the morning of 16 November, the day he was due to appear on *Newsnight*. Again it was typed. BY HAND was again printed on the top right of the envelope. This time, though, it was not a familiar Kafka opening sentence, not a Highsmith passage, not even a phrase or clause. It was another blank sheet of paper carrying only this cryptic message:

J. C

D. N. B.

403

Patrick peered round the noisy, packed Common Room. It looked normal. It was the normal Common Room Patrick knew so well. A Common Room jam-packed with teachers, some needing caffeine, some needing a fresh shirt, some needing deodorant, some needing their ties dry-cleaned, some needing their teeth brushed, teachers dashing in or out, elbowing their way to their pigeonholes, talking loudly, drinking tea, drinking water and grabbing biscuits. A normal Common Room in fact.

He read it again: J. C. D. N. B. 4 0 3.

He tried it another way:

Jay cee
Dec Enn Bee
Four Oh Three

Penn-syl-vania 6-5-0-0-0. Glenn Miller. And it chanted. It could be from a Country and Western song. And it rhymed, not that he thought the rhyme significant. So, more of a crossword clue. This time he was being made to work a bit harder.

J. C? Did he know anyone with those initials? Jesus Christ? Jesus Christ! No. Any writers? It might be a writer. The first three were writers. Kafka . . . Highsmith . . . Edward Thomas. So was it Joseph Conrad? . . . John Clare? . . . How about John Cheever? . . . Or John Cornford maybe?

Or a historical figure. Jack Cade?

DNB . . .

Did not bat? But how could you score 403 if you did not bat? . . . DNB. No, Patrick, this isn't a cricket fan, this is a scholar, a *scholarly* stalker, a bookish crook, and this is a man who is now directing you to the *Dictionary of National Biography*.

He's saying to you that he doesn't just know his Kafka and his Highsmith and the work of Edward Thomas. He's saying that he also knows the by-ways and has met the minor figures. He knows his *DNB*. And he – is he in this room? – is setting you off on another chase. It might well be one of the people watching you now, but don't look round. If he's in the room do not give him that pleasure.

161

As Patrick stood there, feeling the after-shock, members of staff passed in front of him. When they spoke he reacted on automatic, as Patrick Balfour, the headmaster on top of his game, the headmaster at the very top of his profession would. Patrick listened to himself as he responded to each and every one of them.

Heather Bishop, the Head of Strings, smiled at him. Heather was an American, a Patrick fan, and she was still smiling her unforced smile as she approached. She had beautiful smooth skin. Somehow Patrick smiled back. It almost hurt his face.

'Good morning, Patrick.'

'Morning, Heather. Well done, by the way, I loved the Mozart.'

'Why thank you.'

'And the Copland.'

'They did so well, didn't they? I was so proud of them.'

'I was proud of you, Heather, for getting them to play that well.'

'I appreciate you saying that, Patrick. The Copland was a big ask.'

Daniel Radford, the Head of History, was now waiting his turn for a word. Daniel was looking harassed. Life was more than Daniel could handle. The nicest of men, Daniel was deep down an even bigger Patrick fan than Heather, as well as being one of those who believed that Patrick had changed the tone of the school for the better, but having a high-profile historian *and* a novelist *and* a media figure as his headmaster often left Daniel feeling more threatened than encouraged.

'Do you have a moment, Patrick?'

'Yes, Dan, of course.'

Dan's eyes were rattled. 'It's another coursework saga, I'm afraid.'

'Not our friend again?'

'He's taken this one straight off the internet.'

'Why? He doesn't have to, God knows he's clever enough.'

'It's just his way of taking the mickey, of saying the whole thing's beneath him. Why write it if you can nick it? That's how he sees it.'

'Word for word?'

'Word for word.'

'I'll see him. If it happens again I'm going to suspend him.'

'I'm really sorry to bother you with all this. I really thought I'd sorted it.'

'It's no bother, Dan. That's what I'm here for.'

Dan looked quite close to tears so Patrick moved crisply on, trying to comfort himself with the argument that, by visiting the library to consult the *DNB*, he would, in an ironic way, be turning his own private disarray to his professional advantage. By visiting the library he would be showing a bit of the headmasterly visibility that Michael Falconer was always suggesting he adopt. He would be winning his deputy's approval by Being Seen More Around The School. See things around the place for yourself, Patrick. That's what Michael was always urging Patrick to do. And Being Seen Around The Place More, headmaster, lets the whole school know that you are the headmaster. And, believe it or not, headmaster, people do like it. It reminds everyone who is in charge. (Or rather who would be in charge, Michael felt, if only the headmaster spent more time *in* the place and less time writing novels or having affairs or pontificating on the BBC.)

On the stairs up to the library, Patrick passed a gratifying number of colleagues coming down, and as he pushed open the library door and saw the pupils' heads turn he was even more gratified to notice the whispering soon died down.

So they still feel that I count.

They do know who the headmaster is.

Good.

As they should.

Because never in Patrick Balfour's career had he felt more in need of a bit of respect from his school, a bit of respect from his staff and a bit of respect from his pupils. Looking every inch the part, the headmaster set off on a slow headmasterly circuit of the tables and carols. First the lower library, then the upper library where the sixth form usually settled, taking his time, knowing that they were all aware of his presence behind their backs.

He paused to see what Matthew Powell was researching (Matthew was a nice boy, even if he publicly resettled his scrotum rather more often than was seemly) and then he paused to see what Clara Stone was reading (Clara's skirt was a good deal shorter than the school guidelines allowed but resting at about the height that Patrick really liked), nodding his approval at each pupil who caught his eye, leaning over the occasional shoulder and smiling in appreciation at the scholarly atmosphere. The whole scene, he was a little embarrassed to catch himself thinking, would make the most marvellous photograph in the school prospectus.

Did Alice ever use the library? There was no sign of her.

He could see the old leather-bound two-volume *DNB* nestling next to the twenty-two-volume *OED*. He moved in on it. Just before taking it down from the shelf, however, out of the corner of his eye Patrick spotted Max Russell-Jones coming across from his desk by the door.

'And to what do we owe this privilege, Headmaster?'

'Oh, just checking up on something, thank you.'

'Can I perhaps help in any way?'

'No, thank you, Max, I think I can manage.'

Max did a little bow in a mock-courteous manner and swung on his heel. Patrick moved away to a carol, placed the heavy dictionary down, pulled up a chair and allowed his fingers to flick, apparently at random, to page 403. To J. C on page 403.

And there he was. Bottom right-hand corner. Quite a small entry. Joseph Clark.

JOSEPH CLARK (d. 1696) posture-master of Pall Mall . . .

Patrick ran his eye down the entry.

He could not take it all in.

Joseph Clark? Never heard of him.

Posture-master? What the hell was a posture-master? Was J. C a freak contortionist? A posture-master was a man who could contort and dislocate his body so much that even his friends could not recognise him when he passed them in the street.

Patrick's hands were trembling.

Who on earth would come across this Joseph Clark entry? Who would land on this and choose to use it against me, to use this small entry in the *DNB* as ammunition? Well, not Casey Cochrane, that's for sure. Patrick's mind jammed on overload.

At the moment all he could think of doing was to ask the courteous mask of Max Russell-Jones if it would be in order for him to photocopy a page of the *Dictionary of National Biography*. There was something here, something of a curiosity you might say, that interested him. But, first of all, was it acceptable to open such a large dictionary and put it face down on the photocopier?

'But of course, Headmaster.'

They walked through to the photocopier in the library

annexe. Patrick could not stop his hands trembling. Max took the dictionary from him.

'Allow me to do it for you, Headmaster.'

'It won't damage the spine?'

'Not if I'm careful.'

'Very kind of you, Max.'

'Not at all, Headmaster. This page? Page 403, did you say?'

'Yes.'

'Joseph Clark, posture-master of Pall Mall?'

'That's the man.'

Max positioned the large leather-bound book so that the appropriate corner of the page could be copied.

'Would A4 be all right, Headmaster?'

'Fine. Does the name Joseph Clark ring any bells with you, Max?'

'Never crossed my path, I regret to say.'

This is what slowly slid on to the tray of the photo-copier:

JOSEPH CLARK (d. 1696), posture-master, of Pall Mall, although a well-grown man, and inclining to stoutness, was enabled to contort his body in such a manner as to represent almost any kind of deformity and dislocation. The 'Guardian' (no. 102) speaks of him as having been 'the plague of all tailors about town', for he would be measured in one posture, which he changed for another when his clothes were brought home. He even imposed upon the famous surgeon, James Moleyns or Mullins, to whom he applied as a pretended patient. He dislocated the ver-tebrae of his back and other parts of his body in so frightful a fashion that Moleyns was shocked at the sight, and would not so much as attempt a cure.

166

Among other freaks he often passed as a begging cripple with persons in whose company he had been but a few minutes before. Upon such occasions he would not only twist his limbs out of shape, but entirely alter the expression of his face. His powers of facial contortion are said to have been equally extraordinary. Clark was dead before 1697; Evelyn, in his 'Numismata', published in that year, mentions him as 'our late Proteus Clark' (p. 277). A year later a brief account of him was communicated to the Royal Society (*Phil. Trans*. xx. 262). He is the subject of two drawings, by 'Old' Laroon, in Tempest's 'Cryes and Habits of London, 1688'.

With the photocopy in his pocket Patrick left the library. The posture-master of Pall Mall? Contorts his body? Dislocates his vertebrae? Facial contortions? Is he (whoever he is) saying that I am someone who does that, that I am a man of many faces, that I am pretending to be someone, that I steal other people's personalities, that I am always playing a role, is that it? That I am a deceiving Proteus? Or is he saying that he is? Or that we both are?

Patrick recalled something from a book – was it a biography of Ronald Reagan? – something to the effect that the actor 'remembers' forward, the actor projects himself into as yet unspoken lines, while the writer remembers backwards, ordering the past and finding patterns in his own history. As he recalled that passage, as he saw the words halfway down on the right-hand page of the Reagan biography, Patrick also found himself on autopilot. He was walking across the quadrangle.

Why did he not go straight back to his study? If he had been asked that question by Detective Chief Inspector Bevan, Patrick could not have given an explanation.

Instead, on an instinct, he, or his body at least, returned to his study via both the theatre and the Common Room. After all, he had no particular purpose in visiting the theatre, and he had just emptied his pigeonhole in the Common Room. But visit them both he did.

Inside the auditorium it was stiflingly hot. There was a noisy rehearsal in progress, there was some banging backstage and Euan Stuart, standing at the front of the stage with his hands shielding his eyes, was calling out to an unseen person, 'How does that look?' 'Yes, that works,' a voice called back. In another corner a piece of scenery — the back wall of a booklined room — was being painted, and from the top of a hoist one of the lighting boys was shouting down 'Has that sorted it?'

Euan turned, saw who it was standing there in the auditorium, and immediately jumped down off the stage.

'Are you looking for your daughter, Headmaster?'

'Not particularly.'

'She's around the place somewhere, working on her lines.'

'I was just seeing how everything's all going?'

The new Director of Drama was charm itself. 'Oh as mad as ever, all the usual crises, and there's never enough time, is there?'

'But it'll be all right on the night.'

Euan raised his hairy hands in alarm. 'Never, never say that! In this game you must never invite hubris.'

'But Casey sorted out your computer problems?'

'He did indeed; the man's a genius. He's saved the day.'

'What was it?'

'The sound deck, it's all computerised these days, which of course means there's much more chance of a cock-up. But *I* didn't say that.'

'Because you ordered it, Euan.'

'I know, Headmaster, *mea culpa, mea culpa*.'

'And it wouldn't work?'

'Well, for some ridiculous reason it wouldn't play ball with the particular music I wanted. But all's well now.'

Patrick looked into Euan's eyes. Euan looked away.

'Well, I mustn't hold you up any longer, but may I have a look around?'

'Feel free, but do watch your step backstage. Dangerous places, theatres.'

As Euan jumped back up on the stage Patrick said:

'By the way, joking apart, I'm sure it will be a great success.'

'Well, let's hope so, Headmaster.'

After wandering around the backstage area in a rather pointless way and after looking up at the bank of lights as if he actually knew something about lighting and after wandering in to the sound box, which looked like the flight deck of a jumbo jet, Patrick left.

The Common Room was completely empty. And there it was, as somehow he knew it would be: another one in his pigeonhole. He'd only been to the library and over to the theatre but he could see the envelope when he was still three yards away from his pigeonhole, and again it had been hand-delivered. In the intervening fifteen minutes, or twenty at the very most, someone had been back up to the Common Room and placed it there.

Patrick touched the envelope, as if it were a letter bomb. He did not immediately open it. He knew well enough who it was from. No, that's exactly what he did not know, he did not know who it was from. He just knew it was from *him*, from Joseph Clark, the man in his pocket.

He tapped the unopened envelope and leant back against the deputy head's noticeboard, the place for daily business where Michael put his own brisk announcements to the Common Room. Patrick picked up a newspaper which had slipped on to the floor and pretended to read it.

The hot water urn was steaming.

The biscuits had all gone.

There was a new print on the far wall.

No footsteps were coming up the stairs.

His finger slid down the back of the self-sealing envelope.

He unfolded the piece of paper.

So what have we got this time?

This is what Patrick's hooded eyes saw:

TO: PATRICK BALFOUR
FROM: PATRICK BALFOUR

1. *When two sane persons are together one expects that A will recognise B to be more or less the person B takes himself to be, and vice versa. That is, I expect my definition of myself should, by and large, be endorsed by the other person, assuming I am not deliberately impersonating someone else, being hypocritical, lying and so on.*
2. *His whole life has been torn between his desire to reveal himself and his desire to conceal himself.*

Little chance you will have read this book, *The Divided Self* (1960) by R. D. Laing, but you will know the feeling.

18

With his long hair and his pale skin, the long hair and the pale skin of a Pre-Raphaelite beauty, Hugo Solomon was waiting outside Patrick's study, if waiting was the word for so languid a pose. He did not look at all like a naughty boy waiting outside the headmaster's door. Draped against the wall, he was checking his text messages on his mobile. He did not acknowledge the headmaster's approach, obvious enough though Patrick's approach across the wooden hall was.

'Come in, Hugo.'

The boy took his time, easing himself off the wall, and he was still turning off his mobile as he walked into the study some ten seconds after Patrick. OK, Patrick, so our Hugo has known from the cradle the power of seeming unimpressed, but don't let up on the little swine. Patrick's voice was crisp.

'You know what this is about, Hugo, don't you?'

'Mr Radford sent me.'

'And you know why?'

'I'm taking my history coursework off the internet.'

'Yes.'

'Not all of it, though.'

171

'Mr Radford says it is word for word. A complete steal, he said.'

'Did he?'

'Yes.'

The boy, with no hint of anxiety, smiled his no-shit-Sherlock smile. Patrick suffered the smile and swallowed and reminded himself he was already a headmaster on bail.

'Do you want me to change a few words, is that it, do a cut-and-paste job like everyone else?'

'So it *is* word for word?'

'Only that particular piece.'

'That's more than enough.'

'It's only one piece out of five. And all the rest got As.'

'But you've been warned before not to do it.'

'The topic's a waste of time.'

'In your lofty opinion.'

'It's pointless and everyone's bored with it. Even Radford finds it boring.'

'*Mr* Radford.'

'*Mr* Radford.'

Patrick moved away from his desk. He told himself he must behave like a headmaster. He told himself to behave like a man who was used to dealing with all kinds of young people, used to dealing with young people of all types as they go through adolescence, even those young people in his care who he could garrotte.

'Whether you're bored with it or not is not the issue, Hugo. It's that it's cheating.'

'I'll write it out now for you, if you like, without the internet. It's just that I've got a lot on and I was saving myself time.'

'Well, that's an original one, I have to say.'

'I am an original, headmaster.'

Don't lose the plot, Patrick. Stay headmasterly.

'What have you got on that's making you so busy?'

'I'm helping Alice with her play. And I'm doing some research.'

'And what would that be, Hugo, a bit of literary research?'

'Not with you, sorry.'

'What is the research which is much more interesting than your coursework?'

'Everything is more interesting than coursework. And I'm writing a screenplay.'

'Anyway, I'll be doing a bit of writing too, writing to your parents, Hugo, to say that if this happens again I'll be suspending you, and the very next time I'll also be writing to the examination board.'

Hugo smiled and flicked back his long hair.

'That doesn't worry you, Hugo?'

'No, not at all.'

'It really doesn't?'

'No, but it ought to worry you.'

'Why should it worry me, Hugo?'

'Because I don't think it's wise.'

Patrick felt his hands tingle and his mouth twitch. Holding his hands tightly by his side he walked across the study floor to within a few feet of the unmoved boy.

'What did you say?'

'I said, I don't think that is wise.'

'Why?'

'Because if you do that I'll e-mail the exam board the very same day and tell them how much of the coursework in this school is dishonest. Then you'll have to suspend another fifty. Could be more. Could be seventy-five. Who knows, could even include your daughter, not that Al's someone I'd want to land in it.'

'What evidence have you got for saying all this?'

173

'All I need. It's common knowledge.'

'I don't believe you.'

Hugo shrugged. 'You should. And the press will love it. I'll write to a couple of papers telling them which Heads of Department encourage it. I'll tell them which Heads of Department turn a blind eye, and which collude, I'll name them. Name and shame them. It's a matter of public concern. There's increasing media interest in the whole question, some of it stirred up by you.'

Patrick spoke from a dry mouth: 'You wouldn't do any of that.'

'Mind you, if the coursework in this school *was* honest we might not do so well in the league tables. But then you've probably thought of that.' He looked steadily into Patrick's eyes.

'Sit down, Solomon.'

'I don't want to sit down.'

'*Sit down*, I said!'

'I'm not, because I'm not taking any lectures on plagiarism from *you*.'

There was a knock on the door. Patrick stormed over and opened it.

'Yes!'

It was Daphne, her eyes jittery. She looked across at Hugo in a questioning way.

'Is everything all right?'

'It's fine. Thank you.'

'Just to remind you about *Newsnight*.'

'Yes?'

'They're picking you up at eight-thirty.'

'Yes, thank you.'

'And you're due at the Duke of Edinburgh Awards in twenty minutes.'

'I'll be there. Thank you, Daphne.'

He closed the door, and recrossed the carpet towards the boy.

'What was the point of that remark?'

'Which remark?'

'On plagiarism.'

'Oh that.'

'Yes, that.'

Hugo shrugged his fine-by-me smile. 'Do I have to spell it out?'

'Yes, spell out whatever you like.'

'You're sure?'

'I'm sure.'

'J-u-s-t-i-n. Shall I go on? P-e . . .'

'You know him?'

'He taught me. We're friends, yes.'

'Friends? You're still in touch with him?'

The boy rolled his shoulders: you win some you lose some. 'Justin's moved on, and that's OK with me. I still like him.'

'For how long have you been a friend of Justin Pett?'

'Nothing to do with you, is it?'

'I think it is. Did you get involved with him when he was here?'

'"Involved"?'

'Yes, involved.'

'As I said, we were friends.'

'What is all this, Hugo? What are you planning? Are you the one putting –'

'Am I what?'

'Nothing, nothing. To go back to Justin Pett.'

'Only if you want to, headmaster.'

Patrick just stopped himself. With his back to Hugo he paced for a moment in silence. Then, without turning to face him, he said, 'I'll speak to Mr Radford.'

175

'To say what?'

Patrick spat out each word separately: 'I will speak to him in whatever way I like. Get out!'

Before he went to the presentation of the Duke of Edinburgh Awards Patrick checked the staff files and dialled. It rang and rang; there was obviously no voicemail or answerphone facility, but just before Patrick gave up he got this:

'Hell-o.'

'Is that Justin Pett's place?'

'Yes.'

'Could I speak to him, please?'

'Justin's not here.'

'Do you know when he'll be back?'

'Who is this, please?'

'Patrick Balfour.'

'Come again.'

'Patrick Balfour, and I'd like a word with him, could you please tell him I rang.'

'Yes, I'll do that.'

'Will he be back later today?'

'No, he won't.'

'Do you by any chance know when he might be?'

'He's not in the country, I'm afraid.'

'I see. Is he away for long?'

'Well, you never know with Justin, do you? He's in Avignon. Or is it Venice? Or he was. One or the other. Or both.' The voice giggled.

'May I ask who am I talking to?'

'A friend of Justin's.'

'It's really quite important that I speak to him, you see. Do you have an address for him?'

'Justin doesn't really do addresses.'

'Anyway, if he rings could you please tell him I called?'

'If he does, I most certainly will.'

'Thank you so much.'

'Shall I say what it's about?'

'There's really no need, thanks. Has he been away long?'

'Six weeks . . . two months . . . not sure. It feels an age.'

It can't be Justin, then. Unless he's doing it through Hugo Solomon. Which he could well be doing, taking revenge on me through a boy, one of his boys on site. Or through this latest boyfriend who's playing games with me.

'And he could be back any time?'

'That's rather up to him, isn't it? Justin won't be told.'

'Well, thanks anyway.'

'Is that all? I'm sorry I've been so little help.'

'No, you've been most helpful. And I'm sorry to have bothered you.'

'And who is it calling again?'

'Patrick Balfour.'

'I'll just write that down.'

'If you would.'

'Oh, *typique*.'

'What is it?'

'This biro doesn't work. Let's try another one. Ah, that's better. Right, Patrick Balfour called. That's not Patrick Balfour, as in the headmaster?'

'Yes.'

'As in the one who's on telly?'

'I'm afraid so.'

'I've seen you a lot.'

'And I'm on again tonight, if you're interested. On *Newsnight*.'

'That's nice, if I'm in I'll watch.'

'Just one more thing, if I may. You don't by any chance know someone called Hugo Solomon, do you?'

'No, never heard of him. Sorry.'

19

The newsreader looked into Caroline Balfour's eyes and said that *Newsnight* was now starting over on BBC2, that is if perchance you fancy a few good punch-ups, because over on *Newsnight* we can offer you all of that with knobs on. She switched channels and went to the bottom of the stairs calling,

'Alice?'

No answer.

'Alice?'

'What!'

'Daddy's on any minute, darling.'

No answer.

'Aren't you coming down?'

No answer.

'Alice?'

There was no further response, not even the sound of sullen feet padding across the floor above, so Caroline put her herbal tea down on the side table and closed the shutters at the front of the house, shutting out her balcony, her bay trees and most of the London hum. Then, after taking a last look at the ornamental vines on the patio, she closed and locked the shutters at the back.

Back in front of BBC2 she could see, even with the volume down, that the discomfited Minister for Education was in the firing line. She tapped up the volume to hear the predictable jousting,

'Oh, come on, Minister, it's not very difficult. Yes or no?'

To accompany this 'come on' the camera picked up the interviewer's raised left eyebrow.

'I've just explained, if you'll give me a moment, we are having a review on the whole matter of –'

'Not *another* review? Why don't you just sort out the mess?'

'It's not a mess.'

'But it isn't right, is it? The pupils hate the exams, the teachers are up in arms, recruitment is thousands down, the GCSE results are often wrong, the A levels are wrongly marked, more and more schools are appealing against the results, there's no confidence in the AS level –'

'No, it's not right in every detail but we're getting there.'

'You said that last October.'

'And we're still getting there. We're closer.'

The camera picked up the interviewer's right eyebrow.

'Do you, Minister, have any idea – as you might ask the driver of a British train – when we might arrive? This month, next month, sometime, never?'

'You will find that out when you read our review.'

'Oh, this review again –'

'Which will be the most detailed account of educational provision and the most detailed overhaul of the public examination system ever carried out in this country.'

Which was enough for the *Newsnight* interviewer, who now raised both eyebrows and adopted his and-if-you-believe-that-at-home-you'll-believe-anything before swinging towards Patrick.

'So where does that leave you, Mr Balfour? Any the wiser?'

Caroline sat up. God, Patrick looked tired. His face was stretched taut, his eyes set deep with dark lines beneath them. (Daphne had found him slumped asleep at his desk late that afternoon.)

That Patrick started speaking so quietly only confirmed Caroline's sense of a gathering storm. She, better than anyone, knew the danger signs in her husband.

'It leaves me worried. We are already the most overexamined, overtested and overworked educational system in the Western world.'

The interviewer looked unimpressed, snapping in with, 'And the most underachieving.'

'That's not true. The educational achievement of the girls and boys in this country is patchy, varying from the excellent to the competent to the very worrying. Things would be less difficult if we simplified the process.'

'In what way?'

'By massively reducing the examinations and trusting the teachers, who are already the unpaid examiners of a ludicrous amount of coursework, which is not only open to abuse but openly abused.'

'Even in a school as privileged as yours?'

'What does that mean?'

'Well, you're not saying your school is squeaky clean, are you?'

'No, I'm not.'

'And isn't it all a piece of cake when your parents can not only afford whatever fees you charge but also pay for whatever extra tutoring they want?'

'No, it isn't a piece of cake for anyone. The pressures in my school, on both pupils and teachers, are great, as any of them would tell you. If you set yourself the highest standards

181

it's a tough life every lesson of the day. And if you visit my school you will see the most superb work going on in every area. But we're not talking about my school, though if we had all night perhaps we should and you would learn something.'

'We haven't got all night, we've got five minutes.'

'So might I suggest you speak to your producer and allocate sufficient time for the Minister and me to answer the questions properly?'

Caroline ran to the bottom of the stairs. 'Alice! Come and see this! Alice!'

'Well, let me ask you a perfectly simple question. Should we now get rid of the AS level?'

'It's not a good examination but nor is it a perfectly simple question. The Minister isn't a fool. I'm not a fool. Teachers aren't fools. They're some of the brightest people in the country.'

'Why not answer the question?'

'Yes, I would get rid of AS, and I argued against the AS before they were brought in.'

'At last! An answer.'

Patrick smiled, a smile that made Caroline go very still. He leant forward in his studio seat. 'This is just a five-minute hit for you, isn't it, five minutes of TV buzz before you switch to your other colleague or your next topic. You like to make a dismissive comment, to cut people off and come out looking a winner, while those of us who spend our lives in education dealing with the challenging young are demeaned and left to pick up the pieces. Dealing with demanding pupils, as I have been doing today, and running a school properly and sorting out the questions you ask is a lot more difficult than displaying factitious outrage in a studio.'

★

Over in Docklands, Liz Nicholson, with half a manuscript unread on the sofa and the other half splayed on the carpet, was punching the air and splashing some of her glass of Chilean red on to her (happily) red dress.

'Yes! Kick him, Patrick! Kick him in the balls!'

If Roger, her husband, had been at home this goal-mouth celebration would not have been taking place. She probably would have been drinking less and she most certainly would not have been watching her ex-lover, Mr Patrick Balfour, on *Newsnight*. They would probably have been watching European football.

But her husband was not at home; he was now living in Shepherd's Bush, and Liz had just read a good sex scene in the manuscript now lying on the carpet and it was the kind of sex she liked, it rang true, and she was watching Patrick and she was reliving some of the very good sex she had with him as well as missing his mind, his body and his mind, the imprint of his head on the pillow, his humour and his hands, so she gulped her drink, wiped the drops off her dress, wiped her lips with the back of her hand, picked up her handbag off the floor, checked his mobile number in her diary (a year or so ago she would have known it by heart) and excited herself with the thought that it might go off in the television studio, that it might start vibrating against Patrick's thigh right there in his trouser pocket.

'Excuse me for just one moment, would you, I've got a call. Yes, yes, hello? Oh, Liz, hi. Yes, well, as you can see I am a bit tied up, no, of course I don't mind you ringing me, it's lovely to hear you, just give me a moment, will you, to sort out this bloke and I'll come straight back to you.'

But, of course, Patrick was not the kind of man to leave his mobile on while in the television studio, and she left a message, her voice as low and as relaxed and as intimate as she could make it,

183

'Hello. It's me. Now here's a surprise, I'm watching you on TV, even as I speak, and to prove it I'll hold the phone towards the set. Pause for sound effects. There. You can probably hear yourself in the background. Can you hear it? Sound good, don't you? You still look good, too, and you still hit hard. But by the look of it you're not getting enough sleep. Hope the writing's going well. Nearly said "Miss you" but you'll notice I didn't. Bye.'

What's the first thing he remembered of her, the very first thing? Her laugh. No, her mouth, irrespective of whether she was laughing or not, her mouth, even though she often was laughing. Her wonderfully loose mouth, and her laugh and her teeth as she spun aside in the doorway of the National Portrait Gallery and she saw just how soaking wet he was.

Michael Falconer was not yet back at his home in Dulwich. He was too late to see *Newsnight*, though even if he had been back at home, surrounded by framed photographs of his school and his college rugby teams, sitting in his favourite leather armchair with a glass of brandy in his hand, he would not have switched on the television. As far as Michael Falconer was concerned, Patrick going on telly on the same night as the Lower Sixth Parents' Evening was just another form of moonlighting. Patrick Balfour was putting posturing and publicity and self-promotion before duty: as expected.

Just as expected, and just as irritating, were some of the predictably fulsome comments about the headmaster that his deputy had to suffer and swallow during the course of that Lower Sixth Parents' Evening. Michael had heard them all before and every Parents' Evening he had to listen to them all over again.

184

– *Your bloke Balfour seems to be doing a great job.*

– *He's so approachable, isn't he?*

– *My God, it's a different school from the funny old place I went to.*

– *Heard him on the radio the other morning, came over terribly well.*

– *Taking in girls seems to have made the difference.*

– *My son says he's a brilliant head.*

– *Fantastic results again, you're obviously getting the essentials right.*

– *My daughter says he's so inspiring.*

– *Doing you a power of good, that Balfour chap, by all accounts.*

– *Hold on to him, if I were you. Don't want Eton poaching him.*

But Michael was not thinking only of Patrick Balfour. Most baffling of all now, in his view, was the behaviour of Daphne. Daphne, who used to be Michael's greatest ally in the dramas that unfolded behind the study door, had in recent weeks become absurdly protective of, if not downright dewy-eyed over, her boss. And when you think that she had been secretary to the two previous heads, both great men in their own very different ways, it absolutely beggared belief. But if Michael went into the office now for a bit of a natter with Daffers and it got on to any general criticism, let alone anything a bit personal, she either affected not to hear it or said that Patrick had worries enough of his own/was working flat-out sixteen hours a day/wasn't quite himself at the moment/needed a bit of space/had such an awful lot on his plate.

Once, she even suggested to Michael that he might be overreacting. He couldn't believe his ears! Good thing probably that he had never married: he'd never understand women, not even Daffers, who, he had always comforted himself, was a sort of honorary bloke.

185

And there's something else wrong, Michael thought. Not only in the theatre. In me. He felt it again. I know there is. And I must sort it out. Sort both out.

After the last of the parents had drifted away at 10.00 p.m. Michael had stayed in the Common Room drinking a cup of lukewarm coffee, eating the last of the dried-up sausage rolls and listening to Euan Stuart pretending, in his most theatrical voice, that he had just ended his evening in a most unpleasant confrontation. The whole episode did not ring true. To Michael it sounded like a page of dialogue from a bad play. As far as Michael was concerned, Euan Stuart was a show-off, a charlatan and a sham. Conscious that Michael Falconer was not proving to be the rapt audience his story required, Euan quickly joined the little group huddled over the gas fire. At the heart of it, Max Russell-Jones was whispering and Casey Cochrane was brooding. A brooding Casey Cochrane listening to a whispering Max Russell-Jones being joined by Euan Stuart was always a bad sign.

Weary in every bone, Michael thanked the caterers, collecting up a few cups and saucers himself as he did so. Then he went down to the lodge and thanked the porters for the long hours they had put in, especially those who had the nightmare job of dealing with the selfish parents, the overpaid and overdressed spivs who arrived late and parked their monster four-wheel-drives wherever they wanted and at whatever angle they pleased.

Finally, before driving home, Michael walked quickly round the campus to check that all was well on the security front. The security guard said only one classroom window had been left undone and only one major building had been left completely unlocked.

'Yes, I can guess,' Michael said, 'don't tell me.'

The security man nodded.

'The new theatre?'

186

'Yes, Mr Falconer.'

'Put a report in to the headmaster, please, first thing in the morning. And a copy to me, if you would.'

'Yes, Mr Falconer. Good night, sir.'

On his way back from Television Centre Patrick listened to Liz's message on his mobile and then slumped back in his taxi. He could not respond. He was finished. Finished full stop. Feeling dead, he watched London pass by the side window. If only he would sleep tonight: sleep tonight and he could face the world. Sleep tonight and he could handle whatever was thrown at him.

The taxi driver, however, was very far from finished. He was giving Patrick the benefit of his worldly wisdom on waking up late and dealing with women.

'Woke up about five this morning, alarm went off, next thing I knew it was eight and I was well fucked off.'

'I bet.'

'And so was the boss, wasn't he?'

'Was he?'

'Still, that's his problem, mate. Said my old man was ill, didn't I?'

'Did you?'

'Same with women, mate. Innit?'

Patrick was lost. He leant forward a little. 'I'm sorry, I didn't catch that last bit.'

'Women, mate.'

'Yes?'

'Treat 'em like mushrooms.'

'Mushrooms?'

'Keep 'em in the dark and use a lot of bullshit. Best way, eh?'

The driver looked in the mirror to see if his fare, a face he sort of half-recognised, was laughing. His fare wasn't.

187

20

Day or night, Patrick had always walked. As a boy he liked to walk in the middle of the night with his friend Alan. As an undergraduate he spent a month walking in the mountains of Greece with Viola. At night they had read stories to each other. By day they had climbed Ossa and Pelion. How special that made him feel. As a young father he liked nothing more than leaving a pile of school work on his desk in Finley Place and going round the perimeter of Hyde Park with Alice. How special *that* made him feel: holding her seven-year-old hand he would cross Kensington Road and go in at Palace Gate, up along the Broad Walk, pass the palace and Queen Victoria's statue, regaling his daughter with Victorian stories as she skipped along by his side or ran ahead into the Orangery.

At the Bayswater Road end they turned right along the North Walk. If it was dry they would sit on a bench near the forsythia and watch the squirrels running helter-skelter along the railings, squirrels so tame they sometimes ate out of Alice's hand.

'On we go, Alice.'

'I love you, Daddy.'

'I love you, too. Have I told you about Edward Jenner?'

At the Italian Gardens, where they were finely sprayed by a row of fountains and surrounded by stone urns, he told Alice about Julius Caesar and the Roman Empire; then, standing in front of his statue, he told her about Edward Jenner and the smallpox vaccine.

'You know such a lot, Daddy.'

'Not really.'

On the Long Water it was now Alice's turn to show off. She counted how many swans she could see before (more difficult) how many tufted ducks she could see before (most difficult) how many shovelers.

'Right, Peter Pan next and then home for Mummy's chocolate cake.'

When the older Patrick was overrevving and unable to sleep, as he was after *Newsnight*, in those hours when by way of engulfing company he had only his own distressful thoughts, he liked to set off in his mind's eye for a walk across London. It was partly to see how good his memory of the great city was, and partly to avoid the cluster of personalities milling around in his uncontrollable and fragmented head.

This imaginary walking, this disciplined exercise of the imagination, was a technique Patrick had first come across while reading the memoirs of Albert Speer, Hitler's architect and armaments minister. *Spandau: The Secret Diaries*, that was the title of Speer's book. The hardback was still on his shelves in his downstairs study. It was in Spandau Prison, while serving twenty years for crimes against humanity, that the Nazi armaments minister walked. And what a walk he was on! For hours on end, day after day, Speer walked round and round the prison yard, a routine of unimaginable tedium made bearable because he imagined that he was walking around the world.

Patrick's prison yard was his bed.

With his legs tucked up, he would walk around London.

Not steal around in the dark.

He had London all to himself.

Not a soul around.

And all that mighty heart was lying still.

Confident in his isolation.

No smart-arse pupils.

No critical colleagues.

No stolen cars.

Don't think about stolen cars.

No taxis, no women, no mushrooms.

No paedophiles.

No special effects, no Casey Cochrane.

No internet, no plagiarism.

No police cars.

Don't think about police cars.

There was not a soul around.

No other people.

But you have to live in this world with other people, Patrick.

Not alone in my bed, not on my private walk I don't.

With the Thames on his right, and Lambeth Palace beyond, he set off at Lambeth Bridge. Under a full moon he walked, oh the cool night air, towards the Houses of Parliament, a neo-Gothic cardboard cutout, tall and sharp against the sky. Passing the Victoria Tower Gardens, passing Rodin's sculpture *The Burghers of Calais* and the statue of Emmeline Pankhurst, past the Sovereign's Entrance and the Chancellor's Gate, pausing before the figure of Oliver Cromwell, with Churchill in his trench coat coming up on his left in Parliament Square.

Churchill.

Turn to him.

Leave the iron railings.

Walk across the empty square.

Go and stand at his feet.

Think about resolve.

He wouldn't be broken by this.

Where's your mental toughness, Patrick?

Never Give In.

Then turn right towards Westminster Bridge, but don't cross it, keep going along the Embankment. Enjoy the Embankment, enjoy the bit of the Embankment you don't see from your study window. You now have London all to yourself as you never do in the day, you now have the whole of the great city to yourself. And you can go as the crow flies, or, if you prefer as a bat flies, the bats come out from their dark recesses, like you do, like Mr Hyde did, and they have a little look around, curious creatures, bats, they're leather-flutterers, and their webby fingers extend to support a thin membrane which stretches from the side of the neck by the toes of both pairs of feet to the tail – and forms a kind of wing, with which they fly in a peculiar quivering motion, and *that*, if you're ignorant, is a bat upon the wing. But don't let them bite you. Nasty bite, a bat bite.

Over the river, on his right and falling behind him, he now had St Thomas' Hospital and London County Hall. Nothing on the water, no tugs called *Resolve*, no barges, no pleasure boats, no commentary Français, no Italiano, no Español and no Deutsch, just the river in the moonlight. No joggers sweating by and no pleasure boats cruising down to Greenwich or up to Kew. No souvenirs, no pimps, no pupils smoking, no Hugo Solomon, no pick-pockets, no scurrying crisp packets.

He saw a face from schooldays.

Who was that?

It could have been Alan.

But how changed he was!

Patrick felt a little better.

The pain in his stomach eased.

He felt warm. His arms were going loose.

He was that young father again.

He and Caroline were happy.

With the middle finger of her right hand Alice was tracing the bunnies running round the edge of her cereal bowl.

Which bunny is first, Alice, and which bunny is last?

You can't tell, Daddy.

Clever girl!

Holding Alice's warm hand, that lovely seven-year-old hand.

How many tufted ducks, how many shovelers?

Such a different hand from his old mother's hand.

Such a different hand from Viola's, holding him so tight.

Viola held his hand too tightly. She clung to him.

Where was Viola now?

And on the slippy sandunes of Cornwall, warm under bare foot, he was giving Jamie a piggyback.

From the slippy sandunes his feet moved to the springy grass.

Put me down and race me back, Dad.

They raced. You're too good for me, son.

Then Jamie, teeth gritted, was winning his first 1500 metres race.

Look at those wagtails running up and down the stones by the river.

I'm sorry, Caroline: for everything.

I love you, Mum.

I'm sorry about your legs.

I can't pray but I do love you.

I know you do, Patrick. But tell me before I die.

We are all only one second from being disabled.
Damn, I'm coming back up to the surface.
We are only one second away.
Only a nano-second or a near miss from a car crash, only a statistic away from a cancer, only one last gulp from drowning, only a broken milk bottle from being blind, only a paper-thin constraint keeps me just this side of the law, I'm only one provocation away from violence, there but for the grace of God go I, there but for a near-miss statistic go I, so why don't I reflect on my good fortune, or at least on my good fortune until this second, until this nano-second.

And then Patrick tells his mind to run over all the good things that have happened to him, you lucky sod, all the good people I know, watching my friend Alan run wild into the sea in all weathers, he was never afraid of drowning, whatever the weather he stripped and jumped into every river and every sea, all the good conversations, all the sharp mountains and all the long beaches, especially the beach all the way from Rhosilli to Worm's Head on the Gower Coast, the breezy cliff, the awkward stile and the slowly dragging roar, and I'm going

    Albert Speer was still walking in the prison yard
    Patrick Balfour was still walking in his prison bed
    He was walking and he was going
    He was going and he was walking
    And somewhere
    It didn't matter where
    Some where
    Somewhere over the rainbow
    A nightingale sang
    Somewhere
    In Berkeley Square
    A nightingale sang

Some where

Somewhere between seeing the Royal Festival Hall coming up and asking himself is that a glimpse of the distant moonlit St Paul's, somewhere between crushing a crab apple and crushing people, somewhere between being a young married man and a subtle headmaster, somewhere between Cambridge then and London now, somewhere between asking questions and answering them, somewhere between Billie Holiday and Dinah Washington, somewhere between Hungerford Bridge and Blackfriars Bridge, at some point in the bed, at some point between her warm breasts, at some point between her warm legs, he fell asleep, he fell asleep, he fell asleep to the piano and the sax, and as he fell asleep with Art Tatum's fingers and Ben Webster's lips, the waste-disposal clears away the words, the snatches of unconnected and irrelevant songs fade, and don't ask me why, don't ask me how, don't ask me who decides, but he goes, I go . . . I go . . . I go . . . to . . .

Sleep

and at some point all thirty-two of the London Eyes, all the blue ones and all the green ones, were closed and still.

And Patrick dreamt.

He dreamt that two men came and knocked on his door. It was a surprise that they had come knocking on his door. But somehow he also expected them.

They looked at Patrick and came in without being asked and started to search his house. They moved the furniture and turned over the carpets and checked the floorboards. They went into all his cupboards. They pulled down the extension ladder from the loft. He could hear them rumbling around right above his head.

Next they went down to the cellar. It was cold down there, and in the winter, even though he had put wire meshing over the ventilation holes, the rats got in. They rummaged around right under his feet as he sat in his study.

They found nothing. Which was a relief and a terrible prolongation. They were now everywhere. They were pushing open creaking doors, pulling out the drawers of his filing cabinets, tugging old blankets out of his airing cupboards, pulling back dusty curtains and, without a by your leave, ransacking his desk. While they were doing this, he pretended to go on reading.

They moved outside the house and began their excavations: under the garden shed, the garage, under the woodpile and the tarpaulins. Next it was the lawn. It was a perfect lawn and he kept the edges sharp. But they were digging it up like a cemetery.

They came back in to the house, looked at him, and their eyes said you know why we are here. Then they went out. They were not leaving. He knew they were going to find her body but he could not remember where exactly he had buried her.

It might be under the pavement just outside the front door. Sometimes he was sure it was.

But it might not be.

21

Dear Daddy,

I know I'm not meant to know about it but I do, so I need to talk to you. URGENTLY. I'll be in the flat after school today from 4.30 on if you can talk then. Be there. The school can run without you. Tell a lie for once in your life, say you've got a <u>HEADACHE,</u> that's what I do, who cares? There are IMPORTANT things I would like to tell you.

Alice xxx

Patrick did have a headache but he said nothing. He told no lie and he got away from his last meeting just before five o'clock. He crossed a freezing quad. It was the first frost of the winter. Alice heard her father's feet slowing a little as he came up the second flight. She had the door open as he approached the last few steps and they gave each other a brief hug. The kitchen table was covered with her books and files and biros and pencils and rubbers and paper: Alice could claim ownership of a table, could make a place her own, in thirty seconds.

She also, Patrick could not held noticing – and he wished he could help noticing but once a parent-teacher always a parent-teacher – she also had holes in both elbows of her cardigan, holes she was clearly proud of and clearly keen to enlarge.

'Don't let me interrupt whatever you're doing.'

'Are you all right, Dad?'

'Yes.'

'*Are* you?'

'Yes. And you're sounding like your mother.'

'Am I?'

'And my mother.'

'Probably because we're all worried about you.'

'I'd love a cup of tea.'

She moved to the sink. He followed her. Her hair smelt of shampoo. The fridge was humming.

'What are you up to?'

'Working on a script, well, a draft.'

'That sounds exciting.'

'We're workshopping a short play. Hugo's helping me.'

'So he told me.'

Alice frowned. 'That's a surprise, you chatting to Hugo.'

'I wouldn't call it a chat. So what does that mean, work-shopping?'

'Writing it, letting it develop as you rehearse, it's sort of coming out as we go along, using whatever is to hand. It's scarey because you don't know where it's leading you, but it's exciting.'

'What's it about?'

'Difficult to say. It's, you know, pretty personal.'

'Well, the most interesting things usually are. So it's a team effort?'

'Sort of. With more effort from some than others.'

'Sounds like trying to run a school.'

'Oh, poor old you.'

'And is it contemporary, the play?'

197

'It's not that precise. About twenty-five years ago.'

'Great. What's it like to work in, the new theatre? I popped in the other day.'

'Amazing. It feels intimate, you know, you feel they're all there. That it's all alive and true and happening. It feels . . . so close.'

'The audience?'

'The audience, the past, the people in the story, alive or dead they're all there, even if they're dead, you almost feel you can touch them, bring them back to life, that they're real, as real as . . . the people in the audience, it's weird.'

'No, it's wonderful.'

'What is?'

'What you just said was great.'

'Was it? It just came out.'

'And you're keeping up with your other subjects?'

The fridge shivered and subsided.

'Dad!'

'What?'

Alice's eyes were in half-revolt. 'You weren't really interested, were you?'

'But you are keeping up?'

'Dad, don't start straightaway.'

'I'm not.'

'You are.'

'I've been into the theatre and I've asked about your play.'

'It's not a duty, is it?'

'Well, are you? Are you doing any other work?'

Alice exhaled with theatrical volume. 'Yes!'

'Fine, that's all I wanted to know. I'm allowed to ask, aren't I?'

'Once I've finished with this play I'm attacking my French, I promise.'

'And your Politics?'

'*And* my Politics!'

'That's it. Well done.'

'Grrrr!'

The kettle clicked off and she huffily poured the hot water on the tea bag, spilling a fair bit in the saucer. She huffily wiped the saucer with the sleeve of her cardigan.

'Mum said you were brilliant on *Newsnight*.'

'Oh, that's nice.'

'Did she ring you?'

'No.'

'She said she was going to.'

'Perhaps I was on the phone.'

'And you were brilliant on Churchill last week.'

'Oh, I'll have to sit down for a bit!'

'I mean it, you were.'

'Can't handle all this.'

'Don't be gauche, Daddy darling. Learn how to take a compliment, that's what we young gels are always being told . . . So, will you be coming to see our plays then?'

'Plays, plural?'

'Yes, there are two.'

'What's the other one about?'

'They're both about . . . relationships, I suppose.'

'Oooo! As in "re–la–tion–ships"?'

'Yes, don't mock. And how we ruin each other's lives.'

'Do we?'

'Yes, Dad.'

'Tell me more.'

'You're not telling me you've never ruined anyone's life?'

'Have I?'

'I can think of one for a start.'

'Who's that?'

'Don't play games, Dad. Mum's put up with so much.'

'Do you think I don't know that?'

'Why not just say you're coming?'

'Of course I'm coming. When are they?'

'At the beginning of December. They're in the calendar. Don't you read the calendar?'

'Look, I'll be there, I'm famous for turning up. And I got the bloody place converted into a theatre, didn't I?'

Alice was now into her stride. 'But you've got to *want* to come! I want you and Mum to sit together and see me act, and stay and talk afterwards.'

'We will. Promise.'

'You hardly ever do anything together.'

'OK, OK.'

'But you don't.'

'Are you directing as well?'

'Change the subject, typical.'

'Are you directing as well?'

'Sort of me. Sort of Hugo.'

'So he's pretty involved?'

'I know you don't like him but at least he's got ideas.'

She put the tea in front of Patrick and faced him across the table, her fingers tugging at the holes in her cardigan. She fixed him with her eyes. She had Caroline's big brown eyes. Indeed, at some moments she could almost have been the Caroline he had first seen across the tea room in the University Library.

'Moving on, Dad, what are we going to do about you?'

'Aren't you having a cup?'

'*Dad!*'

'There's not much we can do at the moment, Alice, honestly there isn't.'

'Mum says the police are involved.'

'They are, yes.'

'And they came in here! The police, snooping in our flat.'

'They had a reason for doing that.'

'It's disgusting, the whole thing. Some people are really disgusting.'

'The whole thing? How much did Mum tell you?'

'Look, I can handle it, Dad! I'm seventeen!'

'I know, but there are some things you don't want your daughter, even your seventeen-year-old daughter, even a daughter like you, to know, as you will one day come to –'

'But how can they think you did it?'

'If you were a detective you might think so. On the face of it, it looks very convincing.'

'Not to me.'

'Well, your mother could see it.'

Alice's face was now as flushed as Patrick's was pale.

'Except you wouldn't do it. You couldn't do it.'

'And *that's* what loyal wives always say about serial killers.'

'But you've never done anything that bad.'

'Oh, what were you saying a moment ago?'

'That's completely different.'

Alice, unwilling to revisit the newspaper saga, unwilling to see again the page three photographs of her father and Liz Nicholson, nibbled at her biscuit, going round the edges in the manner of one of her earlier heroes, Peter Rabbit.

'So who have you upset the most in your life?'

'Apart from Mum?'

'There's no need to keep on about that. Who? Who have you upset the most?'

'That's where I'm drawing a blank.'

'Honestly?'

'Who knows who we upset or hurt without meaning to? In the course of a life. Who knows what damage we might have done?'

'Interesting, that.'

'Why?'

Alice shook her head and did some circles with her nail on the table top. 'No, nothing.'

'What were you going to say?'

'Well, it's obviously revenge. Look at all those Elizabethan plays. Well, isn't it? They all boil down to revenge of some kind, a grievance, a wrong supposedly righted, an eye for an eye.'

'Or a psychopath. An Iago.'

'You think so?'

'I wish I knew, I can't pinpoint anything else. You don't think it could be a teacher, Al, do you?'

She thought a bit and then slowly shook her head. 'No, not a teacher. They're too scared of you.'

'Scared of me? Don't be ridiculous.'

'Oh come on, you quite like it. There are enough weirdos here, mind you.'

'Are there? Who are they?'

Like Kafka, who could not live without his anxiety, Patrick was now picking away at himself, picking away at his own psychological skin, revealing and concealing, waiting to see if Alice would duplicate anyone on his list. But there was no response at all. She just stayed looking beyond his shoulder and out of the window.

'Dad.'

'Yes.'

'I'm going to move back here with you, full-time. Tomorrow.'

'No you're not.'

'I am.'

'Thanks, Alice, but don't. It's sweet of you but I really don't want you caught up in it.'

'I'm going to. I want to. It might be a good thing in lots of ways.'

'It's not a good idea. Thanks, but it isn't. There's never much food here and I'm always out and you wouldn't eat properly.'

'Don't go on about my eating! It makes me sooo angry.'

'And Mum wouldn't like it, she really wouldn't.'

'That's where you're wrong. She would like it. She has to put up with me and she wouldn't say it but she needs a break. Deep down she'd like me to go.'

'That's not true.'

'We've talked about it. It's all sorted.'

'It's nice of you to sort it but I want to see this through in my own way. Also, whoever got in here to take those photos has a key, and could easily get in again. It's too big a risk.'

'If there's two of us around it's less likely to happen.'

'I said no. I'm sleeping badly, dreaming badly, and walking around in the night. It's better for both of us if you don't.'

She exhaled, though this time not quite as theatrically. 'And there's another reason. All these play rehearsals after school mean I'm getting back too late and then I'm too knackered to do any work.'

'Ah, a bit of self-interest too.'

'Isn't there ever any with you?'

He gave her arm a conceding, admiring squeeze. 'Well, stay here on rehearsal nights, that's fine, but I don't want you here all the time. Not while this is in the air. You're much safer over there with Mum.'

Alice took her arm away from him a bit more quickly than he wanted. 'Dad.'

'What is it?'

'When I said there were weirdos here I wasn't meaning the teachers.'

'Who did you mean?'

203

'I meant some of the boys.'

'Well, there's always a few. They're probably not as weird as they want you to think.'

'They're not scared of you or anybody.'

'It's mostly bravado with teenage boys, too much testosterone.'

'That's patronising, Dad.'

'It's a fact.'

'You always do that, try to make a joke of things. It's such a male thing, it's really sad. We're having a serious chat here and I'm trying to help and you have to make it silly.'

'I was telling you what I believe to be the truth.'

'The ones I'm talking about aren't scared. Aren't scared of anything. The only person they're even close to being scared of is Falconer.'

'I can see that. I'm a bit scared of him too.'

'Well, you shouldn't be. With them it's different, and by the way, Dad, they don't think you're liberal, they just think you're weak.'

His heart kicked in and his stomach fell. 'Well, thanks for that, Alice.'

'I told you, in my letter, I told you it was important that we had a talk. I'm sorry if that hurt you. I'm not telling you what I think, I'm telling you what this lot think. You always said to me you didn't mind as long as I told you the truth. Didn't you always say that to me and to Jamie? Didn't you, lots of times?'

'Yes, and I meant it.'

While I told you lies.

'And you still mean it?'

'Yes. Yes, I still mean it.'

Alice looked troubled. 'Didn't you ever get up to bad things at school, Dad?'

'I expect I did. It's . . . a long time ago.'

'You mean you forget bad things as you get older?'

'Some things.'

'Don't they come back to haunt you?'

The phone rang. It was Daphne. Michael Falconer had been in wanting an urgent word with Patrick, about what exactly he wouldn't say, so was she to put him off? Yes, he'd deal with it later. When Patrick returned to the kitchen table Alice was concentrating hard on the middle finger of her right hand, trying to rub off a smudge of ink.

'Dad?'

'Yes.'

'How many boys were you at school with who stole cars?'

'None. Don't be silly.'

'How many stole credit cards?'

'We didn't have credit cards in those days.'

'You see, you think it's a wonderful school, and in some ways it is, but you don't know what goes on. You see what you want to see. You see the results and the turned-on smiles in the corridors. You see the respect and not the V-signs. You get bound up in the politics and the Common Room and stuff, but the point is you don't *know* what goes on. You don't. And if you smile like that once more I'll scream.'

'OK, what don't I see, what don't I know?'

'I'm not sure how much I can say.'

'Now you're patronising me.'

'All right then, I get a lot of stick because I won't take coke. You didn't know that.'

'No, I did not.' And he did not. His hands were starting to sweat.

'They're into porn on the internet. You didn't know that. Hard stuff.'

'Yes, I did know that, it's a common problem in schools, and we've taken steps to sort it.'

205

'And they're still doing it. In the computer centre. I've seen it. Grim stuff. Wouldn't be surprised if Cock isn't into it too. And now it's going on in the library and in the theatre sound box.'

'Mr Cochrane?'

'And it's the same ones, they'll do anything. They head-butted a kid a couple of weekends ago, not someone here, some random boy just off Leicester Square.'

Patrick stood up and walked round the table.

'OK. OK.'

'Shall I go on?'

No.

'Yes.'

'They sent a piece of pooh in an envelope to a teacher here. On your staff.'

'I don't believe that.'

'Up to you, Dad.'

'I simply don't believe it.'

'Up to you. I know they did.'

'Names?'

'Not about anything specific I said, mind, but in the area, right?'

'Right.'

She looked out at the Thames and the night sky and thought about it. She looked up at her father.

'Go on,' he said. 'You can't just start this and then stop.'

Then she looked down at the ink stain on her middle finger and shook her head, and kept shaking it.

Patrick's e-mail inbox.

Just checking. Have you read *The Divided Self* (1960) by R. D. Laing yet? Should be available on the internet.

22

Liz worked mostly at home on Mondays. Reading closely, with her favourite music on, scribbling notes on the manuscripts. And when Patrick, despite Daphne being in despair over his packed diary, wanted one last discussion about the tone in the final chapters of the Rodin novel, Liz broke one of her rules: she was very busy and she never did this but, if there was no other time he was free, they could meet at twelve noon at her place in Docklands. It wouldn't, Patrick promised, take more than an hour.

And it didn't. In one hour in her upstairs sitting room, over a beef sandwich and a cup of coffee (for him) and a smoked salmon sandwich and a glass of white wine (for her), they put the final touches to the ending. Liz spotted a couple of helpful trims and also suggested that Camille, in one final act of revenge, could appropriate Rodin's first person narrative because hadn't The Master appropriated her art as well as her body?

Absolutely, Patrick said, and it's funny you should say that because that's always the biggest decision for me as a writer: do I go for the first person, which at first sight seems so seductively compelling and liberating and I embrace it and I set off at a rate of knots but the further I move on with it the more I find the first person somehow cramps both the reader and the writer to just the one viewpoint, or do I favour the more conventional third person, the omniscient fly on the wall, which means I can becomes he can, and I can enter any mind or body I wish and that means overall greater freedom? In a way, Liz said, aren't we in a sense getting back to our Classical and Romantic discussion?

'Yes,' Patrick said, determined to make the change she had suggested. 'And you are a brilliant editor.'

He tapped the heavy manuscript into a neat stack and put it back in the large envelope and then locked the envelope into his black leather briefcase, repeating you are a brilliant editor. He looked at his watch and said damn he had to dash, boring of me I know but thanks once again you've been a great help, and Liz said it's been a real pleasure as always and it's going to be a best-seller believe me and she pressed play on Oscar Peterson's *Night Train* and said she would see him down to the front door and she led the way down the stairs. While reaching across to open it she turned and kissed him, her lips loose and full, lips of a kind he had never kissed before. They stayed by the front door, kissing against it, leaning back, and he said he had to go and she said I want you, Patrick. Before he could say a second time 'I've really got to get back' she said 'School can wait. For once it can wait.'

And that was the last thing he said because she did all the talking.

She took off his jacket and put it over the banister at the bottom of the stairs.

He was a millrace of emotions.

By the time she led him back up the stairs and back up

208

to the first landing she was undoing the buttons on her blouse and undoing his shirt.

The bedroom door was open.

They met, rarely and irregularly and always with an eye on the clock. And when he saw her, when she walked towards him, in sun glasses, white T-shirt and blue skirt, her body athletic, he was a boy again. It was easy to get to her place by taxi, it wasn't all that far east, but he didn't want to be put down on the pavement right outside so he often got out a few streets away and walked the last part, then cut through the narrow courtyard (and up her stairs, the stairs up which she liked, in her dominating soliloquies, to lead him). Sometimes, feeling immune, they took a risk — she knew as well as he did the risks for a man in his position, for a public figure — and slipped out to Angelo's, her favourite place in Docklands, where they held hands and talked about books and Alice and Jamie and her own childlessness and Roger's violence and ballet and how much Oscar Peterson learnt from Art Tatum.

'I love talking to you.'

'I love talking to you, Liz.'

'You know what started it, don't you?'

'No.'

'You took my mind, Patrick.'

'How do you mean?'

'Don't play stupid; that's where you had me first, as you know very well, you knocked over my mind, and since then I've had no choice. Angelo, another coffee, please.'

'*Si, si*, Liz.'

Angelo was Sardinian, a shepherd's son, a waiter who had left Cagliari for cold cash and a 'better life' in London, and Angelo, dancing attendance on Liz, said that she was the most beautiful of all his customers and every time she walked in for coffee or hot chocolate, talking away as if her life depended on it, he was a happier man because she transported him to the land of romance: *she make me believe in love*, Angelo said. He also said he'd never seen a better walk on a woman. Patrick agreed.

Sometimes Liz cut out the articles on him in the press. They laughed as they read together gossipy pieces like:

And that's why Balfour's friends ask themselves how-does-he-do-it and why his supporters call him a great man. He is one of the most charismatic men in public life, an inspiration, a man who leads three lives, a headmaster, a novelist and a media star. And is it any wonder his enemies both inside and outside education groan out loud and say 'Did you see who was on TV again last night?' and put their heads in their hands and say 'That bloody Balfour bloke would kill his granny for a bit of publicity.'

'If only they knew about your fourth life', Liz said, doing up her bra in front of the mirror. If someone from the publishing house had rung up to say 'I'm sorry, Patrick, but Liz Nicholson, your editor, has been killed in a car crash' he was not sure he could have gone on living himself.

Sometimes they had happy phone calls. She said he could be so sexy on the phone. She would kneel on the bed in her bra and panties, with her legs slightly apart, moving gently, touching herself as he spoke. Sometimes they had sad phone calls.

'Roger knows.'

'What do you mean he knows?'

'Last night he said, "You're seeing someone, aren't you?"'

'Don't worry about it.'

210

'Oh, this is awful.'

'Why?'

'It just is.'

'You mean seeing me?'

'No, not seeing you all the time, that's what's so awful. Come round now. I want you now.'

And she often asked him, when they were lying in bed together (the bed in which, like Pepys's Diana, she denied him nothing), why he didn't leave his headship and write full-time, put all his energies into his writing and media work – at which he was so good – and leave behind the tedious constraints of headmastering. It's not just tedious constraints, Patrick said. It's the power. You're joking, she said. No, it's the power, Liz, that's what it's all about. None of us, of course, wants to say the word power; we prefer to say that it is a privilege for us to serve as headmasters, that it is an honour to lead, even (God help us) that it is a wonderful opportunity to *facilitate*. But it's the power, Liz. It's the chance to put your mark on your world, or at the very least to leave your footprint in the sand. Better than that, and more insidiously attractive on a daily basis, it's how you're treated. It's the deference, it's the way they wait a few yards away from you, hovering, hoping to have a word, trying to catch your eye. At first, new to the job, or, as they now prefer to put it, 'in my first hundred days', I thought they were taking the piss. You know, all this I'm sorry to interrupt, Patrick, may I catch you for a moment? And excuse me, headmaster, do you have a second, it's rather urgent? Why would intelligent people behave in this craven way? Why would people who run you down in private, why would bitter cynics behave like spaniels in public? It's very simple. Because they fear their careers are in my hands. If they cross me in public they fear they'll be finished here. Fall out with me and they can forget promotion, that's the

211

fear, and, what's more, if they apply for a job somewhere else they suspect that the only place I'll offload them on is somewhere they'd rather not be. Not many jobs carry that kind of autocratic power, Liz. I'm not proud of it but it's true. There's a great bit in Fanny Burney's diary – d'you know it? – where she says there's a kind of deference that kills her, that, after her success as a writer, she sometimes encounters a certain air of respect which petrifies her.

In my study, of course, or on my own territory, and one-on-one, I can be as friendly as the next man, supportive, understanding, sympathetic, kind. One-on-one, touchy-feely, that's me. But when I walk around the school, when I chair a committee, I have teeth. And if I ever forget it for a moment someone will remind me of it by their deference. By their respect.

Talking of touchy-feely, Liz said, reaching down with her hand, and talking of teeth, would you mind if I . . .

That's the sort of way it went and that's the sort of way it was still going when Roger Nicholson opened the Sunday paper, checked up on Sheffield United and read the football pages, and then went back to the news pages, and then turned over and came across a photograph of his wife, the 'beautiful young publishing star Liz Nicholson', and Patrick Balfour holding hands in Angelo's, with the headline:

TOP HEAD AFFAIR.

So it ended unhappily, very unhappily. It ended with Caroline remote and tight-lipped, and with Jamie and Alice upset and confused, and with Roger Nicholson punching Liz so hard in the face that he broke her nose and blacked her eye and she was off work for three and a half weeks. The school governors, after taking soundings from Michael Falconer and other senior members of staff, supported Patrick. Indeed, although he never told Patrick as much, Michael Falconer fought the hardest of battles to save him, and although the story rumbled on for a few weeks, the press soon had bigger fish than a headmaster and a publisher to fry.

'It blew over', as they say, or at least the cloud moved away and well out of sight, though Caroline would never be the same and Liz treasured this letter and sometimes read it alone in her bed.

Dearest Liz,

Some things you never forget or get over, even if you want to, even if you try really hard. And I have tried really hard. Some things you never forget and you're better advised to keep them to yourself, for they have a value, a private value and significance, which you should keep to yourself, pearls beyond price, which you should keep to yourself. They become a yardstick. They are the experiences by which everything else is measured and will always be measured, and you carry them with you; they're part of you. You're humbled by them, even though they are unresolvable; you're grateful to them, even if your faults remain uncondoned and the pain still as sharp. When you lose confidence in yourself you remind yourself how wonderful it was, even the pain, not just the joy, especially the pain, and you remind yourself that this landed at no one else's feet, this pearl.

with my love,
Patrick

23

When Patrick returned to his desk from an even more than usually pointless Heads of Department Committee he picked up a message on his answerphone from Caroline. He rang her immediately.

'Caroline?'

'Yes.'

'It's Patrick.'

'I can still recognise your voice, Patrick.'

'You rang.'

'Yes. It's Alice. I'm not sure what's up but she's behaving rather oddly. The last few days.'

'Do you think it's linked to our chat?'

'It could be. Yes, I think it must be.'

Caroline, always the steady and practical one, was clearly upset.

'In what way? In what way oddly?'

'She said she told you some nasty things and she now wished she hadn't.'

'I can handle what she told me.'

'We're not talking about what you can handle, Patrick. I'm concerned about Alice.'

'Was there anything particular, you know, anything specific about her behaviour?'

'How about she's stopped talking to me? Is that specific enough for you?'

'You mean completely?'

From the muffled sound Caroline could be crying. Patrick went on.

'She isn't talking at all?'

'Not to me at least. She's become very secretive, always up in her room; it's as if she's having a character change.'

'That's what actors practise, isn't it?'

'And listening to some jazz singer at the same time.'

'Sounds like a phase. I went through all that.'

Caroline screamed: 'For Christ's sake, Patrick, will you please find another tone! You're sounding like a bloody counsellor.'

'I don't think I was. I think you're being very aggressive.'

'Look, I wouldn't be bothering you with all this if it was as easy as you're making it sound. There's something wrong with her, and you can either believe me or write your own version of it.'

'I believe you.'

'Sometimes I think you've lost all touch with your real feelings.'

'So do I.'

Patrick could see his e-mail winking. He had a message.

'And you say that kind of so-do-I-thing all too easily.'

'Caroline, calm down, calm down . . . I was only trying to help.'

'Well, you weren't.'

'No, I can see that.'

'You're sounding more and more like someone who spends all day listening to himself. This is not just a minor thing, Patrick.'

215

'When we had that chat, Alice said she wanted to come and stay here but I rather put her off. Was I wrong to do that?'

'No. Yes. Oh, I don't know. The thing is, Patrick, I don't know if you can handle her, not the way you are and the way she is.'

'Would you like to put it to her again? Say that you and I think it's better if she stays here?'

'All right, I'll put it to her.'

'Thanks.'

'If she comes in.'

Patrick put the phone down. He turned to the screen and double-clicked.

> *if we see a light at the end of the tunnel,*
> *it's the light of an oncoming train.*
>
> Robert Lowell

It hit him with simple clear force. He could no longer deal with this alone. He took out his pocket diary and dialled.

'John Bevan speaking.'

'Chief Inspector, this is Patrick Balfour.'

'Hello, Patrick, what can I do for you?'

That singsong voice was back in his life.

'A few things have come up. Could we meet fairly soon?'

'Of course we can, Patrick.'

'When suits you?'

'Let's have a look, shall we?'

'Can you make tonight? Early evening?'

'Tomorrow night's better for me, Patrick. Tonight's a bit of a problem.'

'Tomorrow I can't. What about Friday?'

'Friday? Give me a second . . . yes . . . fine . . . I think I can, between six and seven. Is that OK?'

216

'Yes, where would suit you? Not here in school, if you don't mind.'

'And not here I bet!'

'No, I'd rather not.'

'Tell you what, how about the Rat and Parrot then, on the corner of Montcrieff Street. Do you know it?'

'I do, except my sixth form go there.'

'Kill two birds with one stone then. How's six o'clock?'

'Six o'clock. Yes. Hang on, I'm just putting that in my diary.'

'See you at six, then. The side bar on the left. Might get a seat at six if we're lucky.'

'The bar on the left, fine.'

But now the phantoms were competing. Phone down, diary still out, numbers at the back, work number, home number, deep breath, you shouldn't be doing this, Patrick, you really should not. He stared at the numbers until they all jumbled up. He stared at them until they all fell back into place.

Phone up.

'Liz?'

'Patrick? . . . Is that Patrick?'

'Yes, it's me.'

'It's been a long time.'

'Yes it has.'

They can hear each other breathing.

'You saw me on *Newsnight*?'

'Yes, you were good.'

'Thanks for your message.'

They can hear each other breathing.

'What's up? You don't sound right.'

'I'm not.'

'What is it? You're not ill, are you?'

'No, I'm not ill.'

217

'Are you sure? I don't know why but I'm always worrying about that.'

'Is there any chance we could meet?'

'Meet?'

'Yes.'

'Is that . . . a good idea?'

Patrick held the telephone and stared ahead at the book-lined wall of his study. Books. When had he last read a book? He should not have rung. *Is that a good idea?* No, it was not a good idea. He was not going to say another word, not one single solitary word. He left the ball in her court. He was not going to beg or wheedle or coax. He was long past all that stuff. The question he had asked was, is there any chance we can meet?

'Yes, if you like. Yes, Patrick, yes of course we can.'

'It's serious, Liz, what's happening.'

'Really?'

'And it's got to me.'

'Is it things with Caroline?'

'I can't explain now, I really can't. Not at the moment.'

'I understand.'

'I wouldn't be asking to see you otherwise.'

There was a pause. They were both assessing, both looking at their lives and the likely effect of all this, both on the edge of the cliff and looking out to sea. She asked him,

'When? When suits you? Tomorrow?'

'I can't tomorrow, I'm afraid.'

'Friday? Can you make it around seven on Friday? Seven-thirty's possible for me, but I've got meetings all afternoon, and you know yourself what can happen.'

'Publishers and their meetings!'

'Don't you start. Is seven-thirty all right?'

'Seven-thirty is fine. I'm seeing a policeman at six so you'll find me at my chastened best.'

218

'A policeman?'

'Yes.'

'Whatever for?'

'Just tell me where to meet. Somewhere I've never been.'

I want to hear you laugh.

'Well, there's a little place just up from the Opera House, Frankie's, on the left. A hundred yards further up. Just past Café Rouge.'

I want to hear you laugh.

'I'll be there, Liz, at Frankie's, at seven-thirty, wearing a pink blouse.'

'You silly bugger.'

24

Detective Chief Inspector John Bevan, as Welsh as they come despite the pint of London Pride in hand, was already at the bar as Patrick pushed his way through the side entrance of the Rat and Parrot. The place was hot. It was hot and hoppy and airless and heavy with smoke and sweat and packed tight with early evening drinkers: mostly City types.

Patrick made a clumsy attempt at a handshake, but only grasped two of DCI Bevan's fingers. Damn. What a complete fool a man feels when he does that!

'What can I get you, Patrick?'

It's Christian names.

'A large whisky, thanks.'

'Anything with it?'

'A splash of soda.'

'Any particular one?'

'White Horse, if they've got it.'

'Nowhere to sit by the look of it. I thought we might be lucky.'

'It doesn't matter,' Patrick said.

Bevan then nodded to the corner by the Gents. 'No, we'll be all right, I'll ask the young lovers to budge up a bit.'

'Thanks for this. For coming along, I mean.'

And the young lovers were happy to budge up a bit, allowing the tall headmaster and the podgy detective, the unlikeliest couple in the bar, to squeeze in together.

In the pub setting, in a sweater and cord trousers, Bevan did not look like a policeman or a detective. He looked like an off-duty businessman in his local, a nice, friendly, plump, conciliatory man, an easy-going man whose only aim in life was to sort out any possible misunderstandings and, if at all possible, to sell Patrick some insurance.

'It's Famous Grouse; no White Horse, I'm afraid.'

'That's fine.'

'Can you tell the difference?'

'Definitely.'

There was so much background noise Patrick had little fear of them being overheard.

'Cheers. Average day at school, then?'

'I'm not sure I know any more what that is.'

'Know what you mean.'

'What about you?'

'Not great, no. Some of the Rastis are well out of order. So, what's been going on, then? Something new?'

Patrick took a brown A4 envelope out of his pocket.

'Far too much.'

While Bevan read the notes, the Kafka, the Highsmith, the e-mails, the Edward Thomas, the Joseph Clark, the two R. D. Laing ones, Patrick felt the whisky hit and burn his empty stomach like bench acid.

'Through the post?'

'Only one of them. The others were hand-delivered.'

'To your home in Finley Place?'

'No, to my pigeonhole at school.'

'Your pigeonhole, right. No phone calls?'

'Not yet.'

'Why d'you say that?'

'Just that I'm braced for anything now, any day, any time. It's landmines everywhere.'

Bevan looked hard at Patrick.

'Do you understand them, these notes?'

'In what sense?'

'Do they all add up?'

'I know the books, some of the books they come from, Kafka's *Trial*, and I'm an Edward Thomas fan and one is somewhere in the Ripley novels.'

'Is that the same as the Ripley films?'

'Yes.'

'*The Talented Mr Ripley*. Saw that one, no-limits liar, psychopath and killer. Very good I thought. Have you seen it?'

'No. Should I?'

'Given all this, I would. And you'd never heard of this J. C.?'

'Never.'

'But you have now?'

'Yes, it's Joseph Clark. Late seventeenth century, a very minor figure.'

Bevan read the *DNB* entry very slowly, twice, holding the photocopy between his knees, then folded it and gave it back to Patrick.

'Well, you learn something every day, don't you?'

'You do indeed.'

'Pursuing you with puzzles, isn't he?'

Patrick nodded his enjoyment of that.

'That's very well put.'

'Praise indeed from the headmaster.'

'I was not being patronising, if that's what you mean.'

Bevan raised an eyebrow and wiggled his head.

'I really wasn't,' Patrick said.

'I'll believe you on that.'

Bevan finished his beer in three long gulps, burping slightly before he could put his hand to his mouth.

'Excuse me. Nice pint, that.'

'Let me get you another.'

The detective tapped his round stomach and shook his head. 'Better not, the wife's on the case, got to watch the weight.'

'So, what do you make of them?'

'The plague of all tailors. Changing one posture for another, two faces. Quite a card, isn't he?'

'The one who sent them or Joseph Clark?'

He picked up the brown envelope. 'Both. I'll take these.'

'What will you do with them?'

'Primary evidence, aren't they, and primary evidence is always best. Run a check for fingerprints and typeface, put these through a chemical process.'

'What process is that?'

'Ninhydrin.'

'What does that do?'

'You soak the exhibits in fluid and the finger marks are raised . . . show up in purply pink. Oh, and I want to know the dates on which they all arrived. Dates can be very important.'

'Why?'

'See if there's any pattern. And send me any other notes or letters you get, right?'

'Yes, I will.'

Bevan looked round the pub. 'Entirely alter the expression of his face, that's his point.'

'Exactly. So you don't now think I sent all these to myself?'

The detective's shrug annoyed Patrick.

'You're not still thinking that, are you? You're not still thinking it's me?'

'How could he have known I was coming to your school?'

'I haven't a clue. You're the detective.'

'And you're a writer, so use your imagination. The only people who know about that visit are you, me and your secretary. Unless she's untrustworthy?'

'Daphne! I'd put my life on her.'

'Because I don't like wild goose chases. Or would it be geese? So you're saying this very clever man with no motive has taken to pestering you.'

'Or a fantasist has latched on to me.'

'A fantasist?'

'Yes.'

'Unlikely. Too educated, this bloke. This is all very focused, this Kafka and J. C. stuff. He's got a repertoire.'

'There are some highly qualified fantasists. I've got some on my staff.'

'Who are they?'

'No, I'm not talking about this issue, I'm just saying that some people, some educated people in responsible positions, who do an excellent professional job every day, also live in cloud-cuckoo land. I've got a colleague who says he takes his holidays on safari in Africa when he stays for a fortnight at a B & B in King's Lynn.'

'Fair enough. I bet the breakfasts are better at the B & B.'

'He even talks about the lions and how hot it was in Mombasa.'

They both came as close to laughing as they would that evening. Bevan tapped his glass with the ends of his fingers.

'All right, Patrick, I will have another. It's London Pride. You get them and I'll have another read of these.'

While waiting to be served Patrick checked the other bar to see if any of his pupils were in there drinking. No.

While someone ahead of him was being served he also had to listen to a couple of car salesmen:

'N reg, standard steel wheels, nice deep blue, twin exhaust coming out the arse, an' you know what?'

'What?'

'He wants fuckin' 17k for it.'

'Tryin' it on, mate, in 'e?'

'17 k, that's a fuckin' joke, that is.'

And it isn't the only thing that's a fucking joke, mate. My life is.

When Patrick came back with the pint and a single whisky this time (mustn't be too far gone when he sees Liz) the young couple, who were now kissing, readjusted their bodies slightly to allow Patrick to sit down again. In fact, as luck would have it, from the side the girl looked a bit like a younger Liz. Patrick raised his glass a little to the detective.

'When I left you last time you said you wanted to make some more enquiries about me.'

'Cheers. So I did.'

Bevan sucked a bit of foam off the top of his pint and smacked his lips in appreciation.

'And have you?'

'I have.'

'And have those enquiries thrown anything up, for example that I left the conference at Brighton far too late to have been at that garage? Did you confirm that?'

'You left late, yes, but you could still have made it. Just. You've been booked for speeding twice in the last five years.'

The briskness of this riposte took the wind out of Patrick.

'Someone is trying to destroy me, someone is hell-bent on destroying me, and you think I didn't pay for some petrol! And then I hand in photos like that. And I suppose you now think I'm writing myself letters and sending myself e-mails.'

If Patrick was getting worked up, Bevan was not.

'You might be. It's often done. In a high place but willing to lose it all, that's the mind-set. Chemist rang us up the other day, lab assistant saying he could see some cannabis plants in a photograph. Raided the home, didn't we, arrested three people, recovered the drugs, street value of £15,000. Some people love taking risks, Patrick, and after taking the risk, in the cold light of day, they have to cover up.'

'And sending my son e-mails? I'm doing that too, am I? Making sure my son knows I'm a pervert?'

Equally unbothered by this, Bevan tapped his glass again with his fingernails. 'How well do you know the meat rack, Patrick?'

'The what?'

'The meat rack.'

'I don't know what you're talking about.'

'In Piccadilly. You often go to Piccadilly.'

'Do I?'

'On the way to and from your all-male club.'

'I hardly ever go to my club. I'm not a clubby person.'

'But you often go to Piccadilly.'

'And I go to Tower Records as well and I go to Jermyn Street and I often walk that way to the Royal Academy. I'm a Friend there, and the Royal Academy is not all male.'

'I'm talking about the amusement arcades.'

'I hate amusement arcades.'

'That's where one-parent family boys sell their bums. London, not just London, mind you, even Cardiff, I'm sad to say. And Brighton. They bend over the machines and you buy the meat.'

226

Patrick shook his head in distaste.

'I don't want to know about that.'

'Let's say someone called Darren is one of them.'

'Who's Darren?'

'The boy in your photographs.'

Patrick's eyes blazed. 'They're not my photographs. They were taken by someone else, by someone pretending to be me. It's not very difficult to grasp.'

'And we found this Darren and he recognised your photo. "That's him," he said. "Dead posh, nice suit, and handy at all sorts." Darren had no doubts.'

'I've never touched a boy in my life.'

'So you said.'

Bevan's gaze made Patrick falter.

'Or taken a boy to my flat. Or cruised on Clapham Common. It's not my taste. Believe who you like.'

'It's who the judge will believe, Patrick, that's your problem. You're on video at the garage, you're on video at the shop, and let's say you're identified by Darren, he also works Brighton, Darren does, and you were in Brighton on the day of the bilking. After the conference and after meeting Darren for a bit of mutual down by the marina, I'd say you were in a bit of a state and that explains the petrol. When did you last have sex with your wife, Patrick?'

Patrick had finished his whisky, but the last gulp was now burning back up into his throat. 'If you'll excuse me, I am going. I've got someone to meet.'

'Patrick, I'm as keen to find the truth as you are. There's no Darren.'

'This is worse than a waste of time.'

'Nothing gives me more pleasure than locking up three-star bastards.'

'And I'm one of those?'

'This man's one and I want to get him.'

Patrick stood up. Bevan stood up with him. Patrick said:

'You want to get *me*, as far as I can see that's all you're interested in.'

For the first time Bevan looked a little put out. His comfortable face tightened and his mouth narrowed as if for a silent whistle.

'No, that's not the case.'

'Look, I can't take too much more of this. I'm having terrible dreams, some of them are . . . worse even than the day I'm living. And someone's still out there pretending to be me. Making my life a misery.'

'Sit down, Patrick. Walking away won't help. Please sit down.'

He did, and they sat, not speaking, both staring straight ahead. Patrick's eyes were tired and watering in the smoke. Bevan turned to him and whispered in a completely different tone:

'And is this all round the school?'

'No, and it shouldn't be.'

Bevan rubbed his hands together.

'So let's get after the *doppelgänger*, turn the tables on him, is that it?'

'What?'

'Find out how many Patrick Balfours we've got hanging around the place?'

'You could put it that way.'

'Someone who'd like to spoil things for you, Patrick. Because you'd spoiled things for him.'

'That's how you see it?'

'That sort of thing. So, any names?'

'If I was sure enough I'd give you them, but they're just swimming around in my head, each as good or as bad as the other.'

'Names, Patrick.'

'Each day I think it's someone different.'

'Names. I don't believe you. I want their names. Write them down there. You arouse strong feelings, all successful people do. Face it.'

'I am facing it. I'm going through it every hour of the day and night.'

'Names.'

Patrick took out his pen. Bevan watched him write down Euan Stuart, Max Russell-Jones, Casey Cochrane and Hugo Solomon. Next to the last one he put 'pupil' in brackets.

'So now, at long last, you don't think it's me?'

'I'm keeping an open mind. I'm checking up on you and I'll check up on them. There are strange people all over the place, no doubt about that. It's a very thin line between being a good doctor and being Harold Shipman.'

'You think so?'

'I know so. I also want a covert camera fitted in your staff room, covering the headmaster's pigeonhole.'

'But you can't do that! Can you? Wouldn't I have to tell the bursar?'

'You can give us access in the night; you don't sleep well, you're up there working and you let us in. We'll be in and out. Those boys are professionals.'

'All right.'

'No one will see anything; the camera lens is little bigger than a pin. I'll arrange it.'

'Fine.'

DCI Bevan put Patrick's list of names in the envelope. 'Might even go for some smart water dye around the pigeonhole.'

'Is that a good idea?'

'I'll think about it. But from now on you'll ring me each time one of these comes along, right?'

'I will, yes.'

'And I'm going to read all the books these bits come from. By the way, anyone ever objected to anything in your books?'

'In what way?'

'Objected strongly to anything? Your wife? Any scores to settle?'

'No, they're historical novels.'

'But there's nothing gnawing away? Nothing you shouldn't have done?'

'Not that I can remember.'

'I'm reading *Silver*, by the way.'

'Are you?'

'Going back to schools, what about ex-students?'

'I've thought of that.'

'How many have you expelled? Over the years?'

'I don't know.'

'About?'

'Over the years? Ten, fifteen maybe. Plenty more were eased out, without anyone knowing why.'

'Apart from the people themselves.'

'Quite.'

'Anyone ever threatened you?'

'No.'

'Any messy ones, Patrick?'

'A few.'

'I'd have thought they all were. Think about them. Let me know.'

Messy? Of course they were messy. They were all messy. He could see their faces, their mothers weeping, the fathers stony-faced, facing up to their children, to what they had done, facing up too late. My son is a cheat, my son is a liar, my son is a drug dealer, my son is a shoplifter, my son is a bully, my son is a vandal, my son has sexually assaulted other boys. How *could* you! After all we've given you! After all we've *spent* on you! How dare you! I'll never be able to lift up my head again! Get in the car!

Messy!

Bevan was writing some numbers and an address on a piece of paper. 'You're not going to play it on your own. The letters, send them on, and forward all the e-mails to me. You'll do that?'

'Yes.'

'And I want a copy of your school list, all staff and pupils.'

Patrick put his hand to his inside pocket. 'Have this one. I've got plenty of spares.'

'None of your writing in it, is there? Nothing personal?'

'Come to think of it, I'll send you another one.'

'Because here's a scenario about him, just a thought, nothing more.'

'Go on.'

'You know most of what I'm about to say.'

'I'm not sure what I know any more.'

'You're a success, Patrick, well you are, consistently successful, and you loom large in his life. You're larger than life and even larger in his. Because this guy's a failure. Or at least he feels one. You or I might not see him as a failure, that's not the point, the point is he feels one, and he's clinging to it. It's his failure, and it's what gets him up in the morning, his failure is his security blanket, he sucks his failure, it's what puts a spring in his step, it's *his* failure, and his failure is this doom brain's great secret.'

'How do you know?'

The detective's eyes were on the edge of sarcasm but his voice stayed gentle. 'I don't know, Patrick, I've just told you, it's a *scen-a-rio*, isn't it?'

'And he's likely to be on my staff?'

231

'Well, we know he's somewhere on the inside track, don't we?'

'Yes.'

'And another thing, why don't you talk to your wife more about it?'

'I will.'

'And I'd like to have one more look round your flat again, if I may. Your school one, not Finley Place.'

'Any time.'

'In fact, the whole school. I'll be popping in and out.'

'Any time you like.'

'And the best thing is for you to get on with being a headmaster.'

25

Should he shake her hand, as if meeting a colleague again, or kiss her on one cheek as at a dinner party, or kiss her on both cheeks as he would a close female friend who'd come to stay, or give her a warm open-armed hug like a long-lost brother? It would partly, he supposed, depend on how she reacted to him as he went in. Unless he was there first, in which case he would stand up and move straight towards her.

Right, got that sorted.

He walked on. He was Joseph Clark, the plague of all tailors, the posture-master of Pall Mall. Our late Proteus, Patrick Balfour, unrecognisable to those in whose company he had so recently been, with an irresistible tendency to fall apart, was now out among the other freaks, out on the streets of London.

He walked on, his other side courting the thrills. Walking through the smell coming from open pub doors, through the smell of Chinese sticky sauces, past cheese smells from a deli, then the smell of tarragon and cinnamon, snatches of Italian, bits of Arabic, women's deodorant, aromatic incense shops, rancid trash from a split black bag, diesel and chip fat, smell after smell, was that lavender oil? was that lilies? doorway after doorway, eyes and bodies in doorways looking sideways as he walked away from safety, as he walked away from the headmasterly circuit. Step by step Patrick went, each step a career risk, each step taking him a little closer to the edge of the cliff, smelling the spice and the danger, revealing himself in excess, revelling in excess, the sane are madder than we think going up through Chinatown.

This could go terribly wrong.

Fancy a drink, darling, brushing his arm, come on in.

Chambermaid or duchess?

What would Michael Falconer say if he could see this?

I feel reassuringly alive.

At such moments there is a voice which speaks inside and says this is the real me.

Scaring some life into himself, living on his wits.

What would Mother say?

Oh if she could see me now.

Making up the rules to fit my world.

The flesh negligently leaning –

Not quite a line of Lowell's.

Crisscrossing Shaftesbury Avenue, up Dean Street, Old Compton Street, every which way, Wardour Street, Romilly Street, rejecting the religious formulations, circling the streets, enticing candles and glacial eyes, red and yellow lights, red pools, clasped hands, red pools and puddles, feeling it in his grasp and out of reach, rinsing his imagination of raised knives, his mind now a vacuum, past the Coach and Horses, past Maison Berthaux, a blind man in a coat too big for him is stranded on a corner, people miss him by inches, no one bumps into him, Patrick misses him, just, taking lefts and rights at random, taking turnings he did not usually take, his mind swinging, the clarinet adding a glow, leather shops, the senselessness, the aimlessness, you can be anyone here, you could be so many people here, other lives are being lived and played out here in front of smeared mirrors, the divisible and the distinctive, lives so far from his study, deviating so far from his elevated position, lit lurking illuminated staircases, steps down to basements, men become base by degrees, man or woman, man/woman, cripple/scholar.

Pull yourself together, Patrick.

Go and meet her now!

Patrick, pull your two selves together.

27, Savile Row. He passes West End Central Police Station.

Where the wallet was handed in.

How often was Bevan in there?

Or in Charing Cross Police Station?

How many other police stations are there in London?

He sees the other Patrick Balfour in Hatchard's book-shop.

He sees him handing in his wallet.

Keep going.

He passes the Police Station in Old Burlington Street.

Everywhere is a police station.

The other Patrick Balfour is handing in the photos to be developed.

Keep going.

He passes the Police Court in Marlborough Street.

You're a wasp, Patrick, a wasp drowning in a pint of beer.

Go and see Caroline now.

No, I'm going to see Liz.

No, go to the meat market.

Go on, I dare you.

Go into the arcades.

See what Detective Chief Inspector John Bevan is on about.

235

In a way he was as alive and as adolescent as he had ever been. Was he the only middle-aged adult whose heart still hammered as he walked towards such a meeting, who smelt every smell, whose mind was on a roller coaster, and who still wanted to drive off into the distance with Liz beside him, with Bruce Springsteen and Tom Waits and The Traveling Wilburys, and just drive and talk and listen, talk not lecture, talk not banter, talk not gossip, and catch a glimpse of her each time he turned left? The thing was, shouldn't he have moved beyond all this romantic stuff by now? Shouldn't he have *grown up*?

Patrick stopped at a second-hand bookshop. He looked at his own reflection. His eye was then caught by a name. R. D. Laing. It was one of the shops he had visited on the very day that he had first bumped into Liz, when he ran in from the rain and into her life, when he was looking for Stevenson's fables, but now he went in and bought a copy of R. D. Laing's *The Divided Self*. That was the title that had caught his eye on the pavement. Time for a bit of bed-time reading. He would read it in bed, after he had watched the video of *The Talented Mr Ripley*.

Again he looked at himself in the shop window. At a reflection of the public Patrick Balfour. He checked his tie and hair.

Patrick walked on towards Frankie's sure only of one thing: that it would be great to see her again. There had never been a woman – forget bed, for a moment forget sex and all that – whose voice gave him such pleasure, whose responses and whose company he had more enjoyed. But what was he asking of her now? That she became a shoulder to cry on? Or that she would become an ally, a creative strategist, a mind-reader, a female detective on the case?

He didn't know, *I don't know*, he just wanted to see her, to sit next to her, to sit opposite her. That was enough.

Was that so much to ask? She would be a kind of light at the end of the tunnel, even though he could not see any end in sight, and even though Robert Lowell's mocking lines ruined the pleasure of any comfort that thought might have offered.

Liz was there first and made it easy by walking towards him and hugging him, like a long-lost brother, like a long-lost lover. She held him and said, 'It's so good to see you.'

'You too,' he said.

'I like your tie.'

'So do I.'

'How was your detective?'

'He had his moments. Yes, he definitely had his moments.' He did not let her go. His cheek, a little chill from the streets, was still in touch with her warm one.

Hell, she looks good, I never expected to see her again, never expected to see that walk and those legs again, even though in my mad moments I have wandered all over London, needles, haystacks, crazily persuading myself I have seen her, that I have caught sight of her, that I can smell her as I smell a minty herb on my fingers in the garden, but she never came out of any gallery doors or sat in the corner of any café I was in. How I wanted her to tap my shoulder and say hi as I looked at a painting. But I felt that if I kept going at school, in my own way, working harder and harder, the pain would ease and I would eventually be able to accept or at least to accommodate everything. Month by month, year by year, she would move a little further away into the past. I might have to adjust the rear-view mirror to see if she was still there, still there and still waving, and she was still there, just, but much smaller, much more in the corner, much less pressingly centre stage, and just as I am about to say to myself, yes I can bear it without her

237

when I know that I can't, I find that I am holding her in my arms again.

'I've booked a table,' she said, easing away.

And they sat down and he said please order the food and the drink. She looked at him. I mean it, he said, order me anything, would you mind, I don't care, and she didn't say you look tired; what she said was Patrick what is it, and it was as easy as that first time in the rain, it all came out. Here he was again, when he should have been sitting in the Music School for the Band Concert, here he was again wanting to tell Liz just about everything that had happened. At the police station, the photos, the anonymous notes, the e-mails, the call from Jamie, his sleeplessness.

He did not care what he was eating or drinking. Later that night he could not even remember if there was a tablecloth beneath his hands, he could not see anybody else though the restaurant was full. Even though he had walked the streets he suddenly did not know in what part of London he was or they were. Everything but her presence was a blank. If Detective Chief Inspector Bevan had followed him in an unmarked car and picked him up outside Frankie's and cross-questioned him on his whereabouts and his motives, and asked him why he was taking yet another such risk, he would have been at a loss for answers. All he knew was that he was back with her, sitting with her, and feeling better.

He looked at her as he ate (she ordered him sausages and mash) and as he drank the house red. He looked at her as she ate her flash-fried lamb's liver. He was warm and safe, warm and safe enough (an hour later) to ask:

'Do you think Roger might be doing this to me? Is he capable of this?'

'Roger?'

'And, no, that isn't why I wanted to meet.'

238

Liz did not react quickly. She swirled the wine in her glass, swirling it very slowly along the sides as she did so, and up to and almost over the brim before tilting it upright towards her lips, sipping it and saying:

'I don't know.'

'Is he still angry?'

'Oh yes, he's still very angry. But it's hard . . . to believe he would.'

'But he can be violent.'

She reddened and looked down. 'Oh, yes, he can be violent. But I can't see him planning all this. He's more likely to wait for you and punch you in the face. Get it over quickly. He's never been the . . . psychological type.'

'Unless he's on to a new level.'

'No, it's not Roger.'

'Why are you so sure?'

'I just don't think he would.'

'He's involved with actors. He could easily get one to play me.'

She thought again, and again shook her head. 'No, it's not him. Believe me, it isn't him to do that.'

'Does he ever talk about me?'

'No.'

'Never?'

'Well, he said you ruined his life . . . That you might as well have killed him.'

'That's a bit strong.'

'He often said it. That you took his place . . . displaced him. He felt you took over.'

'But I haven't.'

She put her glass down and sat back a bit. 'Anyway, the thing is, we've parted. Nine months ago now.'

Patrick slowly put down his knife and fork. 'Have you?'

'I suggested it,' Liz said, 'and he agreed.'

'And is it better?'

'Yes. Much better.'

'So I'm not to be sorry.'

'No, don't be. So. So, what about your loyal deputy?'

'Michael Falconer?'

'Yes. He's got plenty of reason to dislike you, or so you used to say. Is he still on the scene?'

'Very much so, but he doesn't have that kind of mind.'

'Whereas Roger does?'

'I was just asking you if –'

'And when it all came out about us, didn't that double-barrelled bloke try to get the governors to sack you?'

'Max Russell-Jones, yes. You're one of the very few people who know that. He's now the librarian. But Michael didn't sign the letter to the governors.'

'Perhaps he just dictated it?'

'Anyway, it isn't as straightforward as that. He's an old boy of the school and he thinks I'm taking it in the wrong direction. Quite a few old boys do.'

'And he disapproved of you making the school co-ed?'

'Oh yes.'

'He doesn't like girls.'

'I don't know about that but he doesn't want girls at the school, no. But they're there and they're staying and in two years' time we'll be fully co-ed.'

'Has he any other reasons to hate you?'

'Michael? Oh yes. He's seething about the studio theatre.'

'That's up and running, is it?'

'Yes.'

'One of your greatest dreams. Well done!'

'You didn't see it in the papers? Big thing in the *Independent*?'

'Must have missed it.'

'But my turning the gym into a theatre said it all for Michael. The last straw. But he still wouldn't do this. Deep down he's decent. Wrong-headed but decent.'

'Deep down he's stuck at thirteen.'

He looked across at her empty plate and empty glass.

'Was the liver good?'

'I didn't notice.'

'That's exactly what I love about you.'

Liz looked away.

'Sorry, shouldn't have said that. Another bottle, shall we?'

'Not for me. I'll get another glass of red for you.'

Liz turned round in her chair and waved to the waiter. Patrick saw the cut of her hair, the nape of her neck. She was wearing her hair even shorter. She turned back, asking,

'Read anything good lately?'

'Not really.'

'Nothing at all?'

'Well, apart from some riveting stuff on erectile dysfunction in the paper today.'

'Don't remember that as being a par-*tic*-ular problem with you.'

'I'm trying to stay ahead of the game.'

She laughed. 'You're an idiot, you really are.'

'Have I ever told you I could spend all day looking at you?'

'Yes.'

'Really? When?'

'Oh, you often did.'

'Damn.'

'And you also told me that Churchill said that to Ava Gardner and that Ava Gardner loved it.'

'Did I?'

'Yes. But it wasn't Ava Gardner he said it to.'

'Wasn't it?'

'No, it was Vivien Leigh.'

'I must be losing my touch.'

'As well as your identity.'

They both liked that. She went on:

'Going back to Roger, you're right; he would know people who could do it, he's got lots of contacts. Forget Roger himself for a minute, but that might be the area to look.'

'And he could give anyone access to TV film of me. Someone could study me on film.'

'But why would he risk getting someone else to do it? And I don't see how whoever it was would get into your flat. That's what makes it an insider.'

'I agree.'

'One of the three you mentioned. Maybe. Or even a bit of teamwork.'

'Teamwork?'

'Yes. Getting together, all doing a different bit. Books one, technology the other, acting the other.'

'Hell, do you think so?'

'They see enough of each other. It wouldn't be too difficult.'

Patrick stared at that possibility. Then he said, 'But not Justin Pett?'

'No. I don't see it.'

'But Roger and Justin worked together at one time.'

'Justin spits fire but he hasn't got the guts. To me this feels a deeper revenge than that; longer lasting.'

'You think so? Really?'

'Yes.'

'Against *me*?'

She put her hands to her head in a hair–pulling–out gesture.

'Yes, and I'm irritated you're making me say it. You're playing dumb and I don't like it. The last thing you are is dumb. How often are you in the papers? When I had my first big success with a book, some of my friends wrote to me, wrote me nice notes, but some never spoke to me again. Lots simply never mentioned it at all. Some never asked me round to their place again. When I was one of the crowd I was fine. When I was a bit of a celeb for a week, when I'd got noticed, when I was called a top publisher, that meant I was up myself. And with you, you can multiply that by ten.'

'Sorry, Liz, my mind's all over the show. I can persuade myself of anything at the moment.'

'And I don't believe that either; you're not like that.'

'Now you're sounding like Caroline.'

'That's unfair on her and it's unfair on me. You're an authority figure, you've got to be tough. Oh, don't look so hurt. Headmasters are, aren't they? You told me so yourself once. Remember? They like to have teeth, you said.'

'Thanks.'

'Oh, come on, Patrick, you told me you were drawn to the power.'

'You've got a good memory.'

'I probably remember every word you've ever said. All right? So let's say there's someone in your sixth form who doesn't like you one little bit.'

'There's more than one.'

'But this one is unbalanced, and sophisticated. Your school is famous for its sophistication. So this kid is all of that, and he's going to a top university before going into the media, and what's more he's twisted. And he hates you. It only takes one to hate you enough. God, I hated some of my teachers, didn't you?'

'No.'

243

'I don't believe you. I saw one of mine in a pub in Camden the other night; it's years since I'd seen him, but I had to get out of there.'

'Leaving a pub isn't a crime. Framing someone and misleading the police is.'

'So you never hated any of your teachers?'

'Not that much, no. Only when a friend of mine was expelled.'

'For?'

'No, no, it doesn't matter. It's all so long ago.'

'You can't start something and then just say that! Are you trying to wind me up?'

She looked around, suddenly distracted. Had she had enough of him and enough of all this? Patrick leant forward:

'Now I want to know about you. Anything great about to be published?'

For a moment she seemed lost for words. Her eyes were older, a bit harder, but searching his for some sign.

'No, Patrick, that's just you being nice. Another time for that. You must be feeling pretty . . . embattled?'

'Not as much as that Israeli bloke.'

'Which Israeli bloke?'

'Didn't you read about him in *The Times*?'

'No, what?'

'He was in this hotel and summoned a prostitute and when he opened the door it was his sixteen-year-old daughter.'

'My God! And what happened?'

'He had a heart attack and his wife's divorcing him.'

'What they used to call a condign punishment.'

'I love seeing you laugh.'

'Do you?'

'More than anything else.'

244

'But, look, Patrick, you'll be careful, won't you?'

'With whom?'

'Just generally, in case there's more to come. He might step it up.'

'Or they might. The three of them.'

'Exactly.'

Liz looked at her watch.

'D'you have to go?'

'Soonish, yes. I've just remembered I have to make a few calls.'

'Bit late, isn't it?'

'The thing is, I've been offered this job in New York.'

Patrick felt an engulfing adolescent panic. 'New York?'

'Yes.'

'You're not thinking of moving there?'

'Yes. A fresh start.'

'Really? Is that out of the blue? Tell me more.'

She put her hand over his. 'I won't, if you don't mind. I really don't want to at the moment.'

'Are you tempted? No, not by me, by New York I mean?'

'Yes to both.'

'Anyway.' He looked around. 'Anyway, thanks for fitting me in tonight.'

'Oh, for fuck's sake, Patrick, that is the most stupid thing to say. Seeing you tonight was about as difficult as it gets but I wanted to do it and I did it and I did it because I think about you all the time, every day. OK? So never say that kind of thing to me again. Ever.'

'I won't. And I'm sorry.'

'You should be.'

He straightened his back, his fingers shaking, trying to do up his top shirt button and fumbling with the knot of his tie. He suddenly felt older. More formal. Further away.

245

Patrick gulped the dregs of his coffee, the last sugar grains sweet on his lips. Liz looked at him drinking his coffee. She noticed the tremble in his hand. They did not speak for a moment. Then she smiled and said:

'So we'll meet again?'

'Yes, we must.'

'It's been lovely. It really has.'

'Yes, it has.'

'And I'm on the case.'

He slept the sleep of the innocent, he slept the sleep of a child. And the next day Patrick was as good a headmaster and as good a man as he had ever been. He was at his desk early and he was professional in his despatch. To Daphne he seemed back to his old self. He dealt with his mail. He returned his calls. He replied to various notes from members of staff.

There was a bounce about Patrick. He was on top. As a husband he rang Caroline and said he was sorry he'd been so difficult. Caroline said it could well be her fault. They assured each other that it was not the other's fault. And Alice was being a bit less difficult. Only a bit, but still.

As a leader he was skilful, effortlessly working the Common Room during break. He apologised for unavoidably missing the Band Concert but Michael Falconer assured him it was wonderful. He thanked the staff for running the extra mile, never the easiest thing in week eleven of a very long term. He was tolerant of the boring colleagues, tolerant of those with whom, as Fanny Burney would put it, he had dawdling conversations on dawdling subjects. He was tolerant even of the Scylla and Charybdis he landed between at lunch.

In bed alone that night he asked himself why he had done such a good job that day, why he had performed so well. He knew only too well why. Even the drabbest tree in November, even the deadest brown leaves, can flare into unexpected colour if the sun comes out. His day at school had been so good, and he had been so good, because the night before he had been sitting with Liz for a few hours. After seeing her he felt warm inside and so much better deep down.

In bed that night Patrick told himself that Auden was so right: the desires of the heart are as crooked as corkscrews.

26

Encouraged by this, Patrick did as he was bidden by Detective Chief Inspector Bevan in the Rat and Parrot: he sent him a school list and he got on with his job. And, for good measure, he also sent him the glossy new prospectus, which included new photos not only of the new computers but also of the prettiest new girls inside the new theatre.

But his hours of pumping adrenalin around the campus did not block off his obsession. Nor did the sets of lower sixth reports which landed on his desk block anything out. Nor did chairing a very long Pay and Conditions Committee. Nor did watching Hugo Solomon, at his arrogant worst, losing the Senior Debating Final which he should have won. The harder Patrick worked, the more he pushed himself, and the more events he dutifully attended, the more inventive his mind became at ransacking his memory and returning by one devious route or another to the strange case of the other Patrick Balfour.

Because, whenever he felt like it, the other Patrick Balfour would return to him.

Liz was right that there was more to come. The next two moves arrived a day apart, and Patrick, as he promised he would, forwarded both of them immediately to DCI

248

Bevan. Unfortunately with these moves there was no evidence on the covert Common Room cameras because it was not in the headmaster's pigeonhole that these arrived. Before going to bed Patrick had checked his Inbox on his upstairs laptop. The new message flashed up:

He was humbled to the dust by the many ill things he had done, and raised up again into a sober and fearful gratitude by the many that he had come so near to doing, yet avoided . . .

. . . And thus fortified, as I supposed, on every side, I began to profit by the strange immunities of my position.

Patrick Balfour

For a Stevenson fan these were no challenge. They were quotations from *The Strange Case of Dr Jekyll and Mr Hyde*. And how obvious was the purpose this time! To highlight or to reawaken the many ill things Patrick had done, to stress that there but for the grace of God . . . Life's near misses. Conscience, once again it was conscience, the undisclosed consequences of actions, the sense of having got away with it – so far. My stalker, my man out there, thinks I have got away with it. But got away with what?

Humbled to the dust was the clearest threat while the second quotation, picking out *the immunities of my position*, focused on power. It struck at the protection that power gives or seems to offer, the self-induced sense of being invulnerable, of being fortified on every side. But Patrick had already been hounded and exposed by an intrusive press. Gowns and furred robes don't hide all, do they? And as for *sober*? *fortified*? Drink? Yes, Patrick drank too much, but he did not dream of being beyond the reach of justice.

Ever since Patrick's father had read him *Treasure Island* at his bedside he had loved stories about the good guy and the bad guy; and Patrick, even as a boy, always found the bad guy, even a one-legged bad guy, more interesting than the good. When Alice was a little girl Patrick carried on the family tradition and sat on the end of her bed and read *Treasure Island* to her. Her eyes drank deep as she listened intently; she sucked her thumb and bit the corner of the sheet until it was soaking wet.

And when Jamie studied *The Strange Case of Dr Jekyll and Mr Hyde* for GCSE English Literature it was with Euan Stuart, wasn't it?

Yes, with Euan Stuart, no less.

It was time for Patrick to revisit the library.

The second e-mail came up on his screen in his study late in the afternoon, the very gloomy afternoon, of 21 November, one of those November days when it is almost dark at 3.50. Patrick was yawning with exhaustion and dying to be rescued by a good night's sleep, a prospect so unlikely as to be comic. Yawning, rubbing his eyes, he clicked on to this:

Let me call myself, for the present, William Wilson. The fair page lying before me need not be sullied with my real appellation.

Or:

Let me call myself, for the present, Patrick Balfour.
Patrick Balfour is reactionary and progressive, he's something and he's nothing. He makes me sick.
And, Patrick Balfour, soon you will be forced to face yourself.

The real Patrick Balfour closed his eyes. He concentrated hard, with his eyes closed. William Wilson? Who the hell was William Wilson? Patrick had once taught a boy called William Wilson. A boy in his first school, in Bristol. He played football. William Wilson? Left back, wasn't he, quick on his feet, gutsy in the physical challenge. A ginger-haired lad from Avonmouth; yes, he could see William Wilson now.

There was a knock on the door. Then a louder one. Patrick did not speak or move. It felt like a knock in another house. No, he knew this story too. He'd read this William Wilson story at school. But how the hell did his e-mailer know, from the huge range of English Literature, which particular books or stories he had read at school? With whom, in his adult life, had he ever discussed his schoolboy reading? No one, not Caroline, not Liz.

William Wilson was a story by Edgar Allan Poe. A tale of mystery and imagination. Patrick read it for prep (it was only about twenty pages) and then they read it round the class. He could remember the classroom they were in. He remembered the William Blake poster on the wall, and he remembered the quotation underneath it: *it is an easy thing to talk of patience to the afflicted.* Each member of the class read a paragraph of the story, alternating with Mr Griffiths, an English teacher who really could read, and Patrick wished Mr Griffiths had read every paragraph, had read the whole story out loud himself as it was so much scarier when he performed it. Most of the class, embarrassed by their own voices, rushed through their paragraphs, happy simply to get as quickly as they could to the full stop and hand the baton on to the next boy.

The problems of William Wilson began when he was at a boarding school, a large rambling Elizabethan house with a fretted Gothic steeple. Someone, with the same name and the same date of birth, arrives at the same school and this Wilson immediately makes the other Wilson's life a misery. Wilson Mark 2 hounds Wilson Mark 1. The

251

second Wilson has a weakness in the faucial or guttural organs which precludes him from raising his voice at any time above a very low whisper.

And what is such an e-mail if not a very low whisper, a below-the-belt whisper? PB2 was a whisperer.

The first Wilson finds his rival intolerable and leaves the school to start a new life at Eton. For a while all goes well, but one night, while he is wildly excited by wine, the whispering Wilson turns up at Eton College too. After Eton, Wilson Mark 1 goes up to Oxford, or escapes to Oxford, or so he thinks, but the other Wilson exposes him there as a cheat at cards. Like a mad comet, Wilson runs away (or chases himself) from Paris to Rome to Vienna to Berlin to Moscow. Finally Wilson Mark 1, frantic with every species of wild excitement, fights a duel with Wilson Mark 2 and kills him. He then catches sight of a mirror at the far end of the room, and looking into it he sees himself covered in blood and mortally wounded. He has killed himself.

Patrick opened his eyes. The bullied and the bullying William Wilsons were still glowing on his blue and white computer screen. That knock on the door again.

'Come in.'

She was standing there. Notepad in hand; she looked as neat as ever, her skirt brown, her blouse beige, her shoes sensible.

'Are you all right, Patrick?'

'Yes, Daphne, why?'

Her voice was private and concerned. 'I've been buzzing you, and then I knocked and you didn't answer.'

'Really?'

'I was a bit worried.'

'I must have nodded off.'

'Shall I get you a cup of coffee?'

252

'Don't tell me, I've missed another appointment?'

'No, it's just that Alice hasn't turned up to lessons this afternoon, and no one seems to know where she is.'

He kept his voice level. 'Who told you?'

'Michael was told in the Common Room, and he came over and told me.'

'I'll ring Caroline. Sorry about that.' Coolly said, Patrick, very coolly said, but the whole thing pressed on his chest and dragged on his heart. He went on, 'All right, Daphne, and thanks for telling me. Sounds as if she's going through a bit of a bolshie patch.'

'Michael thinks it might be the play, the pressure of it.'

Patrick snapped petulantly back, 'Oh, I'm sure he does.'

'And there is something else. About Michael.'

'What is it? What have I done wrong now?'

'You haven't done anything wrong, Patrick, as far as I know, but there's something he can't bring himself to tell you –'

'Oh, really? That's unusual. Michael usually seems to make his views pretty clear to me on everything: co-education, drama, sport, my daughter, you name it.'

'So I thought it would be better if I told you.'

'So you're delivering the bad news?'

'How did you know?'

'Well, it's obvious, Daphne, isn't it? I'm not doing my job, everyone can see that, loyal as you are even you can see it, and the governors have found out about the police, and the phones have been going and Michael Falconer has been feeding them all the worst bits and there's been a meeting at the Athenaeum and the old guard have decided.'

'Patrick, what on earth are you talking about?'

Patrick went to the window and let in the roar of traffic. On the pavement below an old woman was unsteadily exercising her dog.

'It's OK, Daphne, you're the most loyal person I know, but it had to happen. These things always come out, someone somewhere always says something. You think you can sit on it but you can't.'

'Patrick.'

'Yes? You're not going to deny it?'

'Please stop it, Patrick. I mean it. It's beneath you, all this, it really is. The thing is, Michael is ill. He has cancer.'

Patrick swung round. 'Cancer? My God.'

'Yes.'

'Cancer of what? Where?'

'Of the prostate.'

'Sit down for a moment, Daphne, would you.'

'I'd really better not, there's so much on my desk.'

'Please. I'd like you to stay, just for a moment. Please sit down.'

'Thank you.'

'And forgive . . . what I just said. Tell me more about Michael.'

'He's been through all the tests the last few weeks, and it's just been confirmed.'

'The last few weeks?'

'Yes, he got the results of his first blood test on . . . 6 November, in fact he came in when you were, well you know, but he didn't want to worry you with it. Since then it's been more tests, and the biopsy last week has confirmed it.'

'Where is he now?'

'He's across in his study.'

'Should he be at work?'

'He's going in next Monday.'

'Next Monday!'

'They insisted. Operating on the Tuesday in the Kingswood.'

'I'll go across to see him now.'

254

'I'm not sure he wants to talk about it. In fact I know he doesn't because he made that clear.'

'Really?'

'Really.'

'But he told you?'

'Yes, he told me.'

'He can't have found that easy, being the sort of man he is. Sorry, that sounded rude.'

Daphne folded her hands on her lap with a sad half-smile. 'No, it didn't, but Michael and I go back . . . a long way.'

'But he's going to be all right? Well, you know, as all right as −'

'You know Michael. He's a fighter. And as long as they have got it early.'

'Does he seem worried? Well, I mean I know he must be, but how long does he −'

'His main anxiety, Patrick, is making sure all the necessary cover is in place, that everything is properly organised before he goes in.'

'And that we won't be able to cope without him?'

'He didn't say that.'

'No, but he wouldn't be far wrong.'

Patrick wanted to see Michael but he had to respect Michael's wishes. He was feeling empty. He stood up and looked at his father's photograph in the top right-hand drawer. He thought about his father. He thought about him until he saw him sitting in the old summerhouse, under the damson tree, doing the crossword. He thought about his mother. He wondered how Jamie was getting on in Baltimore. He should ring him. He thought about Alice. Why was Alice being so difficult?

Disorientated, he also made a mistake, a big mistake. Or rather his hand did. His hand started to flick through the second-hand R. D. Laing he had bought on the way to meet Liz. Paragraphs stood out, and these paragraphs did stick, they stuck to him like . . . like the wasps' nest stuck on the side of the old summerhouse. One year they had to get Rentokil Man in.

Within the context of mutual sanity there is, however, quite a wide margin for conflict, error, misconception, in short, for a disjunction of one kind or another between the person one is in one's own eyes (one's being for oneself) and the person one is in the eyes of the other (one's being-for-the-other), and, conversely, between who or what he is for me and who or what he is for himself.

Patrick feared that if that sentence, if that sentence in its entirety, ever started to run round inside his head, if that sentence ever moved into what R. D. Laing called his 'mental apparatus', Patrick knew he would have to pursue it, to kick and pursue it, like a boy kicking a can all the way home from school. It wasn't just nasty things like wasps' nests. It was much the same for Patrick when his eye caught a butterfly. He had to watch it, really fix on it, wait until it took off, watch where it landed and trembled, watch where it went, to this flower, to that warm stone, ah, now it's on that pane of glass in the greenhouse, now it's near the squirrels, his eye holding fast to it, following it round and round the garden until it was trembling its way over the wall and he could see it no more.

This was Patrick's next butterfly:

We have our secrets and our needs to confess. We may remember how, in childhood, adults were first able to look right through us, and into us, and what an accomplishment it was when we, in fear and trembling, could tell our first lie,

256

*and make, for ourselves, the discovery that we are irre-
deemably alone in certain respects, and know that within the
territory of ourselves there can be only*

He snapped the book shut. Patrick liked to think he was
good in a crisis, good when self-control was most required,
but he was in a worse panic sweat than when he had parted
company with Alan in bad visibility in the Peak District –
and did not see him again for three hours. By the time
Alan took human shape and appeared grinning through
the gloom, Patrick had reached the land of the far-fetched
and had already written the obituary for the school magazine and the letters of condolence to Alan's parents, the
parents of the boy he loved, and watched his best friend's
coffin lowered into the earth.

No, not Alan.

Don't go there, not now. The dream was bad enough.

Michael has cancer.

You must help Michael.

But a smaller coffin was being lowered into the earth
when his son Jamie, aged eight, suddenly went off ahead in
the Scottish Highlands while Patrick was sitting eating a
Mars Bar on a smooth rock, and they lost touch with each
other, and Patrick suddenly realised that he was alone, Jamie
was not there, where was he, and Patrick scrambled up and
down the mountainside, shouting JamieJamieJamie until
he was hoarse, shouting until he could shout no more, staring down screes and shafts and over sheer drops. When,
defeated and the father of a lost son and how will I ever face
Caroline or life again, he saw Jamie standing by the gate at
the point from which they had set off hours before, he was
torn in half, half wanting to hit Jamie and hit Jamie, half
wanting to hug him and hug him. He hugged him.

27

He washed his face in cold water. He cleaned his teeth and gargled. Then, feeling irredeemably alone, Patrick dialled 4422 on the internal telephone system and waited for the languid voice of Max Russell-Jones.

'Library.'

'Is that Max?'

'It is, Headmaster.'

'Do you have a moment, if I come over?'

'But of course, Headmaster.'

'This isn't too busy a time?'

'No, with the mock GCSEs on the place is an absolute haven.'

'I'll be with you in a minute.'

Patrick wrote down the authors and the titles on a fresh piece of notepaper, from Kafka to Poe, in the order in which they had arrived. Just a list of the authors and the titles but to Patrick they seemed more like a slimy, silvery slug trail, and one that could well be leading him up the garden path.

He set off briskly across the quad to be met at the door of the librarian's office by a heartfelt Max:

'Terrible news about poor Michael, isn't it? Absolutely ghastly.'

'It is, yes. Is it now . . . common knowledge?'

'I'm not sure *how* common, Headmaster, but knowing this place I imagine it soon will be. To be honest, he hasn't been looking after himself for quite some while.'

'No, I suppose he hasn't.'

'And he's lost weight. But can any of us stop the old boy overworking? No, we can't. He's one of life's genuine saints. By the way, are *you* all right, Headmaster? You're looking a bit under the weather this morning.'

Max at his most solicitous was not helping Patrick's churning stomach.

'How are things going up here? Generally?'

'First things first, I'm delighted with the new carpet, Headmaster.'

'It's certainly much quieter.'

'So much easier to creep up behind them when they're eating or talking.'

'You enjoy that, Max, do you?'

'Hugely.'

'And the new bank of computers hasn't changed the atmosphere? It's not taking the library down the magazines and newspapers and video route?'

'Rest assured, Headmaster, this is one library will that not become a corner shop.'

'And no abuse of the internet? No hard porn?'

'Always a difficult one, that. Who knows what people get up to these days – I was going to say in the privacy of their homes, but I meant in front of their screens. But no, I'm not unduly worried.'

'And Casey has issued his firm new guidelines? On plagiarism as well as porn?'

Max chortled. 'Oh, we all love Casey and his firm guidelines.'

Max then leant back a little as if to say surely this is not what you have come up here to discuss, and to invite closure on the question of porn. Patrick accepted the invitation.

'Good. Anyway, I was wondering, do we have all these in stock?'

Faced with the list of titles Max stiffened a little and focused his restless gaze. 'Ah, our Joseph Clark again.'

'Indeed.'

Max opened a drawer in his desk and took out an envelope which he handed to Patrick.

'In fact I've tracked down a bit more about him for you.'

'On Joseph Clark?'

'The whole thing rather intrigued me, to be honest, you coming up here out of the blue like that, so I thought I'd see what I could find, and the British Library sent me this today.'

'That's quick.'

'Yes, jolly good of them, wasn't it? Perhaps this fleshes him out a bit for you.'

'That is kind of you, Max.'

Max looked back at the piece of paper Patrick had given him.

'So, is this a reading list for the Lower Sixth Psychology Option? I hear you're running that next year.'

'No it's not. I haven't got round to that.'

'Some literary quiz you're trying?'

'First, I was wondering if we have all these books, and secondly, a bit of a strange request, has any of them been taken out? In recent weeks, I mean. Say, since the beginning of November.'

Max raised an eyebrow, pursed his lips and swung towards his computer. On every wall were pictures of Prague and Rome.

'Well, let's see, shall we? I can certainly check for you.

260

At a guess I'd say we have them all, except for the R. D. Laing.'

As his long fingers tapped the keys, Max spoke to the screen: 'So, it's not a quiz?'

'Not exactly, Max. More of a teaser.'

'I'm intrigued. Do sit down.'

From his seat across the table Patrick could not see what was coming up on the librarian's screen but he could see Max's elegant cuffs, his manicured nails and his signet ring: the fingers that had written the disloyal letter to the governors, the fingers that had run the extra mile on Joseph Clark. He could see his dark-brown suede shoes.

'Yes. We do have a copy of each.'

'Including the R. D. Laing?'

'Including the R. D. Laing, yes, *The Divided Self*, wasn't it, yes, I was wrong there. Not that I've ever *seen* it here, I'm glad to say, one of those awful sixties gurus, wasn't he? Have you read it, Headmaster?'

'Just dipped into it.'

'Any good?'

'I haven't got far enough to say. And they're all on the open shelves, are they? Not kept in the reserve stock?'

'No, they're all open-shelf books.'

'And they're all in at the moment?'

The screen made a greyish white gleam on Max's cheek.

'Let . . . me . . . see. By the way, if it's teasers you're into, here's another one for you. Do you know which category of books we lose most of in this school? No? Give up? To put you straight out of your misery, I will tell you. It's theology. Worrying, isn't it? Ah, here we are. Well, the only one out at the moment is the Ripley novel and . . . the Poe. No, the Ripley came back in today. Just the Poe is out.'

'Who's borrowed it?'

261

Max, in one of his most irritating habits, echoed Patrick's words with some questioning edge: 'Who has borrowed it?'

'Do you mind telling me?'

'The Poe collection?'

'Yes.'

Max's long dry fingers tapped the keys.

'This is not a disciplinary matter, Headmaster, I trust?'

'I hope not.'

'Because none of us is perfect. It is a few days overdue, I'm afraid, and it was borrowed by a lower-sixth girl, Alice Balfour.'

Neither man moved a muscle.

'And the Highsmith?'

'The Ripley. *The Talented Mr Ripley*, by Patricia Highsmith? *Such* a scary book.' Max's head remained motionless, with not a hair out of place. 'Well, let's say you have a well-read daughter.'

'She took out both?'

Job done, Max swung round in his chair, his voice closer now to the high jokey rather than the languid.

'Oh, a coincidence I'm sure, Headmaster. But are you any further forward on your intriguing list?'

'I'm not sure. You haven't spotted Alice around today, have you?'

'I may have seen her going into the Sixth Form Centre at the very beginning of break. Yes, I'm sure she was in that group.'

'The Sixth Form Centre, thanks.'

She wasn't there. A couple of boys were playing snooker. One looked up from his cue as Patrick entered, then played a shot. A girl, taking a sandwich from its plastic container, stood up and smiled nervously at him. Another boy, aware of Patrick's presence and sensing he ought to make some sort of gesture, slowly took one foot off the aluminium table. A girl whooped as she scored at table football. Hugo Solomon was by the Coke machine, on his mobile. Patrick went out.

Back in his study he rang Finley Place three times. Engaged, engaged, engaged. When he did get through Alice answered.

'Why aren't you at school?'

'I'm not feeling very well.'

'What's up?'

'Just feeling sick.'

'In what way?'

'In a feeling sick kind of way.'

'Did you tell anyone? Your head of house? The school nurse?'

'No.'

'You can't just leave like that. No one here knew where you were.'

'It's not a big deal, Dad, is it?'

'You should have told someone.'

'You can do it now.'

'Is Mum there?'

'Don't think so. I'll have a look.'

She put the phone down. Patrick tapped his desk.

'No, she's not here.'

'But you're well enough to be on the phone for half an hour?'

'Someone rang me. Like you're doing.'

'Does Mum know you're at home?'

'No, I haven't seen her today.'

'Look, I'm not going on about it now, but this isn't good enough.'

'I'm sorry, Dad, I'm just stressed out.'

'You'd better come and live here then.'

'But I asked you that, I asked you a number of times and you said no.'

'I know I did.'

'So what's changed?'

'Look, be at school tomorrow.'

'I was going to be.'

'And some of your library books are overdue.'

He put the phone down.

Slumped in his chair that evening, alone in his flat with a pizza and a bottle of White Horse, Patrick read the British Library photocopy about Joseph Clark. What clue was hidden in or behind all this Crippl'd, Hunch Back'd, Pot Belly'd, Sharp Breasted stuff?

In the Pall Mall at London, lived one Clark (call'd, The Posture-Master) that had such an absolute command of all his Muscles and Joints, that he can dis-joint almost his whole Body; so that he impos'd on our famous Mullens, who lookt on him in so miserable a Condition, that he would not undertake his Cure: Tho' he was a well grown Fellow, yet he would appear in all the Deformities that can be imagin'd, as Hunch Back'd, Pot Belly'd, Sharp Breasted; he disjointed his Arms, Shoulders, Legs and Thighs, that he well appear'd as great an Object of Pity as any; and he has often impos'd on the same Company, where he has been just before, to give him money as a Cripple; he looking so much unlike himself, that they could not know him. I have seen him make his Hips stand out a considerable way from his Loins, and so high that they seem'd to invade the Place of his Back, in which Posture he has so large a Belly, as tho' one of our Company had one of a considerable Size, yet it

264

seem'd lank compar'd with his: He turns his Face into all Shapes, so that by himself he acts all the uncouth, demure, odd Faces of a Quaker's Meeting: I could not have conceiv'd it possible to have done what he did, unless I had seen it; and I am sensible how short I am come to a full Description of him: None certainly can describe what he does, but himself. He began Young to bring his Body to it, and there are several Instance of Persons that can move several of their Bones out of their Joints, using themselves to it from Children.

from the Royal Society, *Phil. Trans.* xx. *262*

Half-drunk, eyes half-closed, Patrick read this. He had never much liked even minor versions of self-dislocation. For example, he hated watching or listening to pupils in class pulling their fingers slightly out of their sockets, or 'cracking their knuckles' by rubbing their finger bones against the cartilages and popping the air bubbles they create.

Of Joseph Clark's tricks, the one that struck deepest into Patrick's mind was his going to the tailor's, to be measured for a new suit, and adopting a deformed posture. Patrick could see it all. Clark standing there with his left shoulder out of its socket and his left arm sloping far down, his left hand rubbing against his left knee, his right shoulder up, his right shoulder blade sticking out, with his hips every which way, looking for all the world like Laurence Olivier in *Richard III* – and being solemnly measured. This measuring the tailor would do, presumably moving round Joseph with all conceivable tact and tactile decorum. Then, some weeks later, when the tailor called for the fitting, with the suit made up, Joseph would reverse the dislocations, this time with his right shoulder down, his right

265

hand brushing his right knee, and watch the tailor, poor sod, aghast at the failure of his work. Brilliant. Brilliant and sick.

Like the person who was after him.

Like the person who dressed up as Patrick.

Patrick shook his head and gave up. He slumped back on the sofa and drank and flicked through the channels, settling on a programme about the SAS and their endurance tests. A group of volunteers, people from all walks of life, were going through hell on earth in the Scottish Highlands. And, what's more, they were going through hell on earth just for the hell of it. Because this particular group did not even want to join the SAS; they just wanted to see if they could pass the SAS test. And they did not mind television cameras recording their suffering and their failure.

For a few minutes the programme annoyed him, as did all those vicarious programmes about macho men with guns or men in prisons or men in uniforms. But Patrick soon felt drawn to the women featured in the exercise, the women who were keen to prove that they could do anything that the men could do. He sat forward. One woman, with blonde short-cropped hair, was reeling and punch-drunk, but she stumbled on, kept going by her team's support. Another woman, with long blonde hair, was a rugby player. One with dark hair could have been a student in any lecture hall. She was full of astonishing tenacity. All were brave and all took the pain full on. They outlasted many of the men.

Stumbling himself, Patrick took Alice's letters out of the bottom drawer of his desk and started to read them. He felt his eyes filling up.

28

'Dad.'

'Jamie!'

'How are you?'

Patrick sat up in his chair, his fingers still a little greasy from the pizza, and turned down the volume with the remote.

'Have you got a cold, Dad?'

'No, why?'

'What are you doing?'

'Just slobbing around really, you know, just . . . well, being a bit of a teacher, I suppose. Hell, you know teachers, Jamie. Lazy sods, always moaning. Spend half their time at home, and that's when they're not on holiday.'

'Had a few, have you?'

'It shows? How's Baltimore?'

'Baltimore's fine. More to the point, Dad, are you all right?'

'I'm OK, thanks.'

'I've just been speaking to Al.'

'Oh, caught her in, did you?'

'She says you're all stressed out. She said you went ballistic with her.'

'Ballistic?'

'Her word.'

'If your sister thinks that me saying a few slightly critical things to her is me going ballistic she has led a more sheltered life than I thought.'

'That's what she said. Ballistic.'

'Look, Jamie, she can say what she likes, and she does.'

'And she said Mum reckons you've lost the plot a bit.'

'I'd ask Mum for her own quotes if I were you. I'm absolutely fine.'

'Well, you're not. I can tell. So, what *actually* were you doing?'

'Me?'

'When I rang. More specifically.'

Patrick sniffed. 'More specifically, Jamie? After I'd thought about what I'm going to say at sixth form assembly tomorrow morning I turned on the telly and I started watching, well, I still am – sound down – watching some women in combat gear running around the Scottish Highlands. There they go. They're amazing, they really are. There goes another one. She's punch-drunk but still on her feet. She's reeling all over the glen. Talk about guts.'

'Doesn't sound like your sort of viewing.'

'Ah now, there you're wrong, son. I'm fascinated by guts, by who's got it and who hasn't.'

'What else have you been up to?'

'Me?'

'You, the man I'm talking to. Anything else?'

'Not much. Well, I've also been thinking quite a bit about Michael Falconer.'

'Oh yes.'

'Thinking I may have got him wrong.'

'I always told you he was a good bloke, Dad.'

'He's got cancer.'

268

'What!'

'Yes.'

'Oh, bloody hell, no. Shit. I'm sorry to hear that.'

'Yes, well, there you go.'

'Him of all people. I just can't see him ill. He's not the type who gets ill.'

'Exactly. Have you . . . rung because you've had more e-mails?'

'No, I'm ringing to ask you to send me everything you've been hit with.'

'Why?'

'Because I want to see it all, and because I hate hearing you drinking on your own, and because I might be able to work it out. I've got a hunch or two.'

'Well, don't worry about me.'

'I am worrying about you and I do. So send it all in an e-mail to me now.'

'Chapter and verse?'

'Yes, after I put the phone down.'

'What's your hunch?'

'Look, I don't know but I think it might well be a kid at school.'

'Why?'

'Something about it, something Al said.'

'Something specific?'

'No, but the only way he could have known my e-mail address was by looking over Al's shoulder.'

'In the computer centre?'

'Yes.'

'Unless you're the server in charge of the whole school network. Then you have access to everything.'

'Whatever. Just send me the stuff.'

'Tell me something else, would you, what did you make of Alice? Generally?'

'Al? Well, you know, usual drama queen.'

'That's all?'

'I reckon.'

'Nothing deeper? Nothing more . . . troubled?'

'Not that I got.'

'D'you speak to Mum as well tonight?'

'No, but she's rung me a few times the last fortnight, keeping me up to speed. But, listen, I'm upset about M. F.'

'I'm sorry I had to tell you that, Jamie. He's just gone in.'

'Tell you what, Dad. He's got it. Guts, I mean.'

'I agree.'

'Anyway, I won't go on now. I'll be back in touch when I've read your e-mail.'

Half an hour later, at the very second that Patrick finished pressing SEND NOW on the e-mail, the phone next to his computer rang. He was expecting it to be Jamie saying what the hell's going on, Dad, get a grip will you. It was an upbeat Liz, her voice energising.

'You've been on the phone a long time.'

'Yes, what you might call a family night phone-in.'

'That's nice.'

'Not altogether.'

'Well, let's say I've never had one.'

'So, have you . . . have you had any more thoughts on New York?'

'At the moment, Patrick, I'm focusing on you.'

'Ah, now *that*, I have to say, is the bit about this whole thing that I am enjoying. The patient can lie back and enjoy it, surrounded by nurses all looking like you.'

'Sometimes you are such a typical man.'

'I'm so glad to hear you say that.'

'Such a sad Romantic. You're not consumptive, are you?'

'Maybe.'

'Putting aside the nursey fantasy for just a moment, how are you, generally?'

'The truth?'

'That's it, Patrick, I'm not family.'

'The truth is . . . I'm shot to pieces. As when you rang.'

'Well, I've been to something today that you would have enjoyed.'

'Tell me.'

'The exhibition at the Imperial War Museum. Knowing you, you haven't been?'

'The . . . Twelve Soldier Poets?'

'You've been?'

'No, but I saw the review in *Time Out*.'

'Well, guess what's there?'

'What?'

'Edward Thomas's fobwatch!'

'Not the one he was carrying when he was killed?'

'Yes, stopped at 7.36 and twelve seconds . . .'

'Wow . . . I must go.'

'Funny how one thing like that can say it all, isn't it, and say it better than the bigger things . . .'

'Absolutely.'

'And he of course made me think of you . . . and *The Other*, that poem of his you told me about. In Angelo's.'

He was back sitting in Angelo's. Back holding her hand.

'Did I?'

'Yes, you did. You know, where Edward Thomas is walking alone and he comes out of a wood, and goes into a pub . . . have I got this right?'

'Yes, that's it.'

'And the landlord says weren't you in here yesterday . . . and Edward Thomas says no, not me, you've got the wrong man, and the landlord says no I haven't got the

271

wrong man it was you all right and you set off that way . . .
and so Thomas finishes his drink and leaves the pub and
starts to follow the direction the landlord gave him. Yes?
Are you still there, Patrick?'

'Yes.'

'Patrick?'

'Yes.'

'You were crying when I rang, weren't you?'

'Yes.'

He could tell her anything. He felt he could reach out
and touch her, even on the phone.

Liz asked very quietly, 'Why?'

'Jamie. Jamie was so . . . And then there's Alice.
Caroline. Everything.'

'Yes.'

'The whole mess. You know.'

'Yes.'

'Moving on . . .'

'Right, moving on,' she said, her voice bright again.
'Have you ever seen *The Passenger*?'

'Don't think so, no.'

'Christ, have you seen *any*thing? The Michelangelo
Antonioni film? The one with Jack Nicholson? No, not
One Flew Over The Cuckoo's Nest, everyone's seen that,
hell, I thought I was talking to one of the London cultural
elite. It was on TV a while back. *The Passenger*? No?'

'No. I was probably writing. Getting on with my own
work. That's what you were always telling me to do.'

'Anyway, Nicholson's this TV reporter stuck in some
hot, fly-ridden godforsaken desert hotel, and on an
impulse he exchanges his identity with a man he finds
dead in the next room.'

'Why?'

'Well, looking at the corpse, he gets the idea that things

can only get better for him and so he drags the dead body into his own room, so that it looks as if he himself is the one who has died. Then he puts on the other man's clothes and pockets his papers and diary and drives away, a new man, leaving himself for dead, as it were. And he follows this new man's engagements in his diary and . . . becomes this other bloke. It's that simple.'

'Ends badly, I bet.'

'Yes.'

'So, what are you saying?'

'As well as going to exhibitions and watching films I've been doing a bit of digging myself.'

'Digging?'

'Well, sort of research.'

'Tell me.'

'All right, this is what I've done. Don't worry, no names were mentioned or anything, but I've got a woman friend who does criminal profiling. She wrote a book about it in the States, bestseller. You know, you try to work out the personality of the criminal who's still at large, like Jack the Ripper or the Washington sniper; you might think it's a load of rubbish and no better than star-gazing, but I just thought it worth a try.'

'Look, I'm up for anything, reflexology, rebirthing, cranial what's-it, let's go for it.'

'Shall I read you what she said? I wrote it down.'

'Yes.'

'We're calling him PB2, Patrick Balfour 2, all right?'

'That's amazing, I've been using that as shorthand too. But the profiler doesn't know it's me?'

'I just told you, Patrick, no names were mentioned.'

'Right, I'm listening, Liz, I really am.'

'But not concentrating.'

'I am now. And I love your voice.'

'Don't try that.'

'I really do.'

'Have you been drinking?'

'Me?'

'Do you want me to read this to you or not?'

'Ever thought about being a teacher?'

'No.'

'Pity. But I'm listening. Fire away.'

'"PB2 is clever, well-read, but in a quirky, obsessive way. Once he gets on to something he pursues it or pursues him all the way. He is a kind of private, psychological stalker. He probably sits on his own and watches a lot of old movies . . . old ones like *Rear Window*, and thinks he's James Stewart, new ones like *The Matrix*. His revenges are mainly in his imagination, so he might seem a quiet, even laid-back person. But the lines between fact and fiction, between reality and imagination, these are lines he does not find easy to draw and to observe. He likes the *idea* of a shoot-out, of a confrontation, but would probably see it in film or literary terms. He probably plays second fiddle to people who are much less clever than he is, while secretly despising them. His revenges may take an oblique form. He's probably left clues in the notes he's sending. He probably wants to be caught. The hunter and the hunted, the criminal and the creator, may well be more akin than we tend to believe."'

'And that's it?'

'Yes.'

'*Rear Window*?'

'Well, you don't respect privacy, you see it all, you see all the things you should never see, the dreams, the dirty linen, the suicide, the lonely woman, the drinker, the perfect murder, the light under the door, the steps coming along the corridor towards your door and no help coming

274

and you've got nowhere to run, only an open window but you can't move. You may not have seen *The Passenger* but you must have seen Hitchcock's *Rear Window*, Patrick? James Stewart? Yes?'

'Yes, and Grace Kelly. How gorgeous was she! And what about a motive? Did your profiler friend discuss that?'

'Only generally.'

Patrick sensed a reluctance.

'And?'

'That's up to you she said.'

'Up to me? What do you mean?'

'A long-term festering grievance of some intensely personal kind. A relationship thing. A family thing. Probably kept a lid on it for years. And now it's suddenly triggered.'

'A family thing?'

'Feeding it, building it up, that kind of thing, apparently that's how it works.'

'Right.'

Patrick stared at the empty pizza carton. He picked it up and crumpled it.

'Anything new your end, Patrick?

'Well, I've just found out that Alice has borrowed two of the books from the school library. Including the Edgar Allan Poe.'

Liz did not immediately respond but when she did she was firm. 'Look, you must tell your detective everything, even any embarrassing family bits like that.'

'Must I? Would you in my position?'

'I would. Ring him tomorrow with that. It may help him to build up a picture. You concealing and hiding things is not what this is about. Or, rather, it may be what this is about.'

'What did you say, Liz? That last bit?'

'You heard.'

It was Patrick's turn to fall silent. He started to breathe more heavily. He reached out for the bottle. He unscrewed the top very slowly. He did not want her to hear it.

'Patrick?'

'Yes.'

'Think about it.'

'I am thinking about it. I will think about it.'

'The other thing you could do, I've just thought of this, is write it down as if you're the other man. Imagine you're PB2. See what you come up with.'

His fingers stopped turning. He sat up straight on the sofa.

'You reckon?'

'Yes.'

'Really?'

'You're a writer, Patrick, and a bloody good one. It might help you to work it all out. Put yourself in his shoes . . . The wallet, the petrol, even the photos.'

'Become the bastard?'

'Yes. It may not be that difficult.'

Patrick laughed soundlessly.

29

Patrick stood alone on the stage of Old Big School. Sceptical as ever of the sound system, he checked the microphone and then waited until the hall fell completely silent. He looked at the assembled company. He had written no speech.

'You will have noticed that Mr Falconer is not with me on the stage this morning. He is in hospital. Mr Falconer is the last man to want me to tell you but I think you ought to know. A few weeks ago I told you about Winston Churchill in 1953. I told you that he showed the greatest courage not only throughout the war but also in how he faced his health crisis. He saw it as another hurdle, perhaps as another invading army which needed to be repelled. Later today I am going to see a man who faces another test of his own courage. You can be sure that Mr Falconer too will never give in. He does not back away. I hope you would wish me to send him all your best wishes. I have placed by the door a stack of Get Well cards. Would you, if you wish to, before you rush off to first lesson, please put your signature on one of the cards as you go out. You may be already grateful to him. You may already have stood outside his door. That does not matter. This is a school, not the Second World War. Whether you know it or not you have all benefited from the attention and the example which he brings every day and every term to this place. He has never missed a school event, a concert or a match. And in the holidays he is here, ensuring everything is properly set up for the next term, checking that all the new educational initiatives are given every chance of success and are properly administered. He always puts himself last and you first. And after you leave he will follow all your careers with real interest. For me he has been a model of straightness and dedication. In all schools there are some quite outstanding men and women on the teaching staff. No man ever cared for this school, for each and every one of you, more than Mr Falconer did – and does. He won't give in. So don't relax. Because he will be back.'

As Patrick walked down from the stage and out they all applauded. Standing outside Old Big School, while they all drifted off to first lesson, he looked at the notice boards of forthcoming events. Rehearsals for the Carol Service. Two new plays in the theatre. Arts Society. Water Polo Final. In the reflection in the glass he saw her standing just behind him.

'Dad.'

'Hello, Alice.'

He turned to face her.

'I've taken the book back. The Poe.'

'Thanks. What got you on to him?'

'Mr Stuart, he likes Poe, he often mentions him.'

'Oh really.'

'So I thought I'd better read some.'

'Which ones did you read?'

'To be honest, I didn't. Haven't had time.'

'I know the feeling.'

She looked at the doors to Old Big School. 'Never heard you like that before.'

'Haven't you?'

'It was good. Different from your usual.'

'Oh well, there you go. Dress rehearsal tonight I see.'

'Yes.'

'Good luck.'

'Got to dash.'

'Alice.'

She turned, her voice irritated. 'Yes?'

'Go and see Granny sometime, won't you? Just for ten minutes.'

'Has she mentioned it again?'

'Yes. She loves it when you call in.'

Michael was in a private room of his own at the end of the corridor on the second floor of the Kingswood. There was a drip tucked into his dorsum, a plastic strip around his wrist and a smell of clean linen. A small trolley, with a few cards and a large jug of water, stood at the side of his bed.

'How are you?'

'Fine.'

'Really?'

'Really. And it's nice of you to come, Patrick.'

'You know me, Michael, always glad to get out of the hard work.'

Michael's brow darkened a touch and he waved a hand as if to say please play the game, headmaster, no need for that, no need for that here, not now.

'Do pull up a chair. And move those papers on to the trolley.'

Patrick did as he was told, and put the package he was carrying on the floor. He pulled the seat a little closer to

Michael's bed. Michael had a crumb sticking to the corner of his mouth.

'You seem nicely set up here,' Patrick said. 'More like a hotel than a hospital.'

'Can't complain.'

'TV, a view, the lot.'

'I suppose it's what I've paid for all these years.'

'So, it went well?'

Michael's face was unyielding. 'That's what they tell me. It's all gone with the surgeon's knife.'

'Good.'

'And I'll be out of here and back in the saddle in no time.'

'How have your nights been?'

'Sleep's never been a problem with me, I drop off all the time.'

As well as the cards and the flowers Patrick's eye caught Michael's green suit on a hanger and his brogues and the frayed Hawks Club tie. And a pile of papers. There was a pile of school papers with his biro balanced on top of them.

'Michael, that's not school stuff, is it?'

'What?'

'That.'

'I know, Headmaster, I know.'

'But you really mustn't.'

'But I'm bored already. Terribly bored. I have to do something.'

'You really really mustn't. If we don't watch you, you'll have exercise books in here next.'

'You got rid of exercise books, Headmaster.'

'Did I? When did I do that?'

'Years ago. Along with the dais. No, just joking. But don't worry about the work, it's what I do, Patrick. It's all

I've got, isn't it? One hundred and seven years, man and boy. That's what they say about me, isn't it?'

'Don't be silly.'

But it was what they said. It was what Patrick said.

'But I'll tell you one thing, Patrick, I misjudged that Solomon boy.'

'Did you?'

'He's just sent me the loveliest letter. It's funny how the rogues, the ones you fight the hardest, often do the unexpectedly nice things.'

'That's true.'

'Though I would stop short of saying that Hugo is basically a nice person.'

'I wouldn't stop short of saying he's a swine.'

'Perhaps you're right. Who knows? But do thank Caroline for her card.'

'I will.'

He didn't even know she'd sent one.

'So, is the old place falling apart without me?'

'But of course.'

'How are things, how's morale?'

Morale was one of Michael's words. *Michael and his morale* was one of Patrick's pet hates. The phrase annoyed Patrick to hell and back. But looking at him lying there, his lips swollen and the hairs white on his chiselled, unshaven chin, how could any of that annoy him now?

'Morale's generally OK . . . ish, I think. Considering.'

Patrick could hardly say his own morale was all over the ocky and at an all-time low. He could hardly say his mind was more often out there than right here. He could hardly say I need your help, Michael. No, he had to talk about everyday things at school. He pictured the school list and the calendar and rewound the last few days and said:

'The Save the Children concert went pretty well.'

'Good, good. How much did we make?'

'Over two thousand pounds.'

'Marvellous. Have to say the choir's never been better.'

'Sorry you had to miss the visit to Goldsmiths' Hall. I know you always enjoy that.'

'Never mind, can't be helped. And the Junior Scholarship, how did the marking go?'

'Fine, no problems as far as I know . . . What else? Oh, yes, we won the fencing.'

All the tubes and bags and bottles in the room started to jump.

'Excellent! We *won*? We beat Eton?'

'Michael, be careful, you'll pull that thing out.'

Michael banged the bed with his other hand. His reading glasses fell off the blankets. As Patrick picked them up Michael was still going:

'*That is* the best news I've heard for weeks. What an effort! I knew we'd fight back. The first time for twenty-three years.'

Patrick smiled. There wasn't a trace of irony in the old bugger.

'I thought you'd be pleased.'

'Pleased? That's put a spring in my step, that'll help my flow. And how's Daffers?'

'Oh, keeping us all in line.'

'Give her my love, won't you?'

'I certainly will. And the governors want you to know, Michael, that you'll be on full pay for as long as all this takes. You mustn't hurry back.'

'No, don't think for one minute you're getting rid of me that easily. I'll be darkening your doors only too soon, I'm already wolfing my food. You ask the nurses.'

Patrick bent down again, this time to reach under his chair. 'In fact, I've got a little something for you.'

Michael looked taken aback and very shy, like a little boy sensing a treat. 'Oh, you shouldn't have. What on earth can it be?'

'It's not very original, I'm afraid.'

Michael smiled stolidly: 'Sounds just the thing for me then.'

Patrick handed over the large package. Michael fumbled on the bed, found his reading glasses and put them on the end of his nose. He started to unwrap it, very carefully, as if he was going to save the paper for another day. As he pulled off the last of the soft white tissue his eyelids fluttered and he paled and clenched his teeth to control his quivering lips. He then, looking confused, took out the cards. When he opened his eyes he averted them but reached out and pressed Patrick's arm. Patrick put his hand over Michael's.

'I wasn't sure if you would like it. I didn't really know what to get.'

'It's . . . not only is it what I need, it's what I've always wanted.'

'I'm so pleased.'

'As for the cards . . . I'll read them later.'

At that second there was a belly laugh outside the door and the nurse, a large redhead, clomped in. Patrick moved slightly away. Inside the room the nurse was still laughing at some private joke. Her face was entirely open.

'Are you all right, Mr Falconer?'

'Fine, thank you.'

'Back rest all right?'

'Perfect.'

'Keeping up your fluids?'

She looked assessingly at him. In response to her gaze Michael suddenly declaimed in a melodramatic way as if he were at a Christmas party:

'*Every day*
In every way
I'm getting better and better.
That's what Emile-the-froggie-Coué used to say, nurse.'

'Emile who? Who's he?'

'A Frenchman. It's now called auto-suggestion, of course, the power of your mind, the holistic bit, telling yourself you're getting better, and I am.'

'No more pains?'

'Just a twinge, nurse, nothing more.'

'Oooh, *what is this*?'

'I've just been given it.'

'It's beautiful. It really is.'

'It is, isn't it? My old briefcase had given up the ghost; well, to be honest, it had become something of a joke with my colleagues.'

The nurse was stroking the leather. 'It's the softest leather. Just feel it, better than my handbag, cost a bomb I bet. And what's this here?'

'My initials, woven into a crest.'

'It's beautifully done.'

'That's the school where I work. Where the headmaster, Mr Balfour here, where he and I *both* work.'

The nurse smiled and nodded at Patrick before spotting Michael's red eyes.

'But you're not getting too tired, are you? You are, you know.'

Patrick left the bedside and walked over to the window, promising, 'I'll be off in a minute, nurse. I mustn't stay too long.'

Behind him the nurse busied around the bed a bit, straightening this, looking at his charts, checking this and that.

'Anything I can get you, Mr Falconer?'

'No, thanks.'

She cheerily moved out, saying she'd be back shortly.

From the window Patrick could see a jackdaw perched on a chimney. He could almost see the end of the street where his mother lived, where his immobile mother would be squinnying through the gloom at the birds and the squirrels. Then there were the big office blocks and the warehouses along the river, and – somewhere out there – the man who was trying to destroy him.

'It's a splendid view, isn't it?' Michael said, his voice back to normal.

'Yes, it is.'

Patrick turned round to face Michael. There was now a pulse, a sense of expectancy in the atmosphere.

'Michael, may I tell you something in confidence?'

'Of course. Do sit down.'

'The nurse won't be angry with me if I stay a little bit longer?'

'No, her bark's worse than her bite.'

'And at least I'll be keeping you away from your marking.'

Michael smiled. 'I'd be delighted if you stayed.'

'Really?'

'Really.'

'Because it's a bit personal, to tell you the truth.'

'I hope I've always been considered reliable, Patrick.'

'Well, the thing is, Michael, over the last three or four weeks, in fact since 5 November . . .'

And Patrick told him, told him man to man, as he had told Liz (man to woman), as late one night (woman to girl) Caroline had told Alice, told him everything, including and in particular, his suspicions of Casey Cochrane, Euan Stuart and Max Russell-Jones. And the question above all that he would like Michael to address, when he felt up to it, distasteful though no doubt it would be to him, the issue he would like Michael to focus on, if he wouldn't mind, was whether any of them could conceivably, as it were, be in what you might call the frame, whether any of them had it in him to do this, to carry it all out, or had any of them ever done anything that Michael knew about that he Patrick did not, or was there perhaps someone else, someone he had not thought of, because the busier and the more out of touch one got as a head it was only too easy to become absorbed in one's own political world and not to pick up the vibes. It's most unfair of me to be asking this, and you may feel it's a bit of cheek, given that we have not always seen eye to eye, but that is where I am now.

All Michael said was, 'Good grief.' And then, 'Goodness me. I saw something similar on TV. Not long ago. How to steal someone's identity, how it's done.'

'There's a lot of it about.'

'Wasn't there something in the papers too?'

'Was there?'

'About some Nigerians running identity fraud in London on a huge scale?'

'I didn't see that.'

'You haven't appointed any Nigerians lately, have you?'

'Don't think I have, not recently.'

Patrick stood up and paced around, paced around the small private ward in much the same way he did in his spacious study. As he glanced over it was clear that while he had been talking Michael had become increasingly uncomfortable.

'I'm sorry to hit you with this, Michael, but I have almost come to the end of the road.'

'I'm not surprised. The pressure must be intolerable.'

'So, what do you think?'

Michael was now red in the face, if not distressed.

'On balance I think it's best if I give you a ring in a couple of hours. I don't want to jump the gun on this one.'

'Fine.'

'And also I'm afraid the pressure on me has become intolerable. I've simply got to have a pee. Or at least see if anything down there is still working. What we in the trade call bladder irrigation.'

He was holding on to himself, gathering himself, and struggling to get out of bed.

'I'm so sorry, I shouldn't have stayed. But you have my mobile number?'

'No. Jot it on that bit of paper, would you?'

Patrick scribbled it and hurried out.

30

On leaving the hospital, Patrick did something he now rarely did. Indeed, in these late November days he was increasingly doing things that he rarely did. This time he followed his feet up Peter's Hill into St Paul's Cathedral. It was not his body. He was watching it go up the wide west steps of St Paul's and paying his entrance fee and refusing the offer of the audio headphone guide and letting someone else do the walking down the nave and looking up at the Whispering Gallery, and all this without giving in to his internal policeman who was getting into his ear with his oh come on, Patrick, this isn't some naff intimations of mortality moment, is it, we're not lighting a candle and having some post-hospital religious flush here, are we, or perhaps even saying a little prayer for Michael?

Say a little prayer for you.

Aretha Franklin song, isn't it?

Shut up.

He walked on, a little thing in the corner of himself, looking around. There was no Handel or Bach reverberating around the nave. Instead, a woman priest's voice, taped by the sound of it, broke in, echoing from high on every pillar. The woman priest's voice asked in a very very very slow voice if all those in the cathedral would care to pause to pause in their daily lives in their daily lives, to be still for a moment in this busy world in this busy world, and to reflect to reflect, and to join together, and to say, in whatever language you choose, The Lord's Prayer.

All around him Patrick watched and listened to this happen. *And forgive us our trespasses, as we forgive those who trespass against us. And lead us not into temptation . . .*

He couldn't agree more, temptation he did not need, and his body wandered off, pausing, strolling, sitting, reflecting, thinking of Michael and the moment their hands touched by his bedside. His eye caught a plaque.

Patrick looked again.

In the 1690s, there was an organist at St Paul's called J. Clark. Indeed J. Clark, it seemed, was one of the cathedral's very first organists. Not Joseph Clark. Jeremiah Clark, but even so.

Move on.

Patrick's eye was now arrested by another plaque. *To the memory of George M Smith March 19 1824 April 6 1901 to whom English Literature owes the Dictionary of National Biography.*

J. Clark *and the* DNB.

Could he never escape from all this? Even in the cathedral he was being pursued.

Communion was about to begin so Patrick went down to the crypt, something he had not done since he was a child. When he was a seven-year-old boy he walked round the crypt holding his mother's hand and she had pointed out England's heroes to her bright little button. Perhaps his love of history began in this very place.

And that, Patrick, his mother said, bending down to his eye level, is Nelson's tomb, and he was a hero at Trafalgar, he had a missing arm, well, no, he didn't have a missing arm because the whole point was his arm was missing, he didn't have his arm at all, anyway you know what I mean, and when Nelson's funeral was held at St Paul's neither his wife nor the woman he loved was there, they weren't even allowed in to the cathedral for the service, what do you think of that, doesn't that tell you a lot, don't treat your women like that when you grow up, will you? What was that, darling? Oh yes, Patrick, a man can love his wife and another woman but we don't want to talk about that at the moment. And that tomb? That tomb over there is Wellington's, and he was a hero, and that is Florence Nightingale, and she, you'll notice, is the only woman allowed down here, and why do you think that might be . . .

Patrick half-stumbled on an uneven flagstone, and stopped. He felt giddy. His head was ringing. There, round the next arch, was a bust of W. E. Henley.

'This,' Patrick said out loud, 'is getting ridiculous. First it's J. Clark and then it's the *DNB* and now it's Henley.'

The bearded Henley looked straight at Patrick. I know you, Patrick Balfour, he said, I know you only too well. I am the Henley on whom Robert Louis Stevenson based his Long John Silver. Louis took great liberties with me in *Treasure Island*, and so did you in *Silver*. You should not take liberties with friends. Friends are far too precious. Friends . . .

Friends . . . old friends . . .
One sees how it ends.
A woman looks
Or a man lies,
And the pleasant brooks
And the quiet skies,
Ruined with brawling

290

And caterwauling,
Enchant no more
As they did before.
And so it ends
With friends.

Patrick stared at Henley as he recited the poem: the
bearded W. E. Henley, bloody but unbowed, Stevenson's
great friend and collaborator, the irascible Henley who
Patrick had been for two years, the Gloucester poet who
accused Fanny Osborne, Stevenson's wife, of plagiarism, an
accusation that brought a bitter end to the friendship.

Patrick steadied himself, fearful he was about to fall. It's
just tiredness, he said to himself, that's all. It's just the strain,
and the lack of sleep. Breathe deeply and your head will
clear. Breathe deeply and you'll be fine. See it as no more
than a bit of jet lag.

*Is it any less difficult to judge of a good man or a half-good
man, than of the worst criminal at the bar? And may not each
have relevant excuses?*

But his head was not clearing. His head was getting
worse. And everywhere that Patrick, a good man and a
half-good man, looked in the crypt, whichever way he
turned, he could see them gathering: Stevenson and
Henley and Fanny Osborne.

After all, as he knew only too well, Patrick The Writer
had but to drink the cup, to swallow the drug of unre-
strained storytelling, and he could leave behind his
respectable desk and indulge a career of crime, let slip the
animal within, tear off all his constraints as Liz tore off his
clothes, tore off his clothes to the sound of Oscar
Peterson's piano, if he swallowed the drug he could meta-
morphose and make love or make war, rape or kill,
describe non-liable lust, change sex, change century, scroll

291

down the menu of myth and memory, suck in any sensation, assume any thick cloak, take on any number of protean identities, become one or two or more, be as many people as he liked, be the humble fly on the wall or the dreadful shipwreck or an omniscient god, exempt himself from any responsibility, appropriate any reach of unequalled glory or vicious depravity, recast history, create new lives or put words they never spoke into dead men's mouths, and, if need be, promise penitence for all this –

In the crypt they moved forward towards him.

Did he himself have any *relevant excuses*?

Rodin and Camille Claudel were there too, his later creations coming on to his stage like Banquo's line. They were looking at Patrick, all five of them. He knew them all so well. He knew their secrets. But the days when he had the whip hand with these characters were now past. He knew what was going on. They had come to demand the final reckoning, to say how dare you, *how dare you*, Patrick Balfour, who the hell do you think you are?

Each face in the crypt, each body, each eye was familiar. Each eye was levelled at Patrick. He closed his eyes. He opened them. Justin Pett was now standing next to Rodin, tapping his silver-handled stick on the stone floor.

Cool though it was in the crypt, Patrick's face was now clammy with sweat. He wanted to steal quietly away from them as they all gathered together and formed up and moved forward towards him like a Greek chorus, a chorus with an individual and a collective complaint to make. But Patrick could not move. He tried to, but Justin Pett, the spokesman, stepped forward and his voice came out of all the speakers in the cathedral.

And he said

For a hypocrite to be a writer is a wonderful calling: to tell the truth by falsehoods. You, Patrick Balfour, shamelessly take people's private property and their private parts and make out they're your own. But it's all too easy putting words into the mouths of real people, entering their heads and their beds, unbidden and unwelcome. Why don't you come up with something out of your own imagination? You should write something original, instead of making real people – those who are dead and can no longer object – say something they never said but which it suits your purposes to have them say. You're misappropriating the funds of the past, Patrick. And all, if I may say so, my dear, without a by-your-leave. Talk about taking liberties!

And don't think you can run away like that.

Yes, you are, you're about to run away, and not only that, you're about to fall back on your safety net. You're thinking Shakespeare, aren't you? You're thinking why can't I do it if Shakespeare did it. He did it all the time. He borrowed this, he borrowed that, he nicked this character and that plot, this Proteus Clark of poets, this Egyptian Proteus, this honey bee was always appropriating his sources, changing inconvenient dates, sucking here and there, annexing history, being everyone and no one, taking liberties left right and centre, I am not what I am, inhabiting other lives, putting his words in their mouths, and because he *had* to be someone, he had to be someone else *to see*. He had to be someone else to fulfil himself. Yes, we know the standard defence, we know all that, Patrick, we've all read Borges' *Labyrinths*, it's all there. We've watched Mike Yarwood being other people, we've watched Rory Bremner being other people. *They clap, therefore I am.*

Patrick looked at his accusers as they moved even closer, tightening the noose around him in the crypt. Their eyes were nailing him down, pressing in on him. Patrick backed away. His legs began to unlock. He turned and his stride

293

began to quicken, then he hurried headlong from their eyes, their nailing eyes, his feet hard on the flagstones, and he bounded up the stone staircase of the crypt two steps at a time, and he started to run full-tilt down the middle of the cathedral nave.

Attendants moved to intercept him but he eluded them. He side-stepped left and he swerved right, kicking over a pile of prayer books. Bemused tourists in headphones stood aside. Worshippers stared, appalled. It was a shocking sight. An old woman, praying, turned with her mouth open to watch the tall man in the dark suit running full-tilt past her and out, out of the west door and down the wide flight of steps into the foggy dusk and the diesel air.

Patrick ran to escape his mind but his mind had no trouble with the pace his legs had set, and soon overtook him.

31

The taxi circled the square and turned into Finley Place. Patrick let himself into number 64 and wiped his shoes. Even though his head was flickering with visions, it hit him, as it always did, how grand the curving staircase was. The curving staircase sobered him. He tried to work it all out. It was as if he had never been there before. It seemed unreal. Was this sort-of grand place really *his* home? Yes, because this part of town was sort-of grand; it was the London of museums and minor embassies, a place of wide pavements and black railings and flag poles and Mercedes parking down the middle of the road.

'Hell-o! Caroline!'

He started to climb. His feet felt twice as heavy as usual. They felt like someone else's feet. Like his mother's.

'Caroline?'

She called down, 'I'm on the phone. Come on up.'

He went on up. And that is Caroline over there, my wife Caroline, my beautifully dressed wife Caroline talking to a customer, and she turned and waved hi to him as he went into the sitting room. It also hit him, as it always did, how grand the sitting room was. High ceilings, huge armchairs, glass-cased cabinets, big fireplace, little polished tables and Vivaldi's Cello Concerto playing so quietly and so discreetly in the background: Vivaldi through the keyhole.

Patrick looked into their sitting room. Her sitting room. Effectively he had gone: *you're a goner, Patrick. In every sense, you've gone.*

That is Caroline over there, that is my wife Caroline in the corner at her small walnut desk, the small desk from which she conducts her ever-expanding OTT business. He kissed her on the top of her head, rather in the way he kissed his mother. She smiled and nodded that she had noticed the kiss on the top of her head and went on listening to her client, her fingers flicking between a quick doodle and a quick pencil sketch of a well-designed garden.

In the kitchen Patrick checked in with Daphne to tell her where he was, to see if all was well at school, and to send her Michael's love. His mouth felt dry. He found a pint glass, ran the tap in the sink until the water was properly cold, filled it and gulped it down. He stared at the oven display panel flashing. Still thirsty, he made himself a cup of tea and took an apple from the bowl. By the look of the fridge Caroline had bought some red mullet for her supper. A little salad and some red mullet. Watching her figure, as ever.

High above the patio at the back, in the space between two rooftops, a plane lowered its way across the London sky towards Heathrow. He munched the apple and stroked the circle of smooth pebbles Caroline had arranged on the side windowsill, the grey and blue pebbles picked up by Jamie and Alice one Easter afternoon on a Norfolk beach. He was not the same man as the man who was on that beach. More to the point, was he the man who had been in St Paul's that afternoon? Had the headmaster Patrick

Balfour really run out of the cathedral like that? He was not sure. Yes, he was. Yes, he had.

Both sides of me were in deadly earnest.

They were fraternising and fighting.

Ten minutes later and no further forward, with Caroline still doodling and still talking to her client, Patrick carried his second cup of tea into their bedroom. Some constraint, some sense that he needed permission, made him stop in the doorway. The bedroom looked like a photograph in a glossy magazine: expensive, perfect, sexless. This was now her space, her room and her room only. The king-size bed, with a bedspread he had never seen before, with a new blue bedspread, was immaculate. On her bedside table was a bottle of Migral.

He backed out and crossed to Alice's room. Far from the usual Alice bedroom scene he found this also neat and tidy, so much so there seemed little evidence that it was a room in which his daughter was now sleeping and working. It didn't feel right. Yes, he was glad to see Rabbit and Kanga propped upright on her pillow waiting for her return, as they always had been, but where were the wet towels lying on the wooden floor and where was the dressing gown abandoned inside out on an unmade bed?

He went in. There was precious little evidence of any academic work of any kind. On the mantelpiece she had propped up some ink drawings, quite striking ones of herself. He had not seen these before.

His eyes could not focus. Patrick picked up the drawings and took a closer look. No, it was all right, he could see clearly now.

Were they self-portraits or were they the work of a friend in the Art School? The Art School – as Patrick Balfour the headmaster was pleased to tell all his prospective parents –

was now a much livelier place, with life classes each Tuesday after school, with a male and female model on alternate weeks. Such a good thing for the boys and the girls to sit together drawing the nude body. Don't you agree? Oh, yes, headmaster, it would never have happened in my day.

And these portraits of Alice were certainly high quality. They were bold and unfussy and confident. The eyes and cheek bones were excellent. They were her. The face was thoughtful. The face was strangely absorbed. This Alice, this daughter of his, was very much her own person. If they were ever framed he would love to have one of these drawings in his study. There was no signature he could find in the bottom corner. He turned them over. Nothing on the back either.

By the way the mirrors on her dressing table were arranged − arranged so that you could see yourself from all angles − the portraits could well have been done by Alice herself. Yes, she had done them! Of course she had, his clever Alice had done them. And the longer he looked at the drawings the better they seemed, though the face struck him more as the woman she would one day grow to be rather than the seventeen-year-old she now was. He put the drawings back on the mantelpiece.

Patrick took his shoes off and walked round in his socks. His feet felt the knots in the wood and the rugs and the uneven floorboards. He looked down on the street, then turned round, moved Rabbit and Kanga over a bit, and slumped back on the pillows. Alice. In her white socks and little shoes as she walked off to primary school. Reading *Peter Rabbit and Benjamin Bunny* to her. Oh, those rabbits. Those naughty rabbits. They'll get into trouble. They'll be caught in Mr McGregor's garden. They're mischievous, aren't they? What does mischievous mean, Daddy? Up to no good, being naughty. Are you up to no good, Alice? Are you, Daddy?

The digital clock radio winked at Patrick. Patrick hated digital clock radios. He wanted to go to sleep but knew he must not. He did not want Caroline to find him asleep before they had spoken. He wanted to ring Liz and tell her what happened in the crypt but if he phoned her now he knew he would be punished. That's how it worked. If he had moved from his place by Caroline's bed in the labour ward when she was giving birth to the baby Jamie or the baby Alice, so soon to be seen for the first time, Patrick believed the child would be damaged in some terrible way. Dreading any deformities, he did not budge.

'Not been opening any drawers, I hope.'

'No, Caroline, not this time.'

He stood up and gave her a hug.

'You're sure?'

'Sure. How's business?'

'Crazy, completely crazy. I'm booked up until March.'

'That's what we like to hear.'

'Sorry to be so long on the phone, she just wouldn't stop.'

'Sounds like some of my worst parents.'

'And I've got a headache coming on.'

'Have you? I should have rung you to say I was coming.'

'You don't have to ring to visit your own home, do you?'

'Of course I don't. I was just . . . being friendly. Just . . . That's all.'

He flapped his hand. His heart sank. Why was it always like this? Why, in whatever mood he tried to start things, why was it always like this?

'Just been to see Michael in the Kingswood.'

'How is he?'

'He's fine and he loved your card. Thanks for thinking of that. Are you free for the next hour or so?'

'I've got to go and see someone, I'm afraid; it could be quite a big commission.'

'Where's that?'

'The Fulham Road. Just off.'

'Fine, just a thought. I'll lie down for a bit, if that's OK.'

'Don't be silly; of course it's OK.'

But Patrick jumped up and walked over to the mantelpiece. 'Did she draw these?'

'No, she's not that good.'

'You always said she was.'

'No, I didn't.'

'You did.'

'I said she was good, which she is, but not that good, and I doubt she's been to much art this year.'

'Why not?'

Caroline's voice suddenly rose. 'Because it's all drama drama drama, isn't it? And when she's not acting on stage she's acting up here.'

'It's like that, is it?'

'Yes, it is like that.'

Patrick told himself to breathe in. Breathe out. And start again.

'So. So, who did do the drawings?'

'Safer not to ask.'

'Why?'

'No, why not, *you* ask her if you like, because if I do she'll only have a go at me for prying.'

'Is it that bad?'

'Yes.'

'I see. Well, I expect you're right, leave well alone.'

Caroline folded her arms. 'Oh I'm right all right, she's behaving appallingly.'

300

'Really?'

'Absolutely appallingly. She's rude to me, she flounces in and out, God knows who she thinks she is. Whenever I ask her to help she either says she'll do it later and never does, or she storms off. The sooner this bloody play is over the better. I'm absolutely sick to death of it.'

'Seventeen-year-old girls, eh?'

Caroline swirled round. 'It's nothing to do with girls. Or boys. Why do boys drink until they fall over? Why do boys break wing mirrors off cars? Why do boys say they've slept with more girls than they have? Why do boys under-achieve at GCSE? Why don't boys shower more often? Why don't boys −'

'Yes, yes, OK, Caroline, got it.'

'So spare me the seventeen-year-old bit. And spare me how difficult it is for a girl to grow up with two such busy parents. There are lots of seventeen-year-old girls who do not behave like our daughter. I go round to lots of homes and meet lots of people with busy lives who have delight-ful seventeen-year-olds, and don't tell me that's because they're putting their best foot forward in front of other people, because Alice wouldn't know which was her best foot even if she tripped over it.'

Caroline, her eyes blazing, her face red, her arms crossed, was now moving metronomically back and forth at the end of the bed.

'OK, Caroline, OK.'

'Because sometimes, as in right now, I don't like her one little bit. I do not like my daughter Alice. How does that sound? Sometimes I wish she'd just go. And just leave me alone!'

Caroline stopped and put both hands on her head and closed her eyes. Patrick repositioned Kanga and Rabbit. Then she was off again, backwards and forwards.

301

'And when she is here she's giggling on the phone with that Hugo boy. D'you know what my last phone bill was? £325, £3 – 2 – 5. And that is not my business line, and you know what, I'm going to leave her a note telling her she's not having any more new clothes because she's a spoilt, conceited brat.'

They sat in silence. Patrick asked,

'Is she seeing much of . . . Hugo Solomon?'

'Ask her yourself. All I know is they read bits out of books to each other and think it's all terribly funny. At my expense.'

'How long have they been doing that?'

'Don't ask me, ask her.'

'Oh well . . . I don't know . . . I saw her this morning . . . she seemed OK.'

'You probably saw her for ten seconds.'

'Look . . . perhaps she'd better come and spend some time with me.'

'Good. Excellent idea. Agreed. I'm all for it. You fix it. I'm off.' She noisily closed the window shutters.

'Caroline.'

'I mean every word.'

'Before you go.'

'What?'

'I've had more . . . more of those letters.'

She turned round. 'Have you?'

'Very nasty ones. And I've sent them all to the detective.'

'How awful. How awful for you.'

'They're on the same lines, only more disturbing. And I'm no further forward. Well, not much.'

'All you can do is tell the police, Patrick. That's all you can do. It really is.'

'I just said I have done.'

'They'll be working on it. And they're the ones who

should be moving forwards not you. You've got a huge job to do without playing the detective yourself.'

'That's what . . . no, no, you're right.'

'That's what what? You were going to say something.'

'No, it's nothing.'

'I wish I could have been more of a help, Patrick. I really do.'

Patrick heard his mouth say: 'No, no, that's fine, you've obviously got more than enough on your plate as it is. Anyway, you'd better be off, and good luck with your client.'

She looked at her watch. 'Yes, I suppose I'd better.'

'Glad it's all going so well on that score at least. And I hope the headache doesn't get any worse.'

'Even if it does it'll go. It always does.'

'And we'll meet up just before the play? On Thursday. It's seven-thirty.'

Caroline nodded grimly. 'I suppose so. Yes, of course we will. I'll be there.'

'And about Alice; look, we did what we thought best, didn't we, we did what we thought best with both the children, didn't we?'

'We did what you wanted, Patrick.'

Words failed him.

32

With his shirt off Patrick was shinning up to the very tip of a phallic column. It was a Doric colonnade. He made it and looked across the mountains of Greece. He was at Delphi with Viola. Suntanned, she was lying far below on the altar at the Temple of Athena, writing something in her diary, writing to her hero-worshipping brother. From high up on the column, with his eagle's eye view, Patrick could see not only the whole archaeological site but also the exact words she was writing. She wrote, Dear Rory, Well, here I am at Delphi, with Patrick The Oracle. Patrick fell off the column but he was caught by the sound of his mobile phone and landed safely on the spongy grass of Alice's bed. He found his phone on the pillow just behind Kanga.

It was Michael.

'Patrick, sorry to be so long.'

'How did you get on?'

'Best pee I've had in quite some while. Most encouraging.'

'Excellent.'

'On the other matter, is it all right to talk?'

'Of course.'

'I'm not interrupting?'

'No, not at all.'

'You sound a bit muzzy.'

'Well, to be honest I was on the bed.'

'Really?'

'Alone.'

'Jolly good, no harm done then. It's just that I hate telephones when it's personal but I'm sure you don't want to drag yourself over here all over again.'

Patrick swung his feet over the side of Alice's bed. He licked his dry lips. 'I'll happily come to see you tomorrow if you'd prefer.'

'No, let's get it out of the way. Perhaps if we do it like the Reading Competition? Working up from the bottom, if you'll pardon the expression?'

The man was incorrigible.

'Bottom up it is, Michael.'

'Have to say I've rather enjoyed it, doing a bit of P. D. James. She's my kind of thing, by the way.'

'P. D. James?'

'Yes, closed community, Church of England, English middle class, know where you stand, and at least they know how to speak. I can't understand a word some of those Scottish chappies write. Is P. D. J. your cup of tea, Patrick?'

'I hear she's very good.'

'Right, are you ready?'

'Yes. Fire away.'

With the phone to his ear, Patrick started to walk around the bedroom. He looked at his watch. It was more than an hour since Caroline had left. By the time Michael finished the call Patrick, listening intently, had walked in and out of every elegant room in Finley Place.

'First of all, then, the non-starter. That is Max Russell-Jones. Not my favourite man, as you know, and he roundly dislikes you, as *you* know, perhaps with some cause, and he's literary enough to have done all this and more, much more, the man's read everything, but no. It's beneath him. He is also a man who will take no risks. He is clever enough to have got any number of jobs, but he's stayed, *and* he's taken on the library. Also the fear of being caught would stop him, I'm sure of that. He has an aesthetic distaste for any kind of lowlife. He'd love to see you fall, there's little doubt about that as we know from your . . . previous trouble, but he wouldn't risk his neck to bring it about. And the point is this man is going to be caught. The police will get him.'

Patrick, now in the kitchen, poured himself a glass of water. 'What makes you so sure of that, Michael?'

'Sure the police will get him or sure it's not Max Russell-Jones?'

'Sure the police will get him.'

'Because he wants to be caught.'

'Interesting. A friend of mine said exactly that.'

'Ah, so I'm not the only one you've taken into your confidence.'

'You've recovered very quickly from the anaesthetic, Michael.'

'I'm a rugger bugger, remember. And at number two, well, equal second really, I have –'

'If there are only three, Michael, these must be equal *first*.'

'Bear with, would you. At joint number two we have Casey and Euan. There's a case – no, wrong word – there's an argument it's more likely to be Casey, because of his involvement in Soho. He's always struck me as a grubby little man and I have very little doubt he's into pornography and I'd never have appointed him in a month of Sundays, as you may remember.'

'I do remember, Michael. And you were right.'

Patrick saw a badly bent paperback half-tucked down the side of the sofa. He pulled it out. *The Collected Poems of Edward Thomas.*

'Thank you for saying so, Patrick. I think I was. I think he has a twisted mind, a dark side. Mind you, I'm prejudiced. In my book anyone who spends all day and every day staring at a screen is in one way or another defective. It makes you dysfunctional. So, yes, I think Casey is up to no good, I see him looking at dirty pictures, but I don't see him getting into your flat with a camera and a boy.'

'He could have used an accomplice. Paid someone to do it. The Hugo Solomon type.'

'He could.'

With his free hand Patrick was gently bending the Edward Thomas back into shape.

'Michael, when you say you see him looking at dirty pictures I assume you –'

'Good Lord, I was speaking figuratively. I didn't mean I've actually been leaning over his shoulder in the computer centre.'

'But you are sure about the porn?'

'As sure as I can be.'

'Any proof?'

'Not that I want to share with you, but it comes from a friend in the Common Room who's as good with computers as Casey is. I put him on to Casey's tail a month ago. No doubt about it. But the point is Casey is practically illiterate, you only have to read his end of term reports to see that, no grasp of language at all, described a boy as reactionary when he meant rebellious, doesn't understand full stops and can't spell. Furthermore, he wouldn't even understand those clues. Which brings me to a man who most certainly would know how to torture you with some barbs from literature and would enjoy it.'

'Euan.'

'Indeed, we come to my equal second, Euan Stuart. The dodgiest of the lot in some ways. He makes my skin crawl. I despise the way he appropriates other people's ideas, even friendships.'

'Interesting you should use that word.'

'Friendships?'

'Well, those too maybe, but I was meaning appropriation.'

Phone still to his ear, having circled all the rooms, Patrick was now back where he started. With his free hand he tidied up Alice's crumpled bed. Michael was in full flow.

'Euan is into make-up. He's an excellent mimic, as we all know, and he's cruel. I've seen him doing Alison Knight's walk and making people laugh with it, and anyone who imitates a disabled woman is beneath contempt. We all know he thinks he should be Head of English and you and I know he shouldn't. Indeed, it was generous of you to give him an allowance as the new Head of Drama, not that I think there should even be one.'

'Thank you for that, Michael.'

'You did ask me to be frank, Patrick. Still, let's keep off that. I also think he's a thief. In fact, I know he is.'

'Go on.'

Patrick stopped and rested one arm on the marble mantelpiece, looking at the drawings of Alice as he listened.

'I went for drinks to his house in September, after the beginning-of-term Common Room meeting. I had a bit of a browse. He has lots of books belonging to Glasgow University Library. A few looked very special.'

'Michael, an awful lot of respectable people are guilty on that score.'

'Are they?'

'Yes. On that score probably half the members of the cabinet would go down.'

'Well, if so it's a disgrace and it says all you need to say about the political class, and all of us in academic life should take a stand on it. As far as I'm concerned taking someone's £35 book is just the same as taking £35 from his wallet.'

'Or indeed from a petrol station.'

'Indeed, Headmaster. *And* Euan misappropriates funds from the drama budget.'

'You're sure?'

'I'm sure.'

'Why haven't you mentioned it to me or the bursar?'

'I tried to, Patrick, but you lost your temper with me before I even got to it, and said you wanted to hear no more from me on the drama scene. So I'm afraid I just thought, oh if he's going to be like that then blow it.'

'But you have evidence?'

'Yes. Which I've been through with the bursar. We wanted to be sure before we bothered you with it. Some recent bills and expenses in the drama department just don't make sense. Euan's siphoning off some cash.'

'But you still don't think he did it? Did all that to me?'

'No, sweaty wee man though he is, I don't think he did. No, Euan's a coward, he hasn't got the guts.'

'I think this whole thing, Michael, is terribly cowardly. I don't see it as guts.'

'Even so, no, I've been lying here for an hour thinking about it and Euan's not your man.'

'So who is?'

'Justin Pett.'

Patrick smiled at his daughter's grown-up face on the mantelpiece. 'Michael, you don't think this is now getting a bit personal on your part?'

'I know what you're thinking. No, it's not because of that, but it all fits.'

Patrick started to slip on his shoes. 'May I stop you there for a moment, Michael?'

'Of course.'

'Because I'm afraid you're wrong. I had exactly that suspicion and I've looked into it and that's why I didn't mention him. The thing is, Justin's not even in the country. I've rung him. He hasn't been in England for some months.'

'He told you that, did he, from wherever he is?'

'No, one of his friends answered his phone.'

'One of his ménage, you mean.'

'Friends, ménage, Michael, whatever.'

'They can't even lie straight in bed, people like that.'

'He was very clear about it, and he took my name.'

'Who is he?'

'Whoever answered the phone. He was quite clear that Justin was abroad.'

'So it must have been Justin's double I saw then.'

Patrick stood up with only one shoe on. 'Where did you see him? When?'

'Twice. Once, a few weeks ago, talking to your daughter and Hugo Solomon. And the second time he was poncing his way across the Tottenham Court Road.'

'Where was he talking to Alice and Hugo?'

'Outside the Royal Academy. In the cobbled courtyard there, under the Reynolds statue. I'd gone along with the sixth form to see the Poussin exhibition. Francesca in the art department kindly offered me a spare ticket, and there he was. Didn't have to speak to him, thank God. Mind you, got inside and found he had written the exhibition notes. Yes, he's your man. He could do it, he would enjoy it, he has nothing to lose, and he wouldn't care about the consequences.'

310

'You think he's that bad?'

'Boys, no morals, filthy mind, filthy mouth. In a word, poison.'

'Thank you for all that, Michael.'

Patrick picked up a small bottle of nail varnish off Alice's dressing table. Troubled in a way he could not define, he looked at the colour.

'I hope I haven't upset you. I know Justin's an old friend of yours.'

'No, Michael, you've been most helpful.'

'I don't sense I have been.'

'You most certainly have. Now you get back into bed.'

'I am in bed.'

'Get some rest then. Please.'

'I will.'

'Or I'll feel even more guilty. And thank you again.'

Patrick could feel one of Michael's short speeches coming on.

'No, Patrick, thank *you*. For coming to see me. For the magnificent gift, which I shall treasure as well as use every day, and most of all for taking me into your trust.'

'I'm the one who should be thanking you.'

'As for all those signatures, from the boys and girls . . .'

33

Imagine you're PB2.

Yes, Liz.

You're a writer, aren't you? So imagine you're him.

A current started to run through Patrick's hands. He could see it all. He could see himself sitting at the table, behind a pile of shiny books, his jacket off, his pen at the ready. And he could just as easily stand in the queue and look across at himself sitting behind the same pile of books. He was there in Piccadilly, on the ground floor in Hatchard's, and there was this queue, quite a decent queue, a morale-boosting queue in fact, because no writer likes sitting there waiting to sign while no one turns up. You feel a right prat.

And surprise surprise, most of those who did turn up were women. There were a few men, but mostly they were well-dressed women between thirty-five and fifty. Women Patrick was glad to see. Most of his fan mail, sent on to his home address by his publishers, was from women. Women who immediately used his first name, women who claimed – no, women who *knew* – that Patrick would understand them. Women he did not know and had never met but women who he imagined were married and had the usual number of children and the usual amount of sex but who lived in the hope that there was more to life than that. Women bored with their husbands, with their rich or passingly well-off husbands, their husbands who bought expensive tickets and then fell asleep in the theatre, their overweight husbands who drank too much and watched telly and played golf and never talked about books or ideas or feelings. Women who might suppose that Patrick Balfour was better in bed than their bloke. Women who said they wished their son or daughter was at his school. Because Patrick Balfour would understand my children, and, Patrick, you would understand me.

Patrick could see the man, unshaven, the one with the Belfast accent, the man who was hanging around there a little longer than all the others, standing to one side, pretending to browse, but quite close enough to hear Patrick speak. While trying to look as if he wasn't really part of it all, in fact he was. A fan who didn't want to appear a fan, a fan who thought it was a bit beneath him, somehow a bit naff, to be a fan.

PB1 was watching himself signing the books. PB2 was watching PB1 and waiting for PB1 to sign his copy(ies).

So ten days' growth and a rinse it would have to be, and before those days were up I decided I had to use every hour Watching People. Let him do the Reading People; I'd do the Watching. And where better to watch than in the street? In the street or on the tube or in the pub I gave myself two-minute exercises. Two minutes to see how much I could memorise of a person's looks and habits. I chose anyone at random. This track-suited black man. This harassed white office clerk. This balding husband. Just two minutes. Then I would walk away, doing

313

everything, every gesture, every movement, doing everything exactly as my randomly selected victim had done. Good practice, that's what it was, and if I was going to fix him I had to be good.

On the day of the signing, I cycled along Piccadilly to Hatchard's. I got there hot, sweaty and unshaven. Which was exactly the look I wanted. A bit wild-eyed. I chained my bike and went straight in. He was already signing his books. I had to control myself. I wanted to run at him and hit him with a club. I wanted to finish him off there and then. Smash the fucker's head in. But I stood there and watched the way he signed his name. I watched him from all angles, the way he sat, the hunch of his shoulders. I hated his smile, hated the way he scratched the back of his hand. His posture. The way he touched his chin, as if he was really listening to all those women, the way he touched his chin and nose and ears. He was just as I expected he would be. The photographs, the hours I had studied him on videos had paid off. Expensive shoes, no doubt about that, could even be handmade. His cufflinks, plain gold, possibly with his initials engraved on them. Yes, I'm closer now. On his cufflinks I can just make out the P and the B. Yes. Now I'm only two away, I can clearly see them. PB. His plain tie, his Jermyn Street shirt. Bet it was Jermyn Street he got it. Suit? Possibly tailored, but more likely off the peg. He has a good enough physique to take the suit as it came. He has a good enough body to take women as they came all over him. His jacket was over the back of his chair. I could see the top edge of his wallet. Simple, black leather, and a simple steal.

I joined the queue, a long line of his kind of women, watching him as we wound and shuffled our way slowly towards the great man. Me and a whole lot of women.

Keep cool. Don't get angry. Don't miss a trick, I said to myself, memorise everything.

Sudden panic. Shit. What was my voice? An adrenalin rush to beat all adrenalin rushes. The accent. I hadn't, believe it or not, thought about that. I quickly decided it had to be Leeds or Belfast. If I have to, I can also do Bradford, I can do Bristol/Bristle, Birmingham/Brummie, a passable Geordie and a glottal-stopped Glaswegian. I also do quite a good chainsaw.

As I stood, the next one to have his book (or, in my case, books) signed, I saw him put his hand on the previous woman's arm, just a little friendly touch. Get your dirty hands off her, Balfour.

He saw me notice his touch and he looked at me, man to man, and smiled. I looked away. I handed him the two copies.

'That's very kind,' he said. '*Two* copies. Would you like me to sign both?'

I settled on Van Morrison Belfast. 'Yes, please.'

'Would you like me to put your name as well or just my own?'

For a crazy second I thought about saying please put *for Patrick from Franz Kafka* on one and *for Patrick from Joseph Clark* on the other, but I saved those up for another day.

'Just yours, thank you.'

'OK, no silly messages, just my name.'

He signed. Patrick Balfour. He signed. Patrick Balfour. The pen. The hand. The ink. Both were perfect performances. He did not wear glasses but I could not tell whether he had contacts. Maybe. But I got his hair parting, just to the left of the crown. And his wallet. Hair colour: brown with a little grey at the temples, what they call the distinguished look, touched with what the journos call a bit of gravitas, a look weighted by a bit of ballast.

315

'Thank you again,' he said. 'I hope you enjoy it.'

He glanced up at me but I moved away and took the books to the far side of the shop, that's me, in a posh Piccadilly bookshop. A plain Belfast man who was understandably shy in the great man's company. He was still watching me so I started to flick through one of the copies as if I could hardly bear to wait. When he started to sign the next person's copy, another panting female, and was engrossed with her, I was free to look at him again.

And there it was on the inside of the back cover, his life in five lines, his achievements. Good mug shot too, tell him anywhere, see him in a crowd. So that was it, then, all done and dusted. I had all I needed, signature, game, set and match.

After a final look at the real Patrick Balfour, and sure that I had got every detail of him right, I, the new Patrick Balfour, left. I cut down into Jermyn Street from Piccadilly, barely a few hundred yards, and bought two Harvie and Hudson shirts. Exactly the same as his. Bloody ridiculous price, I can live for a week on that. But sometimes you have to bite the bullet and needs must. So I coughed up for his plain pink tie. Exactly his.

Then I went up to Oxford Street, to WH Smith's, and bought a Slimpick wallet folder. Which colour do you want the girl asked and I was so wound up I nearly snapped and said what colour did you think I want, you bitch, I want black – and back in my room I wrote 'PB' on the outside of my black Slimpick folder. Into it I put all the reviews of his new book and some recent articles about him. More of the same crap: '*Is this man the greatest leader in education?*' was the headline in the *Sunday Times*. The *Independent* countered with '*Balfour tipped to go into politics*'. My black folder would grow, I knew it would, grow fatter and smugger.

I washed, shaved off my growth and reacquainted myself with my face. Then I took one of the shirts out of its wrappings. Talk about pins and cardboard. I put it on. Then the tie. Feeling every inch Patrick Bloody Balfour, I sat down.

And the petrol? What about that?

I only put in £35 worth of petrol at the Shell garage on the Mile End Road. I wasn't putting more than that in his car. Not when he doesn't even pay for his own petrol. The perks he gets are ridiculous. Free flat, free food, free phone, big salary. With these blokes it's all expenses, all first-class trains. Not that you get there any quicker in first class, you're still being mucked about, but at least the ticket collector and the people who walk past the first-class carriages look at you as if you count, and Balfour counts all right, and being looked at as if you count is about the only comfort left on Connex South East.

Mind you, come to think of it, I wasn't paying for the petrol either. It was Patrick Balfour who was driving off without paying. But I did give the forecourt cameras every chance to have a really good look at me. Me in my big car, and my number plate, and my Harvie and Hudson shirt before I drove off at getaway speed. For an evening or so I toyed with the idea of having a woman along next to me in the front passenger seat, with her skirt up and her knickers showing, to add a bit more spice to the story, to help a bit more with that headline, you know the sort of Sunday thing, just what exactly *was* Patrick Balfour up to that night in the Mile End Road. But I did it alone.

And the photos on the sofa? What about them? How did he get those?

Don't know. Can't see that, Liz.

34

Daphne was hovering. Patrick had noticed she was hovering more and more these days: hovering and looking concerned. Her style had always been to be briskly into his study and briskly out, minimum fuss and maximum despatch. But this time she had brought in a cup of coffee, even though he had not asked for one.

'Caroline rang.'

'Problems?'

'Would you ring her back?'

'Of course.'

'And Michael rang from hospital.'

'And?'

'He was very touched you went. Very.'

'Things are going to be better between us.'

'Oh, and Casey wants to see you, today if possible.'

'About?'

'Abuse of the internet.'

'Not that again.'

'Yes. There's been more in the library, and more in the computer centre. I've pencilled him in for three-thirty.'

'I'm afraid I can't today. Put him off, would you?'

'You've already put him off once on all this.'

'Have I?'

'You know what he's like.'

'I'm sorry about that but break tomorrow will have to do.'

Daphne looked put out. She knew as well as Patrick did that he had a free half-hour in his diary later in the afternoon. Well, he had arranged to ring Liz.

'Is there anything else, Daphne?'

'Yes. It may not be anything but someone came into the office about half an hour ago.'

'Yes?'

'And left a letter for you.'

'Who was it?'

'That's the annoying thing, I had my back turned.'

'Didn't Emily see him?'

'Yes, but she doesn't yet know the names of the whole Common Room. She's only in her second week.'

'She's doing very well already. But it was a member of the Common Room?'

'She *thought* so. She thought she might have seen him around.'

'So why wouldn't whoever it is put the letter in my Common Room pigeonhole?'

'Oh, that's not unusual, people do sometimes drop something off with me, to get it to you as quickly as possible. It just felt odd, Patrick, that's all.'

Perhaps he hadn't put it in the pigeonhole because he knew about the surveillance? So he decided to take an even bigger risk. Because that was part of the thrill.

'What did he look like?'

'Yes, I asked Emily that.'

'And?'

'Well, a bit like you apparently. "A bit like the head" were Emily's words.'

319

Daphne handed the envelope over. On the envelope, handwritten in black ink, was Patrick Balfour Esq. The writing was small and neat. Apart from the back of the sex phone cards this was the first evidence of his hand.

He must get it straight to Bevan.

'And it wasn't marked Private and Confidential, so I opened it.'

'That's fine, Daphne.'

'I thought it might be a reply to an invitation, something like that, but it isn't. Sorry.'

'Don't worry.'

Patrick unfolded the paper. The poem was also written out by hand. What Bevan would call primary evidence.

> And now I dare not follow after
> Too close. I try to keep in sight,
> Dreading his frown and worse his laughter.
> I steal out of the wood to light;
> I see the swift shoot from the rafter
> By the inn door: ere I alight
> I wait and hear the starlings wheeze
> And nibble like ducks: I wait his flight.
> He goes. I follow: no release
> Until he ceases. Then I also shall cease.

'Does it mean anything to you, Patrick?'

'Yes, it does. I know it well. It's the last verse of a long and difficult poem.'

'It's not one I was ever taught, I'm afraid. What's it called?'

'*The Other*, by Edward Thomas.'

'Is it linked, if you don't mind my asking, to that . . . other business?'

Patrick smiled. 'Yes, it is.'

'And are you any nearer getting to the bottom of it?'

'I'm not sure.'

'If ever I can be any help at all, I'd love to be.'

'I know that.'

'I can't bear watching what it's doing to you.'

Daphne was now watching him staring at the poem. Patrick, unknown to Daphne, was staring at the letter 'r'. Everywhere he looked there was that 'r'. In fact, there were fourteen 'r's, each one formed in that particular way. The man was getting closer. Was this the final move from PB2? Patrick's voice, when it came, was mechanical.

'I couldn't have kept going without you, you know that.'

'To be honest, I feel I've done very little.'

'All you can do, if you wouldn't mind, is listen. You're a very good listener, Daphne.'

'I like to think I am.'

'But you haven't heard anything around the place, anything which might give you a clue that something is up?'

'No.'

'Nothing from the bursary staff, nothing at lunch, no nudges, nothing from the works staff, no winks, no whispers?'

'No, nothing. Not until that letter.'

As soon as Daphne had gone he knew it was only a matter of seconds. His mind was turning over any and every stone, tunnelling into his past, uprooting a dead smell. Bent double he got out of the study and turned left. He had to hurry.

Quickly, Patrick.

He had his handkerchief to his mouth.

As soon as he was in the lavatory and had locked the door, he sank down, heaving, with his knees on the floor and his head down over the bowl. He was very sick, sicker than he had been since his drunken Cambridge days.

White-faced, he sat back on the sofa in his upstairs flat – sat back on what he now thought of as *the* sofa – and rang her number. She sounded far away and slow.

'I'm in bed. Have been since lunchtime.'

'One of your bad ones?'

'I can't see.'

'Are they getting worse?'

'Yes.'

'Is it worth getting the doctor?'

'I'll give the pills a chance. The doctor can't do much.'

'I'll come over.'

'There's no point, honestly.'

'I'm coming over, Caroline.'

'Alice can get me anything I need when she comes in.'

'You've probably been overdoing it.'

'No more than usual.'

'I'm sorry about this.'

'So am I.'

'Please ask Alice to ring me when she gets in.'

He rang her number. She took an age to answer. He started to fear the worst. She then knocked the phone off the hook. He heard her fumbling for it. Then she said hello. She said she had been asleep. What time was it? Her legs had gone dead. For a moment I thought there was something wrong. No, only that her legs were dead. Now she had to go to the lavatory. These water tablets, they're no good at all. Go on then, I'll wait. He waited. He waited a long time. She fumbled again with the phone. It makes me so angry, Patrick. You're doing very well,

Mum. It's so humiliating, Patrick, I never know if I'm going to make it. I know, but I'm proud of you. I'm just a carcass, that's all I am. What have you been doing at school? Oh, Careers Evening last night. Alice's play tomorrow. Caroline's not feeling great. A talk on the Serbian war crimes trial today. Did you say Caroline's in Serbia? No, Mum, I said – could you ring later, Patrick, I'm finding it hard to follow you. Yes, Mum, I'll ring later. You don't mind me asking you to do that, do you? No, of course I don't. It's ages since you came to see me. Well, no, it isn't in fact. But you will ring me later? Yes, I'll ring you. I promise.

He rang her number. She picked it up after one ring.

'It's me.'

'Lovely to hear you, Patrick.'

'And you.'

'What have you been up to?'

'Just been to a talk on the Serbian war crimes trial.'

'You get some interesting people into your school, don't you?'

'That's the idea, anyway.'

'Horrible day, isn't it? I hate these grey days. Makes me want to go to Greece, somewhere like that.'

'I'd love to go to Greece with you.'

'Have you ever been?'

'Only once.'

'When was that?'

'Oh, years ago, when I was at Cambridge. When I was young.'

'I've often wondered what you were like when you were young.'

'Pretty arrogant, I expect. Any further thoughts on New York?'

'Not really, no.'

There was a moment's silence. Then he said, 'I've been having terrible dreams. They really upset me.'

'You should write them down. Apparently that helps, helps to take the sting out of them.'

'I might do that.'

'You never saw *The Talking Cure*, did you, at the Cottesloe a while back? The Christopher Hampton?'

'Here we go again.'

'Don't be touchy. It's just that you mentioning your dreams obviously brought Freud and Jung to mind, and it was a play about them.'

'I didn't see it.'

'Ralph Fiennes was in it.'

'That wouldn't be the good-looking man whose photo was in your kitchen?'

'Still is. He helps me get over you.'

'Well, I may not have seen the play, Liz, but I have read Freud.'

'Have you?'

'Well, some of it.'

'Which books?'

'And Jung. Some.'

'How much?'

'Not a lot.'

'*Dreams* or *Memories, Dreams, Reflections*?'

'Yes. That's the one.'

'It's two books, Patrick. Which?'

'Is it?'

'Yes.'

'Fuck.'

'Caught again.'

'Well, I've read enough Jung to be able to talk about him at dinner parties, and that's good enough for me, repression, wish-fulfilment, the latent content, that sort of stuff.'

'No, that's Freud, Patrick, not Jung.'

'Don't tell me they're two different blokes?'

'Anyway, Jung analysed more than two thousand dreams a year –'

'Good God! Poor sod.'

'And next time you're in your school library you might like to look him up, his *Collected Works*, I mean. Libido, eros, dreams, disunity, schizophrenia, Wise Old Man, The Trickster, ego, animus, psychotherapy, the hero, masculine/feminine, The Divine Child, the psychological accommodations of a marriage –'

'Woah there, steady on, Liz, what is all this?'

'I was just reading out the contents page.'

'The contents page?'

'We're reprinting it, it's on my desk at this very moment, all human screwed-up life.'

Patrick looked round his empty flat. It felt soiled.

'Liz.'

'Yes?'

'Tell me something nice.'

'I just did. I said I would like to go to Greece with you.'

'No, I said that. You said you'd just like to go to Greece.'

'All right, one day I would like to see your new theatre. You must be so proud of that.'

'Sometime, when all this is over, I'll show it to you. We'll sit in the stalls together.'

'But listen, you keep going. Right?'

'Just keep buggering on, as Churchill said.'

'You and your Churchill!'

'So I must put on my headmaster's suit and my headmaster's mask and win the war? Yes?'

'That's the one, what Jung calls your social face, your persona.'

'He's not being derogatory, I hope?'

'Not necessarily. But remember, I'm with you.'

'Thanks, Clemmie.'

35

As well as banishing the dais from the classroom Patrick had put an end to the tradition of seats being reserved for the headmaster and his wife at school plays. For a start, Caroline rarely turned up to anything these days so why should they reserve one of the best seats in the house for her? Secondly, whatever his status and profile, Patrick liked at least the appearance of equality. Thirdly, instead of being perched bang in the middle of the third row like some second-rate royal he preferred to sit wherever he could, taking a punt that he wouldn't land next to some bore, indeed hoping he might even nick one at the very end of a row. Not (as his critics liked to claim) so that he could make an easy bolt for the bar or the exit, but because he had more room there for his long legs.

On the moonlit evening of 29 November, twenty minutes before the show was due to start, Patrick looked at the photograph of his father and changed his shirt and selected his blue and white striped tie and put on his persona (the slightly inscrutable one with a touch of hauteur) and crossed the quadrangle to the new theatre. At the box office he collected the two tickets in an envelope marked The Headmaster and handed one back.

As he passed Euan Stuart at the entrance to the bar, Euan said,

'They're not numbered, Headmaster, do sit wherever you like.'

'My wife couldn't make it, I'm afraid. She's got a migraine.'

Euan smiled no surprises there then. But I do have a surprise for *you*, Euan, because as you can see, I've brought my other woman, my girlfriend, my lover, you probably remember her pictures in the papers, don't think you've met Euan Stuart, have you, Liz? Liz, Euan. Euan, Liz. Yes, we're sleeping together tonight. Can't wait. You can probably see the anticipation on my face. Even sitting next to her drives me crazy. Even talking to her on the phone drives me crazy.

The headmaster walked into the bar. Now, Liz, this is the bar. I don't want to talk to any parents so stay very close to my side and talk to me. Monopolise me. Right, so here's an interesting thing. D'you see the bar top, the one those parents are leaning on, see how polished it is, beautiful bit of wood, isn't it, well, that bar top was built by the school's own carpenters, and the wood they used for it was some timber saved from the old gymnasium. It's lovely. Yes, you're absolutely right, it's an irony not lost on Michael Falconer.

But at that particular moment the provenance of the wood on the bar top was not a detail on Patrick's mind. At that particular moment Patrick was suddenly irritated, and not for the first time, suddenly very irritated indeed by the high-pitched girly screaming he could hear all round the bar and the girly billing and cooing and the girly running into each other's arms which seemed obligatory on such occasions. Tell me something, Liz, would you: tell me why it is that otherwise intelligent girls who get into school

328

drama always have to giggle like that? You wondered what I was like when I was young. Well, I bet *you* weren't like that when you were a girl. You weren't, were you?

By the way, I do wish I had known you back then. Isn't it terrible how we want to have known those we love before we even met them? As if we have some retrospective claim on their affections. You look lovely, by the way.

Alone at the end of a row, Patrick did not bother with his programme. With a prick of pride, he craned his neck to look up at the bank of lights, then turned round to see the state of the art sound box, and finally he focused straight ahead at the stage. And in whichever direction he cared to look – and he would be the first to admit this – he was looking in an unashamedly proprietorial way.

Yes, OK, Liz, bugger the modesty and all that, I'll say it. This is *my* theatre. All right, it's not called the Patrick Balfour Theatre, the aforementioned modesty forbids, quite apart from the fact that nobody even bloody suggested it, but that's what in all but name this place is. If I was not the headmaster of this school there would be no theatre. Fact. If I was not the headmaster this school would still be single-sex, sporty and in the second division. Fact. End of story.

Patrick.

Yes, Liz.

No, it's not Liz. It's Caroline. Just pull yourself together, will you?

Yes.

Just listen to you. Your conceit!

Pull your two sides together.

Have you learnt nothing these last few weeks?

The auditorium was soon two-thirds full of casually dressed pupils and formally dressed parents. Two-thirds full was quite an encouraging house for an experimental evening – after all, they weren't here for *The Bloody Boy Friend* or *Guys and Bloody Dolls* or *Bugsy Bloody Malone*. They were here for two new plays, two world premieres, in other words for two plays unlikely ever to be seen again, plays entitled *Well Out of Order* and *Kiss the Skeleton*.

Parents nodded or raised an acknowledging eyebrow as Patrick Balfour, the headmaster, turning round to scan the rows, caught their glances. A few pupils in jeans and T-shirts, with their trainers stuck up on the back of the bench seats in front, waved hi to him. They were making the most of their casual clothes and enjoying to the full their open disregard of the no-feet-on-seats rule, a disregard which Michael Falconer would claim that simply sitting in the theatre somehow invited.

To think, Liz, that last year where we are sitting now, where you are sitting next to me now and looking lovely, with your warm right thigh touching my left, only last year this was, believe it or not, a dreary damp gymnasium, and where these rows of bright blue seats are now last year there were rubber mats and wall bars and white lines and body odour and basketballs and fencers and pectorals and press-ups. And seventeen-year-old boys with flat stomachs and great bodies. Yes, OK that's true, Liz, *and* seventeen-year-old boys with great bodies, but try to keep your mind on higher things, because if this theatre doesn't make my school a better school I don't know what does. Yes, I admit I haven't seen all the things in the West End that you have, that Freud and Jung play for one, but by seeing this theatre through to its completion I've made this school a more civilised place, a more creative place.

Euan Stuart, with large sweat patches under his arms, was now coming along the side gangway, eyes roving, hairy hands visible, to see if they were all ready and up and running, doing his last-minute directorial sidle by, just before he called through to front of house to give the all-clear.

'Such a pity Mrs Balfour couldn't come, Headmaster.'

'Yes, she's very sorry to miss it.'

'Alice's play is on second, but it should be well worth the wait.'

'I'm looking forward to both the plays,' Patrick said.

Euan then added, in his most confiding and for-your-ears-alone tone, 'She's worked her socks off for this, she really has.'

'That's very nice to hear.'

'And perhaps we'll see you in the bar afterwards.'

'Thank you, Euan.'

And I'll tell you something else, Liz. That man is a thief.

You're joking.

I'm not. Michael Falconer told me.

He seemed nice enough to me.

Seemed is the point.

The lights in the auditorium were now dimming.

The best that could be said of the first play, *Well Out of Order*, which took place in front of a black drape, was that it was well titled. After a few reasonable gags it descended with embarrassing speed into sub-Beckett. Three people were sitting around a bucket peeling potatoes and saying portentous things while a boy in a green beard rode a bicycle, its front wheel high in the air, back and forth across the stage.

Patrick and the play soon parted company. His mood plummeted. Was a project that fell so badly at the first hurdle the sort of stuff that his school in his theatre should be putting on? I'm really sorry, Liz, I really am, you shouldn't be having to sit through this drivel. Don't be silly, Patrick, give it a chance, it's very much the sort of thing teenagers do. No, Liz, no it isn't. What this is is the sort of crap which gives drama a bad name, what this is is the sort of stuff which shows Euan Stuart and the drama department missing every target except its own foot, what this is is the sort of self-indulgent rubbish which would more than justify Michael Falconer ripping the catheter out of his dick and the drip out of his dorsum and putting on his Hawks Club tie and breaking through the fire doors and leading his storming pack of rugger buggers and hand-picked hammer-bearing weightlifters, all hellbent on returning this building to its former testosterone glories. No, Liz, we must put an end to the endgames. No, Liz, better basketball and BO in the old gym than sub-Beckett bicycling back and forth across the stage in my new theatre.

Patrick did not have a clue what was going on, though three rows behind him Max Russell-Jones, presumably tuned in to this variant of absurd middle European drama, appeared to know. And the audience knew that M. R-J knew. The audience knew that M. R-J knew because M. R-J was laughing loudly throughout the play. Laughing like that made M. R-J feel very switched on and laughing like that made Patrick very angry. It reminded Patrick that whenever he went to a Shakespearean comedy there were always women with English degrees in the front stalls chortling at every unfunny pun, starting usually with a very knowing little collective titter at line one.

Patrick pulled the plug and hunched down deeper in his seat so that the head of the person in front completely obstructed his view of the stage. Then, to make absolutely sure that none of it got through to his collective uncon-scious, he closed his eyes.

That's much better. Now, Liz, I'll just undo your bra, that's it, and put my hand there, just there if I may, that is very nice, perfect, come a bit closer, yes, perfect, you know nothing quite beats the moment you first touch the softness of a woman's breast, and I'm going to spend the rest of this dreadful play enjoying yours, but you will nudge me, won't you, when *Well Out of Order* is well and truly over. If in doubt wait until Max Russell-Jones – he's The Laughing Cavalier three rows behind – wait until he is shouting 'Bravo, bravo' as if he has just witnessed a new Olivier in a new Stoppard.

When the lights in the auditorium came up, and the clapping stopped, Patrick opened his eyes and sat up in his seat and peered down at the programme. There wasn't much information. The second play was simply

Kiss the Skeleton

Girl/Woman: Alice Balfour

This was, it seemed, a one-girl/one-woman show. And the one girl/one woman starring in this show was, it seemed, his daughter.

Breathe deeply.

Are you nervous, Patrick? Yes, Liz, wouldn't you be? Yes, but you must be very proud of her too. Oh, I'm not sure of that but I am sure, by the way, Liz, that you've got great breasts and I hope you're proud of them. I don't think of it like that. Well, you should. It was like being in the back row of the cinema again. Did you like it? What do you think? I felt young again. Me too. It takes me back.

Once again the house lights dimmed. The black drape was flown and the stage lights now came up to reveal a beautifully painted book-lined study/bedroom. Thank God for small mercies, Patrick whispered, because what we may be looking at here, Liz, what we may be being shown here, Liz, is – and I hope I have got this right – is no more or less than a book-lined study/bedroom. And if that is so, if we are indeed seeing a bit of your actual verisimilitude, then Thank you, God, for this bit of realism, and thank you, Liz, for sitting next to me tonight with your bra off, and yes you may call me old-fashioned but I do tend to prefer plays that I can understand.

Shh, stop it, or I'll be one of those giggly girls.

In front of the bookcase, along the back flat and facing the audience, there was a single bed. Backstage left, next to a door, there was a fridge. Backstage right there was a table, covered with student files and a pile of books and essay notes and a stapler and a box index, all these items sprayed around an old typewriter. On the floor there was a frayed rug and a record player. The furniture and the overall style were dated, possibly twenty years or so ago. Possibly more. Anyway, not now.

Patrick glanced round the auditorium. His arm, draped over the empty seat next to him, jumped. His heart jumped. He saw that Detective Chief Inspector Bevan had eased himself into the back row. He looked again. And no, it couldn't be . . . Jamie was sitting just beyond Bevan. Jamie! Jamie? He looked. No, it wasn't Jamie. Who was it? The spitting image. It must be the brother of one of the girls. But that was Bevan, no doubt about it. Had he arrived just to see Alice? Bevan caught his eye but made no other movement. Patrick looked back at the set.

His heart began to settle.

Out of the window on the back flat, a very well-painted window, you could see a lawn and Gothic façades and a distant chapel, all suggesting a college or an ancient university of some sort. More to the point, and much more arresting, was the music, with the surface sounds of a crackly old vinyl record. It stole in as Alice sat up on her bed, then lay half back, leaning on her elbow. It was 'September In The Rain', the opening bars of Dinah Washington's song, which swept Patrick back to a different kind of pain, back to his youth, not so much back to the back row of the cinema and fiddling with the clasp of her bra, but back to university days.

It was so long since he had heard the song, shaking his head at himself in disbelief,

> the leaves of brown
> came tumbling down
> that September
> oh that Sep-tem-ber
> in the rain

How music picks you up and transports you to your September, do you find that, Liz, how it transports each of us to a time and a place, each to our own. Just that first sound opens up and brings back to life the sights and the smells and the people. The years drop away. Is there one human experience which is so specific yet so universally and so intensely shared?

And that's Alice?

Yes, Liz, that is Alice.

She's lovely.

Thanks. I think so too.

Alice got off the bed, took an upright chair from the table and moved it down stage centre. She sat on it, facing the audience, and as she spoke she started doing her hair, as if in front of a mirror. From the very first words she had the unhurried poise of a natural actor.

'That's not my music, it's his. I was into Brahms and Mahler and Wagner. But once he put it on and played it to me . . . it became mine. Or I became its. It took me over. He took me over. So did Billie Holiday and Dinah Washington. If you didn't know the song, well, it was Dinah Washington, the Queen of the Blues. She was born Ruth Lee Jones in Tuscaloosa, Alabama, but changed her name in 1942. She's dead now, long dead, Dinah Washington. It was drink and sleeping pills. 1963. As is Billie Holiday; it was drugs. 1959. A different year, but yeah yeah, the same old story.'

It's a risky theatrical convention, don't you think, Liz, this sort of asking yourself questions out loud. Don't you, as a regular theatre-goer, as a person who sees plays about Freud and Jung, feel that? Whenever the playwright uses this approach, I worry about what will happen if any of the non-suspension of disbelief literalists out there in the audience start calling back unhelpful answers. In fact, this did happen once. Honestly. I was there. No, honestly it did. I was in a Dublin theatre late one night, well Caroline and I were both there, and this soliloquising actor on the stage was musing to himself and saying 'Am I right or am I right?' and a drunk in the front row stood up and said 'By Jaysus, you're bloody right there *and* you're bloody right.'

Concentrate.

Is Bevan still there?

Yes.

And Jamie isn't?

Of course he isn't.

Wasn't Euan Stuart looking at me then? Checking up on me?

Alice, his daughter, looking well into her twenties rather than seventeen, and seeming much taller, checked and assessed her hair in the invisible mirror, and shrugged in a who-cares-too-bad-if-it-isn't-right way. She said:

'No one else in our lot played that kind of music. They didn't even know it existed. And the fact that it wasn't mainstream, that it wasn't on at every party and in every room, made it so . . . special, so . . . *him*. Every time I went to his rooms after lectures or before we went to the pictures he played something like that. The kind of music that was around before rock and roll blew it aside. And to be into that made me feel different, discriminating, minority, at an angle. And I wanted to be at an angle. Angular. *At* Cambridge *and* angular. Wow, now isn't that the double whammy!'

Patrick stirred. He resettled his legs. He moved his arms. He could not get comfortable. Alice paced the boards, picked up her essay, skim-read a bit and then put it down.

'It was always in his room that we met, never here, never' – she looked round – 'in mine. I don't live here any more, in fact, but I wanted you to know the . . . setting. Well, that's not quite true, he did come to my room but I'll get on to that later. The point was, colleges were single-sex then, and a girl could visit a bloke but a bloke couldn't visit a girl. It would strike you now as strict. If it didn't make you laugh in disbelief.'

She glared at the audience.

'Don't laugh.'

But Patrick was not laughing. There was a band of pain tightening across his chest, and it was tightening more with each sentence. How in God's name can this be happening? How in God's name could she be saying these things?

No one was laughing, not even Max Russell-Jones, as Alice walked to the record player and took another LP out of its sleeve. Patrick could not see the title but he did not need to. He remembered the purple and red cover only too well. Alice lowered the needle. Patrick remembered the room. It was Viola Hutcheson's room. He was back there. He remembered everything. The music began.

It was Billie Holiday, *Mean To Me*.

Alice looked up from her kneeling position next to the record player.

'Have you ever been in love?'

337

Patrick was finding it hard to swallow.

'Because I hadn't been before and I haven't been since. In love at nineteen. Dumped at twenty. So what? Yeah? That's what you're thinking. So what, Viola, it happens? Getting dropped is all part of the learning curve. Grow up.'

Patrick tried to undo his collar. His fingers would not work. Looking askance, he saw Euan Stuart eyeing him across the auditorium. Looking the other way he saw John Bevan. But Bevan's eyes were firmly on Alice and on the stage.

'If you've been there, you'll know the pattern. Doesn't return your calls, doesn't answer your letters, isn't where he said he'd meet you, stops coming to the lectures you've got used to going to together. And yet somehow you knew it from the very first moment. It's like you're out on your own, walking in a wood in late September and you hear a leaf falling, to your left or right or just behind you as you walk, just one leaf clipping the other leaves as it comes down, and you know, in a month or more the whole lot will be all over. That leaf was dying foliage.'

Alice stormed across the stage and savagely cut off the music. She shoved the Billie Holiday vinyl hard back in the LP cover. She put Billie Holiday back in her place.

'That just makes it worse, all that. So why make it worse? I'll tell you why. Because you *want* to make it worse, you *want* to wallow. It's not a pretty sight, self-pity. I remember on TV once a man with multiple sclerosis was being interviewed by some in-your-face bloke who said "But isn't all this rather self-pitying?" and the MS man said "Of course it is, you pillock, what do you expect?" I cheered.'

Alice paced around a bit then swivelled towards the audience.

'Anyway, I'll tell you how we met.'

The Civil War, Patrick thought. It was the Civil War seminar, and I was showing off. I was always showing off.

'It was a day heavy with atmosphere, with little air, and I remember thinking . . . don't worry, this will clear. This could still be a nice day. The pollen will be better later.'

Her hay fever. Yes, Viola's bad hay fever. *You're in my spot, honey.* Surely everyone could hear Patrick's breathing and his heart bumping? He could no longer mask his distress. He could no longer make out all the words Alice was saying. Surely the headmaster-watchers in the audience could hear his heart going hammer and tongs? Surely everyone was now looking at him? Alice was sitting forward on the chair centre downstage, with her story to tell.

'It was in a faculty seminar on the role of religion in the English Civil War. Normally I didn't go to seminars, I just went to my weekly supervisions and some lectures. Only the really keen crowd went to seminars, about ten or so. The ones who got or wanted to get firsts. Usually it was we girls who were so keen and . . . it was a hay fevery day and my eyes were itching. And there he was. He was . . . there. He spoke so fluently, so confidently. He held the floor and made the issues come alive, more than any teacher or lecturer had ever done.

'And I knew he wasn't talking to the room. Hay fever or no hay fever he was talking to me. He had me . . . in his hand, in the palm of his hand, before he touched me. He had nice hands.'

She looked at her hands, the backs of her hands, then her palms. Then at the bones of her feet, and started to paint her toenails.

'I painted my toenails vermilion.'

She threw her arms open in abandon. She pirouetted. She did a forward roll. She stood up, arms out, like an

Olympic gymnast awaiting the applause and the judges' score.

'And suddenly we were . . . going out. And within a week we were singing Dinah Washington and Brook Benton duets. We'd do alternate verses of 'A Rockin' Good Way (To Mess Around And Fall In Love)', and I'd do Dinah's ad-lib *you're in my spot again, honey*. When I was with him I felt so . . . buoyed up, no pun, I felt I was riding this great wave of hope. Whatever the water, however rough, I could bounce along, I could ride it. That's how I felt. We didn't have any money, not that we were poor-poor, but we just got by. As the young do. And we were happy. Looking back perhaps we were *too* happy. How does it go, *don't be too happy, kid, because when the happy happy bust they do bust hard.* Forgotten who wrote it. All I know is I . . . *ached.* With an incurable ache. And I couldn't tell anyone, except my little bro. My devoted little bro. I told Rory everything, but he was just too young.'

Alice tried a brave I'm-not-crying smile, then covered her face in her hands. But she quickly recovered her poise, and strode round the stage with a manic energy, recreating the scene.

'We spent every hour together, reading, listening to his music, listening to my music, eating burnt toast and yoghurt, smoking, drinking wine. And making love. They're such ordinary phrases, aren't they, such everyday events, yet it is a miracle to me, just as, they tell me, having a child is. Not that I've had one. Not that I was allowed to have his. So, there we were, and then there we weren't. Perhaps I wasn't good enough in bed, whatever that means. I keep reading articles in magazines about being good in bed. She was, he was. He was great in bed. She was great in bed. I don't think you should write it. I don't think you should say that. Who knows how good you can

340

be in bed at seventeen, at nineteen, at twenty-nine, at fifty-nine, all you can do is try to express what you feel and hope, somehow, that you come across as good in bed. Perhaps I was terrible. Perhaps I was OK. Perhaps I was variable. *I don't know, do I!'*

Not fifteen feet from Patrick, Alice walked up and down the front of the stage, almost pleading with the audience.

'Do you?'

You could hear a pin drop. Patrick's head was thumping too. His heart was about to burst and his hands were trembling and his head was about to explode.

Thank God he was at the end of the row.

He tried to swallow.

How does anyone *know* all this!

He was unwell, he would leave.

He couldn't. Alice would never forgive him.

You can handle this.

Turbulence has hit the plane, that's all.

This is a fear you can master.

Above all, do not spoil Alice's big night.

You are not having a heart attack.

You are being attacked.

Which is different.

This is the final attack.

The final attack. Patrick felt his chin sag. His neck felt loose, as if he had fallen into a drunken stupor. He could hear nothing clearly. It was all muzzy and all so far away. He was no longer there. Nor did he know how long all this went on. When he raised his face, when he forced his chin to come up, the pain was still in his chest and his eyes would not clear. When they did he saw Alice looking straight at him. How much had he missed? How much more had he been attacked? Alice was looking straight at her father. Or so it seemed to her father.

341

'Anyway, all I know is that I loved him to bits, and he did me. For nearly a year. And then he met her. He's still with her, I'll give him that. But then she is rich. And she is in magazines now. And he is famous.'

She laughed an empty laugh and turned upstage to the fridge and took out a bottle of wine. It was already open. She held up the bottle.

'He told me about wine too, as well as the early Italian Renaissance. We sat by the roadside, trying to hitch, our backs to wheatfields. The smell of melting tar. We went to Siena and Assisi and saw the Giottos. We went to the Uffizi in Florence. The Ponte Vecchio. Then we went to Greece. And do you know the best bit of Greece? No, it wasn't any of the famous sites. It was lying in his arms listening to the sheep bells and the goat bells. Every tenth sheep and every tenth goat has a bell around its neck. Did you know that? And as they wander along you hear that haunting sound. It couldn't get any better.'

She shrugged oh–couldn't–it.

'Did he leave me because he was bored? No, he left me because she was rich. I saw her in the University Library, walking along with him. I was sitting behind a stack of books and they couldn't see me. The cardigan she had on must have cost a fortune. And her shoes, and her bag. And the worst thing was, the very worst thing was, she looked . . . nice. Auburn hair, but not pleased with herself. I wanted to hate her. All I could think was *you're in my spot, honey*. He had a good singing voice, Brook Benton or whoever, and he was a great mimic. If you closed your eyes when he was taking someone off it was as if they were in the room. Perhaps that's part of his success, his protean success. He can be other people.'

She pulled out the cork. She poured a glass, but did not drink it. Even the unselfconscious way that Alice pulled the cork and did not drink the wine was class. At no moment in the play did she seem self-conscious or aware of the audience. Even in his great distress Patrick could see the quality of her acting.

'To go back to sex for a minute. I'm tugged both ways on this topic. It's overrated, it's a ridiculous obsession, it's all anyone writes about, it sells newspapers, it topples politicians, it gets huge advances, while you're getting your hair done you can read about forty ways of doing it at the weekend. It's ridiculous and overrated and we ought to get on with our lives and keep it in proportion. That is one tug. The other tug is . . . when you see someone across the room, you go, you seek each other out, it pulls you like a magnet, and when you're in it, in its thrall, it shapes, defines, makes and ruins, overrides, that's it, it overrides your day. And *what a diff'rence a day makes, just twenty-fours hours.* Another Dinah Washington song.'

Alice picked up a pile of books from the table and sat with them at the front of the stage. She flicked through a couple of the texts, as you might while writing an essay, as if you were looking for an apt quotation.

'At school we read *Romeo and Juliet,* I expect you did . . . such *young* lovers, and we read *Antony and Cleopatra,* such middle-age wrinklies, but still such fools, and we wrote such knowing essays about them, as if we knew all about young love and middle-aged love, what a joke, and then there was Ophelia and Hamlet − did they do it, those young lovers? Was she driven crazy because it was all over for her, while Gertrude and Claudius were half-pissed and hard at it in their middle-aged adulterous bed?'

She looked up. She put the plays open face-down on the stage.

'Well, that was literature. This is life. All right, you can say no it isn't, it's a play, but I'm backing you not to go

343

down that knowing route, I'm backing you to say that in this case literature *is* life, and I'm . . . I'm begging you to come with me. All the way to the end.'

She picked up the glass of wine off the floor beside her and drank some.

'As I said, I saw him with her in the library, I saw them from behind the book stack, and I knew it was all over. All I could lose I lost. I saw the engagement announcement in *The Times* and in the *Daily Telegraph*. I wrote, it wasn't easy, but I wrote to congratulate him. Them. To congratulate them. I saw their children's births announced. Same papers. Their children. Not my child.'

She then stared into the mirror again to check her face. She looked at herself, at the contours of her teeth and lips. She now looked older, more in her thirties than twenties, and desolate. Her eyes were heavy with black runny make-up. Viola Hutcheson was crying. Alice Balfour was crying. Then she sniffed and messily wiped away the tears with a paper tissue.

'This triple mirror has seen a lot. He liked us to make love in front of it. In the middle of the night he climbed over the college walls, the all-female college walls, and up the drain pipe and over the flat roof. Talk about Romeo. Talk about Juliet. *Tree at my window, window tree, my sash is lowered.* That's not Romeo, that's Robert Frost. At first I was shy in front of the mirror. But shyness soon passes. He didn't reply to my letter, of course. I wrote to him when he got his first book published. But I didn't send it. I've still got it. Here. I remember reading in a history book the phrase *the rapacious appropriation of the abbey lands*. It stuck, as such things will. Funny things, phrases, phrases like *stripped to the waist*. That's a funny phrase. And I can still see him, *stripped to* —'

Another tissue. She rolled it into a hard, wet, white ball. Her face puckered and swelled.

'He loved me, dropped me, used me and . . . appropriated me. I was an annexe. And on he goes, from glory to
glory. And the biggest joke is, he's taken to telling young
people how to behave. I saw him do it . . . on television.
He may be . . . unscathed, but, with his record, he should
know better.'

That hollow laugh.

Patrick closed his eyes.

Don't laugh like that, Alice.

'In the years after him I worked for a charity and then
before moving to Canada I worked in a bookshop, a small
one in Portobello, Edinburgh. I even sold his first book to
people. I felt sick each time I opened the back flap and saw
his face. His books were on the shelf. But I'm not against
success. I often think, did I duck the challenge of doing
something bigger? If it was an essay at school, the question
would be 'Was the fall of the tragic heroine a weakness of
character or was she the victim of fate?' In a way I felt I
had nothing much left, the well was dry. But I wrote
something myself. I wrote all this down. "So this is just
revenge, isn't it?" the in-your-face interviewer asks me on
TV, and I say "Of course it is, you pillock". The apples are
now all full of wasps. And I'd rather kill myself than kill
someone else. Which is what he did.'

She moved towards the bed with her glass and got
something else from her jeans' pocket. Was it a bottle of
pills? She did not let you see exactly what it was but it
seemed to be something special, something saved up for
this moment.

No, Alice, no, don't.

Viola, don't. No, you didn't. I don't believe you did.

This is a play. This is play-acting, that's all it is, play-
acting.

You didn't, did you?

345

Viola! You mustn't.

Alice sat on the edge of her bed, drinking from the glass and then scratching the nail varnish off her toes.

'And, however famous or distinguished or much more famous and much more distinguished he becomes after I've gone, I hope one day he has to sit there and squirm. And sees my fridge is empty.'

She looked back at the fridge and then out at the audience.

'Don't use the milk. The milk's off too.'

Then Alice lay back on the bed. The needle bit and the vinyl scratched and Dinah Washington, the Queen of the Blues, started to sing:

> What a diff'rence a day makes
> Just twenty-four hours

And then Alice was singing softly along with Dinah, singing along with the Queen of the Blues, counterpointing that gospelly, jazzy, original voice with some gently English phrasing. The last sound in the darkness, as the female duet faded, was of a glass falling on to the stage floor and breaking.

Then silence.

Then – all around the auditorium – the acclamation.

Alice, in a spotlight on the very front edge of the stage, with the fridge door still open at the back, bowed once from the waist down, and was gone. She did not come out of character and smile or look grateful for the applause. She just stared, accusingly. Then walked off. They clapped and clapped for her to return to the stage, she must come back, she deserved more applause, come back on, Alice, come back, Viola, come back on.

But she did not come back.

36

He did not know how long he had been there. Perhaps five minutes, perhaps ten. With the lights fully up in the auditorium, Patrick stayed where he was, the only one left in his seat. His ears were ringing. His legs did not want to move.

    – You knew, didn't you?

    – Knew what?

    – You knew it would be a body blow for her.

    – Did I?

    – Oh yes.

    – Not that big.

    – You did. You sensed it even if you didn't know it.

    – Not that big.

    – Not sure I believe you.

    – Believe what you like.

    – Come on.

    – Anyway, you can't stay with someone on that basis. You can't.

    – She'd never get over you, and you knew that.

    – I didn't. I did not know that.

    – But she told you she couldn't live without you. Fact.

    – Yes, but lots of people say that.

– Do they?

– Yes, that's what lots of people say.

– Is it?

– Yes, in bed. When they're young. When they're in love.

– Have a lot said it to you?

– No, of course not, but you know what I'm –

– But she didn't say it like lots of people say it, did she?

– Maybe. I can't remember.

– And she didn't just say it in bed. She said it midday, matter-of-fact.

– Maybe.

– No maybes. *All I could lose I lost.* Her words.

– So, so how does Alice know all this?

– How do you think?

Patrick peered slowly round. DCI Bevan was nowhere to be seen. At the end of Alice's performance the detective must have slipped away as quietly as he had slipped in. Only a few parents were still there, heads together, peering in at the sound box. Some stragglers were chatting with Max Russell-Jones, dawdling under the glowing EXIT. Two boys were going along the rows with black plastic bags, bending to pick up the sweet papers and the Coke cans and the programmes left under the seats.

Patrick looked down at his folded programme.

He turned it over.

He read it again.

That sentence standing on its own at the very bottom.

Thanks to Hugo Solomon and Rory Hutcheson.

Her brother! There was a gentle tap on his shoulder. He jumped. Close to his ear was the softly stroking Scottish voice of Euan Stuart.

'Drink, Patrick? Do join us in the bar. There's someone I'd like you to meet.'

'In a minute.'

But it wasn't a minute. Within seconds Patrick leapt up from his seat and grabbed Euan's elbow.

'Where is he?'

'Who?'

Patrick jabbed at the bottom of the programme. 'You know damn well who!'

'I'm sorry?'

'You appoint the staff here now, do you?'

'No, of course I don't. What is all this, Headmaster?'

'Who the hell do you think you are?'

'I'm afraid I don't know what –'

'I have to know who is on the campus. And so does the bursar. For legal and for security reasons. D'you understand?'

Euan wrenched free his arm and wiped some sweat from his face. 'Yes, of course I understand that but –'

Patrick shook the programme in his face. 'How much did you pay him, Euan? Rory Hutcheson?'

'Just his expenses. He said he'd do it for nothing. And he did.'

'Where is he?'

'I don't know. Having a drink with Alice I expect. That's what he said anyway.'

'Did he know my daughter was at school here? Before he came?'

'I don't know.'

'Before he started to help you, did he mention me or Alice?'

Euan rubbed his forehead. 'I don't think so, no, not that I can remember. Does it matter?'

'Go and get him.'

'Now?'

'Yes, go into the bar and bring him here. Now. Just him.'

'Right.'

Euan pushed through the door. There was laughter from the bar. Euan returned, his face white, his tongue wetting his upper lip.

'Can't see him. He's not there.'

'Alice?'

'No, I couldn't see her either.'

'So where is she?'

'Probably still taking her make-up off.'

Euan's voice was now high and strangulated.

'Where does he live, Euan?'

'Stays with friends I think, not far from the Albert Hall, the Cromwell Road.'

Very close to Finley Place. He's been close to Finley Place. He's set the whole thing up from start to finish. Very close to our home, as close as he can be to Alice, close to where the films were developed, right on our doorstep.

'Is that all you know?'

'That sort of area anyway.'

'You've never visited him?'

Euan spread his hands. 'No. Why should I?'

'That's only a few hundred yards from our house.'

'Is it?'

'You must know that.'

'How would I? I've never been invited to your house.'

'So he doesn't have his own flat in London?'

'Not as far as I know. Look, they're probably just round at the pub, celebrating.'

'When did you two meet?'

'Oh, years ago, up in Scotland when I –'

Patrick pushed past him and jumped up on to the stage. Backstage, he dodged the ladders and the prop table, hurrying through the semi-darkness and round behind the cyclorama. He knew the layout. If need be he could have done this blindfold. He knew it from countless hours poring

350

over the conversion plans, from even more hours walking round the hard-hat site with architects and builders.

Pressing light buttons as he went he leapt down the back basement stairs three at a time. He hammered on the door of the girls' dressing room.

'Alice? Alice!'

He went straight in.

There was no one there. Just some make-up and flowers and little scribbled messages and scent and coat hangers and crushed cartons of orange juice. On the wooden seat in the corner there was the bottle of vermilion nail varnish.

Patrick, cursing himself, checked the other dressing room, the boys' one. Empty, just a pair of boxer shorts and a T-shirt and a jacket draped on the back of a chair and coffee stains and body odour. He went into both toilets. Stale cigarette smells.

No one.

Had he missed something? He returned to the girls' dressing room. He could see his palm print was still there on the Formica top. He picked up a small bottle of Evian and drank from it. He opened all the drawers. More make-up and a large box of tissues. Propped on a high windowsill were some good luck cards. He read them. Break a leg cards, good luck darling cards, I'm sure it will go well cards from parents and boyfriends. One was still inside its torn-open envelope:

A,
You'll be great. Don't worry about it. Be there afterwards.
Usual place.
    R x

Make the friendship.
Seal the friendship.

351

Abuse the friendship.

Patrick was burning. Still clutching the bottle of water, he ran back up the other staircase, his feet echoing in the stairwell. He pushed out through the stage door in to the night air and to the small car park tucked round the back. It was coming on to rain. There was just one car, Euan's Passat, and a bike chained to a railing.

She could be anywhere, in any flat, in any hotel, in any car – if he's got a car.

They could be in a taxi.

Or a hired car.

Or a van he sleeps in. A white van with ropes and a mattress.

Revenge on the mattress.

The rapacious appropriation of the abbey lands.

He hurried round past the English department to the front of the theatre and looked through the big windows into the bar to see if Alice was now in there. She wasn't. Perhaps she was coming round the other way. There was no semblance left of his headmasterly control, none of the gravitas facia. He was in a total panic.

'Ah, Headmaster, everyone's been looking for you.'

It was Max Russell-Jones.

'Alice was superb, absolutely superb. What a girl!'

Patrick did not speak. The swimming pool! He tracked back across some wet grass and jumped a flower bed. That's where she was, she was in the swimming pool. Floating on the top. He could see her. He started to run.

A Welsh voice stopped him mid-flight.

'Patrick!'

Patrick turned. It was John Bevan walking towards him, windswept and breathless.

'I've got the car outside. Come with me.'

37

All I could lose I lost.
As long as Alice is alive, I don't care.

As Bevan drove him west along the Embankment he rang Caroline. She would have taken some pills and be in bed asleep. There was no answer. He left a message.

'He's been under surveillance, our Mr Hutcheson,' Bevan said, indicating, and the Volvo turned right, 'but I didn't want to make any mistakes at this stage.'

'So you knew where he was staying?'

'The hotel, yes. The Ashgrove.'

'Just past Waitrose, on the Cromwell Road?'

'That's the one.'

'That's where he meets Alice?'

'Yes. We've got someone there now.'

'You've been watching the hotel?'

'On and off. There are lots of places he goes.'

'Do you know he's there now?'

'I'm hoping he will be, yes.'

'But you don't know?'

Bevan looked in the rear window. 'I'm hoping.'

'And he was using my name? Not four hundred yards from my home?'

'Yes.'

'And you've known all these weeks?'

'No, only recently. But I knew he'd be in the audience tonight, or backstage, following the script.'

'So you knew his real name?'

'Yes, we did. It's all been teamwork. He's an actor, you know, never made it, he'd been to drama school but a couple of years later he's hanging around for a few walk-on parts, good-looking enough but never got to play the major roles.'

'A frustrated actor.'

Bevan overtook a bus.

'A couple of times I went to look round the school. And the Joseph Clark impersonations, they got me think-ing – acting again – and I was in the theatre, looking at the possibilities, you know, and something in there felt a bit creepy.'

'In the theatre?'

'Yes.'

'Strangely enough, my deputy said something very like that. Some weeks ago.'

Bevan now indicated left, talking as he did so. 'And I'd done some time lines, to see if there was any pattern of days in the letters arriving. Patterns can help. Then I picked up a rehearsal schedule for October and November, and the dates of the rehearsals and the dates of the notes in your pigeonhole tallied.'

'Right, I see.'

'Next time I was in there, in the theatre, I heard the name Rory. And here's a funny thing, I just thought I'd check out the Rorys, but I couldn't find any on your school list, not one, not even among the students, but I asked the technician there, and he said this one wasn't a pupil, he was a friend of the Head of Drama.'

354

Patrick was staring straight ahead. 'Rory Hutcheson.'

'Knew him well, did you?'

'Hardly at all. Well, a bit. He came up to Cambridge a few times.'

'To see his sister?'

'Yes. We're talking over twenty-five years ago. Or more. I liked him.'

The traffic slowed to a halt.

'There you go. Anyway, next thing, I looked up *Spotlight*, the actors' directory, you know, all the actors and their photos. And there he was, and a bit like you, Patrick, I have to say. More than a passing resemblance.'

Patrick said nothing.

'You know what it's like for actors, Patrick. Plenty of time on your hands, time to brood on the death of a loved one, to apportion blame, plenty of time to read the papers and watch videos, all the time in the world to learn the lines, to build up a scrapbook of his own.'

'Rory kept a scrapbook on me?'

'I'll say he did! For years.'

'Years?'

'Since his sister's death.'

'When was that?'

'Fifteen years ago. That was the first cutting, the obituary notice from Canada. The rest are about you. Hundreds of newspaper cuttings and photos. Popped into his hotel room, we did, when he was out, gave it the once over, and there it was, the scrapbook. And her diaries. A small pile of them.'

'Diaries? Do you think Alice will have seen those?'

'He also attended that conference you spoke at in Brighton. Well, the first part of it.'

'Brighton?'

'He moves around a lot, we know that, uses other

names, it's not just you he pretends to be, so that he's never really known. Bit of a chameleon, you might say.'

'It's all coming back to me.'

'What?'

'Rory couldn't make up his mind whether to go to art school or drama school. He was good at both. Viola was always going on about how creative he was.'

They were at some traffic lights. Bevan's fingers drummed the driving wheel. Then his hand squeaked on the glass as he wiped the inside of the windscreen. Eleven-thirty at night and the streets were full. Patrick, avoiding eye contact with his own reflection, let some air in. He lowered his window a bit too much, then closed it, then opened it a couple of inches. As the car moved forward he asked,

'How did he know that you'd come to see me?'

'That very first day? To your school?'

'Yes.'

'November the fifth? He may have got lucky there . . . remember he was already in the school, he'd started in early October, doing as much or as little as he liked, and of course the work gave him irregular hours, just what he wanted, close to you but no pattern, dropping in and out, even weekends, knowing you'd not know him and would be too preoccupied to ask even if you saw him around.'

'Because he knew I'd only be looking for familiar faces?'

'That's it, boy, he'd planted the three bombs, and he knew we'd pick them up and act.'

'And that's the Kafka? An obvious point of call.'

'Yes. And the anonymous notes would have bothered you at any time. Horrible things, anonymous notes.'

'They are.'

The traffic was even heavier. Come on, come on, let's get there.

356

'Rory knows how your mind works, Patrick, no doubt about it.'

'You think so?'

Bevan went on talking in his clear, unhurried way. Instead of being behind the wheel he could just as easily have been sitting in the side bar of the Rat And Parrot.

'You're his new part. Before he begins all this, he's read all your articles and your books, and his first hit more or less coincided with my visit. No, he wasn't watching out of a window, he was just banking on it happening and it does and then he gets giddy and just keeps sending stuff. Eye for an eye. Revenge, it's like a drug. Like sex.'

He had done those drawings on her mantelpiece! No wonder they were so good. Done them before getting into bed with her, it's so erotic being drawn, drawn into bed. Or tying her up in a van?

Rory knows how your mind works, Patrick.

And I do his.

So you want to know how it began, Balfour, don't you?

Yes, Rory, I do.

It began with me reading my sister's diaries, and every page she wrote cut me to the quick. What she went through with you, and what she went through after you. And the photos she kept. You and Viola sitting on a wall, outside a pub. Grantchester by the look of it. Viola and you, arms round each other, on the Backs at Cambridge. Viola sitting in a punt, you punting. You and Viola at a May Ball. Viola in front of the Parthenon. Looking at the photos fury would flood my veins and I'd stare at them until you disappeared. Until I'd cleansed her life of you.

I read your novels to see if you were juggling with her still. See if you were getting the last bit of mileage out of all she had given you. Every chapter I asked myself: will it be here, will it be on this page or the next that she appears, that I would see my sister enter the story dressed up as a lover or a wife or a mistress? All you had to do was change the colour of her hair, give her a different name, make her taller or shorter and – she was a 'character' in a Patrick Balfour book.

But you didn't. Or at least you haven't yet. She isn't there. Which leaves me thinking. It leaves me thinking something even worse. That you have edited her out. Airbrushed her from your history. Dumped her in the trash can. Which in my book, Balfour, is even worse than appropriation.

I can't get even a walk-on part but your name, Balfour, your name is appearing more and more. When I'm shaving you're on the *Today* programme. I'm staring at your face in the mirror, with my razor in my hand. You're on *Start The Week*. When I'm making a quick omelette at lunchtime you're on *The World At One*, not only in my face and in my mirror but in my ear, everywhere I turn there's your name, and your name's an insult to my sister, her name's on a gravestone in Toronto, it's your name should be on a gravestone, Balfour, because you're an insult to *her* name.

You're a serial offender; first it's Viola, then it's that Liz Nicholson, and she even looks a bit like Viola, if Viola had been lucky enough to live to her age.

But then you made your mistake. That interview in the *Independent*. I knew if I waited long enough you would make a mistake. The interview came out on the very day the theatre opened. Talk about publicity, you and your theatre. And there were these two photographs. I cut it all out, the article and the photos. One is a half-page shot of you, one of those huge black and white close-up portraits, and I put it on the screen and I blow it up even bigger, even bigger than my face in the shaving mirror, before I blow you up. I can see each individual hair on your face. The smaller photograph is of you standing outside the theatre, your theatre, flanked by four smiling sixth-formers, two smiling boys and two smiling girls. One of them is your daughter. Alice. Just a bit younger than Viola was when you met her. Bang. And then it said Euan Stuart was Head of Drama there, BANG. Euan Stuart. I remembered Euan from Glasgow days, bit of a creep but we acted a bit together, and bang, bang, I thought I'd give Euan a ring, long time no see, see if I could be of any use, see if I could put my hand on Mr Balfour's shoulder, *the hand on the shoulder, the policeman's badge.*

Patrick looked, as if hypnotised, at the blue and red lights on the dashboard. When he looked at Bevan he was stifling a yawn: a copper driving a car, a copper doing his business. Bevan took a sweet out of a tin and popped it into his mouth.

'I knew it was him,' Bevan said. 'But until tonight I didn't really know why.'

'And that was?'

'He wanted to expose you to your daughter. In public.'

If Alice is safe, Patrick said to himself, I'll never complain again, never moan again, I'll never do anything wrong again. Promise. *We've got to get to her as soon as we can.* That man, that failed actor, the man who inveigled my daughter into playing Viola, or his version of his sister, is probably now whispering in her ear. Before killing her. *Someone spoiling things for you, Patrick, because you spoiled things for him.* That's how Bevan put it in the Rat and Parrot. An eye for an eye, that's his endgame.

Patrick shook his head a little, no, he kept shaking his head, no no, Rory won't do that, he wouldn't do that, he's

359

not that evil. He was a nice boy. Patrick unscrewed the plastic top and drank from the small bottle of Evian. He offered it to Bevan.

'No thanks. You all right, Patrick?'

'I'm OK. And my car? What about the bilking?'

'Rory dresses up like you, gives your clothes an airing, hires the same model Volvo, same colour, and puts some stick-on plates on, same number as yours. That one is easy.'

'You might have said that when you arrested me.'

'I thought it was you doing the bilking, Patrick.'

A perfect Joseph Clark cameo.

'So what about the photos?'

Bevan whistled his almost soundless whistle.

'The photos? More difficult that one. The keys to your flat and the photos? Your guess, Patrick, is as good as mine.'

Is it? My guess is as good as yours? All right then, my guess is that

Alice always leaves her bag on the seats in the auditorium, about three rows from the stage, a few seats in. Whenever she comes through the door for our rehearsals she always calls hi Rory and waves to me and comes straight to where I'm sitting and plonks her bag down. Tell you what, she fancies me more each day. The older man thing? Probably. And why not? The friendly older man, that's me. And I'm fun. Someone you can say anything to. Not some boy who'll grab her tits first up. Plonks her bag just behind where I'm sitting with my notebook and my script. Sometimes I'm next to Euan, sometimes on my own, directing her moves on stage, stressing this word or that. I keep chipping in, keep her aware of me. I touch her up with comments and notes and saying why don't we do that bit again, it's great and it's lovely but just let it flow a bit more, yes? Let it breathe, yes? just a bit, let it sound as natural as possible. You're going to be great, Alice. You are great, believe me. Be yourself in your own room, you know, walk around as you walk around in your own bedroom, when there's no one watching, know what I mean? *That's* it. *Ex-act*-ly. Make it feel *private*. Because this is a very private piece, a solitary, passionate piece. You feel that too? Good. It's heartfelt and it's got to burn slowly. You know how strongly we can feel on our own, how dramatic it feels to be us inside our heads? I turn to Euan and whisper, she's got great legs, Alice, hasn't she, and she knows it. Euan nods. And Alice knows I'm whispering to Euan about her, and she loves it. With the lights in her eyes, I watch her do her stuff and I stretch my arms up to look at my watch and ease back in my seat and dangle my arm over the back of the row and slowly slip my fingers in and take the keys . . . I tell Euan I have to pop out for a bit. Won't be long, Euan, just remembered the trousers I should have picked up from the cleaners. I get a copy of all her keys made and hurry back and as I come in I can hear the Dinah Washington track, his music, my sister's music, and Alice is saying the line *All I could lose I lost* and for a moment I freeze. If she says her keys are missing I'll find them somewhere on the floor but she's still up there, she's never been off the stage, and Euan is standing next to her, as close as he can get, getting a bit of quality time with her, and he's making a point about not moving too much as I drop the keys back in her bag. Piece of piss.

The only sound was Bevan sucking his sweet.
　'Bloody hell.'
　'Something wrong, Patrick?'
　'No, I was just thinking.'

'Don't worry, we'll get him.'

'And the photographs, the boy? How the hell did he do that?'

Bevan nodded at the road ahead: 'He took digital photos of your empty flat, then had some tart of a boy superimposed, as if he was on the sofa. Not difficult, not difficult at all on a computer. I saw something similar done last week, special effects stuff, and it's almost impossible to tell. Funny world, isn't it?'

The sort of stuff Casey Cochrane does? Was Casey in on it in some way? The trips to the theatre? Then it clicks.

'And while he's up there,' Patrick said much louder than he intended, almost triumphantly, 'while he's up there in the flat, he makes some phone calls to the sex lines, and that's how those calls showed up on my number.'

'Yes. And that was one of the things that worried me most.'

They were now coming up to the Natural History Museum. Nearly there. Not two minutes from Finley Place. This was a world he and Caroline knew all too well. A world he and Jamie and Alice knew. Cullens and Starbucks, Partridge's and Café Flo. When the children were little these were the pavements he walked day and night, every season of the year, either going down to the Gloucester Road shops for milk and a paper or going the other way up to Kensington Gardens.

Be prepared, Patrick, for whatever it is you have to see. Be prepared. That's all you can do. She's taken something herself, that's what she's done. In his hotel room. She's finished it all like the play. Some sort of sick poetic justice. It was exactly the sort of thing she'd fall for, a drama queen's ending, *in this case literature is life*, that was the line he had written for her. That was her fate and his punishment. He'd encouraged her to go the same way as Viola.

'What I still can't see,' Patrick forced himself to say in a balanced voice, 'is why Alice has been taking out those books from the library?'

'Interesting one, that. This man has a hold on her. She sees the books Rory's reading in his hotel room and he tells her they're great and she should read them and . . . you must know what it's like, Patrick. In a sense, he's teaching her.'

'So, has he got a record? Done anything before this?'

'No, no record, doesn't mean he's done nothing, of course. Just means we haven't caught him before.'

'But he's dangerous?'

'He could be. When we get there I want you to stay in the car.'

'I thought I'd be coming in with you.'

Bevan tapped the steering wheel very lightly with his finger tips, his voice patient and tactful. 'The thing is, I don't know what I'm going to find, do I? And, given that it's a potential crime scene, I don't want to contaminate it, and above all, if your daughter's there, I don't want to provoke anything. All right?'

'Yes, of course.'

Bevan's phone went. Patrick watched his face. Bevan listened and then spoke quietly.

'Yes. Yes. Got that. Right. Right. Yes.'

Patrick felt Bevan brace himself. Bevan looked in the rear-view mirror, turned the steering wheel hard right and did a sharp U-turn. Someone leant on his horn.

'What's happened?'

'They're not at the hotel. We're going back.'

Patrick closed his eyes to shut out the pounding.

38

She was lying just inside the glass door. Her body had twisted as it fell. Patrick could see that much, and the hand-held phone on the carpet. He could also see the bruises. He could see no more because Bevan did not let him any closer than the bedroom door. Patrick felt Bevan's hand on his arm; with his eyes still on her body, he felt himself being drawn steadily and firmly back and away.

Bevan had told Patrick in the car that he would not allow him into the room. If a crime had been committed, CID and Forensics would need to finish their work first. And a pathologist was on his way. There might need to be a postmortem.

A young uniformed policeman, his nose red from the cold, was inside the porch.

'Any sign?' Bevan asked him.

'No, sir.'

'No sign of any break-in? French windows?'

'No. No windows, no doors, no nothing.'

Bevan looked at the policeman and then at Patrick. His tie loosened, he was pacing slowly, rubbing his finger on his lips, as if ticking off things in his mind. He spoke again to the policeman.

'Probably had a key. And Mrs Balfour rang when?'

'Twenty-three nineteen. To say there was an intruder but he'd left.'

'Left?'

'Run out the door and left it open. She said she woke up and he was standing over her.'

'That's all?'

'She was very frightened.'

'I bet she was.'

'She said something about her son, not clear what, dropped the phone and that was it.'

'Joseph Clark.'

'Sir?'

'Nothing, just something to Mr Balfour here. It's his mother.'

'I'm sorry, sir,' the policeman said to Patrick.

'Any other calls from here?'

The policeman took out his notebook.

'Checked that. Only one, a minute or two before she rang us. 020 7112 8989.'

'That's my number,' Patrick said. 'She rang my home?'

'She did. We tried it. But no one's in.'

'My wife's not very well. She'll be asleep. Shall I try again myself?'

'If you like,' Bevan said, taking the policeman to one side and leaving Patrick to himself.

Patrick dialled and waited. His hands were now beginning to shake. Again there was no reply. When he put his phone back in his pocket he could hear the two policemen muttering, and the faint whirr of his mother's fridge. That had always been part of the web of sounds that made up her place, the whirr of a fridge that he noticed was often a bit grubby but never got round to cleaning. He knew what she would have in it. She would have in it what she always had in it: a few slices of cooked ham and some small pieces of cheese. Some sliced bread. And a few eggs. Probably past their sell-by date. And tomatoes. She liked those new tomatoes on the vine they sold these days. Though even those she said weren't as good as the ones Dad used to grow in his greenhouse.

I'm sorry I didn't clean the fridge, Mum.

Or sort out the dripping tap.

No more cooked ham.

No more cheese.

As the details flooded in, Patrick stepped out into the hall to hide his distress and to escape the repeating phrases.

No more coffees, Mum, no more brandies.

Patrick closed his eyes as the phrases started to string themselves together and go round and round. No more opening the french windows to watch the birds, no more fumbling for your glasses, no more struggling along the edge of your bed and into your wheelchair, no need now to change the mothballs under your folded blouses, no more gardening programmes, no more not quite making it to the loo.

Now they'll be making enquiries about you and putting out alerts and doing a postmortem.

When *no more you no more you* attached itself to the string he started to shake badly. He put his hands into his pockets. Bevan came over again to Patrick and spoke quietly:

'Our Mr Balfour checked out of the hotel early this evening.'

'But he was at the play?'

'He wouldn't have missed that.'

'You're sure?'

'He was there all right. Somewhere. Probably very close to you. And then came straight on here.'

'You think so?'

'Having dressed up as you. He knew you and I would be going west, looking for Alice, knowing this would be the last place we'd ever think of.'

Patrick absorbed that, then looked at the floor: 'I thought he'd finished. You know, finished with me.'

'So did I, Patrick.'

'I thought the play was his last move. Not this.'

Patrick waved a hand at the bedroom. Bevan nodded.

'Not . . . my mother. It doesn't . . .'

'No, it doesn't.'

'Alice must have told him about her. Do you think so?'

'Looks like it.'

Her last moments. It was everything his mother had always feared most, only worse, everything she had always feared since the day Dad had died – and more. She had always hated the nights. She always slept with her bedside light on. Did he call out, Mum, it's Patrick? When she woke she would have seen the man straightaway, the son she was so proud of, seen her son Patrick in his blue suit and pink shirt. Is that you, Patrick? She would have smiled. What a surprise, dear, you gave me quite a shock, what time is it, I didn't hear you come in, what are you doing here? What was Patrick doing here, Patrick what are you doing here now, staring at her like that, what are you doing staring at me like that? Are you all right, Patrick? There's nothing wrong, is there? Pass me my glasses, would you?

Patrick!

Patrick, say something.

I caused this.

If it hadn't been for me, this would never have happened.

Patrick saw him standing over her bed, looking down on his mother. And what did he have to say to her? What terrible accusations did he want to make? Would she have called out to Dad for help? Trying to get across to the

367

door, every move an agony, what words were ringing in her ears, what were the last thoughts and feelings she had about her son, the son who loved her? She died appalled, she died thinking the unthinkable. To die thinking your son was . . . it was the worst, the most soiled of deaths.

'You know the top drawer of your mother's bedside table . . .?'

'Yes?'

'It's open. Any reason why that might be?'

'My letters to her. That's where she keeps them.'

Wrong tense.

Kept them.

'Right.'

'She could have been reading them. She said she often did in the night.'

'I see.'

'You know, if she felt a bit low.'

'Anything else? In the drawer?'

'Some photos of my father, bound to be.'

'Yes.'

'And ones of Jamie and Alice. She dotes on Alice.'

Doted.

'And that's all?'

'Well, I know she used to keep my manuscripts in there . . . Or they may be in the sideboard now. My pencil drafts.'

Bevan looked at the tips of his fingers.

'It's empty.'

'He's taken the letters? Everything?'

'The drawer's empty.'

His signature.

'Do you think,' Patrick asked, 'you could get me a glass of water?'

'Of course.'

Patrick crouched slowly down, his knees sagging as if he had been punched below the belt. After a few moments Bevan touched his arm and gave him the glass of water and the briefest of encouraging smiles.

'Don't worry, Patrick, we'll get him.'

'Will you?'

'He's out there and we'll get him.' Bevan waved his hand as if to cut any further discussion. He was now looking out of the window. 'Patrick,' he called, 'come here.'

Patrick straightened up. Just behind the parked patrol car, a taxi had pulled in with its indicators flashing. Alice was getting out. She turned to pay the fare then started half-running, half-stumbling, towards the flats. Bevan moved quickly to the door.

'Let's catch her before she comes in.'

Seeing Patrick and the detective walking towards her Alice stopped in her tracks, wild-eyed with horror. Her hand went to her mouth.

'No!'

'Alice.'

'My God, Dad, what . . . what have you —?'

'Alice,' Bevan said, 'I'm Detective Chief Inspector Bevan. I'm afraid you can't go in at the moment.'

Alice did not look at Bevan or even acknowledge that he had spoken. She was waving her hands and recoiling from Patrick, her voice a low moan.

'Dad . . . Dad.'

'Something's happened to Granny.'

'She left a message . . . you . . . you were in there . . . what . . . have you done?'

'We've just arrived here,' Patrick said.

Alice pointed vaguely behind her. 'Granny left a message, I heard it when I got in. She said she woke up and you were there and we were to come as soon as —'

'Your father's been with me all evening,' Bevan said, 'at the play and since. Where have *you* been?'

Alice reeled round to Bevan, glaring at him. 'Me?' she said with a kind of disdain. '*Me!*'

'Yes, you. Since the play ended.'

She put her fingers into her hair. 'Since the play? I went for a drink.'

'Who with?'

'Then I went home. And got that message. And came here. To see Granny. I've got to see her! *I've got to see Granny!*'

She tried to move past Bevan into the flat but he caught her wrists and pulled her round.

'Who were you with?' Bevan's voice was sharp with impatience.

'No one.'

'You drank on your own? Where? Which pub?'

'He didn't . . . he didn't turn up. So I went home.'

'Your friend Rory Hutcheson?'

Her eyes were wide. The detective repeated the question.

'Rory Hutcheson, Alice?'

She was moving her head slowly from side to side, staring. Bevan went on.

'Did you try the hotel? The Ashgrove? Did you try his room before going home? He wasn't there, was he?'

She stared at him.

'Alice, listen. Did you see him at all after the play?'

'No.'

'Do you know where he went? Do you know where he might have gone? Alice. After he left here, where would he have gone?'

'Here?' Alice looked from Bevan to Patrick and back. 'After he left *here*?'

'Yes.'

She pushed some strands of damp hair away from her puffy eyes. Then her face crumpled. 'No, no, no, no.' Moaning, she put her hands over her ears and turned hard away and faced the wall.

Bevan nodded at Patrick. After a moment Patrick said: 'You do realise it's him, Alice, don't you? The whole thing.'

She did not reply.

'When did you know, about the play? Alice? Did you know it was me?'

'Sort of,' she whispered.

'When?'

She shrugged.

'When, Alice?'

'It seemed to fit. When I put it all together.'

'And he told you?'

'Yes. Last night.' Then, from somewhere deep inside, she said, 'Is Granny dead? Dad? Is she?'

'Yes.'

'Was she killed?'

'We don't know,' Bevan said. 'She might have been.'

When she spoke it came out in slow gulps. 'I'll never forgive myself.'

Patrick could not speak.

Bevan left them standing there and went back inside. Patrick saw that lights were now coming on in other flats. A curtain twitched, hovered and then fell back in place. Alice's shoulders slowly began to heave. Then she started to sob. Patrick put an arm round her.

'I don't know where he is, Dad, I really don't.'

There was now an acknowledgement of a kind in her voice.

'All right,' he said. 'All right, you don't.'

A white van drew up at the kerb. Patrick saw a man and a woman get out, open the back door of the van, and pull on white overalls. As they carried heavy cases up towards the flats he spoke to Alice again.

'In a minute or two I think we ought to go home, don't you? And tell Mum.'

'I want to stay with Granny. You go home.'

'I'm not doing that.'

'I want to stay here. Even if I can't see her.'

'All right. We'll stay for a bit.'

'I don't want to go home.'

'I said we'll stay for a bit.'

'When can I see her?'

'When they tell us,' Patrick said. 'There's a lot to do.' Patrick kept his hand on her shoulder.

The man standing outside that block of flats with his arm round his daughter had the same name as that other man sitting in his study on Guy Fawkes Day, the man writing that difficult letter to those difficult parents about their difficult son. But he felt a world away. Now there was no sequence or shape to his thoughts, let alone any ability to rearrange the phrases. Now there were just names in his head, and all that those names carried, and they came whirling, overlapping, singly or together, in any order:

Mum, Viola, Caroline, Alice, Liz

Alice, Caroline, Liz, Viola, Mum

the pain and the presence of one adding to or displacing the others.

How could he bring things together now? *Could* things ever be brought together? He stared into the wintry night, feeling some warmth from Alice's shoulder, knowing only that he must try.